C000259462

REIGNITING CHASE

A STANDALONE GAY ROMANCE

JEANNE ST. JAMES

Copyright © 2022 by Jeanne St. James, Double-J Romance, Inc.

All rights reserved.

No part of this book may be reproduced in any form or by any electronic or mechanical means, including information storage and retrieval systems, without written permission from the author, except for the use of brief quotations in a book review.

Editor: Proofreading by the Page
Cover Art: Golden Czermak @ FuriousFotog
Beta Readers: Author BJ Alpha, Alex Swab, Sharon Abrams

www.jeannestjames.com

Sign up for my newsletter for insider information, author news, and new releases:
www.jeannestjames.com/newslettersignup

Warning: This book contains adult scenes and language and may be considered offensive to some readers. This book is for sale to adults ONLY, as defined by the laws of the country in which you made your purchase. Please store your files wisely, where they cannot be accessed by under-aged readers.

~

Dirty Angels MC, Blue Avengers MC & Blood Fury MC are registered trademarks of Jeanne St James, Double-J Romance, Inc.

~

Keep an eye on her website at http://www.jeannestjames.com/or sign up for her newsletter to learn about her upcoming releases: http://www.jeannestjames.com/newslettersignup

Author Links: Instagram * Facebook * Newsletter * Jeanne's FB Readers Group * BookBub * TikTok

CONTENT WARNING

Discussion of depression/grief
Discussion of suicide/loss of a former spouse

"Every end is a new beginning."
~ Anonymous

PROLOGUE

ESCAPING THE DARKNESS

Chase

THE FORD BRONCO RAPTOR was put to the test as it rocked and rolled up the dirt lane. As best as I could, I skirted the massive potholes filled with mud from the last storm, overgrown weeds and brush encroaching on the path making it even more narrow, and long, deep ruts reminding me of miniature versions of the Grand Canyon.

I had traded in my Audi A8 for this very reason.

Buying the four-by-four had been the right choice. The real estate agent had warned me about the lane, not to mention the amount of snowfall the area received in winter. I had taken that warning seriously.

Especially after the agent sent me pictures. Tons of pictures.

Of everything. Not just the run-down lane.

Pictures that anyone in their right mind would have them immediately walking away from the property. No, not walk, sprint.

As much as the agent wanted the commission, he also wanted to be upfront with me since I was buying the property sight unseen.

A risky buy for sure.

A risk I was willing to take for privacy and some peace.

I needed a fresh start in a place where no one knew me or about what happened. The remote cabin on a mountain right outside of Eagle's Landing, Pennsylvania, seemed to be the perfect spot.

I hoped so.

I needed to find my mojo again as soon as possible. It had been gone as long as...

I slammed the brakes on that thought before it festered.

I bounced wildly in the driver's seat as the Ford crept up the last few yards of the lane and finally arrived at the edge of the clearing.

A clearing that needed just as much work as the dirt lane.

I paid the agent to have someone trim it back as best as they could, to have the shabby shingled roof replaced with metal, install a large emergency generator—since power failure up on the mountain was a given—and have the five-hundred-gallon propane tank filled. But the rest... I had decided to tackle that after I arrived, either by attempting to do the work myself or hiring local people. *Attempt* was the key point since I didn't have any kind of construction experience. I'd never done any handiwork around my previous homes before.

There was a first time for everything. Luckily, YouTube was full of tutorial videos for everything under the sun.

I figured being forced to do some manual labor could be good therapy. It might also help spark my creativity. That had been in the toilet since... that day. The day I was trying not to dwell on.

After shifting the Bronco into Park and shutting down the engine, I stared at what was in front of me. My "new" home.

At that moment, I realized I had really lost my fucking mind.

Now that I was seeing the cabin in person... reality smacked me across the forehead with a sledgehammer. It appeared way worse in person and I hadn't even seen the inside yet.

For a second, I wasn't sure I should.

"What the fuck are you doing, you idiot?" My whisper replaced the silence in the Ford's interior. "What the fuck were you thinking? Why did you ever think you could do this?"

Jesus Christ. I should turn my Bronco around and...

6

No. I should first burn that rat-trap cabin to the ground, *then* turn my Bronco around, head back down the mountain, find a comfy motel and then another place to live. Tell the agent to sell the two hundred acres of wooded mountain land to someone who could build something better from scratch. Someone other than me.

I had bought this property mainly because the amount of acreage surrounding the cabin ensured I'd have no neighbors. Plus the fact it butted up against a huge pond or small lake, however the hell it was classified. No matter what it was called, it was a nice sized body of water.

As a bestselling author, I should know how to describe things better. However, right now, I didn't give a shit about accurate descriptions. Instead, my focus was on how the hell I would survive here.

I scratched at the week-old growth of stubble on my face as I contemplated both my next steps and the cedar-plank-sided cabin before me.

"Fuck," I muttered under my breath and shoved open the driver's door, unfolding myself with a groan.

My forty-fifth birthday had come and gone a few months ago without any fanfare, but left behind gifts I could've done without. Aching bones, insomnia, stiff joints, blurry vision and more.

But all that I had expected. Growing old alone, I had not.

I blew out a sharp breath. I needed to stop procrastinating, go inside, check out the cabin and see if it was possible to sleep there tonight or if I'd have to backtrack into town and find somewhere better. At least until I could make the cabin somewhat habitable.

With a hand clamped around the back of my neck, I ground it back and forth and gave myself a short and to the point pep talk. "Let's do this."

The wooden steps creaked as I climbed them up to the porch. They weren't spongy and I couldn't see any obvious rot or broken boards, so that was reassuring. The wood porch was tiny, but then from what I'd seen in the photos, the door I was approaching was the rear entrance. The true front door faced the ten-acre lake.

Lake *something*. I couldn't remember what it was called.

Not that it mattered. Since I owned it from shore to shore, I could name it whatever the hell I wanted.

Lake Leave-Me-Alone had a nice ring to it.

I dug out the key the agent had overnighted to me from the front pocket of my jeans. I had never met him since everything had been done virtually. Even the closing.

As I went to slide the key into the lock, I realized the door wasn't completely closed. It was open barely a crack. Did one of the workers leave it open? Or had it already been open and nobody cared enough to close it? They probably did the work they'd been paid for and left as soon as possible.

The hinges creaked as I pushed open the thick, rustic wood door.

Mental note: Grab a can of WD-40 next time you're in town. If that doesn't work, a can of gas and a lighter will solve the problem.

Standing before the threshold, I sucked in a few deep breaths of the warm, clean mountain air. So different from where I just came.

The air wasn't the only thing different. I paused to listen.

So was the quiet.

No traffic. No voices. Pure fucking bliss.

The only sound, besides the birds and small mammals scurrying in the underbrush, was the one in my head telling me on an endless loop that I was crazy to buy this place.

Maybe all the silence wasn't the best idea. My own internal voices might become amplified, maybe even deafening.

On the trip here, I'd listened to a couple of long audiobooks since my thoughts tended to drown out music. With audiobooks, I was forced to concentrate. A good, well-written mystery was able to pull me from those dark, wandering thoughts and into someone else's story. One other than my own, both the crime thriller I needed to write and the depressing Nicholas Sparks story I was currently living.

But it also reminded me that I needed to rediscover my creativity. I sure as hell hoped this place would help with that.

That was the whole point of moving to this remote area.

When I stepped over the threshold, I had to stop myself from turning around and escaping as fast as possible. The pictures didn't make it look this bad. Now I wondered how long ago they were actually taken and why the agent hadn't provided a virtual tour. But in truth, the agent hadn't been lying. It certainly was an old hunting cabin that was, at this point, not much better than camping.

Unfortunately, I knew nothing about roughing it or living off the grid. Even though it was debatable whether this cabin was actually considered off-the-grid living. Mainly because it had a well with a working pump, as well as water already tested and deemed safe. It also had electricity and soon would have satellite internet so I could get back to being productive.

If that was actually achieved, my literary agent might do some backflips. So would my reader base, who'd been clamoring for the past two years for the next book in my bestselling series.

When it came down to it, so would I, since writing was my sole source of income and my royalty payments had been slowly dwindling every month I went without a new release.

While I currently had a nice cushion in my bank account, it would be quickly eaten up by getting the cabin and its sparse amenities into shape.

No matter what, I'd have to actually *write* a book first. And with all the endless work that came after the first draft—editing, cover art, marketing, and more—it wasn't like it would be published soon after.

I was giving myself six months to write the next book in my popular crime thriller series. By the time it hit my readers' hands, it would probably be a year and a half from now. If not longer.

I didn't want to think about it. I might be dead broke by the time I received my first royalty payment on a new book, depending on how generous the publisher's advance was.

My publisher had been hesitant to give me one this time after I'd spiraled into a dark place. They told my agent Randall that once at least three "well-written" chapters landed in their hands, they'd consider sending an advance.

Just fucking great.

Grudgingly, I couldn't blame them since severe writer's block had crushed some authors' careers. I held out hope it wouldn't end mine.

Hence, the reason I stood where I currently did.

Shoving those depressing thoughts aside, I concentrated on the depressing view directly in front of me instead.

At first glance, it appeared as if no one had been inside recently except for local wildlife.

I walked deeper into the twelve hundred square foot cabin. It wasn't a bad size for me since I'd be living alone and I didn't need much in terms of space. A place to lay my head, a place to eat and somewhere to write.

The cabin had only two rooms walled off—the bedroom and bathroom—but other than that, the floor plan was completely open. Dust kicked up as I wandered around the main area of the cabin, inspecting everything a bit closer and making a mental checklist of what needed to be done.

It wasn't long before I realized I should actually write it down since the list might be longer than my brain could handle.

The little bit of furniture the previous owners left behind was covered in an inch of dust or was broken. All of it needed to be either tossed or broken up and used for firewood. The kitchen cabinets were empty with the doors hanging wide open as if the contents inside had been stolen or packed up and removed.

Ghost-like cobwebs clung in every corner.

Every window was cloudy from years of neglect. One was completely shattered and would need to be replaced. Actually all would need to be replaced with new double-paned windows to help keep in the heat come winter. Even with the light early spring breeze, drafts could be detected when I ran my hand along the edge of the nearest window frame.

I shook my head and spotted scat on the floor. Lifting my gaze, I saw why. A half dozen bats clung to the open rafters above having a little afternoon siesta.

Fuck.

Besides the bat shit, I recognized what animal the little black grains of rice come from. A small rodent related to Mickey.

"You're all getting your eviction notice in the next day or so," I warned the bats and any mice listening. "Freeloaders."

I continued around the main living space. Luckily, the large fireplace built out of mountain stone seemed to be in good shape. As was the thick, wide wood mantelpiece over it. At least something wouldn't need replaced or repaired.

Actually, the structure of the cabin was basically sound. It had "good bones." Most of the repairs would be cosmetic or to make it more energy efficient. The wide-planked wood floor boards simply needed a good scrubbing, as did the kitchen sink and appliances.

Luckily, that was something I could easily handle on my own. I didn't mind using a little elbow grease.

The filthy woven rug in front of the hearth needed to be tossed. Firewood scattered on the floor needed to be neatly stacked. The pile of cold ashes in the fireplace needed to be removed and a chimney sweep would be hired to avoid any fires in the flue.

I peeked my head into the bathroom. Since it was the only one, it was a decent size. It didn't include a tub, only a stand-up shower stall missing a shower curtain, a filthy window, a toilet that needed scrubbed, and a free-standing sink marred with hard water stains.

Next to the bathroom was my bedroom. Also not a bad size since it was the only one. A broken metal bed frame sat in the center of the room, and an old wood dresser was against one wall. I was afraid to open the drawers since I was sure families of mice had turned it into a condominium complex.

But it was the large windows in the room that caught my attention. They might be dirty now, but through them the view of the lake was spectacular. I imagined myself opening them wide and hearing owls, fox and even loons at night, along with getting a breeze.

I added several ceiling fans to my list. One for the bedroom, as well as a couple for the main living space.

My king-sized bed would fit perfectly in that room, as well as the dresser I brought along and waited to be unloaded from the U-Haul parked at the bottom of the mountain.

Both my SUV and the enclosed trailer were packed full with only the necessities, like clothes and my bed. Everything else I had given away to organizations that helped veterans and the homeless after selling my house on Long Island.

After stepping out of the bedroom, I headed to the back door— No, the front door—to find it had been left unlocked, too. Pulling it open, I walked out onto the covered porch that spanned the whole length of the cabin and stared out at what I now owned.

The spectacular and breathtaking view of the lake from that wide porch had called my name when I had scrolled through the pictures on the real estate listing. Beyond the lake were more trees and the mountain continued rising as a backdrop.

That picture perfect view had been what sold me on the property and blinded me enough to ignore the rest of the issues.

I imagined myself in a rocking chair, enjoying my morning coffee. Or setting up a little place on the porch to write.

The tension I'd been holding suddenly disappeared and my shoulders dropped a couple of inches. My spine softened and my thoughts immediately became clearer.

This. This was what I needed.

At least once the major work was done.

Like the rest of the cabin, the porch needed a fresh coat of stain and a protective coating, something I could handle on my own.

I glanced over to my right to find a three-sided open shelter half-full of firewood along with a stump clearly used for splitting that wood. After descending the three steps, I made my way around to the front of the cabin—no, the back—to where I was parked.

On my route back to the Bronco, I paused at the large propane tank along the exterior cabin wall on the same side as the kitchen to check the gauge. Thankfully, it was completely full as promised.

I kept going until I stood next to the Bronco and gave the outside of the cabin another once over.

My home.

It would do. It had to.

I undoubtedly needed a change and this would definitely be a major one.

If moving here didn't help, then I'd need to face the fact I was helpless.

But for now, I needed to head back to town, find a place to stay for the night and buy a bunch of cleaning supplies so I could tackle the filth.

Before I could do that, I needed to empty my packed Bronco and only take an overnight bag and my laptop along. When I come back tomorrow, I'd begin cleaning as best as I could, then attempt to tow the U-Haul up the lane from where I left it at the bottom without it breaking an axle.

Also while in town, I'd ask around at both the diner and motel to find someone to replace the windows. In the meantime, I'd buy some plastic sheeting to cover the broken one to keep the bats and critters out.

I also needed to rent a post office box.

Damn. The list was endless.

By the time I had the cabin in a somewhat livable condition, the words better be ready to flow.

If not, I needed to find a new career.

CHAPTER 1

Chase

I PAUSED the fork halfway to my mouth. So far, I had only made a small dent in the diner's belly-busting breakfast special. It was criminal how much food the server had delivered for five bucks.

Five freaking bucks. On Long Island, it would have cost me at least fifteen.

For only two more dollars, the coffee came with unlimited refills. If I could mainline that welcomed caffeine right now, I would.

My whole body ached and I was exhausted, not only from sleeping like shit in the motel but from tackling the seemingly endless job of cleaning the cabin from top to bottom. I didn't want the furniture I purchased down at a mom-and-pop store in Picture Rocks to be delivered until the place was completely spotless and all my unwanted roommates had been effectively evicted.

While I liked bats and knew they were beneficial, I just didn't want to share the same space with them. If they returned to sleep in the rafters today, then I needed to find how they were getting in since I had secured the broken window with plastic-sheeting.

But all of that wasn't what made me pause my eating, it was the man across the diner who wouldn't stop staring.

Like me, he also sat alone, but unlike me, he seemed to know everyone in the diner. A local just like the rest of the patrons and employees there.

The first morning, all eyes had turned in my direction as soon as I walked through The Eagle's Nest's door, but now the waitresses were used to seeing me since today was my third day eating in the diner, for both breakfast and a late dinner.

The food was good, the prices fantastic and attentive, friendly service even better.

Even one of the thirty-something-year-old waitresses had tried flirting with me. She had no idea she was barking up the wrong tree. Even if I was on the dating market, she was playing on the wrong team. While I had the utmost respect for women, I simply didn't want to sleep with them.

However, the man who kept staring at me was most likely not on my team, either.

Was he staring because I was simply a stranger in a close-knit community where everyone apparently knew everyone?

It couldn't be because I was gay. While I had never hidden it, I also didn't flaunt it and most women, when I broke it to them gently, were shocked to find out the truth.

Most men, too.

I'd heard, *"My gaydar must be broken,"* more times than I'd ever wanted to.

Even so, dating wasn't on my agenda anytime soon. Or ever, since I had no plans on dating anyone ever again.

Life would be easier that way. Plus, at this point, being a team player didn't matter, I preferred to remain a free agent.

Ignoring the man, I finished shoving the forkful of scrambled eggs into my mouth, wondering when the guy would get bored with watching me and lose interest in whatever had caught it in the first place.

Trying to ignore the rude man, I stabbed a piece of sausage, also shoving it into my mouth and chewing. Sucking down half a cup of black coffee, I hoped the guy would simply fuck off.

Finally, unable to ignore him anymore, I dropped the fork on my plate with a clatter, tipped my head down and rubbed my forehead. I steadied my breathing in an attempt to lower my quickly rising blood pressure.

I only wanted to eat in peace. I wasn't here to make friends, or even enemies.

I wanted to be left the fuck alone.

But of course that wasn't going to happen.

This was exactly why I left Long Island, everything I knew and everybody who knew me. I wanted to live somewhere no one knew me or my backstory. I had gotten to the breaking point, swallowed up by pity on one hand, or people thinking it was time I "got over it" on the other.

I'd never get over it.

Not fucking ever.

"Fuck!" screamed through my head when the dark-haired man rose from where he sat at the counter. After throwing a few singles next to his plate, he turned and headed away from the entrance and toward my booth.

Of. Fucking. Course.

Dread rose from my gut into my throat and began to choke me. The man might have recognized me somehow.

Lifting my coffee cup, I used it to hide my face, but peered over the rim to keep an eye on the approaching man. My muscles and spine stiffened more with every step taken closer to where I sat.

Trying to mind my own business.

Trying to eat breakfast.

Trying to exist in peace.

Maybe the guy was headed to the restrooms right past my booth. If only I could be so lucky.

Attempting not to be too obvious, I quickly scanned the man

from head to toe.

He might be in his late thirties or early forties. Possibly three or four inches shorter than my six-foot-two. Solidly built, he had broad shoulders and a trim torso that tapered down to his hips. All he needed was a flannel shirt and an axe to go along with his thick, dark beard and he'd be the poster boy for a lumberjack.

As he moved, the short sleeves of his snug T-shirt caught on his bulging biceps. His thighs appeared thick in his worn jeans. And his pecs did not bounce with each step. *Hell no*, they flexed.

The man was serious about his physique.

I used to be fit mentally and physically, too.

Now I felt nothing but broken. As if the patched-up pieces had been glued together so I could appear whole.

One wrong move and I'd easily shatter all over again.

I raised my gaze back up to the man's face when he stopped at my table.

As much as I didn't want to admit it, the man was handsome with his strong jawline covered in a full, but well-trimmed, beard. Not a gray hair could be seen on his head or his face. His dark chocolate eyes framed in thick, black lashes held curiosity.

And maybe something else. But I might be imagining that.

It was hard to read a stranger's intentions and I wasn't about to try.

While I had been checking him out, one corner of full lips pulled up in a half-smile. It came off as friendly but cautious. Like he was trying to hand a treat to a stray dog that might snap at him at any second.

Me being that snapping stray.

"Sorry, I didn't mean to stare." His rich, baritone voice was tinged with steel when it rumbled from him.

"But you did anyway."

The man's head tipped to the side slightly while turning the tables and searching my face.

I picked up a forkful of hash browns slathered in ketchup and shoved them into my mouth in an unspoken message of *"Can't you see I'm eating and don't want to be bothered?"*

"I was trying to place you. You look familiar."

I almost choked on my mouthful of food. "Doubt it."

His thick, dark eyebrows pinned together. "No, I know you from somewhere."

"You don't." I took a long sip of coffee to wash down the crispy, shredded potatoes. However, my breakfast was now sitting like a cement block deep within my stomach.

"You're right. I don't know you personally. I said you looked familiar." The other corner of the man's mouth now curled up until he wore a friendly, but slightly roguish, smile. "What's your name?"

Hell no. I wasn't doing this.

As hot as the man was… As much as the guy could be my type….

I gritted my teeth together. I no longer had a type.

I had no interest in the man before me. None.

I wasn't looking for a "buddy." I wasn't looking for a lover. I just wanted to be left the hell alone. "You don't know me. I'm new to the area."

"I only asked for your name. This town is small. If you're here to stay, everyone will eventually learn it anyway."

I slowly inhaled, filling my lungs completely as I tried to keep myself wrapped tightly.

"Why is it some big secret?"

A muscle in my jaw popped. I unclenched it. "It's not."

Mr. Nosy cocked an eyebrow. "Then?"

Jesus Christ. He was right. Eventually everyone would know my name whether I wanted them to or not. At least they'd know my real name which was different from my pen name.

If I told him, maybe the guy would leave. "Chase."

"Is that your first or last name?"

"It's my name."

The formerly friendly smile fell flat as he studied me for a few seconds. Finally, he said, "Got it," and sharply rapped his knuckles on the table, making the utensils jump. "Have a great day, *Chase*." When he turned, he added under his breath, "*Asshole*."

Since I'd been choking my fork with white knuckles, I loosened my grip, stabbed a piece of cold sausage link and shoved it into my mouth as the man walked toward the exit.

The fucker bugged me for my name but managed not to give me his.

Didn't matter. I didn't need or want it.

I observed the long strides the nosy man with no name took to the cash register by the front entrance, where he stopped and waited until my waitress, wearing a huge smile, hurried over to help him.

I found myself scanning the man again, this time from the rear, taking in the broad expanse of his back, his tight hips and that ass snuggled perfectly in well-fitted Levi's. I told myself I was only checking out the guy's ass because my eyes had been automatically drawn to it when *Mr. Nosy* slipped his wallet from his back pocket.

When I took a bite of toast, it tasted like sawdust since I'd lost my appetite. As I chewed, I watched my waitress and *Mr. Nosy* exchange words as they finished the transaction. I sighed softly in relief when the man finally walked out the door without another glance back at me.

Thankfully, he must have gotten the message.

I forced more of the breakfast down since I'd need the fuel to do all the work I planned to do on the cabin today. Once I finished draining my cup of coffee, the waitress magically appeared with a full pot. "Refill?"

"No. Thank you. I'll just take my check."

The waitress' warm smile only grew larger. "It's already paid for."

My eyebrows stitched together. "How? That has to be a mistake."

"Nope," she answered in her chipper voice. "Rett covered it."

Rett?

She must have recognized the confusion on my face. "The gentleman who stopped over to welcome you to Eagle's Landing."

Jesus. That hadn't been a welcome. The word "welcome" never even came out of that Rett guy's mouth. Not once. He only wanted info to feed his damn nosiness.

I glanced out the booth's window to the parking lot.

"If you need anything else, just holler."

I half-nodded, distracted...

By the man standing next to a dark blue Chevy truck with the driver's door hanging open. But he wasn't climbing in. Instead, he faced the diner and stared back at me through the window, a crooked smile once again on his face.

Smug bastard.

With an upward jerk of his chin, the lopsided smile turned into a grin large enough to be seen from the next state and *Mr. Nosy* hauled his ass up and into the cab of the Chevy.

My heart pounded against my chest as the truck pulled out of the parking lot and disappeared from sight.

WITH MY ASS settled in one of the cushioned wood rockers that had been delivered yesterday along with the rest of the furniture, I stared out over the still lake. A mist rose off the water, giving it an eerie look.

Being early spring, the morning air still had a slight bite to it. I sipped at the steaming mug of black coffee, simply breathing in the fresh air and taking in my peaceful surroundings.

Breathe in the good, breathe out the bad...

A variety of birds singing, a distant high-pitched bark of what might be a fox and some chipmunks scurrying among the dead leaves in the nearby tree line filled my ears.

I even heard the call of what sounded like a loon out on the water. I'd have to do some research about what kind of wildlife lived in the area so I could identify all the sounds. I might even have to buy a pair of binoculars to spot some eagles, the whole reason for the nearby town's name.

With my feet kicked up on the railing, I took another long sip of the black-as-night coffee, letting it warm me up from the inside out while the caffeine worked on pulling me out of my haze.

I'd finally had a decent night's sleep, mostly because I'd fallen into bed exhausted. Last night, I barely had enough energy to strip off my clothes before collapsing on the mattress.

The past few days had been spent thoroughly cleaning, putting my bed together, putting the delivered furniture in place, going grocery shopping to fill the now spotless and no longer nose-wrinkling, stomach-churning smelly fridge, emptying the U-Haul and taking the long trip to the nearest rental place to return it.

Hardest damn physical work I'd done in a long time.

However, every muscle now ached and every joint complained. A good reminder that I needed to get back on track with working out. Writing was a sedentary job and I needed to find a way to keep active and flexible.

Hiking around my property and swimming in the lake might do it. But when I checked the temp of the water yesterday with just my hand, my balls went automatically into hiding. They wanted no part of that frigid water.

Since the lake wasn't too deep, my hope was in a few weeks the water would warm up enough for me to brave more than dipping in a few fingers.

I also needed to grab a tackle box and rod down at Harry's Hardware in town to try my hand at fishing. When I was in there to buy the plastic sheeting for the broken window—along with some tools and nails to fix some of the shit that had been broken, more cleaning supplies and some other oddball stuff—I noticed hardware wasn't the only thing Harry sold. He carried all kinds of outdoor stuff, like sporting goods as well as any landscaping equipment I would need.

Harry was happy to see me. My credit card wasn't as happy to see Harry.

Back on Long Island, I had hired a landscaper to take care of all the yard work and to keep the gardens weed-free. I also hired people to fix stuff. Here, I planned on doing as much as I could myself and learn as I went.

However, now that the satellite internet had been installed two days prior, I no longer had an excuse not to get back to writing.

None.

I couldn't procrastinate any longer. If I didn't string words together to create a good story my readers would buy, I wouldn't get paid. Simple as that.

And if I didn't get paid, Harry would eventually be unhappy because my ass would be flat broke. Then I might turn into some hermit mountain man who had to live off the land.

Actually, that didn't sound so bad right now.

Oh yes, I was officially delusional.

Unfortunately, reality was calling my name. And reality's name was Mac.

I glanced over at my laptop sitting on a small table nearby. I hadn't opened it once since arriving in Eagle's Landing.

Not at the motel. Not since I moved into the cabin.

It taunted me.

Or haunted me.

Depending on how I looked at it.

I needed to find my words.

Somehow.

While writer's block was normal at times for every author, it didn't normally last for two years.

Reading fiction had always helped spur my creativity in the past, but I stopped reading books when I stopped writing. And the only time I had listened to audiobooks was during the long drive from Long Island, New York to Sullivan County, Pennsylvania.

Maybe it would help if I held an actual paperback in my hands. Smelled the print and the paper. Heard the flip of pages. Got lost in the words…

And, of course, dug out my reading glasses since I now struggled to read the print.

Another sign of being over forty. I grimaced.

Over forty-five.

Hell, creeping up on fifty.

Maybe today I'd crack open my Mac and if the words didn't come, I'd head into town tomorrow and grab a few books at the local bookstore I spotted off Main Street.

I scratched at the back of my neck as I tried to remember the name. I'd only gotten a quick glance at it on my way back from Mountainside Market, the only place in town for groceries.

What was the damn name of it?

Did it matter? Probably not since I remembered where it was located.

Not only was my eyesight turning to shit, so was my memory.

However, there were some memories I'd never forget. My fear was the good ones I wanted to hold onto would fade away, the bad ones I didn't want to remember would stick with me forever.

I sighed.

Maybe the bookstore had the rest of the series I started listening to in audio on my trip. The books had managed to catch my interest —not a small feat—because they were very well-written and had intricate plots.

Plus, I was dying to know what case the bumbling private investigator, Dexter Peabody, whose antics actually pulled a chuckle from me a few times, solved next.

"The Next Page!" burst from me in a shout, causing nearby birds to squawk and fly away and chipmunks to run for cover.

That was the name of the bookstore I had passed.

So damn fitting.

If they didn't have the series in stock, maybe they could order them in and I could use reading a few chapters every night as a reward for getting my daily word count finished.

Now that sounded like a good plan.

I would just need to stick with it.

CHAPTER 2

Chase

THE SMALL COW bell hanging inside the door clanged as I opened it. The two-story building was older, but in excellent shape, with brown painted wood siding and a huge wood sign in the shape of an open book above the door with the name The Next Page carved into it.

The building reminded me of an old-time country store with a covered wooden porch out front with wrought iron benches and large cream-colored painted framed windows to bring in natural light.

How this bookstore survived in this small town, I had no idea. Even in towns with much larger populations, the big box bookstores, as well as online e-book sales, had put so many mom-and-pop bookstores out of business.

However, this one in the middle of nowhere somehow managed to survive.

As I stepped into the *quiet-as-a-library* interior, my nostrils flared and I inhaled the smell of books. The familiar scent was almost as soothing as breathing in the fresh mountain air up at the cabin.

I was surprised to find nobody manning the register to the right of the door. Theft probably wasn't a big issue in this town and on the chance that someone did steal, it was probably easy to figure out who the culprit was. One benefit of laid-back, small town living.

Eagle's Landing certainly had a different vibe from where I used to live.

After only a few days I knew I'd never go back to living in an area where the population was jammed together like sardines. Worse, the traffic on the Long Island Expressway tended to be a snarled mess. Here most traffic jams were caused by wildlife crossing the road.

It would also be hard to find such a quaint, quiet bookstore like this still in business. Stepping inside was unexpectedly comforting and, if I had to admit it, a little motivating.

Rows of shelves filled the store and more lined the perimeter. Every one of those shelves was packed solid with books neatly organized by genre and even broken down into subgenre with clear signage. With a quick glance, I thought they might even be alphabetized by the author's last name under each category.

Before I could check closer, a large black and tan German Shepherd loped up to me from between the rows with his mouth hanging open, his tongue hanging out and a bushy tail up in the air wagging back and forth. The dog circled me once before using his muzzle to nudge my hand for attention.

"What's your name?"

With his tongue now flopping out of the side of his mouth, the friendly, furry greeter turned his deep brown eyes up to me and whined his answer as I scratched his head.

Unfortunately, I didn't speak canine.

"Timber!" A deep voice called from the back of the bookstore.

Timber the GSD ignored whoever was calling him and sat on my foot instead, then leaned into my leg while staring up at me in adoration since he was now being scratched behind the ears.

"Sorry. Normally, he doesn't bother customers unless they have a treat and—"

Fuck whispered silently through my head as a whispered, but audible, "Fuck" came from the man appearing before me.

"Timber," *Mr. Nosy* called again, patting his denim-covered thigh. "He's fine."

"I'm more afraid of you taking a bite out of him than the other way around."

Only about ten feet separated us as we stared at each other.

"Chase, right?"

Shit. I tipped my head in answer. "You shouldn't have paid for my breakfast the other day."

"It was nothing. One way to welcome you to the area."

"Maybe I'm just passing through," I lied.

"It doesn't take long for people to pass through Eagle's Landing. There's not much to keep them here."

"You live here."

Rett shrugged one shoulder. "I don't need much."

Sucking on my teeth in an attempt to reduce the annoyance creeping up my spine, I glanced around the store to avoid Rett's eye contact. "I assume you work here?"

"You could say that."

Ah, Rett was now being ambiguous, the same as I had been with him at the diner when it came to answering questions. The man was trying to make a point, even as subtle as it was.

With a huge yawn, Timber finally unpinned my foot from the floor, wandered off in a lazy pace and disappeared back to wherever he had come from.

"So, why are you sticking around town? Are you a felon on the run?"

While I was in hiding, it wasn't from the law. I debated if I should even answer, but the man was going to find out the truth soon anyway, if not by me than by someone else. Another joy of small town living. "Bought a place nearby."

"Figured that." One dark eyebrow rose. "Where? I don't

remember seeing any places for sale in town. And no one has talked about moving."

What, was he the town gossip? Did he have his finger on the pulse of Eagle's Landing?

But just like my name, it wouldn't be long until everyone in the town with a tiny population of about two hundred or so also knew where I lived. Even though those facts wouldn't stay a secret, I wanted to remain as anonymous as possible for as long as possible. Especially when it came to my career.

If I was lucky, no one in this town or the surrounding area ever heard of my pseudonym or had read my books.

"Coleman Lane."

With his brow dropped low, Rett raked fingers down his beard and I caught myself mesmerized by the whole thing. I silently groaned at my own reaction.

"Coleman Lane? There's only one cabin on that mountain road because it isn't a real road, it's a private lane. And it certainly isn't a house, it's a," he grimaced, "hunting cabin. Or used to be."

The man was certainly a genius. A regular detective. "Right."

"You up here to get it ready for hunting season? Are you a hunter?"

I was so not in the mood for small talk. I only stopped in for some reading material. Like at the diner, I wasn't here to make a friend, especially with someone who asked too many questions. "Sure."

Rett didn't appear to believe me. No surprise. "So… what do you do for a living, Chase?"

Sweet baby Jesus. "Mind my own business."

A half-grin twisted Rett's lips. "A professional conversationist, then?"

"I'm just here for some books."

"I have plenty of books." Rett swept his hand around. "If you haven't noticed, a whole store full. What do you like?"

"Quiet."

Once the grin slipped off his face, Rett stared at me with

narrowed eyes for a long, awkward moment before he nodded. "Like at the diner, I hear you loud and clear. Feel free to browse. I have a little bit of everything. I'm here if you have questions."

"Are the books priced?"

"Yes."

"Then I won't have questions."

Rett stared at me for a few more seconds. While his face was unreadable, his eyes were clearly calling me an asshole again.

Should I feel bad for acting like an asshole? Probably. Did I? No. My privacy was important.

With another sharp nod, Rett turned on his heels, stepped behind the front counter and perched himself on a stool. "I'll be here if you need me."

I wondered if the man always had to get in the last word. I decided to put that to the test. "Thanks."

"You're welcome."

Jesus. I was right.

With a shake of my head, I headed down the closest aisle, then took my time eyeing book titles, pausing here and there, pulling out random books and reading the back copy before sliding them back into place.

The bookstore owner certainly did stock a variety. I was pleasantly surprised to find there was even a dedicated and clearly marked LGBTQ+ section that included both fiction and non-fiction. I wasn't expecting to find that in this area, but that wasn't what I was looking for.

On a bookshelf along the far wall I found the shelves that held thrillers, suspense novels and crime thrillers. My eyes zeroed in on my own titles right next to a few of John Grisham's.

Shit.

At least one copy of each book in my serial killer series was on the shelf. The first book had three copies in stock. On the shelf right below them was the first series I ever wrote when I was new to publishing. A few copies were missing from that ten-book series.

While the older series was what originally put me on the map, my newer Detective Nick Foster series had launched my career into orbit.

But that rocket was quickly barreling back toward Earth and would crash and burn if I couldn't get the next one done soon. Especially if my agent fired me and my publisher broke ties.

The next shelf over held mysteries, what I'd actually been searching for. The audiobooks I listened to on my trip west were written by Everett J. Williams. Luckily, I spotted quite a few copies of each book in the series and a tiny laminated sign above them stated they were autographed copies.

That made me pause. Did the bookstore owner buy them autographed or had the author stopped in to sign them?

Interesting.

Maybe the owner was simply a big fan of the author. I wouldn't be surprised since the books were really good. Not to mention, addicting.

Since I'd already listened to the first two, I grabbed the next two paperbacks in the series, then wandered around the rest of the store to make sure I didn't miss anything before checking out.

I came to a complete halt when I saw that the very back of the store was mostly wide open, as in no shelving in the center of the floor like at the front and center of the building. Butted against the middle of the back wall was a raised platform no bigger than five by five with a microphone and stand at the front edge.

Possibly for book and poetry readings? For local musicians?

Huh.

I had to assume since the town was so small there wasn't much when it came to entertainment. I figured on the days or nights someone was performing, folding chairs would be set up in the empty floor space for the audience.

A Keurig coffeemaker with a stack of disposable cups and a wide selection of beverage pods sat on a small table directly to the right of the platform with a sign that told customers to help themselves. To the left of the tiny "stage" was an open stairway blocked by a white plastic chain and a small metal sign hanging from it that said "Private."

Tucked into the other corner to the right of the platform was an antique wood desk sitting at an angle with a large computer screen sitting on it. Also on the desktop was a pile of what looked like used spiral notebooks along with a Ball canning jar jam-packed with pens. A bunch of sticky notes covered the wall behind a newer gamer's chair that did not match the desk's style whatsoever.

Scratching my head, I stared at the set-up. It made me realize I really needed a better set up for my own writing. I couldn't work all day in a rocking chair. My body would hate me for it. I needed a real desk with a supportive chair, but I also needed to find a spot to put it so I had a view of the lake and the mountain beyond. The whole reason I bought the Coleman cabin.

Adding another room onto the back—no, *front*—of the cabin would work as an office, but I liked the open-air covered porch, too, and wanted to keep it as-is. However, a temperature controlled all-season room would let me see the mind-clearing view and allow me to write in all kinds of weather.

I could always add it to the side, right off the bedroom, and have it installed before winter. I could even open up the back of the fireplace so it was two-sided and…

I shook those thoughts from my head. I needed to get back to being productive first and get the first three chapters sent to my agent so I *could* afford to do all that.

I sighed and took one last glance around before heading back toward the front of the store where Rett, and now Timber, waited.

As soon as I stepped up to the counter and set the two books down, Rett's eyes zeroed in immediately on my wedding band.

Shit.

Quickly curling my fingers into my palm, I dropped my hand to my side and out of his sight. I didn't want more questions from *Mr. Nosy.* Especially about my ring. Or my marriage.

Or, *hell*, about anything.

Even after two years, I couldn't make myself remove my wedding band, despite how many people told me I should move on with my life.

I was. But in my own way. Like moving to Eagle's Landing to get away from all of those same people when I hadn't fucking asked for their goddamn opinion.

I also didn't need people in this *new-to-me* town riding my ass about how unhealthy it was that I wasn't capable of letting go.

I would do it when I was good and ready. Not a moment sooner.

Or, *screw everyone*, I might never do it at all.

Whether I did or didn't was no one's business but my own.

It was *my* life and I wanted no one to tell me how to live it.

Like *Mr. Nosy*, now standing directly behind the counter instead of sitting in the corner on the stool. His brown eyes lifted from my reading choice to my face.

With his lips rolled under, the man appeared to be fighting back questions or comments, or maybe even judgment. It took him a few seconds, but he finally got out, "They're signed."

No shit, Captain Obvious. "I noticed."

"That's book three and four in the series. Are you sure you don't want to start with the first two books? I recommend you read them in order."

I took a slow, deep inhale and the fingers of my right hand automatically curled, too.

Rett's eyebrows rose up his forehead and he lifted a palm. "Sorry I asked. Read in whatever order you want. I was just trying to be helpful."

"Don't."

With a tip of his dark head, Rett pulled the two books closer, flipped them over and scanned the ISBNs with a barcode reader. "Do you need a bag?"

Not unless you're going to wear it to keep from asking so many damn questions. "No."

"Can I tell you one more thing?"

Jesus. "Must you?"

Rett's lips twitched. "I would be remiss in my duties if I didn't."

He would be "remiss" in his duties.

Right.

I sighed, cocked my head and waited.

"Once you're done with them, you can trade them back in."

Now, that *was* interesting. That was why so many books on the shelves looked lightly read. The Next Page must be similar to one of those paperback exchange stores. While that meant the author was missing out on royalties, it also made physical copies of books more affordable to the public and encouraged more reading. Especially if there wasn't a library nearby. "One for one?" slipped out before I could stop it.

Rett's smothered smile grew. "Two for one."

I frowned. While that was a decent deal, trading in used books didn't make much money, if at all, versus selling them outright. Now, *my* curiosity was getting the best of me. "How does the store pay its bills?"

"The store doesn't, but I do."

Wait a minute... "You're the owner?"

"I am." *Ah,* there was the same smugness I saw in the parking lot of the Eagle's Nest.

"Are you the only employee?"

"I am. Well, Timber and I."

At hearing his name, the steady thump of the Shepherd's tail hitting the floor could be heard from behind the counter.

How could the man afford to pay the bills, taxes, maybe a mortgage or lease on the building, along with all the rest of the expenses, when there was no way it got enough business to sustain itself? Maybe this Rett was independently wealthy and owning a bookstore had been a pipe dream.

Doesn't matter, Chase. Mind your own damn business just like you want him to mind his, too.

33

Words to live by.

But, despite everything, I had something in common with the irritating man in front of me. Books were an important part of our lives.

Even so, that one commonality wasn't enough to become friends. "What's my total?"

"Since you're a new customer and you're buying two, I'll give you a deal. Just give me thirty."

I slid my wallet from my back pocket, cracked it open and pulled out two twenties. Grabbing the two books off the counter, I left the money in their place. "Keep the change."

"For what? That seems like a pretty big tip for my stellar customer service."

Christ, when the man smiled—even when it was a smart-ass smile—it drew me in. I shoved that discovery back out.

I was never getting involved with anyone again. "My breakfast."

Rett shook his head. "That was my treat."

"I don't need you buying me breakfast."

"Of course you don't *need* it. I was trying to be friendly."

"I don't need you being friendly."

"Fair enough. But since I was going to give you some friendly advice next, I'll call it smart advice instead."

I mentally groaned. He certainly liked to push it.

"Even though you said you were a hunter," Rett lifted one skeptical eyebrow, "my advice is, if you don't own one already, you might consider buying yourself a rifle or shotgun."

I never owned a damn gun and getting one hadn't been on my radar. "Why? Will I need to use it on you?"

"Only if you consider me as dangerous as the bears, bobcats and coyotes up around your cabin. If you aren't aware of it, you're in the Allegheny Mountains now. We've got all kinds of critters around here."

Like nosy bookstore owners. But the only way Rett would be dangerous to me was if the man was gay. Since he was straight, I had no problem keeping him at arm's length. Despite how much Rett was my type. *If* he was gay.

But he wasn't.

Thank my lucky stars.

Plus, you don't have a type, I reminded myself. Not any longer.

"Critters who would like to eat your face off," Rett added.

Before I could respond, the cow bell over the door clanged, drawing our attention to a woman entering and carrying a couple of books.

With an excited, high-pitched bark, Timber scrambled out from behind the counter and the gray-haired woman, possibly in her late sixties or early seventies, pulled a dog biscuit from the pocket of her bright pink, ankle-length skirt.

"Here you go, Timber." Directing a beaming smile at the dog while he practically inhaled the biscuit, she said, "Luckily, I remembered at the last second to bring along a treat. You never would've forgiven me if I hadn't." Once no evidence of the treat was left, she looked up and her gaze sliced between me and Rett, causing an extra crease to join the rest already on her forehead. "I'm sorry, I didn't mean to interrupt you gentlemen."

"You didn't, Dolly. I was just chatting with the newest resident of Eagle's Landing."

She stepped up to the counter and gave me a thorough once-over. "Oh, I haven't seen you around town yet." She jutted out her hand and I had no choice but to take it without appearing ruder than normal.

I did not miss the amusement in Rett's eyes, but I ignored it.

The older woman gave our clasped hands an unexpectedly firm shake. "I'm Dolores Monaghan, the mayor's wife. You can call me Dolly."

"And an avid reader," Rett added with a wink to Dolly. "She alone keeps the store in business. As well as Timber's belly full of treats."

"I'm retired. What else do I have to do?" she asked with a gleam in her eyes.

35

"You told me it's a full time job keeping Chet in line."

"Yes, that's true," she said with a laugh. "Next to every successful man stands an even stronger woman." She winked at me. "That's my version."

It was probably a very accurate version, too.

I gave the older woman an awkward smile. She had to be at least a foot shorter than me, if not more. Not only was her long skirt bright pink but she wore a bright lime green blouse, a pair of purple Crocs and rainbow-colored striped socks.

Obviously, Eagle's Landing wasn't any kind of fashion mecca.

Dolly once again set her blue eyes on me. "And *your* name?"

A soft snort came from behind the counter.

I closed my eyes for a second to prevent them from rolling out of my head and down one of the aisles. "Chase."

"Ah yes, Chet did blather on the other night at dinner about a new resident in town who bought the old Coleman cabin. It's Chase..." She snapped her fingers. "Chase Jones, right?"

Shit. "Yes, that's right."

"Well, welcome to the most boring town you'll ever live in. Even our gossip is boring."

"I'm perfectly fine with boring."

"Good, then you'll love it here." She turned back to Rett. "Whelp, handsome, I'm trading in these two books and picking up the last one available in the series. Too bad the next one isn't out yet. They're almost as addictive as yours."

They're almost as addictive as yours.

My heart did a little tumble. Had she recognized me?

No, she wasn't saying that to me, she was saying that to the man behind the counter.

Huh. He must be some kind of writer. Or wannabe writer.

Everyone and their brother thought they could write a book. They thought it was so damn easy. *Hell*, if it was, I would've banged out the next book in my Nick Foster series two years ago.

The truth was, it was far from easy. Writing a good book was difficult and could be mentally taxing, depending how intricate the plot was.

But if Rett was a writer, that also meant I had one more thing in common with him besides our love of books.

Son of a bitch.

Rett shot her a grin. "That's kind of you, Dolly, but my writing doesn't even compare. I only wish I had the same level of talent as this author."

Dolly wagged a finger at him. "Oh, don't sell yourself short, handsome. You might not be an international star yet, but you certainly are a local one." With that and a wink, she turned and headed toward the wall of shelves that held the crime thrillers, suspense novels and mysteries.

With a frown, my eyes flicked to the books Dolly had set on the counter.

For shit's sake. They were my books.

My books.

I needed to get out of there. Like ten minutes ago.

Without another word, I bolted out the door.

I heard a deep, "Hey!" right before it shut behind me.

CHAPTER 3

Rett

WHAT THE HELL?

Chase Jones—if that was even his real name—acted like he'd seen a freaking ghost. And, even weirder, he had rushed out of the store like one was chasing him.

The man was...

Not odd... different.

He seemed not only closed off and even anti-social, he was...

I wasn't sure how to describe it.

Broken, possibly. Or emotionally damaged by the way he looked, the way he spoke and how he interacted.

Just like the other morning when I first spotted him at the diner, dark half-moons still marred his face under the dark brown, but dull, eyes.

He seemed emotionally empty inside. Clinging to life by only his fingernails.

He was either hiding something or running from something.

Either could be possible and both would be a good reason for him to move to Eagle's Landing and buy the Coleman cabin. Most folks looking for a new beginning didn't move to a remote town that only provided the bare minimum. Someone in hiding usually did.

To be fair, it could be that Chase, prior to moving here, had no clue about small town living and would eventually regret it—if he already didn't—because where he chose could be considered hiding in plain view. He picked a place where *everyone* would learn his name and, unfortunately, his personal business.

In Eagle's Landing, no one escaped that.

Did I love the area? Of course. I wouldn't want to live anywhere else. But like I told the newest resident, I didn't need much. And while the town might be small and lacked amenities, it had a huge advantage over a large town or city living. Despite everyone knowing everything about you, those same people created a tight knit group and even considered each other family. That was a given, whether you wanted it or not.

Unlike in more populated areas, here no one needed an official invite to picnics, barbecues, parties, or whatever. The assumption was, if there was a gathering of any kind, everyone was invited and no one was excluded. No matter what.

Even if it was a baby shower. Or a high school graduation party.

All you had to do was show up, bring a covered dish and enjoy the company.

The local businesses, like Harry's Hardware and The Roost, the only bar in town, would keep a running tab for the locals. If asked, I would do the same in my store or even let someone borrow books if they couldn't afford to buy them.

Our town did not center around money or material things, it centered around being a community that supported each other as best as we could.

If someone was in trouble, we all stepped in.

If someone was sick and couldn't shovel or plow their own driveway, then phone calls would go out and eventually someone would show up to get that work done.

But besides how closed off Chase acted, what also caught my

attention was the wedding band on his left ring finger. Because it was a plain gold ring, it couldn't be mistaken for anything else.

However, the newcomer had been alone at the diner.

When I had asked Marlene, the waitress at the Eagle's Nest said that he'd been coming in for breakfast and dinner for days and every time he did, he'd been by himself. He also spoke to no one in the diner but the staff serving him and even then, it was only the bare minimum. He wasn't rude to them, but he wasn't warm, either.

Basically, the man seemed to be shutting everyone out, no matter what effort they made to be friendly. A reason had to exist behind that kind of behavior.

On the other hand, Chase could simply be one of those people who took a while to warm up to strangers.

When it came down to it, the real question was, why should I care?

If the man wanted to be left alone, then that was what he wanted. I really had no business trying to do a deep dive into someone doing whatever he could to keep others at surface level. Even though that went against every fiber of my being. I'd always been naturally curious and liked to dig into mysteries.

Especially a mystery like Chase Jones.

But then, it was also why I loved writing those types of novels, too.

Chase had asked how the store sustained itself. I hadn't lied when I said it didn't. I was lucky enough that my book royalties paid the bills. By living above the store, and also beneath my means, I made it all work.

I was happy, my readers were happy, and my bookstore customers were happy, too.

Unfortunately, I never got a chance to tell Chase that the two books he bought were *my* books. That I'd written them right there in The Next Page.

Not that I needed the recognition. I was simply excited to witness someone interested in reading them besides my local fanbase.

Dolly appeared from between the book shelves with Timber on her heels.

My dog loved the woman. However, Timber wasn't very fickle and would love anyone who carried dog treats in their pockets. Clearly, the way to my Shepherd's heart was through his stomach.

That would also work for me, too. Unfortunately, as a gay man in a tiny town full of straight folk, nobody was knocking down my door with a homemade casserole and a bottle of wine.

"I wish Anson would hurry up and publish his next book. It's been over two years since he published this one!" Dolly complained, slapping a book onto the counter.

It was the last book available in the Detective Nick Foster series written by one of my favorite authors. "I agree. I wish he would, too."

"Since you're also an author and a bookstore owner, do you think you can reach out to his publisher and ask for some sort of timeline?"

Uh no, I couldn't. I was not making that unforgivable *faux pas*.

"You can't rush perfection, Dolly. Authors sometimes need a break. You know how mentally taxing it can be to come up with fresh plots good enough to suck in readers."

Dolly reached over the counter and patted my arm. "Yes, I know. I need to learn some patience. But the series is so gosh picking good. What about your next one? You know I'm dying to read it early."

"I promise as soon as I write those two final words: 'the end,' it'll be in your eager hands. Then you can rip it apart with that red pen of yours so I can fix all my mistakes."

Dolly shot me a smile. "You don't make mistakes, handsome. A big publisher should be knocking down your door, too. Really, so should the Hollywood folks. Wouldn't that be wonderful? Seeing your books come to life on the big screen?"

With all the horrible books to movie adaptations out there? I didn't need my book babies butchered like that. "I don't need all that. I'm doing just fine the way things are."

"True. And if those Hollywood folks come calling, we might lose you and we can't have that."

"I don't plan on going anywhere. I love it right here."

Dolly winked at me. "Well, we love having you, handsome. We just need to find you a good wife so you can bless us with some babies."

I mentally groaned. A wife and babies were not on my bucket list. Even though everyone in town always insisted that their cousin's sister's daughter's best friend would be a perfect match. I would force a smile, nod my head and tell them I was perfectly happy with remaining single.

I gave Dolly that same smile in answer. I needed to ring up her purchase before she continued to harp on how I needed to find a good woman and make a family.

I wasn't looking for any woman, good or otherwise and I certainly didn't want to have sex with one. I fought my shudder.

I told Chase that I'd been staring at him across the diner because he looked familiar. While he did, the familiarity also had to do with what I had always been looking for in a partner.

At first, the man had caught my attention because *he* fit my type. Then after unabashedly staring at him for a few minutes, I thought I recognized him from somewhere. Chase looked strangely familiar.

From a past life maybe.

I didn't know and couldn't explain it. It could also boil down to wishful thinking.

One day my future Prince Charming would ride into my little town and…

I sighed. Obviously, I needed to stop reading gay romances. They were giving me unrealistic romantic expectations.

If only finding my future "hero" was as easy in real life as it was in novels…

But then, it was called fiction for a reason.

I grabbed the UPC reader attached to the store's point-of-sale system and flipped the book over to scan the ISBN on the back.

The author's small black and white photo next to the short bio on the back cover stared back at me.

I blinked, thinking I was seeing things, picked up the book and squinted to take a closer look at the photo. Then I rubbed my eyes to make sure I wasn't imagining it.

I wasn't.

Son of a bitch.

"I knew he looked familiar," I muttered under my breath.

I quickly skimmed the generic bio. Of course it included no detailed information on the man who recently rushed out of my shop like Michael Myers was chasing him with a butcher knife.

"Who?"

I glanced up at Dolly, almost forgetting she still stood waiting.

Holy shit. My eyes flicked from her back to the book in my hand.

Chase Jones was actually C.J. Anson, the *New York Times, USA Today, Wall-Street Journal* and international bestselling author.

Holy shit.

Holy. Shiiiiiiiiit.

We had a freaking legend amongst our midst.

I had read every one of Anson's blood-rushing, nail-biting twenty-two crime thriller novels from cover to cover, trying to absorb even a smidgeon of the man's talent.

He hadn't said a word. Not one damn word.

Was that why he rushed out of the store? Was he afraid of being discovered?

Dolly's brow was pulled low in concern. "Are you okay, handsome? You suddenly went a bit pale. Do you need to sit down?"

"I'm... fine." I snapped myself out of my stupor, finished ringing Dolly up and handed her the only copy of Anson's latest book I had left in stock.

She tucked it against her chest like it was precious and gave Timber one last pat on the head. "I'm sure I'll be whipping through this one in the next couple of days. I'll see you when I trade it in, if I don't see you before."

I made a mental note to order more copies. Of *all* the man's books. I needed to dedicate a whole bookshelf to the man, have him sign them all and promote them as written by a local author.

Without a doubt Chase would tell me to fuck off.

Luckily, being an author had given me thick skin. "Okay, Dolly. Say hello to Chet for me."

"Will do, handsome."

And then the mayor's wife was gone, leaving me standing at the counter, still a bit dazed from the fact that one of my most revered authors had not only moved to my town, he'd been in my bookstore and we'd actually had a conversation. Not the best conversation but an exchange of words nonetheless.

Funny… I expected to be a lot more excited about meeting *the* C.J. Anson. But I wasn't. In fact, I was kind of disappointed, because…

My "unicorn" author, unfortunately, turned out to be a complete rude asshole.

~

I STARED at the computer screen with my fingers hovering over the keyboard. I'd gone over the same sentence at least twenty times but something about it was off.

For the past four hours I'd been writing without a break. My brain was telling me to step away from the computer and my current work in progress, take Timber for a long walk, then come back and tackle my word salad again once my mind was clearer.

I'd probably feel stupid once I returned and the problem with my sentence structure or word choice smacked me right in the face.

Before I could even rise from my chair, the cow bell above the door clanged, indicating I had a customer. Or someone coming in simply to chat.

Timber, who'd been curled up at my feet under the desk, unwound his lanky body and with a soft *woof* headed out to the front to see if some kind soul had brought him an afternoon treat.

"I'm in the back," I called out.

Most of the locals knew where to find me and I rarely got customers who weren't local. I waited for an answer to see who had entered, but none came.

Since that made the fine hairs on the back of my neck stand, I pushed to my feet with a groan to see who came in. At forty-one, sitting for hours at a time made my body go on strike. It also liked to remind me often that I wasn't twenty-one anymore.

That was another good reason to take Timber for a walk. Fresh air would do my stiff body and my mushy brain some good.

I headed toward the front of the store only to find neither Timber nor a customer. Glancing out the window, only one vehicle was parked out front. A new Ford Bronco Raptor.

I knew exactly who it belonged to.

The sound of Timber's nails on the wood flooring came from the area where both C.J. Anson's and my books were shelved.

Should I even bother? He was only going to tell me he didn't need any help.

I grinned. Of course I should. Even if just to annoy him.

I peeked around the corner and saw Chase scratching Timber behind the ears and my dog's eyes closed in ecstasy.

I'd have that same reaction, too, if he scratched me like that.

Apparently I needed to have a little discussion with my dog about loyalty. If someone didn't like his dad, then Timber shouldn't like that person. That was Canine Behavior 101.

"Well, look who couldn't stay away," I said dryly.

Chase's brown eyes rose from Timber to me as I walked between the shelves to get to where they were.

"I don't need any help."

Of course. If the man was anything, it was being consistent in his grumpiness. Two could play at this *let's-be-a-dick* game. "I didn't ask if you did."

"But here you are anyway."

"Well, if you weren't aware of it yet, it's my store."

"You made that clear the other day."

I hiked my eyebrows up to the top of my forehead. "Did I? I wasn't sure."

Chase grunted and turned to stare at the books. *His* books. Was he here to sign them?

That would mean Chase would have to admit he was C.J. Anson. I had a really strong feeling he wouldn't.

Hmm. I couldn't put a finger on why I had that feeling. For some odd reason, I just did.

Living in this area as long as I had, I'd been taught that you never run from a bear. You made yourself as big as possible, faced them down and created a lot of noise. You challenged them and hoped they backed down. Running would only get you hurt or killed.

Chase was that damn bear.

"Tell me, are you always this…" *Miserable.* "Personable? Or are you only like this with me?"

"Why would you think you're special? I'm like this with everyone."

I thought he might not have any redeeming qualities, but clearly I was wrong. He had the brutal honesty thing going for him. Even if it was only him being honest about being an asshole. "Why?"

"I don't like when people put their noses where they don't belong. If you're friendly with people, that gives them an opening to ask a lot of questions."

I noticed him spinning the wedding ring he hid the other day as he continued to stare at the shelves of books, most likely hoping I'd give up and wander away.

Whether he liked it or not, I was not running from the bear, I was standing my ground.

I studied Chase's profile. He clearly hadn't shaved since he'd been in here the other day. Growing out his beard made sense though, if he was trying to remain "undercover." The photo his publisher used on the back of his books must have been taken at least ten years ago when his face had less lines and was clean shaven.

He also had been wearing a dress shirt under a very sharply-styled fitted vest. Unlike the stretched-out, stained T-shirt and the mud-splattered jeans he currently wore.

Honestly, if I hadn't been a huge fan of his, I might have never recognized him. Now I wish I hadn't. Like the other day, disappointment filled me when it came to the author I previously held in such high regard.

I would've killed for him to be my mentor. Now I just leaned toward smothering him with a pillow to put him out of his misery. Especially since he was determined to spread that misery to everyone around him.

"So... that moat that you've dug around yourself... Just how deep is it?"

"Deep enough to drown." He twisted his head toward me and immediately I saw how tight his jaw was under the growth of whiskers. "So, here's some advice... it's best to stay out of it."

"I'm a damn good swimmer."

"It's not the water you have to worry about."

Apparently.

There came a time in every battle where you had to admit defeat. I had reached it. However, I wasn't finished fighting the war.

Why I felt the need to make the guy open up to me, I didn't know.

He was hurting and I had this crazy urge to help him. But I wouldn't know how to do that unless he gave me more than he currently was.

He was either protecting himself or a secret. Or both.

Since he was now a resident of Eagle's Landing, I had plenty of time to keep chipping away at him. Eventually he'd crumble, it was just a matter of time.

I could wait.

But in the meantime... "Are you here to trade in the books you bought?"

"No."

I waited patiently, not saying anything else but not leaving, either. I'm sure that annoyed him, too.

He sighed and gave me the side-eye. "If you must know, I'm here to buy more."

"More of the Dexter Peabody series?"

"Yes."

"You liked them?" I desperately tried not to squeal like a five-year-old girl. One of my favorite... correction... *former* favorite authors liked my books enough to keep reading them!

"I'm only partway through the third book but since the writing is as consistent and engaging as the first two books, I'm going to say yes."

That had to be painful for him to say, but... Be still my heart.

He frowned. "Are you surprised?"

I shouldn't be, but what author didn't suffer from imposter syndrome?

I had since the day I sat down to write the words "Chapter One" in my first book. I thought writing would be a hobby, a way to express myself creatively, instead it turned into a lucrative career.

Could I live off my royalties in New York City? No. But here in Eagle's Landing I could pay for everything I needed and even put a little aside. Plus, support a bookstore that would be in the red otherwise.

"Have you read them?"

I quickly pulled a blank mask down over my face. "Uh... Yes. All of them."

"Then you'd agree."

Of course, *I* thought they were good. No, not good, freaking *great*. Others must agree with me since they had stellar reviews and the royalties I made on them were enough to pay my expenses.

Holy shit. Chase Jones might be a dick, but at least he had good taste.

Even better, the great C.J. Anson had complimented my writing instead of ripping it apart.

However tempting it might be to blurt out that I was the author of those books, I kept that bottled up since I was afraid if Chase found out it was me who wrote them, he wouldn't read the rest of the series.

And I *desperately* wanted him to read the rest. Because once he was done, I planned on rubbing it in his face that I wrote them. I couldn't wait to see his reaction.

I smothered my grin.

"Since you insist on *helping* me..." He shoved a book at me.

I automatically grabbed it and he began removing all of his books from the shelves and I took them as fast as he handed them to me. "What are you doing?"

"Buying these."

"All of them?" I winced when my question ended with a high-pitched squeak.

"Are you allergic to money?"

Are you allergic to people? "Of course I like money but..." I was now struggling to hold a stack of twenty books and he wasn't done yet.

He removed all his books from the second shelf, too. This time he didn't give them to me, he piled them in his own arms.

Once both shelves were stripped bare, he pushed past me and I reluctantly followed him up to the register where he dropped them all on the counter.

I did the same and stared at him. I made sure my mouth wasn't hanging open. "Why would you buy them all?"

"Do you always question your customers on their purchases?"

"I would if I thought they lost their minds."

"Well, you can rest assured I know what I'm doing. Ring me up."

"But—"

"Ring me up," he said a little louder and a lot more forcefully. "Or are you refusing to sell the books to me?"

I shrugged. "You want them, you can have them. I can always order more." I added a grin onto that second statement.

"I'm going to ask you not to."

That made me pause. "Why? Why don't you want anyone reading them? Do they offend your delicate sensibilities in some way?" I knew exactly why Chase Jones didn't want them on the shelf. But until he admitted who he was, then I was going to act like I didn't know.

"Hardly."

"You know Dolly is a huge fan of this author. She's going to be upset that they're all gone."

"She'll get over it." He yanked his wallet from his back pocket. "Ring me up or I'm just going to throw some cash at you and hope it's enough."

I stared at him and he stared back in a silent challenge.

When my eyes narrowed, so did his.

When I didn't move to ring him up, one of his dark eyebrows lifted ever so slowly.

"I have a suggestion for another book for you. I think I have a copy in stock. It's called, *How to Win Friends & Influence People.*"

"I don't need that."

"I disagree."

"Then we'll have to agree to disagree."

Oh, he was a real peach.

"Ring me up."

"That book might even teach you the importance of the word 'please.' I don't remember because it's been so long since I've read it."

When he started to count the books piled on the counter, my attention got caught on his moving lips as he silently figured out the amount he owed me.

"When are you going to admit it? Or should I continue to pretend I don't know?"

He finished counting silently and then lifted his eyes to mine. "Admit what?"

I grabbed the top book on one of the stacks, turned it until the back copy was facing him and tapped his photo using my middle finger.

His gaze dropped to where I was pointing, his expression went from irritated to totally blank, he licked his lips and then pressed them together tightly.

His tongue sliding over his full lips affected me way more than it should... since he was a dick.

And I doubted he even liked dick. At least, more than his own.

Even if he did, I reminded myself that he had a stick shoved so far up his ass, there was no room for anything else. Like someone else's dick. Someone else possibly being me.

I tipped my head to the side. "You're really taking this whole remaining anonymous thing to an extreme by buying up all your books."

"I have my reasons."

"They're not good ones."

"That's not for you to decide."

Finally I said, "You're right." Since this was just another skirmish in what might be a drawn out war, I could let it go for now.

I heard him release a relieved sigh when I began to scan all the books and put them in an empty box I had behind the counter.

We didn't say another word to each other until after I gave him the total and he paid.

Normally, I'd offer to carry the box to the customer's car, but Chase was more than capable of carrying the heavy box himself.

But after he grabbed it, he slid it to the edge of the counter and paused. "Any more used copies come back, put them aside for me. I want them."

"So, what do you plan to do with all of them?"

"Burn them."

"Why?"

"Because I don't want anyone to know I'm here. Who I am."

"Why?" I repeated.

"You don't need to know that. Just do what I'm asking."

"You're not asking, you're ordering me."

"Then do what I'm ordering."

"I know you're new around here but... I don't take orders from anyone."

"Let's make it a request."

"That I can disregard."

"Of course, you can." Chase leaned in and locked his eyes with mine. "But you won't. As the author, I'm requesting you hold any copies of my books for me."

"Instead of buying and burning them all, I'd prefer if you would sign them instead."

"No."

"You'll be heralded as a celebrity around here."

"I'm not a celebrity," he growled. "That's like saying Stephen King or George R. R. Martin is a celebrity."

"They aren't?"

"I consider them talented artists. Creatives. Not celebrities. They shouldn't be put on that pedestal."

"Why not?"

His brow dropped low. "Why do you constantly question me?"

"Why are you so damn irritable all the time?"

"Why do you feel the need to be in my business?"

"I don't," I answered, matching his energy. "And you're standing in *my* business right now."

"That's not the same."

"You do know that anyone can easily find your picture online. Or even at the back of the e-books."

"Right, but that takes work. They're less likely to realize it's me."

"You're fooling yourself."

"And you may be right. Let me be a fool then."

"Like I said, Dolly's a huge fan."

"Great, then if she figures it out on her own, I'm sure she'll respect my privacy."

"Just so you know, she's the town's gossip hub."

"Great," he muttered. "When she brings back the copy she bought the other day, put it aside."

53

"Fine. How should I let you know I have it? Smoke signals? Carrier pigeon? Pony Express? Or do you want to leave your number?"

Any other customer would've chuckled at that. Not Chase Jones. Oh no. That would mean cracking a smile. Or being friendly. Or recognizing the fact that I had a great sense of humor.

"I'll stop in the next time I'm in town."

Of course. "I can't wait!" I exclaimed with feigned excitement while bouncing on my toes.

With another grunt, Chase heaved the heavy box into his arms and steadied it against his chest. I could at least hold the door for him, but decided to remain behind the counter and watch him struggle with balancing the box and getting the door open.

If he wanted help, he could ask for it.

Oh yes. Two could play the *let's-be-a-dick* game.

However, I think Chase was too much of a pro at it for me to ever win.

CHAPTER 4

Rett

I SHOULDN'T STOOP to his level and actually felt a twinge of guilt doing so. However, I didn't remember ever dealing with anyone so outright miserable.

Everyone seemed to like me. Just not Chase.

Why did I care?

I didn't.

Bullshit, if I didn't I wouldn't be risking the axles on my damn truck as I dodged large craters and deep valleys while driving up Coleman Lane.

I was better than that. I don't remember ever being goaded to the point it turned me into someone petty or rude. Chase deserved a medal because he was the first person to achieve it.

I really wanted to forget about him and continue on with my life before he so rudely interrupted it. But no matter how hard I tried, I couldn't.

I thought about him a lot. An actual disturbing amount.

Especially for someone acting as though he didn't like me as a fellow human being.

Most likely it wasn't an act. He could be the type of person who simply hated everyone, hated life in general and even himself.

Nobody was fixing that and I had no idea why I thought I could.

But again, here I was, driving directly up to the bear's den to poke the grumpy occupant like the total dumbass I was.

Today I came bearing gifts to try to soften him up a little. To "officially" welcome him to the community.

That was my excuse, anyway.

I told myself no matter how rude he was, no matter how hard he tried to push me away or shut me out, I would be the better person. I would simply drop off what I was bringing him, smile and then... move on. If he wanted to remain a dick that would be on him, not me.

I was going to be the better person.

I was. I swear.

Even if I had to work damn hard at it.

I also told myself that I didn't need him to be my friend. I didn't need him to be anything. I didn't even need him to be my favorite author anymore.

Suuuuuure.

It had been about three years since I'd driven up to the Coleman cabin. In fact, the last time I did, I had taken the state police with me to do a welfare check on Mr. Coleman. He had only moved permanently into the hunting cabin after his wife died a few years earlier.

Three years later he began coming into town less and less and eventually, the old man stopped coming completely. That wasn't like him. When Chet and Dolly asked me to check on him, they suggested the police go along, just in case of what might be found.

I was glad they did. I stayed outside while the two state troopers made entry and it wasn't long before they came back out, the rancid smell of a decomposing body clinging to their uniforms.

As soon as the cops called the coroner, I got into my truck and drove away. I went back to town to break the news to the mayor and his wife, who, in turn, spread the word to everyone else.

To die alone like that… Almost as if you'd been forgotten.

That had stuck with me. It also made my heart ache. And, of course, I was sorry I hadn't checked on him sooner.

If Chase kept pushing people away like he was, I was afraid he might end up the same. Alone and forgotten.

I maneuvered my Chevy through the roughly cleared patch of ground at the top of the lane and parked it next to the Bronco.

"Stay in the truck," I instructed Timber when I shifted the truck into Park and climbed out.

Timber answered me with a little *woo woo* sound of disappointment. That told me he'd listen to my command but he wouldn't be happy about doing so.

I stared at the cabin before me. It definitely looked a bit different since the last time I stood in almost the same spot.

The small back porch had been cleaned up. It looked like the windows had been replaced. The roof was now metal and in a lot better shape than when Mr. Coleman lived in the cabin.

From where I stood, all it needed was some landscaping and it would actually look like a home instead of a hunting cabin. Or *former* hunting cabin.

Hunting cabins in the area usually only had the basics and weren't used all year long. And sometimes "hunters" only used their cabins and hunting as an excuse to escape their wives and family for a week.

Thwack.

Thwack.

Thwack.

I might not be an outdoorsman, but I certainly knew what chopping wood sounded like. Since it was only May and winter was a long way off, I had no idea why Chase would be chopping wood now. Unless he was only trying to get a jump on it.

I followed the sound around the right side of the cabin, pausing only to quickly check the propane gauge to make sure Chase had filled it. He had.

Next to the huge tank sat what looked like a new generator. Smart. When the electricity went out—and up on the mountain that was a guaranteed occurrence during some of the crazy storms—he'd have a backup.

New roof. New windows. New generator. A full propane tank. Evidence that the man was digging in his heels and staying a while.

I even spotted a new satellite dish on the roof. Most likely for internet service. With Chase being an author, having access to the internet was crucial. I couldn't do research, publish or market my books without it.

Thwack.

Thwack.

Thwack.

As I continued to follow the sound, my eyes scanned the area near the firewood lean-to. It wasn't coming from there. The old stump Mr. Coleman used to split wood still remained where it was, but no Chase.

As the sound continued, I twisted my head to the left and toward the "front" of the cabin, the side that faced Eagles Lake, the small private lake Chase now owned.

On the opposite side of the cabin at the edge of the surrounding woods was another huge stump. A chainsaw sat on the ground off to the side, and with his back to me was...

A shirtless, sweaty, very focused Chase.

I figured he'd be writing when I drove up. *Holy hell*, was I wrong.

So, so wrong.

I'd never been so happy to be wrong. Under his glistening skin, his muscles flexed and rippled with each strike of the ax. Each lift and fall of his arms.

It had been a month since Chase had come into The Next Page when he bought all of his own books.

Apparently, that month of living in the woods had done a body good.

Really good.

The *I had to wipe away the saliva that caught in the corner of my mouth* type of good.

Hot damn.

Why were the men who caught my attention always straight? Or a dick? Or both?

With my shitty luck and also being hindered by living in Bumfuck, Pennsylvania, I was afraid I'd never find my soulmate, once again unlocking that fear of dying alone.

While Chase might not even be close to being my soulmate, that didn't mean I couldn't appreciate the fine masculine specimen before me.

From the two times he was in the store, I knew he was at least two or three inches taller than me, his body naturally bulkier, his shoulders a bit wider. Even from what little I could see of his face, it didn't look as ragged as it had been the last time he'd been in town.

It could be the physical exercise he was getting, which was apparent from the small mountain of split firewood next to him. It might also have to do with him being outside and getting lots of fresh air.

Of course, I needed to get closer to verify my observations and to give him what I brought as sort of an olive branch.

As I moved closer, I realized he had no clue I was there. He hadn't heard my truck come up the lane or me walking toward him because of his constant chopping.

He didn't stop or even pause once while I watched. He split one piece of firewood right after the other like he was on a mission to beat back demons with that ax.

The closer I got, the easier it was to see the sweat beading on his forehead and rolling down the sides of his face. To see the muscles surging under the wide expanse of his back. The way his flexing thighs filled his jeans.

I swore his legs were thicker than a month ago, too.

If I didn't know any better, at first glance I would think Chase was some wild mountain man living off the land, not a bestselling author of crime thrillers.

He made one hot mountain man, even if his hair was getting a bit shaggy and his beard a little too long. A pair of scissors could fix that easily enough.

His chest was thickly furred above his pecs and that black wiry hair stopped just before his sternum to pick up again below his naval to only disappear past the waist of his jeans.

That was one hell of a trail I wouldn't mind blazing.

I ran my tongue over my lips, fighting the urge to lick the sweat off those pecs, even knowing it might taste bitter from his acidic attitude.

Hell, I wanted to do much more than give him a tongue bath. But Chase *was* holding an ax. And up here no one would hear me scream if he decided to use it on me for ogling him like a depraved, sex-starved gay man who had a thing for bears.

Which, apparently and very unfortunately, I was.

Without a pause in the swing of his ax, he called out, "You done?"

I lifted my eyes just as slowly as I had lowered them. I still had time to appreciate the man since he hadn't turned to look at me yet. "Done with what?"

"Your latest assessment."

Shit. Busted. "I have no reason to assess you."

He slammed the ax into the large stump so it got wedged in the center. Releasing the handle, he turned to face me and pulled off his leather gloves. "Then don't."

I can't help it if I appreciate the view. As much as I don't want to. "Can I ask you a question?"

He reached for the T-shirt hanging over a nearby branch and I almost shed a tear when I thought he was going to pull it on.

He didn't. Thankfully, he only used it to wipe the sweat off his face. "No."

I asked it anyway, since apparently we were still playing the *let's-be-a-dick* game. Even if I had to accept a loss, it would still be satisfying to get in a few good hits. "When's the last time you smiled?"

His expression changed from empty to totally closed off.

"I can tell you used to smile because you have permanent lines at the corner of your eyes."

With his shirt now tossed over his shoulder and his hands plugged on his hips, he turned to face me completely, his dark eyes locking with mine. "Why the hell are you here?"

If eyeballs were capable of shooting lasers from them, I'd be dead.

"I haven't seen you in town in weeks. I got worried." I might have missed him going into town but that was my only plausible excuse to check on him. And when I asked around, no one else had seen him, either. Not anyone at The Eagle's Nest, Harry's Hardware or even at The Roost.

"I don't need anyone worrying about me."

"Maybe not. But just because you don't need it doesn't mean it won't happen."

"I've been busy."

"Apparently." My eyes flicked to the huge pile of split wood that still needed to be stacked, then I glanced back over my shoulder to the almost-full lean-to. "If you haven't noticed yet, you have enough firewood for the next three winters, Chase. Or do you prefer C.J.?"

He ignored my question. No surprise. "I don't do it for the firewood."

Who splits firewood for the hell of it? It wasn't fun. It was back-breaking, blister-causing work. "Then what are you doing it for?"

"I do it…"

That pause was telling and gave me my answer.

He did it as an outlet. A form of therapy. To chase away whatever ghosts haunted him.

Whatever those were.

But if it helped, it helped. It must since the half-moon shadows under his dark brown eyes were now gone. Seeing him head-on, I confirmed his face didn't look as gaunt, either. His eyes were no longer empty, even if they held a bit of annoyance in them right now. For both disturbing him and asking questions he didn't want to answer.

In fact, I was pretty sure if I asked him what color the sky was, he would purposely not answer. Simply to make a point.

No matter what, there appeared to be a little bit more life to him now. Unlike when I first spotted him at the Eagle's Nest. He had looked like he'd been run over by a damn bus.

Maybe not physically, but emotionally.

Something or someone had damaged this man. Whatever it was, whoever it was, was most likely the culprit in why the next book in his series had been delayed.

Whatever happened had knocked him off track.

The sun glinted off his wedding band. If I was a betting man, I'd guess it had something to do with that.

A wedding ring without a spouse. Maybe it had been an unwanted divorce on his part and he was having a tough time letting go.

Not all parties in a divorce wanted one. In fact, some fought a divorce hard. They wanted to make the marriage work even when they shouldn't.

But if that was true for Chase, then it made sense to move to a new place in a remote location where no one knew him. A place to hide out to heal without anyone breathing down his neck.

A place to lick his wounds.

Like an injured and surly bear.

His repeated sharp demand of "Why are you here?" shook me from my thoughts.

"No one had seen you in town for the last month, so I decided to check on you. You might be new to the community but that doesn't mean you aren't a part of it now. You are, no matter if you want to be or not." When his jaw shifted, I kept going but spoke a little faster before he chased me off his property. "I also brought you a few things as sort of a welcoming gift."

"I don't want gifts."

The man was nothing if not consistent. "You might want these."

When I moved even closer, I could pick up the metallic scent of the sweat beginning to dry on his skin, mixed with the aroma of the split wood and spring blossoms on the trees.

I widened my nostrils and tried not to be too obvious when I took a deep inhale, pulling that intoxicating mix again into my lungs. I also kept my hands busy—and more importantly to myself—by removing items from the plastic bag I'd been holding.

I handed him the book Dolly had finished reading. *His* book. "You wanted all copies. Dolly returned this a while ago but since you didn't stop back in, I was holding it for you."

He glanced at the book in my hand for a moment before lifting his gaze back to mine. Was he surprised I did what he asked... or ordered? Maybe.

He took it from me. "I'll get you some money."

"I don't want it. Here. This is for you, too." I held out the fifth book in my Dexter Peabody series. "Since you said you liked these, I figured I'd bring this up to you. You had to have read the other two by now."

Again, I didn't tell him that I was the author because I wanted him to keep reading my books. He might act like a dick but I still couldn't fight the thrill of an accomplished author like C.J. Anson reading and enjoying books from a much smaller author like me.

Especially an author I had deep respect for. Or used to, anyway.

Even so, simply seeing my book in his hands when he took it from me, made me want to bounce all the way back down the mountain like Tigger from Winnie the Pooh.

When he lifted his face again after staring for an awkwardly long time at the two books he now held, his jaw softened a bit and his eyes lost some of the annoyance they'd been holding.

Holy shit, I made a dent. It might be a small dent but it was progress.

I pulled the flyer out of the bag next and held it out to him.

He stared at the single sheet of paper like it was a rattlesnake for far too long.

I shook it to encourage him to take it, but he still refused. "This is a list of what's going on in the bookstore for the month. In case you're interested." I shrugged. "If not, you can use it for a fire starter."

When he still didn't reach for it, I slapped it against his chest, doing my best not to linger over his heated skin.

"It's a good way to meet everyone," I added.

When he finally reached for the flyer, whether to peel it from his still sweaty chest and throw it back at me, or because he was interested, he used his left hand since his right hand was already full of books. I held onto the flyer for a second and while I did, I tipped my head down to his ring and decided to take a risk with my next question. "Divorce?"

When I released the flyer, he scanned the list of live events I had planned for the bookstore in May.

While reading the flyer, he grumbled, "It's none of your business."

"You're right. It's not. I'm sorry for bothering you. I only came up here to give you those books, invite you to the bookstore's activities and officially welcome you to Eagle's Landing…"

"Then you did what you came to do. Now you can—"

I pushed on, talking over him before he totally shut me out. "Also to let you know that if you need anything, just ask. Everyone around here is more than willing to help when and where they can. It's one of the benefits of living in a small town like ours. We've built a solid community and we all step in when needed. So, if you thought you'd be able to hide up here, you picked the wrong place for that. Especially after Mr. Coleman died up here alone. We don't ever want that happening again."

At least I didn't. I hadn't taken a poll with the rest of the town's residents, but I could safely say I spoke for them, too.

Chase's gaze sliced over to the cabin, then back to me. "Coleman died in the cabin?"

"Unfortunately. I was here with the police when they found him. I guess the listing agent didn't tell you." Not that they were obligated to disclose that information.

"No foul play, right?"

I could see his wheels turning as he considered what I just told him. He wrote crime thrillers, so of course someone dying from anything other than natural causes would catch his interest. As it would mine.

"No. It was a combination of old age and bad health. He lost his wife years earlier and I think he came up here to spend the last of his days in his favorite spot. Who could blame him since it's beautiful up here."

Chase turned to face the lake, giving me his back. I could barely hear his murmured, "Yeah."

Not only was the view up at the Coleman cabin beautiful, so was the *naked-from-the-waist-up* man before me. He was working on sculpting his body into a work of art.

I could appreciate art like that. Like him. Even if he was straight as an arrow.

"Divorce can be almost as hard to deal with as death, since you're losing someone you love, the person who was supposed to be your partner in life."

Why was I pushing him? Why did I feel the need to get him to open up to me? Why did I want to take on a challenge that I knew would be no better than banging my head against a wall?

Was it because we were fellow authors and that alone should create a bond or spark a friendship between us?

Or was it because I finally found someone to discuss the trials and tribulations of being a full-time author? Someone who would understand my way of life? Who understood my passion?

"Not divorced."

Those two words were a small nugget of info I was surprised he gave me. No, not surprised, floored. It made me optimistic that I might be making some headway.

"I'm a widower."

Fuck. "I'm sorry about your wife."

With his back still turned toward me and the flyer from The Next Page crushed within his fingers, Chase only nodded.

I counted the heartbeats pounding in my ears as I waited to see if he'd say anything else. To expand on the bomb he just dropped.

When he finally turned back around to face me, his expression was once again as blank as a fresh page in one of my many spiral notebooks. "Are you done?"

"I—"

"With what you came up here to do?"

"Yes, I—"

"You know how to get back, then."

I was being dismissed.

I jerked my chin toward the flyer he was choking in his fist. "Think about it. You're welcome to do some readings of your own books."

His face still gave me nothing when he said, "That's not going to happen." Then he turned on his heels and headed toward the cabin.

I stood and watched his long strides increase the distance between us in record time. Without a glance back at me, he climbed the porch steps, entered the cabin and shut the door.

Effectively shutting me out.

Message received loud and clear.

But since he didn't rip the flyer up in front of me, I hoped I at least planted a seed. Now it was on him to help that seed grow into an olive branch. Or kill it with a lack of caring.

I'd be a fool to think he liked olives.

CHAPTER 5

Rett

CHASE JONES ENDED up being a more common name than I expected. Every time I took a break from writing or helping a customer, I would dig through pages of pages of results from my online search.

Of the closed-off man.

Of the author.

Of the widower.

While I had no problem finding "Author C.J. Anson," what came up was always basic and only had to do with his writing or books. Most of it was old information from past book tours, press releases and things of that nature. I even stumbled across video clips of him signing books for his fans at scheduled events, or from when his public relations team arranged for him to go on a talk show to promote an upcoming book.

But everything I found was from years ago and nothing current.

He looked different in any and all photos and videos I found. Happier and lighter. Not dark and grumpy like a grizzly bear who went into hibernation with a thorn still stuck in its paw.

Chase had definitely gone "underground." From the limited

investigation I could do, it looked like things changed about two years ago.

Even in some of the C.J. Anson fan forums, some asked where the author was, what happened to him and when was his next book coming out. Some readers were concerned about him, while others were more demanding and extremely angry since he left them hanging for so long without a new Nick Foster case to solve.

I didn't get the attitude of the second group. As one who read his series more than once, I knew firsthand that none of his books ended in a cliffhanger and if the next book was never written, those readers weren't out anything.

Because of angry "mob-like" mentality, it made sense for him to go into hiding to escape those demands and that pressure. My guess was, his publisher was riding Chase's ass, too, since he made them a nice chunk of change. And like his readers, they probably felt as though they were being screwed over.

In truth, Chase owed them nothing. Not his publisher, not his big-time agent, not even his readers. He owed it to himself to take a break if and when he needed it. Even if that break was two years and counting.

While I was just as anxious to read the next book in the series as everyone else, including Dolly, I wouldn't make death threats or threaten a writer with any kind of violence like some of the comments I unfortunately read on these forums. Some were downright scary. I couldn't imagine the kind of emails his agent or publisher received. Some of them had to be even worse.

This was a case of fiction being mistaken for real life. People forgot that characters in a novel were just that. Fiction. Nothing more, nothing less.

Imaginary people born and continuing to live in an author's mind.

Though, it could be said that the passion his readers had toward his work was a testament to how well Chase wrote. How much his words sucked a reader into a story. They felt as if they were solving a serial murder case alongside the handsome, intelligent Detective Nick Foster.

Honestly, if I had the power, I would snap my fingers and a real Nick Foster would walk through the front door and sweep me off my feet. Or sweep me off to bed.

But as much as I could fantasize about that, I knew where the line was drawn between fact and fiction.

And one fact I now knew was that Chase was a widower. That led me to start searching online for obituaries. However, I couldn't be positive that Chase Jones wasn't a fake name. And if it was, I was wasting time I could be using to finish my next Dexter Peabody book before my deadline.

C.J. Anson wasn't the only author with clamoring fans. Maybe I didn't have quite the number he had, but my readers, once hooked on my bumbling private investigator series, were pretty loyal.

I was damn lucky to have them, too. Without my readers encouraging me to write the next book, I wouldn't be able to keep the bookstore open, or even pay my bills.

With a drawn-out sigh, I scrolled through the tenth page of results after googling the terms: Chase, Jones, obituary and New York. One of the facts mentioned on C.J. Anson's "About the Author" page on his very professionally done website was he lived in New York. Unfortunately, the Empire State was big.

I understood the need to keep his most personal details private for his safety. Most authors did. And after reading some of the threats of violence against him just for taking so long to release the next book, I'm glad he had.

My eyes skimmed the search results as I continued to scroll, waiting for something to jump out at me. Why did Jones have to be such a common last name?

By the fourteenth page of search results, I was about to give up for the day when something caught my eye.

Survived by his devoted husband Chase A. Jones.

In my head I could hear the squeal of tires as I slammed on the brakes, threw it in reverse to scroll back up, clicked on the link to open the complete obituary, leaned closer toward the monitor, and reread that single line.

Survived by his *devoted husband Chase A. Jones.*

Chase Jones had been married to another man. His *wife* wasn't dead. His *husband* was.

My heart did a little *thumpity-thump* in my chest.

Chase was *gay.*

Holy shit.

The obituary was for a Thomas P. Jones. Skimming it, I couldn't find a cause of death, only that he died suddenly. I assumed that the death was unexpected, too, since there wasn't any mention of an illness.

I also noted that it listed Chase's parents as Thomas's survivors but not Thomas's own parents. That was odd.

In lieu of flowers, the obit asked that donations be made in Thomas's memory to The Trevor Project.

The Trevor Project.

I donated to that non-profit once a year when I had a little spare cash, since the organization focused on suicide prevention and crisis intervention for LGBTQ+ youth. However, that didn't mean that Thomas died by suicide, it could just be a non-profit Chase or his husband liked to support. For good reason.

I didn't want to speculate on his cause of death. How it happened wasn't my business, even as curious as I was.

That wasn't the point I needed to focus on. The focus was that Chase had gone through a huge loss and that was most likely the reason for the state he was currently in and why his writing had suffered.

When my brother had died in a tragic motorcycle accident eleven years ago, it had devastated me.

Losing my younger brother also put me off my game when it came to writing. Like Chase, I was pulled into a dark space for months. I questioned life, I questioned everything, including what was most important to me. Eventually I shook it, but it had been a struggle.

Even so, I couldn't imagine losing a soulmate like that. It had to be like losing a limb. A part of you totally ripped away, leaving you no longer whole.

When Evan died, I was already living here in Eagle's Landing, so I was extremely lucky to have a support system in place within the community. But maybe Chase didn't have that. It could be he was trying to work through this loss all on his own.

If so, it now made sense as to why Chase still wore his wedding band and why he grappled when dealing with people. Also why he left New York and came here, to a town where he had nothing or no one.

And somewhere no one would know him.

Except I knew.

But the question was, what should I do about it, if anything?

IN THE DISTANCE, I could hear the clang of the cow bell as I read out loud. I didn't know if it was someone coming in late or leaving early. Either way, I made a mental note to disable the cow bell before the next weekly event. It usually wasn't a problem if I forgot, but in the rare occurrences that it happened, the bell could be distracting.

Like now.

I scanned the folding chairs set up in front of the tiny stage and when I didn't notice anyone missing, I figured it was the mayor stopping back in to pick up Dolly. Chet never missed an opportunity like this to go face-to-face with the residents of Eagle's Landing. Besides being a great mayor, the townspeople loved him enough that he'd run unopposed for that spot for the last twenty years.

However, not the avid reader that his wife was, Chet rarely stuck around for book or poetry readings. Most of the time he just dropped Dolly off, then headed down to The Roost to have a few beers until whatever event I was having at the bookstore was over.

As the latecomer appeared from between the rows of shelves and slid quietly into a seat at the back, I stumbled over a sentence at the end of chapter four from my current work-in-progress. It wasn't like my store's events got a packed house, so Chase sneaking in at the tail-end of me reading from my first draft didn't go unnoticed.

I did my best to ignore him as I finished up, opened up the floor to questions and then encouraged people to grab more coffee, as well as a freshly-baked cookie as they browsed or to take along with them on their way out.

As a side hobby, I loved to bake. It not only made me happy, it made the store and my apartment above it smell mouth-wateringly delicious. So, every week I baked something from scratch for the attendees as a thank you for taking the time to stop in. By doing so, it showed they supported the store and the weekly "headliners," be it an author, a musician, or even a child reading a story they wrote.

While this week it was chocolate chip cookies, next week it could be brownies, banana bread or even a cake. It all depended on my mood and by the end of the half-hour long reading or performance, the platter was usually picked clean.

I liked to think the weekly events I held both filled their mind, as well as their bellies.

"Don't forget that I have a stack of pre-signed books at the register. I'll be up there shortly to ring up anyone with purchases," I called out, even though most people didn't linger afterward.

From the table nearby, I grabbed my water and chugged down half the bottle since doing a reading was thirsty work.

Plus, I had gotten a little thirsty at seeing Chase slip in at the last minute.

While I had tried to concentrate on reading my own words clearly, I had a difficult time ignoring the man I now looked at with different eyes knowing he played on the same team as I did.

Besides the both of us being authors and readers, we were both gay and single. Chase moving to Eagle's Landing could very well be kismet. *If* Chase didn't have heavy clouds hanging over his head. But the fact was, he did and he'd be emotionally unavailable until those dark clouds cleared.

I doubted that would be anytime soon. A good indicator was him still wearing his husband's ring, even though the man died a little over two years ago.

Chase was still that "devoted" husband.

While everyone dealt with losing a loved one differently and also at a different pace, after losing Evan, I had learned about and went through the five stages of grief myself: denial, anger, bargaining, depression and finally, acceptance.

I couldn't imagine it was healthy for him to still be stuck in that fourth stage, the darkest stage, even though I had been warned that part could last the longest and be the most difficult. However, until Chase accepted the loss, he couldn't move on. And I didn't mean move on in a way he'd forget his husband, but more like adjust to living without his "other half."

Maybe he simply needed a shove toward the last stage of acceptance.

"C'mon, boy," I called to Timber while patting my thigh. Stepping off the low stage, I headed toward the front of the store.

When I couldn't find Chase, I was disappointed that he'd snuck out just as quickly as he'd snuck in and before I got a chance to check in with him.

But what I did find was a half dozen event regulars still gathered near the register, sharing gossip and news, as well as updates about their families.

I stepped behind the counter to ring up books as I listened to the gossip, chatted with the locals and listened to them gush about the chapters I read tonight, all of them excited to get their hands on an early signed copy. Once everyone had their purchases in hand, I hugged the ladies goodnight and shook hands with the men.

It didn't take long until Timber and I were the only ones left.

Finally the store was quiet, but I still had work to do. Besides cleaning up, I needed to put away the folding chairs and take my dog out for a walk. With a glance at the clock, I realized it was already close to nine. Since I'd had a long day of writing, I was ready to curl up in bed to watch an episode of—

The cow bell clanging stopped me in my tracks as I was making my way to the back of the store. I glanced over my shoulder and did a double-take.

Chase was carrying in a big box.

Of what? Split firewood?

Whatever it was sounded heavy when he dropped it onto the front counter. As I headed back toward him, Timber ran ahead of me, immediately planted his furry, traitorous ass on Chase's foot and leaned into him, giving the man the hard to resist "pet me" eyes.

Chase's hand automatically went behind his ears to oblige my needy German Shepherd while the man kept his eyes on me as I approached.

If I sat on his foot and gave him those same puppy dog eyes, would he rub me, too?

Nah, he'd probably try to drop kick me across the room.

"Did you stop by to take Timber on his last walk of the day?" I asked with one eyebrow arched.

"I'm not here to walk your dog."

No shit. "I was surprised to see you show up, even if you were late."

"I was bored." He placed his hand on the edge of the box that had the top flaps cut off. "I also wanted to return these to you."

Return?

I peeked in the box. It was every book he had bought when he came in and wiped out his own shelves.

I lifted my gaze from the box's contents to him. "You didn't burn them." We were barely standing two feet apart. "You couldn't, could you?"

My body started to vibrate from the inside out. He smelled like the woods. Not a manufactured cologne of sandalwood or forest or some fake scent, but actual trees and leaves and grass. It was intoxicating.

"I'm against burning books."

Even the deep rumble of his gravelly voice twisted my insides.

I had found him attractive before, but now that I knew he was gay, my libido had gone into overdrive.

Unfortunately, while the man might be hot on the outside, he was bone cold on the inside.

"Even your own," I concluded. "I'll refund your money or you can trade them in. Your choice." When I went to move behind the counter to get to the cash register, he stopped me with a hand to my forearm.

"I don't need a refund. Give them to someone who can't afford to buy books."

As soon as my gaze flicked down to where he held me, he released me immediately. "That's very… generous of you."

"I didn't need them staring back at me."

"Books don't have eyes."

"You know what I mean."

"I do, actually. You couldn't burn them and you also don't have the space for them up at your cabin…" I knew that wasn't the reason, but unlike him, I was trying to be nice about it. "So, you brought them back here for someone else to enjoy. That's very nice of you."

He grunted. "All right, then…"

When he turned to leave, it was me grabbing his arm this time to stop him. "I'd love for you to sign them."

"No."

"And feature you as a local author."

"No."

"And for you to do a reading."

"Not going to happen."

"Oh, it will. I'm pretty damn persistent."

He cocked a dark eyebrow at me. "And I'm pretty damn resistant."

75

"For some reason, I find that hard to believe," I said dryly. "When you're ready, you'll do a reading and everyone around here will be thrilled when you do." I said that with a lot more confidence than I actually had.

"You don't give up, do you?"

"I just said I'm persistent. Did you miss that part?"

Chase grunted again but he didn't move to leave. He continued to stand there. But once again he was spinning his wedding ring. He probably did it out of habit without realizing it.

I glanced at the clock. My internal battery was drained and I considered cleaning up in the morning, but I knew, once I came downstairs tomorrow, I'd regret not cleaning up tonight.

"Okay, well…" I began in an effort for him to get a clue about leaving.

"What were you reading?"

Whoa. Was he actually trying to start some real dialogue? If so, that might be worth losing out on some sleep and Timber missing out on his walk. I could put my dog out back in the small area behind the store I had fenced for him.

"You only heard the last couple of sentences, but I was reading from the book I'm currently writing."

His eyebrows stitched together and the corners of his mouth tipped downward. "You never said you were an aspiring author. The flyer said tonight's reading would be from Everett J. Williams' latest book."

I pinned my lips together to keep from laughing at the way he begrudgingly said that. When I had control of myself, I answered, "It's not like you gave me a chance. And, honestly… the way you act around me, I didn't think you'd care. But I'm not an aspiring author, I'm actually published."

CHAPTER 6

Chase

"I'm not an aspiring author, I'm actually published."

In the two times I had been in the store previously, and also when he came up to my cabin, he never once mentioned he was also published.

"I'm an author, too," were four words he could've said at any time. He didn't. But he could be right... If he would've told me, would I have even cared?

I'd been living up on the mountain for a month now and was starting to feel things I hadn't in a long time. That meant I was no longer as numb as I had been.

It could be from the fresh air and exercise I was getting. I figured if I got back to taking care of my body, my mind might benefit, too.

And that was one reason I came into town tonight. I had a twinge of guilt over my selfishness of buying up all of my own books so no one else could read them. Mostly for fear of my identity being revealed.

Another reason for stopping in at the bookstore was to see if Everett J. Williams was the one actually doing a reading from his book. I wanted to meet him and tell him how much his books were helping to pull me out of a very long funk.

I'd been disappointed to find it wasn't the author himself. I should've known that someone else would be doing the actual reading instead.

However, Rett's statement got my attention. "What do you write?"

"Mysteries."

I frowned. I read mysteries. "Which ones are yours?"

He pointed to the stack of books on the counter next to the box of my own books I returned. "The ones that are signed."

I forced my expression to remain neutral since that wasn't the answer I'd been expecting. "*You're* Everett J. Williams?" Apparently I hadn't been paying attention and, instead, had been caught up in my own problems too much to notice the obvious signs.

He shrugged. "In the flesh." He gave me a smile that didn't quite reach his eyes. Obviously, he didn't like me and I totally understood why.

I reminded myself that I wasn't in Eagle's Landing to make friends, so it shouldn't matter if Rett liked me or not. I was no longer ten years old and needed validation from others. I was an adult wanting people to respect my privacy. It was that simple.

In turn, I'd respect the privacy of others.

However, in addition to being a jerk to him, I was also a complete idiot and my view of the world around me had been so narrow that I completely missed the fact that the name Rett could be a shortened version of Everett. My excuses could be that I hadn't known Rett's last name and his photo wasn't on the back of the paperbacks, or that I hadn't done any research on the author of the series I was currently reading and enjoying.

All of that was true because I had no reason to dig further. I supposed now I did.

"Does your signature make them worth more?" The question was lame since I'd been on plenty of book tours and to signings myself, so I already knew the answer.

Truthfully, I should leave. I wasn't sure why I was extending this conversation by choice since conversations always led to questions.

Questions I wasn't willing to answer.

"Depends on who you ask," he answered.

He was once again matching my energy of being distant. "I'm asking you."

"Then no."

I knew for a fact that was untrue but maybe he wanted to challenge me by getting me to argue.

"But can you sign one of yours?"

I was surprised. "You want me to sign a copy for you?"

"Sure, since you used to be one of my favorite authors."

Used to be.

Damn. I deserved that. "And now?"

"Let's just say I have a hard time separating the creator from the art. So, actually, if you're going to sign any, I prefer you sign them all. My customers would love that more than I would. Dolly might even buy some to keep on her shelf instead of trading them back in."

I wasn't ready to do that. If I signed more than one copy for him personally, I was afraid someone—including Dolly, the mayor's wife and town gossip—might discover who I was by pestering Rett on how he obtained those signed copies.

I wasn't ready for anyone to know I lived here, other than Rett. Even though other people could easily figure it out since Rett did, most people didn't hone in on the small details and most likely wouldn't put two and two together. Just like me when it came to figuring out that the man before me was Everett J. Williams.

My assumption was Rett hadn't told anyone that Chase Jones and C.J. Anson were one and the same. And for that, I had to be appreciative. I steered the conversation away from signing my books so I wouldn't sound more like a callous dick than I already did. "Your writing is good."

Rett tipped his head. "I dabble. I'm not as proficient as you."

The man didn't dabble and I wasn't lying. His writing *was* good. No, it was excellent. The best I'd read in years. Rett had real talent. Enough for me to keep listening on the long, boring drive from Long Island. Enough for me to want to finish reading the whole Dexter Peabody series.

Books rarely kept my attention anymore. Actually, not much did. But his series had. I even considered reading or listening to the author's whole backlist, if he had one. That alone was a compliment toward the quality of his writing.

"Also unlike you, I haven't made any kind of bestseller list. My readership isn't nearly as large as yours, either."

"With the quality of your work, I'm surprised. The truth is, your writing is stellar and I'm impressed. It takes a lot to do so."

"*Noooo*. Really?" he asked with a twist to his mouth.

I stared at those lips, then closed my eyes and shook my head to cast away any thoughts about how they would feel against mine.

You're not here to make friends, Chase, and you're also not here to find a lover.

I moved to Eagle's Landing for two reasons... To escape the deafening noise in both my head and surrounding me, and, more importantly, to write. That was it. I didn't want attention and I didn't want sex with anyone other than my husband.

Unfortunately, the second part was now impossible. All I had left was our intimate memories. The memories of how being with Thomas made me feel, both in bed and out of it.

He'd been what some might consider my "one true love." No one could ever replace him and I wasn't willing to even try by finding someone else. The loss of my husband had left a hole in my heart so great no one would ever be able to fill. Anyone who tried would fail. I acknowledged the fact to even try wouldn't be fair to the person trying.

If all I had left were my memories to keep me company at night, I was okay with that. Actually I had to be, since anything else wasn't a choice.

For that reason, I shoved away any sliver of attraction to Rett and steered my attention back to publishing, a much safer subject. "You should get an agent. You're that good."

"I don't want an agent."

Why wouldn't he want an agent? His career could explode with the right representation. "An agent could sell your books to one of the big five publishers."

"I must have missed where I asked for your advice."

Oh yes. He was certainly giving me back the same energy I had given him in our previous encounters. Of course, I deserved it and couldn't hold it against him. "Being with a publishing house could do great things for your career."

"Maybe. But I'm quite happy to publish my own books." When he shrugged again, it drew my attention to his broad shoulders.

"As an indie," I murmured a bit distracted.

"Despite what some believe, it's not a dirty word. There always seems to be contention between the two factions. The reality is, traditionally published books aren't any better than indie published, if done right. And honestly, it's the best way to go these days. I can write and publish as fast or as slow as I need to. I can write what I want. I have full creative control over all aspects of my work, including the cover art. Unlike you. And let's not forget, you have an agent and publisher breathing down your neck along with demanding, inflexible deadlines."

It was impossible to say a word to contradict any of that. He was right about this, as well. While having a big publisher and an agent did help take some of the burden off me, it also increased the stress. Especially right now.

Publishing independently meant more flexibility. Any stress would be my own making, not from anyone else.

And the money... There would be less hands in my earnings and more royalties going into my own pockets.

Maybe with my next series I'd try going that route. My current publisher had first right of refusal for the rest of the Nick Foster series, however long it ended up being. So, if I continued writing my bestselling series—and I'd be crazy not to—then I needed to stick with my current publisher since I was currently locked in.

"Even though I don't get the big advances like you, I also don't have to worry about earning out that advance. I don't have to worry about an agent taking a slice of my hard-earned pie. I might not be a household name like Agatha Christie, I still make enough to not only pay the bills, but to keep the doors open on this bookstore."

"Why?"

His brow dropped low over his very dark eyes. "Why what?"

Originally I had thought they were dark brown like mine, but tonight they seemed much darker. Borderline black, even. It could be the store's lighting. I was tempted to grab his chin and tilt his head toward the overhead lights to confirm if what I was seeing was right.

"Why keep the bookstore open if it doesn't make you a profit?"

"This bookstore..." He shook his head. "*Any* bookstore is a treasure chest and the books are the spoils. To me and many readers, they're more valuable than the most precious metal or rare gem. As you know, books, even fiction, expand the mind. They sweep people away on journeys they might never take otherwise. Because of that, I take any chance I can to get more people to read. From the kids in the local schools to the folks at the senior home. If they can't afford a book, I'll lend it to them. The bottom line is, this store brings me joy and it gives others joy, too. That's all I care about. To me that joy makes me richer than having a lot of money."

His heartfelt passion about books and reading was unmistakable. I found it fascinating, just like I had when he read aloud earlier. His voice had a rich, soothing timbre and it only took the few sentences I heard for him to suck me right into the story. After that, I regretted not coming earlier to listen to the whole reading.

But again, I was trying to avoid getting into any deep conversations with the locals to prevent awkward questions or coming off as rude. Unfortunately, something I tended to do, whether I meant to or not.

People with good intentions were always trying to tear down the walls I had set into place for good reason.

For me to survive.

For me to wake up the next morning and the next.

Did I want to? No. Not when it meant I had to live another day without Thomas.

But would I make the people I left behind suffer with guilt the way I did now? I knew how that kind of loss felt, how devastating it was, and I didn't want to do that to anyone else.

That made me lock those walls tightly into place as a way to bind together my splintered pieces. So I could continue on.

Day after day. Night after night.

Taking one step in front of the other through the darkness. One day I might find the edge of those shadows and when I did, I'd let myself step back into the light.

However, I would not let anyone push me there before I was ready.

That was another reason I left Long Island. My friends and family were well-meaning, but they had no idea just how smothering they could be.

My agent also wanted the best for me because, in turn, it benefitted him financially. But his "concern" about me getting back on the writing track could be smothering, too.

Before leaving Long Island, all I wanted to do was stand in a corner with my back to the wall and snap and snarl at everyone.

Some days, I still did.

Like the day I met Rett at the diner.

My attention was pulled back to the man still talking. "As you know, with the popularity of e-books bookstores have closed left and right. And still are. E-books are easier and cheaper to obtain. Another benefit is you can carry around thousands of books in one device. So, if I didn't have my author gig, this bookstore wouldn't make it. Owning it is more of a guilty pleasure that also doubles as my office. Being located in this small town means the store isn't busy and since I'm rarely interrupted, it gives me plenty of time to write. Even better, I get to live upstairs with my dog as my constant companion." He waved a hand around at the full bookshelves. "I'm surrounded by something I love to do. Both reading and writing. For that, I don't need an agent, a big publisher or to be some big-time author. I'm content as things are now. Unlike you."

Unlike you.

Those two simple words were cutting, even though his tone had remained level and he hadn't sounded the slightest bit angry during his whole speech.

Once again he was annoyingly right. But I wasn't going to admit to him that I was far from content and wasn't sure if I'd ever be again.

Basically, I stood alone in the center of a seesaw, trying to balance it. If I leaned too far one way or the other, I'd take a hard fall.

Moving to Eagle's Landing was supposed to help me find balance again in my life. It had been missing since the day I found Thomas dead. The second after that very discovery, everything in my life had come crashing down around me, as well as turning it upside down and inside out. That tragic moment had become my very own ground zero.

Before then, Thomas had been sitting on one side of that seesaw and I sat on the other. The two of us had balanced each other out. Whenever he was sinking, I worked on raising him until we were once again even.

We were a team and I thought we'd been content.

The same as Rett said he was. The man was living his life simply and he was happy. He had a business he loved, even if it couldn't survive on its own. He had a writing career apparently successful enough to pay the bills and, of course, a loyal dog.

What I noticed he didn't have was someone to sit opposite of him on his life's seesaw. He was balancing in the middle all by himself.

The same as I was now doing. However, he seemed way more successful at it.

My seesaw kept tipping from one side to the other and every time it did I overcompensated to correct it. At this point, I needed to either straighten it out or jump off completely. Because I was so damn tired of fighting to keep it level.

"All right, well…" It was time for me to leave. I had been here too long as it was. Especially since I was starting to actually like the man standing only feet from me.

I respected him for who he was, his passion, and how he lived his life with what seemed like no regrets or complaints.

While I was drowning in regrets.

"The truth can be uncomfortable, can't it?"

Now *he* was being the asshole. Yes, I might deserve it but I didn't have to stand there and take it. However, I had come here tonight to meet Everett J. Williams. It just so happened that Rett was the man I came to see.

I needed to thank him for sharing his words with the world, and more specifically with me. Unfortunately, those words struggled to come out of my mouth. Mostly because of the paralyzing fear that he'd want to know *why* his books were so important to me.

Instead I said, "Thanks for bringing me the next Dexter Peabody books. Indie or traditional, it doesn't matter, just keep writing them. When I'm caught up I'll be back for the rest of the series."

He nodded and I turned to leave, hoping that as soon as I stepped outside, the pressure building in my chest would be somewhat relieved.

The walls around me—the store's, not mine—seemed to be closing in and creating a box around the two of us.

A box I couldn't remain inside. Not now. Not ever.

His next question stopped me dead in my tracks. "By the way, how's *your* writing going?" Proof this man was a lot more observant than I was. I was afraid he could see straight through me to the turmoil inside along with everything else I kept hidden away.

Unfortunately, the truth was my writing wasn't "going." While it wasn't a complete failure, the words weren't flowing as easily as they should. My stress over it only made the writer's block worse.

I now had more firewood than I'd ever need for a long time because I had gotten hyper-focused on splitting wood when I needed to focus on my writing instead. I found myself using it as a form of therapy, as well as a way to release my pent-up rage because life was so damn unfair.

But that needed to change since the book wouldn't write itself, as much as I wished it could.

I stared at the man before me. If we were friends, he'd be the perfect person to bounce off ideas. The same way I used to do with Thomas.

That could be a reason why I was struggling so much to write. My partner, whose opinion and introspect I valued, even though he wasn't a writer, was gone. He not only left a hole in my heart but one in my creative process, too.

Even so, Rett and I weren't friends and my treatment of him in the past had pretty much guaranteed we wouldn't be in the future. When he'd been kind, I hadn't. I had no one to blame but myself.

Nothing new.

Could I make an effort to fix that? Possibly, but that might open the door to him witnessing just how messed up I was. I wasn't ready to allow anyone to dig that deep.

"It's coming along," I lied.

With the look he shot me, it was obvious he didn't believe me. "How many cords of firewood do you now have?"

Even though I had no idea how much a cord of wood was, I answered, "Plenty."

He nodded, his expression back to being unreadable. "If you want, Harry will buy some from you to sell to the people who come to the area to camp, fish or hunt. He sells firewood in small bundles. It would be a win-win situation for the two of you."

Why was I getting the feeling this man, one I only met recently, knew me better than he should?

Another good reason, besides my attraction to him, to keep him at arm's length. "I'll keep that in mind."

"If you need to use my truck to haul it into town, let me know."

Now we both stared at each other in awkward silence.

He was once more offering an olive branch, even when I didn't deserve it, and it was up to me to either finally accept it or push it away again.

My first instinct, as it had been for the past two years, was to shut him out. Not to let him past my defenses to a place I was most raw and vulnerable.

I finally murmured, "Okay, thanks."

He reached past me to grab a business card for the bookstore and when he did, his arm accidentally brushed against mine.

My skin prickled and heat rocketed south into my lower belly, confirming my fear of finding him tempting, despite the fact he was most likely straight.

My mind had to be playing tricks on me.

I hadn't let anyone touch me since Thomas died. Not even a simple hug. I haven't allowed any physical contact from my family or from anyone. If I let someone touch me, I was worried I'd simply disintegrate into a pile of dust. Then a strong wind would come along and blow that dust away until nothing of me remained.

Not even a grain of that dust.

Not one damn grain.

His nostrils had flared and his eyes turned even darker when his pupils expanded. The fine hairs on his forearms rose along with goosebumps.

What the hell? He had a reaction to that simple, accidental touch, too. How could that be?

In a stiff, jerky motion he turned away, grabbed the pen lying on the counter and scribbled something on the back of the card.

When he turned back to me, he didn't meet my eyes. "That's my personal cell."

I took the card from his hand, careful to avoid our fingers touching, and stared at the neatly written numbers. "Why do I need that?"

He lifted his gaze but as soon as I met it, he looked past me. "You probably don't but I'm giving it to you anyway." His voice now had a deeper rasp to it than previously.

Jesus. Our accidental brush had affected him the same way as it had me.

Could he be gay, too?

I wasn't going to ask. I didn't want to know. If he was...

No.

No, even if we somehow became friends, eventually that would be more than enough. I didn't want a lover. I no longer wanted to *feel* anything for anybody. Opening myself up to that kind of relationship would be more of a risk than I was willing to take.

My thumb brushed back and forth over his business card. Did it still feel slightly warm where he'd held it?

What the hell, Chase! Stop it.

I sharply flicked the card with my index finger and nodded. "Thanks. I'll try not to bug you too often."

Rett released a soft snort but still avoided meeting my eyes. "I have no worries about that."

He didn't think I'd ever use it.

He was probably right.

"All right, well..."

"I need to lock up." He wanted me gone. Maybe our reactions had been just as uncomfortable for him as it had been for me.

"Right," I murmured and turned toward the door.

I didn't stop moving until I was out of the store, in my Bronco, out of town, back up the mountain and back inside my cabin.

Back in my safe space.

Because apparently that bookstore was not that.

CHAPTER 7

Rett

ONCE AGAIN I was going somewhere I wasn't wanted. I already knew it and was doing it anyway.

Not once had Chase reached out to me in person or via phone. He probably had thrown out my business card the second he left my store three weeks ago.

That was the last time I saw the hibernating bear after he went back up to his mountain cave.

I had put the returned books back on the shelf—still unsigned, of course—and on occasion found myself standing in front of that particular bookshelf. The lie I told myself was I needed to check the stock of both his books and my own, even though I had an excellent point-of-sale system that automatically kept track of inventory.

I would catch myself lost in my own head while running my fingertips lightly along the spines of his books, pretending as if I was dragging my fingers along his warm skin.

Of course, doing that to his books didn't have the same effect on me as when our arms brushed that night.

Touching him had been like touching fire. Sparks had shot through me, sending scorching flames spiraling from my head to my toes, as well as sending blood running south into my cock.

While my reaction had knocked me for a loop, he seemed deeply troubled with his own reaction to our very simple, but accidental, brush.

Of course I found him attractive. Only his exterior, not his interior. And I hated that I would take any valid excuse to touch him more. With consent, of course.

At the end of each day, once I closed the store, shut down my computer and clipped a leash onto Timber's collar to take him out for his nightly walk... Once I let myself think back on that very moment... My imagination ran wild and I had a tough time reining it in.

I pondered what it would be like if he said yes to us touching... kissing... even more.

I never had such a single, simple touch affect me so much. So much so, I actually found myself falling into a slight obsession over the man.

If I stood in front of the shelf long enough, I'd eventually select one of his books to pull out and turn it over so I could study the outdated black-and-white picture again.

Taken at a time when he seemed to be a lot happier than he was now.

When he'd most likely been married, but before his husband's death wrecked him.

Even though we hadn't discussed it, I assumed that was what made him so anti-social.

Losing his life partner had caused him not only the expected heartache, but it crushed his creativity and even made him run away from his home in New York. Most likely where he'd been surrounded by caring friends and loving family.

Something he did not have here. Somewhere he had no one.

No one to support him. No one for him to talk to. No one to care about him.

Chase was obviously hiding in Eagle's Landing so he could continue to lick his wounds from a two-year-old loss. Most likely hiding from the people closest to him concerned he hadn't moved into that fifth stage of grief yet.

I had done more research about the loss of loved ones after the night he showed up for the reading. In addition to what I already knew, I learned the process of grieving was unique to everyone and the stages weren't set in stone.

When I lost my brother, I apparently had been a textbook case when I went through the five typical stages. But then, I'd never been one to wallow in any kind of sorrow. I had also never been one to scream about life being unfair. I went through every day with my eyes wide open to that fact.

I accepted what I didn't have the power to change. I did my best to change what I could not accept.

If life was fair, I wouldn't have lost my brother in the manner I did. I also wouldn't be alone and would've found my soulmate by now. I would be a bigger name in the mystery genre and not have to fight so hard to claim a small corner of it.

Especially after the great C.J. Anson informed me my writing was "stellar." While hearing that was exhilarating, particularly coming from a prestigious author like him, it didn't make my small measure of success any easier.

After parking once again behind the cabin, I was in no rush to get out. I shut off my Chevy and stared at the rear entry where it appeared as though nothing had changed since the last time I'd been here.

It made me wonder if he'd done a bunch of work on the inside. If he was around—I assumed he was since I was parked next to his Bronco—I might try to break down some of his walls by asking to see the inside.

On the other hand, he could get pissed at me coming up here uninvited and for bugging him again, and tell me to go fuck off.

While doing my research, I read that people could regress back into earlier stages of grief. They could boomerang back and forth between the different stages, too. My guess was that Chase was bouncing between the anger and the depression stage.

It was quite possible he was stuck in a never-ending loop he couldn't free himself from. A little shove might be beneficial.

A shove from me, of course. Because apparently I liked to torture myself by attempting to make a better connection with a man wanting none at all.

While I had heard him loud and clear, that didn't mean I would listen. But that also meant I had to be prepared for anything he threw my way.

As I sat in my truck, I donned invisible armor, ready for battle.

I'd admit it. I was dumb for doing this. But we were both authors and if we didn't stick together...

Sure, Rett, keep lying to yourself. You know why the hell you're up here. And it isn't to deliver the next two books in your series and to tell him that you finished the first draft on your latest.

Or to ask him if he could beta-read my work to get his opinion before I send it to my editor.

I shouldn't value his opinion on my writing, but it was difficult not to. And truthfully, I'd be honored if he would want to read the unedited manuscript and give his thoughts, good or bad.

Furthermore, I would absolutely shit myself if he volunteered to write a forward for it. How amazing would it be if the world-renowned author C.J. Anson told readers why they should read my book?

Settle down, you dolt, that wasn't going to happen. You're expecting too much out of someone who wants to share little to nothing.

For the hundredth time, I wondered if he'd always been like this or it truly stemmed from the loss of his husband. I might never know that answer if he never finished grieving.

But to be stuck in that perpetual loop for the rest of his life…

It would be as sad as Mr. Coleman dying up in this cabin alone.

Chase shouldn't be alone. My opinion, of course, because I'm sure the man wouldn't agree.

I told Timber to stay put, got out of my truck and jogged up the steps to the back windowless door. I noticed the newly-installed windows at the back of the cabin now had curtains and while they were drawn open, I didn't want to shove my face against the glass to peer inside. Instead, I did what most civilized people would do and used the side of my palm to pound on the door. My knock ended up sounding more like a dull thump due to the thickness of the wood.

Doors were simply not made like that anymore. Whoever originally built the cabin, maybe even Mr. Coleman, had handmade the doors, too, out of solid cedar. Most likely to be black bear proof.

However, the bear in this case lived on the other side of the door.

I impatiently shuffled from foot to foot as I waited, carefully listening to see if I could hear footsteps approaching. The cabin wasn't large, so if Chase was inside he would only be feet from the door.

I pounded once more with no response.

Tired of waiting, I decided to head around to the front. Maybe he didn't hear my truck bitching and complaining as it fought its way up Coleman Lane.

My guess was Chase probably wouldn't fix the lane's condition since it deterred visitors from showing up unexpectedly.

Unwelcome visitors like me.

I did notice a new "no trespassing" sign installed at the bottom near the road. But, of course, like the dirt lane's shitty condition, I ignored that, too.

I paused at the corner of the cabin, glanced back at Timber sitting in the passenger seat with his head out of the window, his ears perked in attention and his tongue hanging out of the side of his mouth.

His eyes were laser-focused on me. Even from where I stood, I could see the pleading in his eyes to come with me.

I was a sucker. "All right. Let's go!"

With a short, excited yip, he leapt from the open passenger-side window and hit the ground running. When he got to me, his tail was held high and sweeping back and forth in joy for including him on my little search.

"I swear you're just as obsessed with the man as I am, traitor," I muttered to him under my breath. As I continued to move, Timber circled me quickly, then followed closely on my heels.

I headed around to the front of the cabin, and when I didn't find Chase on the rustic covered porch, I climbed those steps and knocked on that door, too.

Timber sat at my side as I waited, looking back and forth from me to the door, as if he was saying, *Just open the door, fool. What are we waiting for?*

"Well," I answered him quietly, "if the man bought a shotgun or rifle on my recommendation, I really don't want to get blown away. How about you?"

Timber glanced up at me, licked his chops and I swear gave me a nod in agreement.

I sighed.

Having complete conversations with my dog was nothing new. It happened a lot since I lived alone.

Correction. Timber and I lived alone.

I'd probably be lonely if I didn't have him as my constant companion.

Huh.

I shoved a stray thought away and after pounding on the wood door again, I heard dead silence.

Chase wasn't inside. As I turned to scan the immediate area for some signs of him, I noticed the woodshed stuffed full of firewood, as well as some neatly stacked in piles closer to the cabin and along the sides of the lean-to.

I also spotted a downed tree had been chain-sawed into much more manageable sections and piled next to the stump Chase had been using to split wood.

Timber and I might be slightly obsessed with Chase but Chase seemed to be obsessed with wood. Since he wasn't around to see it, I didn't bother to smother my grin over the childish joke that ran through my head about the man and his wood.

I scanned the area again. The blue sky was vibrant today, with only a lone white puffy cloud in the distance near the top of the mountain that rose beyond Eagles Lake. Birds were chirping and chattering and doing whatever birds did during the day, the light spring breeze was warm against my skin and the sun reflected off the still water.

I frowned.

I was wrong. The water wasn't still. It had a dark spot moving through the water with ripples following behind. A turtle? A beaver? Ol' Nessie, the Loch Ness Monster?

"Let's go," I ordered Timber, keeping my eyes on whatever was swimming toward shore. Whatever it was still had a ways to go before it reached land.

Coming off the porch, I walked the half length of a football field between the lake and the cabin with Timber eagerly trotting by my side.

That was when I saw it. A towel thrown over the back of a lone plastic Adirondack chair sitting at the water's edge. I could picture Chase sitting in the chair and using it for quiet reflection or even an inspiring place to write.

That made me think that I should find a special spot in nature to sit and write, too. The fresh air might do me some good rather than writing all day in the back corner of the store. A change of scenery might give me some fresh ideas.

Timber's whine drew my attention. He was watching the moving object come closer, then he let out a sharp cry and began to dance along the muddy and rocky shoreline.

I narrowed my eyes and looked closer at what clearly wasn't a turtle.

When that "object"—consisting of two eyes, shaggy dark hair, and a beard—lifted from the water, my breath seized.

Just the person I came to see. Didn't he know about all the dangers in lakes like these? And, worse, he was swimming by himself.

I was only glad that Timber didn't like water, otherwise my traitorous dog wouldn't have waited and would've taken the plunge to meet his new best friend halfway.

I shook my head, then simply breathed when Chase was finally close enough to the shore and at a place he could touch the bottom.

I choked on my own spit as he emerged from the water and continued to approach us as it got more and more shallow. As I swallowed, my Adam's apple got stuck on the way up and after a second finally dropped like a rocket returning to Earth.

The man was completely naked.

Bare-assed naked.

A bare bear.

My brain began to glitch like a short-circuited electrical wire.

He walked out of the water like a freaking king with not one ounce of embarrassment, his gaze on me not faltering with each step he took.

He did not hide himself from my wandering eyes, either.

But *holy shit*... His body... He'd done a lot with it in the three weeks since I saw him last.

Apparently, swimming, like chopping wood, did a body good.

Now only if it had done the same with his mental health...

But I wasn't looking at his brain right now, I was looking at something else.

I shouldn't be.

I couldn't help it. Especially with it bouncing between his two solid, lightly-furred thighs.

"Water's cold," Chase muttered.

I cleared my throat and lifted both eyes along with a solitary eyebrow. "Is it?" If he looked like that with shrinkage from the cold water, then...

I clamped my bottom lip between my teeth. *Jeeeeeesuuuuuus.*

He was forced to stop walking before he reached me due to Timber in full herding mode, circling Chase so closely the dog might cause him to trip. My Shepherd was also yapping in excitement at an ear-piercing pitch as he tried to draw the man's attention but Chase was focused on me instead.

He sucked on his teeth before murmuring, "Yeah."

"Then let's get you warmed up." I forced myself to move and snagged the towel off the chair next to me. I held it up and open.

Because I was helpful like that.

"What are you doing here? I don't remember extending an invite," he said dryly, ignoring the towel and my generous offer at warming him up.

"You did. You must have forgotten."

"I'd remember if I did."

"You just said you didn't remember."

"I also asked what you are doing here. You haven't answered that yet."

"I will," I assured him. "Do you want your towel first? Or do you prefer to air dry?" That last choice would be mine if given one, but I doubted the man wanted my opinion.

"I've got nothing to hide."

"Clearly not," I said under my breath.

I was hoping he'd step into the open towel and let me rub him dry. That hope was quickly dashed when he pulled it from my fingers and roughly scrubbed it over his hair, removing the excess water.

I would've thought the first thing he would've done was wrap it around his waist to hide his nicely-sized package from my wandering eyes, but clearly that wasn't an issue with him.

With his damp, shaggy hair standing up in more directions than it should, he dried off his face next, then his broad shoulders and bulging arms, rubbed the terry cloth down his torso—his abs now a bit more defined than the last time I saw him without a shirt—then took his time to dry off each leg completely before finally wrapping that damn towel around his waist.

A sigh of disappointment slipped from me before I could corral it.

When he was done securing the towel at his hip—I made a mental side note about how his Adonis Belt, the muscular V at his hips, appeared more defined than previously, too—he lifted his brown eyes and locked them with mine. "Was that assessment for my well-being, too?"

I scratched the back of my neck, then shrugged. "Nope. That was for me. Thank you for that."

He tipped his head to the side. "You haven't seen another naked man before?"

"I've seen plenty, just none like you in person." And that was very true. None of the men I'd ever slept with in the past looked anything like Chase.

While I hadn't had sex with trolls, no one else had compared to the man before me. It would be great to find a man who was the perfect package. As attractive on the inside as on the outside.

He reminded me of the time I bought a new coffeemaker for the store. When I opened the box, excited it finally arrived, I was disappointed to find the item inside damaged.

With Chase's eyebrows knitted together, his gaze took a slow roll from my face, down to my boots, only pausing at the erection I didn't bother to hide. Trying to do so would've made it more obvious.

I wasn't ashamed of my attraction to him, anyway. We all made mistakes we had to live with.

Furthermore, if he hadn't wanted me to check him out, he would have covered up sooner. He didn't and had taken his time on purpose. That was the strange part. Especially when he acted as though he didn't like me.

"What are you?" he finally asked.

It took me a second to figure out what he was asking. "The same as you."

I swore he stopped breathing and morphed into a Michelangelo statue. He didn't even blink for the longest time.

Then, as if someone flipped a switch, his head jerked and the rest of him came back to life. "What does that mean?"

"You know what that means."

His lips turned down at the corners and his eyes narrowed on me. "How do you know?"

Shit.

How did I answer that without making him think I was stalking him? Even though I had been when I searched the obituaries. "It was a guess," I fibbed.

"Then your guess is wrong."

"It's not. A straight man doesn't normally show off for other men."

His jaw shifted and he growled, "You think I was showing off?"

It was time to put him on the spot, the same as he had done to me. "Weren't you?"

"Why are you here? You need to answer that question before I consider answering yours. Did you come up here to check on me again?"

"It's been three weeks," I stated matter-of-factly.

"I hadn't paid attention."

"Don't you get bored being alone up here for weeks at a time?"

"Do I look bored?"

"No, you look…"

He cocked an eyebrow.

"You know how you look," I finished in a rush.

"I haven't given it much thought."

I have. I sighed. "Can we start over?"

"Why?"

"Because we could be friends."

"I don't have any openings in that department," he announced, patted Timber on the head, gave him a quick scratch behind the ears and then began the short trek back toward the cabin.

I stood there for a second and watched him go.

With my dog trotting on the man's heels, wagging his tail.

Traitor!

I sighed again, then shouted, "We have a lot in common."

"No, we don't," he shouted back over his shoulder, not stopping.

I jumped into motion and chased after him. I was worried that if he went inside the cabin, he'd lock me out. That wasn't just a worry, there was a real chance of that happening. "We're both authors." *Dumb.*

"So?"

"Timber is loyal to us both." *So weak.*

His step stuttered and he paused, looked down at my dog, then continued up the porch stairs. "That's two things."

"We're both men." *For shit's sake*, that answer was even worse.

With his back to me, he shook his head.

"*Gay* men."

He paused again, this time with his hand circling the door knob, but he remained facing the door.

"I've been the only gay man in this town since I moved here over a decade ago."

He stayed frozen in place.

I continued quickly since I now had his attention. "I haven't shared that with anyone." That was true. Everyone in town only assumed I was straight, the reason they kept trying to push their single female relatives on me.

If someone came out and asked me, I'd tell them the truth. But not one person ever questioned me on why I remained single and shrugged off all attempts at their matchmaking.

Chase released the knob and turned toward me just as I reached the bottom of the porch steps. His face was expressionless. His eyes guarded. His body stiff. "I never said I was gay."

I didn't climb those steps. I stayed at the bottom and licked my lips, giving myself a second to think of an excuse on how I knew he was gay.

He added, "And even if I am, that's no one's business but mine."

"I agree. It's why I never told anyone."

"You just told me."

"Because I can relate."

"Again, I—"

"Now we share a secret." *Holy shit, what was I? Ten?*

"I don't have secrets."

Was he serious? "None?"

"It's only a secret if you don't want anyone to find out."

Right, and Chase was lying about not having secrets. But I didn't want to let the cat out of the bag about me discovering his late spouse was a man.

"What about pen names?" I should just go back to town since I clearly lost any skills I had when it came to effective communication.

Something flashed behind his eyes but he quickly hid it. "You don't have one. You use your full name."

I hadn't told him that. I never told him my last name really was Williams. And I certainly didn't tell him my real middle name or initial.

"And you know that how?" I asked, somewhat surprised.

Even though his face was now blank, the slightest flare of his nostrils gave him away. He'd looked into me, just like I had done with him.

Interesting, but why?

"It's obvious," he finally answered. "It's also on your business card."

Shit. "You didn't throw it out?"

"Why would I throw it out?"

Because you can't help being a huge dick sometimes, that's why. "You can use the number on the back at any time."

"That won't be necessary. Now, I need to get inside to change."

He was dismissing me, but I wasn't done with him yet. "I'll wait. I have something in my truck to give you."

"Whatever it is, I don't need it."

"I also have a favor to ask."

"Do I need to remind you that we're not friends?"

"Not yet." Okay, I was stubborn to a fault. I knew it and now Chase was learning it, too.

He dropped his head and stared at his bare toes. I couldn't resist glancing down at them, too. He had really nice feet and I noticed a few dark hairs decorating his big toes. He had the perfect amount. Manly but not cavemanly.

I don't know why the hell I found them sexy—I've never paid attention to feet before unless they looked like cloven hooves—but with Chase, I did.

He shook his head, sighed and lifted it again. When he did, I made sure my eyes were above his waistline. *Hell*, above his neck.

I chalked up being so damn thirsty over this man due to not being with one in a long time.

The last date I had was at least a year ago. Ever since I moved to Eagle's Landing, I had to find dates in more populated areas like Williamsport, Scranton or Wilkes-Barre.

But all of those were short-lived. More flings than relationships. Just more of a reprieve for the lack of intimacy and another man's touch until I found the next one. For one reason or another, none of the men I had dated or simply hooked up with withstood the test of time.

That time lasting no more than a few weeks at best.

I was one who enjoyed the challenge of coming up with original storylines for my books. I applied that also to men. Chase was definitely a challenge I couldn't pass up. I probably should but I was now committed to at least making him my friend if nothing else.

He would be my friend, *damn it*, whether he wanted to be or not.

I would be his huckleberry.

I rolled my lips under. I might be losing my mind.

I scrambled up the steps after he ignored what I said, turned and opened the door. "I would love to see what you've done with the cabin."

"I'm sure you would," he grumbled, stepping inside.

As soon as I followed him across the threshold, he stopped short and spun around, blocking my way and making me jerk to a halt. "I didn't invite you in."

My gaze followed Timber as he trotted around the small cabin, sniffing everything. "Then I'll just grab my dog…"

Chase shook his head, more out of frustration with me being pushy than him saying "no."

"And I still need to give you what I brought for you," I insisted.

"I don't need anything."

I figured he'd say that. Anything to be a grump. "It's the next two books in my series. I'm not sure how far you've gotten yet."

"You didn't need to do that."

"Of course I didn't, but I wanted to. I respect you as an author and I'm thrilled you're enjoying my books. Besides from the locals, I rarely get feedback on my work. Of course, I get reviews, but I rarely read them because they're more for other readers than for the author. And while some can be uplifting and encourage me to keep writing, some can be downright cruel and make me question every word I write."

All authors dealt with that same issue, but it didn't make it any easier. Every book I wrote was like my baby and to hear someone tell me my baby was ugly…

"Do you read your reviews?" I asked him, wondering if he tortured himself like that. I've read some of his reviews. It didn't matter if I thought his series was genius, others might not. And some comments could be not only uncalled for, but downright nasty.

"No," he answered. "My publisher would drop me if my books

were garbage. Since they want me to keep writing, I have to assume they're good."

Look at him now being humble, unlike his naked stroll out of the lake. "You know they're good."

"My opinion isn't the one that matters."

No truer words.

Without readers we weren't authors, we were strictly writers. Being brave enough to publish your work and then actually selling those books was what made us authors.

Anybody could write, but not everyone had thick enough skin to publish and take harsh criticism of their work, whether valid or not.

Life in the book world was no different than the real world. It could be cruel.

"Well..." He inhaled deeply and glanced over at his bedroom. "I need to change. Thanks for stopping by."

"Saying that last part had to hurt, didn't it?" I asked. "How about while you change, I run out to my truck and bring in the two books I brought for you."

"If you must."

"I must," I insisted.

He stared at me for a few seconds and even though his expression was carefully blank, I was sure he thought I was some whack job. I normally didn't force myself into someone's life like this, but... It was clear Chase needed a friend.

He just didn't realize it yet.

Eventually he would. I was confident about that. And also that I was the perfect person for the job.

He just didn't realize that yet, either.

As soon as he went into his bedroom and closed the door, I leaned down to Timber, sitting by my side but staring in the direction Chase disappeared.

"Stay here," I whispered to my four-legged companion. "This way he won't lock me out. I doubt he wants me to leave you behind."

At least I hoped he wouldn't kidnap Timber. Though, my dog

probably wouldn't care. He'd probably curl up on Chase's bed at night and sleep as if the man had been his daddy since a puppy.

"Traitor," I said under my breath, bugging out my eyes at him.

My dog should be ashamed, but he only gave me a smile and a soft *woof*, causing me to roll my eyes at him.

What made it worse was when I headed out to my truck, he didn't even worry that I was leaving.

I *should* leave him behind, that would teach him.

CHAPTER 8

Chase

I DIDN'T UNDERSTAND the man. He just wouldn't give up. No matter how many times I made it clear I wasn't open to his friendship.

I didn't need a "buddy" and he was trying to elbow his way into that spot.

However, now knowing he was also gay…

Was kind of dangerous.

I'd admit I was attracted to him and he would normally be my type, but I wasn't willing to put myself out there. Whether platonically or otherwise.

I should shower to rinse off the lake water but I'd do that once I was sure Rett was gone. Otherwise, he'd probably rush into the bathroom, check the temp of the water and offer to scrub my back.

I closed my eyes, shook my head and after a deep inhale in an attempt to settle my growing annoyance, I opened my bedroom door, hoping he got the picture and left.

The first living, breathing thing I spotted was Timber sitting right outside my door. As soon as Rett's dog saw me, his bushy tail swept back and forth against my wood floor and he grinned up at me with his long tongue hanging out the side.

He was just as goofy as his damn owner.

The German Shepherd got to his feet and nudged my hand when I stepped around him.

I'd never been a dog person—*hell*, I'd never been an animal person at all—but Thomas and I had owned a cat. On his insistence and against my will. I didn't want one, but having the finicky feline seemed to help Thomas deal with his depression somewhat.

The cat loved him, but hated me. Every time I tried to pet her in an attempt to live in harmony, she hissed her disdain at me, so I left her alone. Then Thomas died and it was only me and the cat who hated me. She even took offense when I tried to feed her. I began to worry she would kill me in my sleep.

Cats could be evil like that. She probably blamed me for Thomas's death.

It got to the point Sammie the Siamese sat by the front door, crying at all hours of the day and night waiting for Thomas to come home.

She wasn't the only one heartbroken. Or lonely. I missed Thomas just as much, if not more.

Watching the poor cat suffer only made it worse for me. Even though my parents were both in their late sixties, they opted to take Sammie and the cat was now living a happily ever after ending.

Me, not so much.

I'm sure my parents would've loved it if I had moved along with the cat into their home in Panama, too. But no…

I was forty-five and the hell if I was living with my parents or even close by. It's not that I didn't love them, I did and was very grateful they were my parents, but I didn't need them up my ass constantly about "moving on" or trying to set me up on dates with their friends' gay sons or grandsons. Or, *hell*, even with their gay friends.

Just no.

At first they let me grieve in my own way, but after a while they got worried and began to tell me to seek help. Kept flying up to Long Island to convince me in person it wasn't healthy for me to not move forward with my life. Advised me that I would do better to move out of the house that held too many memories.

So, I did. I finally moved.

To Eagle's Landing.

To this very cabin on a mountain in the middle of two hundred acres.

To be *alone*.

Unfortunately, I wasn't alone right now. I had both a four-legged visitor and a two-legged pest in my cabin. I needed to get rid of them both and get back to writing. I hadn't hit my word count yet for the day and I needed to.

If I didn't stick to the structured writing plan I had set up, I'd get even farther behind in my current novel.

The problem was, even though I set my daily word count goals to a very conservative number, I wasn't even making that. I found myself sitting in front of my laptop, losing track of time, sometimes even staring sightlessly over the lake. Finally, out of frustration I'd get up, go for a hike, chop wood or take a swim.

Or... pick up where I left off reading the current Everett J. Williams' novel I was engrossed in.

I shouldn't be so harsh on him, but I was worried if I gave him even an inch, he'd take a whole damn mile. For me that mile would be like walking barefoot over my nephew's Legos in the dark. Every step torturous, even as numb as I normally was.

My gaze went from Timber at my feet, to the two Dexter Peabody books—the items Rett must've retrieved from his truck—on my reclaimed wood dining table to the man himself as he inspected everything more closely than he should.

When I swam in the lake, I usually did it naked so I wouldn't have swim trunks to add to my laundry pile. Since I didn't have a washer and dryer in the cabin—and probably never would due to space—to reduce the trips into town to use the small laundromat next to the diner, I tried not to dirty too many clothes.

I had one pair of jeans I wore strictly for dragging dead, downed trees out of the woods, as well as chopping and stacking split firewood. Those jeans could now stand up on their own.

Sometimes I rinsed stuff out in the old farmhouse kitchen sink and hung the clothes out to dry on the porch, but that wasn't the same as using a real washer with quality laundry detergent.

I had purposely taken my time walking out of the lake, hoping my nakedness would make Rett uncomfortable and chase him off.

Of course it didn't.

Instead, he looked at me like I was the Sunday brunch buffet served at The Eagle's Nest. However, Rett's visual inspection of me made him look far more hungry than the after-church crowd fighting over a chafing dish of sausage links.

"You're still here," I grumbled, even though I shouldn't be surprised that the man couldn't take a hint.

He quickly closed the door to the kitchen cabinet he was snooping in and turned with a grin. Not even an ounce of embarrassment on his face for being caught. "I told you I had something to bring you." He jerked his chin toward his books on the table.

My eyes landed once again on the paperbacks. I moved closer to the table and lifted the cover on the top one with a single finger.

Of course.

He'd signed them. I did everything in my power to keep my expression locked down as I read the inscription in his obnoxiously neat handwriting.

To my former favorite author,
Maybe one day you'll achieve that top spot again.
Good luck.

I shook my head and bit back a sigh. "Thanks."

"Anytime. *Sooooo,* anyway," he cleared his throat, came closer to where I stood and waved his hand around, indicating the cabin's interior, "the place looks great. I've never seen it look so clean."

That was because before I began obsessively chopping wood, I had been tiring myself out by scrubbing every inch of the cabin from floor to ceiling. If I wasn't exhausted come nighttime, I couldn't sleep. And if I could fall asleep without being exhausted, I ended up dreaming.

I did whatever I could to sleep dreamless.

Sweet baby Jesus, he was still babbling...

"And all the improvements you did will help come winter. The winds can be wicked and the snow deep. Have you thought about hiring someone to plow the lane when it snows?"

"No."

"You should. You don't want to be stuck up here for days with no way to get out."

Being stuck alone in the cabin didn't sound like a bad thing.

"Especially if there's an emergency," he added.

I swore the man liked to hear himself talk. "Thanks for your concern, but I'll be fine."

"I guess you should be used to rough winters in Jericho."

My head jerked in his direction and I narrowed my eyes on him. To know that, he had to have done some digging beyond the limited bio I provided for the back of my books and my author website. I had purposely used a general "New York" location instead of the more localized one of Long Island when it came to where I resided. But nowhere in that bio indicated I was gay. Nowhere in that bio stated I'd been married and was a widower. And definitely, *nowhere* did it say I had lived in Jericho.

That was information my readers didn't need to know. My personal life and relationship were no one's business, so where did he...

Fuck!

The obituary. That had to be it. He had found Thomas's by using my real name.

Fuck, fuck, fuck. I should've used a fake name when I came to Eagle's Landing, but I never would've guessed someone in this town would actually google me.

I stared at the man who would.

Not only would, who did. "Why?"

His eyebrows lifted. "Why what?"

I pressed my lips together, clamped a hand around the back of my neck and ground it back and forth. I closed the distance between us, keeping our gazes locked so he knew I meant the warning I was about to tell him. "Keep whatever information you dug up to yourself."

"I—"

I raised a palm to stop any excuse he'd try giving me. "Don't even. To be honest, it's a bit creepy."

Rett huffed out a, "Like you've never googled anyone."

Of course I had, but he didn't need to know that. "I came here for anonymity. I moved here," I pointed to the floor, "to be left alone."

"I get it. Your secret's safe with me."

I hoped that was true. "Make sure it is. Now... I need to—"

"Do you mind if I check out the rest of the changes you've made so far?"

I frowned.

He quickly explained, "The only room I haven't seen yet is the bedroom. I promise not to climb into your bed." A short laugh followed.

Who said that kind of shit?

This man was crazy. Absolutely bat-shit crazy. And so damn inappropriate.

I took a deep inhale in an attempt to cool my irritation at the pushy man. I kept telling myself over and over he was only trying to be friendly. But that didn't mean I had to like it and I really had a difficult time believing he didn't want anything more. If he did, I wasn't willing to give him that.

I didn't even want to be friends since he'd be one of those annoying ones you barely tolerated. You only did so because your significant other, your family or your close friends were friends with him, too, so you had no choice. Friends by association.

However, here I had a choice.

I sighed. If I said no, would I sound like a complete bastard?

Did I really care if I did?

In actuality, would it hurt for him to see my bedroom? Maybe he'd leave once he saw what he wanted. "Fine. But make it quick."

He gave me a lopsided smile that was far too sexy than it should be and beelined to my bedroom, most likely worried I'd change my mind.

I thought about it since watching him step into my most intimate space in the cabin made ants march up my spine.

I immediately followed him because I wouldn't put it past him to start digging through my damn underwear drawer. Leaning against the door frame with my arms crossed over my chest, I watched him take a quick spin around the small bedroom. There really wasn't much to see other than the new ceiling fan I had installed, along with the new, bigger, draft-free windows to get a better view of the lake.

Other than that, it was just cleaned up and full of my furniture.

"Looks so much more livable than it used to. It feels more like a home now."

A home you're invading.

But I agreed with his assessment. It now felt like home.

I had my king-sized brass bed set up with all new bedding. I had only brought the frame, mattress and box spring with me from the Jericho house. I had donated all the bedding since Thomas had done most of the decorating and it reminded me too much of him.

I never wanted to forget him and I never would. But to sleep under the same bedding now as when we did as a married couple…

I couldn't.

Especially since it had held his scent.

Damn it.

My eyes stung unexpectedly. Even though it had been about two years, it still felt like yesterday. Why did his loss still affect me so much? Why couldn't I "move on" like so many people urged me to do?

Again, I didn't want to forget him, I only wanted to lessen the sting of losing him.

I thought moving here would put me on that path. Instead, it dropped me in the middle of Rett Williams' path. And he kept trying to run me over.

As authors, I swore we had to be a little touched in the head to be able to write the stories we did, because it was the crime thriller author in me who asked, "Is this where they found him?"

Now who was being creepy? But changing the subject was a good way to get out of my head and keep from drowning in my sorrows.

Neither of us wrote sappy Hallmark type romances. We wrote gritty stories about murderers and bad people doing horrible things and our goal was to bring those people to justice in an *on-the-edge-of-your-seat,* entertaining type of way.

Only Dexter Peabody, P.I., was a goofball, unlike my more serious serial killer hunter Detective Nick Foster.

It came as no surprise that Peabody acted like he did now that I've met the author behind the character.

That author turned toward me.

"Coleman," I clarified when his mouth opened and nothing came out. I must have finally found something to throw him off his game.

His expression turned grim. "I think so, but I didn't come inside. I let the Troopers handle it."

I wished I hadn't gone inside, either, that day. I wish I wouldn't have that particular memory burned into my brain for the rest of my life.

I regretted that it was me who found Thomas, but on the other hand, I would've regretted if it hadn't been me and someone else had come across him instead. Or if I hadn't seen him one last time.

Only… I was relieved nobody else saw him like that. He deserved so much better.

My husband didn't deserve the shitty hand he'd been dealt in life. He hadn't deserved the abuse that had driven him into a pit so deep and dark he had an impossible time pulling himself out.

I did my best to help. To offer him a hand to lift him up and out of that pit. Only my help hadn't been enough.

Jesus, I loved Thomas so fucking much.

Why did life have to be so damn cruel?

Why did some people get to easily skate by in life while others paid dearly?

I swallowed, trying to loosen my closed throat, and I blinked the sting away.

I would *not* allow Rett to see me vulnerable. I would *not* give him any reason to be more "concerned" about me than he already was. It might encourage him to stick his nose even deeper into my business. He would use his "concern" as an excuse to keep checking up on me.

I shook myself mentally and quickly patched up the crack in my resolve.

Do not let him see you break.

My grief completely paralyzed me at times. To the point I wanted to dig a hole and bury myself in it. The days I didn't think I could live one more without Thomas.

Yes, I should move on or at least accept the fact that whatever I did wouldn't change the outcome of what happened. Of losing the only man I had ever loved. The one who took my heart with him, leaving a gaping hole behind.

With a frown, Rett stopped in front of the built-in closet in my room and jerked a thumb at it. "What's with the missing closet doors? Are you having them redone? I noticed the one in the bathroom's missing, too."

No surprise that while I was changing he'd been poking around in my bathroom. Did he dig through my medicine cabinet, as well?

But, *damn*, I never thought I'd have to answer that question because I never expected anyone to be in my bedroom, or, *hell*, my cabin. And if there was, I hadn't expected it to be someone so intrusive.

Even the workers I had hired to do some of the improvements weren't so damn nosy.

"Do you need help rehanging them?"

I couldn't suppress the jolt that shook me to my core at his question. To anyone else, it was a simple question. To me it was so much more.

I needed to rein in any emotions he was stirring up, whether he was aware of it or not.

He needed to leave. Now.

He was watching me closely when he finished with, "It'll be easier with an extra set of hands."

I didn't need his help. I didn't need anything from the man except for him to leave me alone. "They don't need a door."

"Sure they do. Closets are the perfect place for hiding all the mess..."

Closets are perfect for hiding...

"You can just throw stuff in and shut the door." He mimicked closing a door, then turned toward me, his frown gone. "Do you need some made? I know someone who—"

"No."

"But—"

I cut him off with a firm, "My closets don't need doors."

His frown was back. "Why wouldn't you want doors?"

Goddamn it! Because I'm afraid of what I'll find when I open them.

I sucked in air until my lungs were completely full and then blew it back out of my nostrils. "I need to get back to writing."

"Oh? How's the new book coming?"

At least that got him off the subject of doors. Thankfully. "It's... coming along," I lied.

"That didn't sound very convincing."

When he approached where I leaned against the door frame, I straightened and dropped my arms to my side. "Then good thing you don't need convinced."

"If you ever need to bounce any ideas around for your next bestseller, I'm available."

"Good to know." I swept a hand behind me toward the main area of the cabin, hoping he'd take the hint to get out of my bedroom and head back to town.

Or wherever. Anywhere but here.

His gaze slid from me, out the door to the rest of the cabin and back to me. He nodded.

Did he finally get a clue?

"Let's go, Timber," he said to the dog still sniffing around my room and snuffling through the stuff at the bottom of my doorless closet.

Timber's head snapped up and he trotted over to us with his tail up and wagging slowly.

I hesitated in the doorway because I wanted to make sure he actually left my bedroom. And if he didn't, I would herd him out like a German Shepherd. However, my bite would be worse than my bark.

When Rett slipped past me, our arms accidentally brushed again, just like at the bookstore.

My reaction this time was even worse than the last.

This time a fire ripped through me, catching me off guard once again. No, it wasn't simply a fire, it was a fast-burning wildfire fueled by high speed winds burning through every inch of me.

Every cell in my body locked solid.

I couldn't move.

Couldn't blink.

Couldn't even take my next breath.

All I could do was watch Rett's Adam's apple slowly roll up his throat, hang there for a second, then roll back into place.

The sound of him taking a sharp inhale spurred the fire inside me.

It must've done the same for him since the hair on his arms rose along with goosebumps. His wide eyes, now locked with mine, were darker than normal since his pupils had dilated.

We remained frozen in place. Both of us in the doorway. Barely inches from each other. Only a slight gap between us. One move in any direction would have us touching again. One of us leaning in would be enough to press our bodies completely together.

He was too close.

Way too close.

Close enough to see his pulse pounding in his neck and his nostrils flare the slightest bit.

Close enough to pick up his scent.

To feel his heat.

To make out his nipples through the soft cotton of his T-shirt, hard enough to cut glass.

The air I'd been holding in my lungs rushed from me, my temples began to pound. My blood began to rush.

And as soon as my heart began to beat again, so much faster than normal, I said, "You have to go," louder than I meant to.

Rett licked his lips and I followed the motion, finding myself wanting to do it for him.

Wanting to feel his lips.

Touch the short wiry hairs along his jawline and around his mouth.

Test the coarseness of his dark hair between my fingertips.

Sink my teeth into his wide shoulders, his neck, his…

What. The. Hell.

No.

No.

Absolutely not.

No fucking way.

I should not be having any kind of reaction to this man.

He was nothing but a pain in my ass.

He was already trying to wedge his way into my life. I needed to shove him back out.

I had no room for him.

Not as a friend. Not as...

Anything.

"Is something wrong?"

Now he was purposely being obtuse.

"Only that you're still here," I forced up my constricted throat. My heart was also still thumping out of control and pumping blood to somewhere it shouldn't.

I did not want this man.

I did not need this man.

I only needed to convince my cock of that since right now, it was disagreeing with me.

We'd have to agree to disagree.

I waited for him to move out of the doorway to give us some much needed space. When he didn't, when he continued to stand there with his lips parted slightly and his eyes locked with mine, I broke the visual contact and slipped past him, making sure we didn't touch each other again, even by accident.

I finally could breathe when I reached the center of my cabin and had a few feet between us.

Keeping my back to him, I avoided seeing the interest in his dark brown eyes but listened to him moving past me, giving me a wide berth. When he finally came into view again, both he and Timber were standing by the door.

With his back to me, Rett hesitated with his hand on the door handle. He stood there for far too long. Like he was waiting for something. Or trying to remember something. Or even trying to figure out what to say.

Finally, with a small shake of his head, he opened the back door and stepped out onto the small porch.

Before he had a chance to shut the door behind him, I followed him and Timber outside to make sure he actually left the property and didn't hang around lurking.

Then I remembered something he had said earlier.

Before I went inside to get dressed.

Before that touch...

Even though I would regret it, I asked it anyway because now I was more than curious. Especially since Rett hadn't mentioned it again and he didn't seem to be shy about saying whatever he thought should be said.

As Rett walked down the steps and toward his truck, I called out, "You mentioned something about a favor. What was it?"

He paused halfway to his truck and turned back to face me. His cheeks had some color in them, not from our touch, but now I think it was more from aggravation.

Most likely from me.

I didn't care. It was better if he got sick of trying to win me over and left me alone. If he didn't see that now, he would soon. I'd make sure of it. I couldn't have what happened between us at the bookstore and now in my bedroom happen again.

"It doesn't matter."

Oh yes. The man was definitely annoyed with me. Or with his reaction to me. The same as I was with my reaction to him.

"Okay." I shrugged, pretending not to give a shit about the favor. "Thanks for the signed books."

I turned to go back inside and a strange noise coming from him made me stop and glance over my shoulder. When he didn't say anything, I continued to head inside, but once again he made me pause.

"I..."

I turned completely around this time with an eyebrow cocked and my head tilted, waiting for him to get out whatever this favor was. While I was curious, I wasn't going to beg him to tell me.

"I finished my latest book."

What did he want, a cookie? Or to brag, since I was so damn far behind in my own? "Okay?"

"I was hoping..."

Fuck. "That I'd read it," I finished for him, the tension increasing in my chest. I should've known.

No, you shouldn't have asked. You should've let him leave instead of inviting him back into your life by opening that damn door yourself.

He nodded, wiping his hands down the outside of his thighs.

Well, look at that, he'd been nervous about asking. The man who didn't seem to have a filter.

"Yes. I know you're busy with your own writing. And you haven't—"

I cut him off abruptly. "Do you have a copy with you?"

His mouth opened in surprise, then snapped shut and he shook his head. "I can email it to you. I'd just need your email address."

"If I give it to you, will you finally leave me alone?"

His mouth thinned into a slash for a split second before saying, "That's not very nice."

"When and where did you get the impression I was worried about being nice?"

"I didn't get that impression. My impression of you is far from nice."

Damn. That slap-back almost made me grin.

"I haven't read the rest of the series yet. Will it matter?"

His brow furrowed. "Wait... You'll read it?"

I released a sigh. "If there won't be any spoilers for the Peabody books I haven't read yet."

"There won't be. Like the rest of the series, he works on a completely new case in each book."

I nodded. I did the same with my books, too. Each book in the series could stand alone. You could start at any point along the way and move backward or forward.

"Fine. I'll read it when I get a chance. Are you in a rush?"

"I can wait since I don't have it up for preorder yet. But as soon as you're done reading it, I will."

But he needed my email.

If I gave it to him, that would be one more way to wedge his foot into the door.

Worse comes to worse, I could open a free email account and use that. This way if he got to be too much of a pest, I could delete the account. "Is your email on your business card?"

"The store email is."

"I'll send an email to it so you have mine."

He smiled.

Actually freaking smiled. A very large, genuinely happy smile.

I once again stopped breathing.

Where he stood in my clearing, the sun had already been shining on him but when he added that smile?

It became blinding.

But my attraction and reaction to him was disturbing.

I forced myself to turn and go back inside.

"Hey!"

Christ on a cracker, what else could he want from me? I already agreed to do something big for him. Something time consuming and would eat into my own writing time. In addition to that, it would turn my love of his books into work, taking away some of that reading pleasure.

With a stifled sigh, I turned back one more time.

"Can I ask one more thing?"

No. I groaned under my breath. "I'd prefer you didn't."

Of course he ignored that. "Why don't you have any pictures displayed of you and your husband?"

Oh hell no. We weren't going there.

"Have a great day," I ground out and spun on my heels to go back inside and lock him the hell out.

"That didn't sound very genuine," he called out as I slammed the door shut and threw the slide lock.

CHAPTER 9

Chase

I HEARD THE SHAKE, rattle and roll of a truck coming up the lane first. Then the very recognizable bark of an excited dog second.

With a grimace, I took a last glance at my screen and saved my work before closing my laptop and getting to my feet. I didn't need to go out front to know who was once again trespassing without my permission.

Shit. How could he get my permission first? I'd given him no way to contact me other than in person. He probably thought I purposely didn't email him when I only just remembered I had forgotten. The reason I'd forgotten was because for the first time since losing Thomas, I actually found myself in a writing groove and was taking advantage of it while it lasted.

Another bout of writer's block could be lurking around the next corner. That threat made me stay up late and get up early to do nothing but write as long as the words were coming easily.

I was grateful they'd been flowing like a broken dam.

Spending all the time I did outside when the weather was nice, along with the stunning views and peaceful atmosphere must have finally spurred my creativity like I'd hoped it would.

But the quiet I'd achieved was about to quickly change.

Again.

I stepped off the front porch and rounded the cabin, heading to where I could hear Rett ordering Timber to stay in the truck and the dog back-talking by whining and woofing softly.

"I know you do, but I'm not sure it's reciprocated." Rett's response to Timber's complaining drifted over to me as the man, his dog and his truck came into view when I rounded the back corner.

My step stuttered at seeing Rett standing by the passenger door, patting Timber's head sticking out of the window. Once again, the dog's tongue hung out of the side of his mouth in his typical goofy way.

"You speak dog?" I called out, asking the equally goofy owner.

Rett quickly turned in my direction and Timber let out an excited high-pitched scream when he saw me, making his owner wince.

It hurt my ears from where I stood, I couldn't imagine having it done directly next to me.

"I speak Timber."

"Timber's not a dog? You could've fooled me."

"Timber wants to act like he's not a dog, as you can clearly see."

I *mmm*'d and took two more steps, stopped before I got too close and planted my hands on my hips. "What are you doing here?"

"Do you mind if I let him out?"

I shrugged one shoulder. As soon as Rett opened the passenger door, the German Shepherd leapt from the cab, rushed over to the tree line and lifted his leg. Once he was done, he rushed over to me and poked my thigh with his nose.

While I might not speak dog, as he stared up at me I could read his *poor-me*, puppy dog eyes.

I dropped a hand from my hip to scratch behind his ears, causing him to sit on my foot and those eyes to half-close in pleasure as his tail slowly swept back and forth across the ground.

"For some reason my dog likes you. He's usually a better judge of character."

In my past life, I would've chuckled over that comment, but the truth was I rarely laughed anymore. "I guess his judgment is about as good as yours since you keep showing up at my place. Even when you're not wanted."

Rett's lips curled up slightly at the corners and he turned to reach into his truck, pulling out a thick manilla envelope and a pack of…

Pens?

After slamming the truck door shut, he strode toward me, his solid, long legs eating up the ground between us.

Yes, it was pens. A *dozen* red pens.

Why the hell would I need…

I groaned.

The manilla envelope must hold his manuscript. Because I forgot to email him, he printed the damn thing out.

I bit back a sigh.

With only Timber's black and tan body separating us, Rett stopped and lifted one dark eyebrow. "I would've emailed this to you if you had actually emailed me like you said you would."

My eyes flicked to the envelope he held up between us.

The man was certainly determined. However, I couldn't fault him for that. Gumption was always needed in life to get ahead. He certainly had it in spades.

"Therefore," he continued, "I figured you preferred to go old school and I printed the first draft for you, instead."

"I don't waste paper like that."

Thomas had always been big on saving the environment. He was horrified the time I printed out a three-hundred and fifty page novel —one-sided to boot—only to mark it up, make the necessary changes in my writing software and then toss it into a metal trash can to burn it.

I never did it again.

Very few things made Thomas happy.

His cat Sammie.

Me being environmentally aware.

Him reading my books.

Us snuggling together in bed to Netflix and chill.

The list was short.

It wasn't like he didn't want to be happy, but his hard wiring had been severely damaged when he was young. All from his goddamn awful parents. May they rot in hell, even though they both still lived and breathed. Unlike their first-born son.

I wasn't surprised when they didn't show up for our wedding since our love for each other, along with our marriage, were what they considered an abomination.

I shouldn't have been surprised, and was actually relieved, when they didn't show up for his memorial service, either. Of course, I didn't invite them but one of Thomas's childhood friends told them about it.

I'd been on edge that day, expecting them to show up and create a scene. To spout nonsense about us being sinners and that Thomas had deserved what happened to him for how he lived his life.

It was for the best that they didn't show up, otherwise I probably would've punched his father, strangled his mother and ended up in jail.

Truthfully, it would've been worth every minute I spent behind bars.

"I normally don't, either."

Huh?

Oh damn, my mind had wandered. We were discussing printing out manuscripts, right?

He lifted both brows. "It only took me repeating that a half dozen times to yank you back from wherever you disappeared. Welcome back."

Timber was now leaning all of his weight into my leg and crushing my foot while Rett still held the envelope up in the air.

I snagged the manuscript and pens from his fingers. "Do you

expect for me to need a dozen red pens for this?" I shook the envelope.

"From the little I've gotten to know of you, yes. You'll probably use more than twelve, if it's warranted or not."

Even though he was half-teasing, the other half was serious.

"Am I that awful?" I already knew his answer.

"Yes."

"Then why are you here?"

His expression turned one hundred percent serious when he said, "Because I have a feeling you weren't so awful before…"

Before I lost Thomas.

He was right.

Between the two of us, Thomas had been the dark and I had been the light in our relationship and in our lives. Definitely a yin and yang situation.

Now… My light had been snuffed out.

I saw a flicker in the distance, I just couldn't reach out and grab it. When I tried, it slipped through my fingers every damn time.

A whine at my feet made me glance down. Someone wanted attention. Just like his owner.

Would it hurt to have a friend? Someone who understood the ins and outs of writing and the publishing business? Someone who understood what it was like to be gay?

Someone who understood what it was like to be alone?

Though, Rett wasn't quite alone, he had Timber.

And the residents of Eagle's Landing.

I didn't even let myself have that.

Staring at Timber's head, I murmured, "The time before feels like a lifetime ago."

"But you were different."

I raised my gaze from the dog to his owner. Pressing my lips together, I swallowed down the lump that had risen into my throat. "I will never be the same."

I closed my eyes and regretted those words the second they

slipped past my lips. This man had been trying to break down my walls from the second I met him. I was afraid he might be succeeding.

Apparently, persistence paid off. Rett was proof of that.

Damn it. My goal to hide any vulnerability from him was now busted.

"You okay?" His hand landed on my arm.

I'm never okay. I cleared my throat and opened my eyes.

Little bursts of lightning spread from where his fingers held me. It reminded me of when I was a boy and shuffled around the carpet in my socks, then touched an object to get that little *zap.* I considered it a thrill at the time and, even though I knew what would happen, it still made me jump, then burst out in squeals of laughter.

Today I wasn't laughing.

And the look of concern on Rett's face was gone. He stared at where he touched me but didn't remove his hand. In fact, it tightened.

Then his thumb made a quick back and forth movement.

A caress? Was that what he was doing?

I yanked my arm from his grip, pulled my foot from under Timber's weight and took a step back so I could breathe. "What are you doing?"

"Making sure you're all right. You went ghost white. I was worried—"

"Bullshit," I growled, trying to rein in my spinning emotions.

I took another step back and lifted the manuscript. "I'll take a look at this when I get a chance."

I was trying not to panic over whatever Rett was pulling from me every time we touched. But I was beginning to reel from it and was worried if I let loose, I'd be flung so hard that whatever I collided with would smash me into a thousand pieces.

I couldn't let that happen.

I needed space.

Time.

And to be alone.

I avoided looking at him as I made a wide berth and strode over to the rear porch with a quickness. I'm sure it appeared as if I was being chased by a monster.

Because it was true. I was.

And I needed to escape.

"Chase, wait!"

"No," I shouted, not caring what he thought. Not caring if I was rude.

The only problem was, I'd been so lost in my head and didn't realize he'd been on my heels.

Before I could close the door behind me and shut him out, he was there. In my doorway, in my cabin. Forcing his way into my life.

He needed to leave. And I needed to avoid contact with him. If I ignored our reaction to each other, it might go away. *He* might go away.

"Rett—" I couldn't look at him. I didn't want to see what was in his eyes or what was on his face.

"Are you pretending you didn't feel that?"

Yes, of course I am! "I'm not pretending anything. I don't know what you're talking about."

"Bullshit," he echoed. "I felt it. You did, too. Like at the store and the other day in your bedroom. You can deny it all you want but it's there."

I scraped my thumbnail across my forehead. "There's *nothing* there." I was not only trying to convince him, but myself.

"You only refuse to see it."

"You're making things up."

"I'm not."

I stopped in my tracks and spun on him. "The fuck you aren't."

He was only inches from me. Close enough to lift my hand and touch him. But that would be stupid. It would be like swiping my hand through an open flame. It would hurt and I'd regret the burn afterward.

"When's the last time you've been touched? Allowed anyone to touch you or hug you? Or simply comfort you?"

His whispered questions made my chest tighten, made my heart thump heavily. "I don't need any of that."

"Yes, you do. We all do."

"Maybe *you* need that, I do not."

"Why are you so goddamn stubborn?"

Because I have to be. I have no choice.

I'd been barely hanging by a thread for the past two years, it wouldn't take much to snap it. If it broke, I'd never be able to repair it.

Rett was a threat to that unraveling thread.

Even though he would normally be my type, I kept trying to convince myself that I no longer had a type. That I wasn't interested in any man. Gay, bi or...

The man standing too close.

"You need to go," rumbled out of me. An order. A warning. A last chance.

"There's nothing wrong with what you're experiencing when we touch, Chase. Not a damn thing. You're allowed to hurt but you're also allowed to feel. Let yourself have that. Let yourself heal. It doesn't mean you'll forget him. You never will. He's still in your heart and always will be."

"You don't..." I shook my head. "I don't have to explain myself to you."

"You're right, you don't. But despite you denying it, there *is* something between us."

"You're imagining things."

His head jerked to the side and his jaw tightened. "You're wrong and I'm going to prove it to you." He closed the gap between us.

"I don't need proof, I need you to leave—"

Before I realized what was happening and could fend him off, Rett's hand wrapped around the back of my head and he yanked me forward, slamming our mouths together.

Our lips colliding was an explosion, stunning me for a second. Almost the same reaction I had the first time I kissed Thomas, but...

Different.

Not better, not worse...

Unexpected.

His lips moved over mine and his tongue slid over the seam of my mouth, demanding entry.

My heart began to pound. All the tiny hairs on the back of my neck now stood at attention.

And my blood was pooling somewhere it shouldn't.

For a moment I pushed all thoughts out of my head because they were conflicted.

Push him away. Pull him closer.

Pin my mouth shut. Allow him inside.

My cock had responded instantly, but my brain was sluggish. Confused.

I shouldn't want this, but I also wanted more.

I should be pissed at the gall of the man kissing me.

I needed to stop him.

My hands went up to his chest, but instead of pushing him, my fingers curled into his shirt.

All it took was my mouth to open just the slightest and his tongue was pushing its way inside. Sweeping and tasting every corner. Tangling with mine.

For a moment I forgot who I was, where I was and who I was kissing.

I missed this. The touch. The rush of adrenaline. The intimacy.

Both perfect and imperfect at the same time.

Wanted and feared.

His fingers dug into my scalp, the other hand squeezed the side of my waist.

His whole body vibrated against me.

Or was that me? Was I the one shaking? The one about to unravel?

Then his erection pressed to mine.

His erection pressed to…

His erection pressed…

To mine…

Fuck!

The fog cleared from my brain and I landed hard right back in the center of my cabin with a man I didn't want to be attracted to. A man I shouldn't be kissing. And who shouldn't be kissing me.

What was he doing?

What was I doing?

This was wrong. *So* damn wrong.

I didn't want any of this.

I didn't want Rett.

Damn it, I didn't.

I couldn't.

I wouldn't.

I gripped his shirt even tighter, swung him around, yanked my mouth free and put all my weight behind pushing him away.

With a sharp intake of breath, he lost his balance and stumbled back.

As if in slow motion, I watched his foot get caught against one of the chairs, making him fall.

I jumped forward and reached out to grab his wildly flailing arm before he twisted, trying to save himself from falling backwards.

He failed.

The thump of his head against the corner of the solid farmhouse table made me cringe and bark out a, "Fuck!"

Then his knees gave out and he crumpled to the ground.

I stared at the man on the floor.

His eyes were closed.

Jesus fucking Christ! I quickly dropped to my knees next to him. "Rett!" I grabbed his face and turned it to me.

Was he faking it to get back at me? Or did he really pass out?

I tapped two fingers sharply against his bearded cheek. "Rett!"

Son of a bitch!

I gently turned his head until I could see where he struck it and immediately saw the blood.

What the hell did I do?

I quickly parted his short, dark brown hair and was relieved to only see a tiny cut. But that didn't mean there wasn't more damage underneath from the contact.

Like a concussion.

Fuck! I hadn't meant to hurt him.

But that was exactly what I did.

CHAPTER 10

Rett

I wasn't sure where I was sleeping but wherever it was wasn't very comfortable. Worse, my head was propped up on a very lumpy and hard pillow.

That same head also throbbed like I had a bad headache.

I needed to find a more comfortable place to sleep. This wasn't it.

I opened my eyes and closed them instantly.

Was that two heads hovering over me?

I cracked my eyes open again. Enough to try to make out what it was without the light stabbing like a butcher knife through my noggin.

No, even with my blurry vision I realized it wasn't two heads, unless they were identical twins.

Two of Chase would definitely be one too many.

Right now, it may be two too many.

The man was on his knees next to me and it took me a few seconds to realize the pillow under my head wasn't lumpy because it was a crappy pillow, it was Chase's lap.

And I was lying on the hardwood floor.

None of that made any sense.

I winced again at Timber's loud whining. From the corner of my eye, I could see a blurry black and tan four-legged figure pacing back and forth. Then a second later my dog's blocky head pushed between us, and his long snout poked my cheek.

Chase pushed him out of the way. "Timber, no. Not now. Go... Go... Somewhere."

Timber, in fact, did not go "somewhere," he plopped his ass down next to Chase, his head swinging back and forth between me and the man leaning over me.

I tried to ask, "What happened?" but my words came out sounding more jumbled and muffled than they should.

Or was that the cotton in my ears?

My head was still spinning and I had no idea how I got on the floor. Or why.

Worse, my head throbbed with its own heartbeat. And he was pressing on the back of my head with something. Damp cloth? Washcloth? Something wet.

Did I have a cut? Whatever it was, it stung like hell and throbbed to the same beat as the rest of my brain.

"You tripped."

I frowned and shifted to get up.

"Don't move." Chase held me back down with one hand pressed to the back of my head, the other pressing against my shoulder.

"What did I trip over? Timber?" My dog was notorious for being where he didn't belong, including under my feet. Sometimes I swore he was trying to take me out.

"The chair." His lips thinned out.

"I tripped over a chair?" I usually wasn't that klutzy.

When I reached behind my head, Chase smacked my hand away. "Don't touch it."

"It hurts."

"That doesn't mean you should touch it."

I bit back my urge to roll my eyes and say, "Okay, Dad."

Because he was far, far, *far* from my father. Especially with the things I wanted to do to the man…

Yeah, no. Chase was definitely not even close to being the same as my dad. On that note, I also wasn't one to call other men Daddy.

I would normally be thrilled to have my head in his lap like this while he cupped it, but not in this situation.

"Do you want me to take you to the hospital?"

"Am I bleeding?"

He pulled a damp paper towel away and showed me some evidence of blood. "It's only a cut."

"Large enough for stitches?"

"No, but you'll probably need a few aspirin."

"Are my pupils blown?"

I held my breath when he leaned closer and stared directly into my eyes.

Damn. "Are they?"

He shook his head. His own pupils were wider now and his nostrils slightly flared.

"Then, no. I don't want to go to the hospital. My insurance sucks."

"I'd pay for it."

I narrowed my eyes on him. "Why? I only tripped, right?"

"Right."

A flash of memory ping-ponged through my foggy brain. I pressed fingertips to my lips in an attempt to make that memory clearer.

Lips…

Yes, it had something to do with my lips.

Did he punch me in the mouth? No. My mouth would be bleeding and it would hurt.

I remembered my lips tingling… And…

Holy shit.

Everything came flooding back to me.

The kiss I was losing myself in. A hard impact against my chest before I lost my balance…

My heart stopping and then leaping into my throat as I fell backward.

From where I now lay—mostly on the floor and with my upper body on Chase's lap—my eyes flicked to the corner of the table where apparently I'd left a bit of DNA behind. A few hairs and a little bit of blood.

"You pushed me." If that sounded like an accusation, it was meant to.

He had shoved me away, made me fall over the chair and crack my damn head open.

All over a simple kiss.

Okay, maybe not such a simple kiss. It had actually been the hottest kiss I'd had in a very long time.

Maybe even ever.

He might want to deny our attraction—or connection, or whatever we had that created the small explosions in my center—but it was there. No denying it.

Well, Chase denied it.

But he couldn't deny that he'd been as hard as I was during the kiss *and* he'd been kissing me back.

All before…

He could've killed me. *What an asshole.* "You could've killed me," I repeated out loud.

Those very same lips I kissed twisted. "Obviously, you didn't die."

"But I could've."

"But you didn't."

"I only tripped over the chair because you *pushed* me."

He grimaced and at least had the decency to look guilty. "I didn't mean to hurt you, it was an automatic response."

"That's not the typical response to a kiss. I could've died."

"We went over that already. You're still breathing."

"Lucky for you!" Planting a hand on the floor, I pushed myself up.

"I wouldn't say that you still breathing labels me as lucky." He pushed me back down. "In fact, I'd say it's the opposite. Because if you can breathe, you can talk. Stay there."

"No. You're dangerous."

"I'm not."

"Proof says otherwise."

"You shouldn't have done that," Chase mumbled. "I... panicked."

Of course he panicked. His initial reaction and his hard-on proved he liked it. He only wasn't happy about it. "You hit me over a kiss?"

"I didn't hit you. I simply pushed you away."

"Semantics."

"There's a clear distinction between the two."

"Says you."

A loud sigh filled the space between us. "Let's get you up and moved somewhere more comfortable than the floor."

I rose enough to sit. "I should go."

"I'm sure you're still dizzy." He tried to push me back down but this time he was unsuccessful. "You probably shouldn't drive."

I'm sure it killed him to tell me that I shouldn't leave. "I don't want to be where I'm not wanted."

"That hasn't stopped you before."

I guessed that was true.

"You should rest."

"Where? On a wood floor?" I asked. Because the man didn't even have a damn couch. He had a very comfortable-looking chair—possibly a recliner—in front of the fireplace, but other than that the furniture in his place was slim pickings.

He glanced around, and a muscle ticked in his cheek when his gaze landed on his bedroom door.

Oh no...

"Let's get you somewhere more comfortable. Since I don't have a couch, you'll have to use my bed."

No. No.

That wasn't smart. But then kissing him without asking first wasn't smart, either. "Help me up and out to my truck. I can drive."

"You shouldn't. Not yet."

"I'll be fine."

"You're not fine," he practically shouted. Clearly a sign of him losing his patience.

Well, he wasn't the only one.

Surging to his feet, he left me on the floor sitting up. A second later, he leaned down, hooked an arm under my armpits and around my back. "Help me. I can't lift you on my own."

"I don't want to lay in your bed."

"Believe me, I don't want you there, either."

Just for that, I now wanted to sleep in his bed all night.

He assisted me to stand and as soon as I was on my two feet, my brain took a couple spins around my skull and my vision darkened around the edges. "Whoa."

"Told you. You should listen to me."

I would've rolled my eyes at that if I didn't think it would make me pass out. "That's arguable."

He sighed, gritted his teeth and I leaned into him as he helped me the few feet to his bedroom. Once we were inside, he sat me on his mattress. Then, as soon as I scooted back and got my ass settled, he lifted my legs and slid them across the bed until I was in a reclined position.

His bed was really damn comfortable. I'd have to ask him about the brand of mattress.

He tucked his two pillows under my head, careful to avoid the injury. "Stay there. Don't move. I'll get you ice." He spun on his feet and jetted from the room like his ass was on fire.

"Pour some whiskey on that ice," I called out before wincing from yelling.

Chase grumbled something but I couldn't make out what he said.

I sighed. Well, this wasn't how I expected my evening to go.

As much as I had fantasized about being in Chase's bed, none of those fantasies included me being in it by myself or having a slight head injury. Caused by the man himself.

"I don't have corn or peas. This is the best I can do."

"I thought you were bringing me a whiskey on the rocks."

"You're getting frozen spinach." He stepped closer and set the bag of frozen vegetables on the bed along with a dry wash cloth, unscrewed the cap on a bottle of Aleve and shook two pills out onto his palm. "Take those."

"You want me to swallow them dry?"

He squeezed his eyes shut for a few seconds and as soon as he reopened them, he marched back out the door with a jaw that could cut glass.

I made sure to smother my grin when he came back less than a minute later with water.

"That's not well water, is it?" I asked, eyeing the glass.

"Are you fucking kidding me?"

I rolled my lips under, grabbed the glass from him, popped the Aleve into my mouth and chased it with a mouthful of what tasted like spring water. At least he hadn't scooped it from Eagles Lake so I would die of dysentery.

"Lift your head up."

Like the good patient I was, I did as I was told, though I added a groan for good measure.

He avoided my gaze when he curled over me and reached around to press the frozen spinach to my head. I gasped softly when the cold hit my wound, immediately pulling his eyes to mine. Most likely against his will.

We locked gazes and neither of us breathed.

Or moved.

I dropped my eyes to his lips when his tongue appeared and swept across them.

Oh yes, he was thinking about that kiss, too.

I was tempted to taste those lips again but I didn't want to tempt fate. I wouldn't put it past him to kick me while I was already down.

I winced at the pain radiating from my cut. "I can tell you've never been a nurse."

"If you hadn't kissed me you wouldn't need a damn nurse," he ground out. "You caught me off guard. I wasn't expecting that."

Unless he was pushed, he might never be ready. But I wasn't going to point that out because he'd deny it.

I'd already learned he was stubborn like that.

The bed shook violently when, from out of nowhere, Timber jumped on it and, after a big yawn and a few circles to find the perfect spot to settle, he curled up next to me, claiming Chase's bed as his.

Unfortunately for me, and fortunately for Chase, that broke the spell between us. He pulled away and ordered gruffly, "Hold that in place."

I'd prefer if you held it for me.

When I reached back to take it from him, our fingers brushed, and again, he acted like I'd burned him.

He straightened and stepped back from the bed, wiping his hands down the sides of his jeans, acting like I had cooties or something.

"Too late. You're already gay. You can't catch it from me."

"That's not funny."

"You might not realize it yet, but I *am* funny. I have a great sense of humor. You're just too miserable to recognize it."

"Definitely not funny enough to do standup on that little stage at the back of your store."

"Maybe not. But now that you've mentioned it, I'll consider it."

"I'll save you the trouble. Don't. If you did, the residents of Eagle's Landing might chase you out with pitchforks and torches."

I grinned. "Well, look at that, you *do* have a sense of humor somewhere in that deep, dark pit of yours. Maybe you should be doing standup comedy yourself. Dark comedy, of course." I patted the bed beside me. When he stayed where he was, I assured him, "You're safe. I promise to never kiss you again."

Before he could hide it, something flashed behind his eyes at my statement.

Proof, once again, he hadn't hated that kiss. But like he said, I had caught him off guard by doing it.

Understandable.

And he was probably pissed at himself for liking it.

Again, understandable.

Him shoving me away was a knee-jerk reaction. "I forgive you."

He cocked his head and stared at me, his dark brown eyes guarded.

"If you'll forgive me," I added, "since I shouldn't have done that. I'm sorry. Hopefully me kissing you won't leave you with long-term PTSD that you'll need years of therapy to get over."

He pressed his lips together.

"And I hope you won't hate me."

His eyes flicked to Timber curled up next to me, giving him the priceless gift of black and tan hairs on his comforter.

"And that you'll still want to beta-read my manuscript."

Chase's eyes sliced from Timber back to me. "Do you ever shut up?"

I shrugged. "I don't get to see a lot of people during the day, even when the bookstore is open. That causes me to ramble when I'm around living, breathing humans. Though, it's debatable whether I would consider you as a living or breathing human. I've had better conversations with a rock."

"Then why do you keep trying?"

Because I'm trying to break down your walls. And once I commit to something, I don't quit until I achieve my goal. Determined? Yes. Foolish? Maybe. "I'm guessing you were probably a decent guy in your past life. We also have a lot in common, whether you recognize that fact or not."

He surprised me when he finally sat on the edge of the bed. The bed had hardly moved with his weight, so I had to assume it was memory foam or something similar.

"About time you took a load off."

"I'm only sitting because I'm tired of standing."

That was bullshit. I could tell he was slowly loosening up and open to talking more. It had to be my teasing that was breaking through his crusty exterior. "You don't have to sit in here with me."

"If I don't watch you, I wouldn't put it past you to try on some of my clothes."

"You're bigger than me."

"Not by much."

I studied his profile. He had his head turned away from me and was petting Timber's hind leg since it was closest to him.

"You like dogs."

"I've never owned one."

Ah yes, he was finally engaging in small talk. I needed to keep it going. "What made you pick Eagle's Landing?"

"This cabin. The amount of land. The view. And the unbeatable price."

"A perfect spot to hide."

He turned his head and we locked gazes. "Apparently not."

I grinned. "Some people are more determined than others."

"No shit." He blew out a soft breath. "Are you still feeling dizzy?"

"Are you trying to get rid of me? I offered to leave earlier. You're the one who insisted I stay."

"You hit your head pretty hard."

"I must have been pushed pretty hard."

"I apologized."

My eyebrows shot up my forehead. "But did you?"

His brow furrowed. "Didn't I?"

"I'll waive your apology if you answer one question."

"Just one?"

"It's a pretty big one."

Immediately I could see him starting to tense up and shut down, so I hurried to ask it. "When's the last time you've had any," *sex*, "kind of," *sex*, "intimate contact?" *Sex?*

144

"That's not your business."

"You're right, it's not. But I'm making it my business."

"You shouldn't."

"But I am. So, answer or I want you on your knees begging me for my forgiveness." I tried to keep a straight face and not grin since I would never ask him to do that.

Hold on. Did he actually roll his eyes at me? That was a good sign. I was starting to see some human tendencies.

When I nudged him with my elbow to encourage him to answer, he shifted farther away, but twisted slightly toward me, instead. He was no longer petting Timber, his hand was now pressed to the bed very close to my calf.

I imagined what it would be like if he curled his fingers around it and gave it a gentle squeeze.

Then slid up…

Stay on track, Rett. "My question was about intimacy. I'm still waiting for the answer."

"What's it to you?"

I pointed to the floor and with a deeper voice than normal ordered, "Knees or answer."

He sighed and raked his fingers through his hair, mussing it up even worse than it already was. I don't remember it being like that before *"the kiss"* so it was most likely from when he panicked, thinking he hurt me badly. "I don't know."

"Yes you do."

"Not since…" He pressed his lips together, giving me my answer.

"So, no one since your husband."

Chase shook his head and stared across the room.

Holy hell, that was over two years ago. "How about this… When's the last time anyone has touched you?"

"I just said over two years ago." The irritation in his tone was clear and the fingers of the hand he had near my leg curled into the bedding hard enough to turn his knuckles white.

"Not in a sexual way," I clarified, "I meant simple physical contact."

It took him too long to answer. To me that was telling. Painful, too, but not as much as it was when he answered, "When my family hugged me at his funeral."

Again, over two years ago. "You've had no physical contact since then?"

"No, and I don't want it, either." He unclenched his hand from the comforter and began to pick at a loose thread.

The silence stretched between us.

Was he afraid he would feel something and would no longer allow himself to be numb? Why did he want to keep himself so closed off from everyone and everything?

That wasn't healthy.

"Being a monk isn't good for the prostate. Or your mental health."

Chase's brow dropped low. "Are you still trying to be funny? If so, once again you're failing."

"I wasn't trying to be funny and I'm not joking about this."

More silence.

I wanted to keep him talking. I was creating fine cracks in his armor, I just needed to keep picking at them, making them wider so I could slip through.

I had this crazy need to prove to him what he was doing to himself—living in a bubble and trying to avoid the rest of the world —wasn't healthy.

"It's been a while for me, too," I confessed, hoping if I gave him something personal about myself, he'd be more willing to open up.

Chase's dark and disturbing eyes pinned me in place. "What?"

Being the only gay man in a straight town meant I had no friends or buddies to discuss anything to do with dating or sex. "You know, sex. Touch. Losing myself in someone else. The intimacy. Shared pleasure. The shared whispers. Shared dreams and secrets. All of it. I miss it."

All of that confession was one hundred percent true.

"So go get it. Nothing's stopping you."

"You're right. Nothing's stopping me," I murmured. "Except myself." I hesitated for a second, then added, "The same as you."

"But you want it. I don't."

"You do, Chase. You're just trying to convince yourself you don't. You shouldn't starve yourself from enjoying intimacy or another's touch. You know you can have that without getting tangled up in a relationship, right?" *Hint, hint.*

"Simply having sex with someone can get complicated."

"It can, but only if you let it. Did you ever hear of friends with benefits?"

"That can get messy, too."

"True. It could." Anything to do with sex or intimacy could. But it was better than avoiding it completely. "Did you ever think that risk could be worth the reward?"

He surged to his feet because I was pushing him into a zone he wasn't comfortable with. He strode over to the windows overlooking the lake and stared out, keeping his back to me.

Timber had lifted his head and released a little noise but as soon as he made sure both Chase and I were still close by, he tucked his nose back into his fluffy tail, closed his eyes again and let out a soft, satisfied groan.

I ran my hand down his back. "I remember everything about the kiss now, Chase. I remember how it started out. Yes, at first you were surprised but then you were into it. Until you remembered you shouldn't be. That stems from guilt. Do you think you're cheating on his memory? If so, you're not."

"Don't try to analyze me."

I never lost a significant other, but after reading Thomas's obituary, I had thought long and hard about how that might feel. Losing your life partner, your soulmate. The person you vowed your fidelity to for the rest of your life.

Thomas was gone, but Chase had been left behind. Their "forever" had been cut too short. I didn't know how or why, but that part didn't matter. What mattered was how Chase had taken that loss.

Not well. That was to be expected. But to still be so stuck after two years?

Either Thomas had to be his love of a lifetime or he was blaming himself for his husband's death for some reason.

"I'm only telling you what I see. What you're blind to."

"What you're saying is, you think I should have sex with you." He still stood in front of the window staring out, but now he was white-knuckling the frame with both hands.

"Well… I mean… I wasn't volunteering to be a fuck buddy but… Hell… I wouldn't say no. But I'm talking about with anyone you find yourself attracted to, not me."

"Good, because I'm not attracted to you."

I grinned at his back. "Do you think I believe that? Or are you trying to convince yourself?"

He spun around. His expression hard, his eyes even sharper. "You seem fine now. It's time for you to leave."

Damn it. I might have pushed a touch too far.

But it was a step. It might be a small step but it was better than nothing and I believed it was in the right direction.

However, it was hard to tell since Chase blew hot and cold.

I was hoping to get more of the hot from him but it would take time.

Luckily, I had all the time in the world.

CHAPTER 11

Chase

I KEPT my shit together when I helped Rett and his dog out to his truck.

I kept it together when I watched him drive away.

I kept it together as I walked back up the porch and into my quiet cabin.

No dog. No Rett.

Just me and my thoughts.

When I got back inside, I spotted the manila envelope, along with the box of red pens, on my table and beelined to it because I needed something to distract me.

From the man. From the kiss.

From the fact I could've easily gotten lost in Rett simply by us pressing our lips together.

I also needed to find something to help keep my shit together. If I couldn't find my words today for my current book, then diving into his manuscript might help.

Because the very edges of my tight control were beginning to fray. And I didn't want to keep picking at that loose thread like the one on my comforter.

The one Rett had been lying on.

Due to me injuring him.

I hadn't meant to but I hadn't lied when I told Rett I panicked.

I definitely panicked. Not because he kissed me without asking, but because if I hadn't shoved him away, I would have taken that kiss further.

And that would be dangerous.

Rett was dangerous.

The fact was, I wanted him.

The fact remained, I couldn't have him.

The man had mentioned being "fuck buddies." I wasn't sure if he was serious about that or was even offering, but if he was, I wasn't jumping on the offer.

One reason was, I couldn't imagine Rett only being satisfied with that type of relationship. He was all up in my business now, if he was in my bed, too? It could be worse.

But more than that, I couldn't bear to lose again.

Not my heart.

Not someone I cared for.

Not someone I loved.

Sex and even basic companionship could easily grow into love. That was a valid risk. Not too many people I knew could keep the two separate, even if it started that way.

Of course it was possible. People could have sex without all the intimacy that went along with it. But usually with random strangers, not someone they knew personally and had sex with on a regular basis.

Was keeping sex impersonal possible for Rett? Highly doubtful.

Even though the kiss had only lasted a few seconds, the worry of falling for the man could very well last a lifetime.

Despite the fact I pretended I didn't like him, I did. Even despite the fact he was annoying and not as funny as he thought.

I liked more things about him than I disliked.

The way he looked. The way he smelled.

The way he loved his dog.

His books.

His upbeat attitude.

The fact that he kept a bookstore open for the residents of Eagle's Landing, even though it was taking a financial loss. The fact that he hosted weekly activities at that same shop so the locals had something to do.

He was kind. He was caring. He was…

No.

Absolutely not.

After opening the large envelope, I slid out what seemed like a whole ream of paper. I doubted it was five-hundred pages but he didn't have them numbered. However, his books typically ran on the longer side, depending on how much trouble Dexter Peabody got into during his investigation.

Actually, when reading them, I wouldn't want any of his books to end if I didn't know the next one was available and waiting for me to start reading. However, the one I held in my hands *was* the end.

At least until he wrote the next one.

Of course, that made me hyper-aware of how long my own readers had been waiting for my next book and why they were so impatient.

My first instinct had been to say no to beta-reading his manuscript. I really shouldn't take the time out of my writing schedule to read and mark it up. But if I had told him no, I figured I'd regret it later.

I had been enjoying his books. Of course, now I knew where Peabody got his *dorkwardness*—Peabody's own description of himself in the books—and sense of humor.

From the author himself.

I couldn't say Rett was really a dork, or even awkward, but he did have a way about him that was endearing, just like Peabody.

Though, I would never tell the man that.

It was bad enough he was like a glue trap. One I had stepped on by accident and couldn't free myself from, no matter how hard I tried to shake it free.

I was afraid that if I allowed it, he would quickly become a habit.

First as a fellow writer. Then as a friend. And after that...

It was a slippery slope I didn't want to find myself at the top of.

I had slipped enough with that single kiss. It might not have lasted long, but it was long enough for me to catch myself and remember whose lips were pressed to mine.

Not Thomas's, but Rett's.

Not my husband's, but a man I hardly knew.

Of course I missed intimacy, but did I want to get involved with another man, even as "fuck buddies?" No.

I couldn't afford to get involved in another relationship.

Rett said it wouldn't be considered cheating and while technically he was correct, it would still feel that way for me.

I had promised Thomas "'til death do us part." Only, I hadn't expected for his death to come so soon. It should've come after we were old and gray and we both had to gum our food, use a walker and hearing aids.

I expected us to grow old together. To both have age spots, wrinkles and dentures. Instead, I was forced to grow old without him.

He left me.

He left me alone.

He left me broken.

He left me not wanting to ever have anyone else.

I loved him with all my heart, but that heart and mind had been shattered when I found him.

When *I* found him. The worst day of my life.

"Why don't your closets have doors?"

I closed my eyes.

"Why don't your closets have doors?"

I sucked oxygen deep into my lungs and held it until it burned.

"Why don't your closets have doors?"

Pressure built inside of me, causing my skin to tighten to the point I thought it would split. My vision narrowed and I began to suffocate. I desperately gulped air to try to relieve that pressure.

Clutching my closing throat, I dropped his manuscript onto the table and stumbled my way to the front of the cabin.

I needed air.

I needed space.

I needed my husband back.

But instead of Thomas, all I could see was Rett.

All I could feel was his lips on mine.

The second I burst through the door and onto the front porch, I stumbled to my knees, sucking in the night air even as my throat continued to narrow and my heart continued to knock a hole in my chest, as an invisible band circled it, getting tighter and tighter by the second.

It was happening again and nothing I did would stop it.

I had to suffer through every damn nightmare, through every flashback, through every panic attack.

My only option was to ride it out.

Helpless and lost, I sat back on my haunches, curled over my lap and dropped my head into my hands.

Desperate to forget. Afraid to forget.

Wanting to move on. Afraid to move on without him.

My torso felt as heavy as lead as I struggled to sit up.

As I drove my fingers into my hair.

As I began to pull.

And pull.

And pull.

Trying to distract myself from the agony. Anything to pull me from this dark pit of despair.

To remind myself I still lived.

My heart still beat. My lungs still pumped.

But other than that, I remained a shell. An empty shell.

Rett was trying to change that despite my resistance.

He was trying to break open that shell, bring life back into me.

The problem was, it was working.

However, I couldn't have one without the other. I didn't get to pick and choose what I let inside.

If I felt one thing, I felt it all.

Even what tore me down and ripped me apart.

I wasn't ready.

I wasn't ready.

I wasn't…

Throwing my head back, I screamed at the top of my lungs.

My fingers kept ripping on my hair and I screamed and screamed and screamed, trying to release my rage. The awful ache.

I couldn't stop.

Those tortured screams carried over the water. And soon one scream blended into the next as they bounced back to me, becoming amplified. Deafening.

Driving into my head. Into my heart. Piercing my very center like a spear.

I screamed until my voice was raw, until my throat felt like it was bleeding.

Every scream scraped my insides like a rusty spoon.

Until I had nothing left inside me.

Until I was safely back to being an empty shell once more.

Back to being numb on the inside.

The only way I could survive.

CHAPTER 12

Rett

I SCRAMBLED for my cell phone when it buzzed. I had it plugged in to charge overnight since I was done working for the day and currently had myself propped against the headboard while watching a movie and mindlessly running my fingers along Timber's back. Knocked out cold and snoring, my sleeping companion was sprawled out next to me on the mattress, taking up most of the bed. Like normal.

Usually, I didn't get texts or phone calls this late at night unless something major happened and a mass text went out to all of Eagle's Landing residents. Texts received at this time of night could be a fire. A deer vs car collision. Coyote sightings. A black bear break-in. Or a life-threatening injury.

Basic gossip usually waited until the sun was shining. Emergencies did not.

Unplugging the phone, I swiped it from my nightstand and quickly slipped on the reading glasses I kept next to the bed. Once I closed up the store for the evening and took Timber for his last walk of the day, I removed my contacts.

While I could watch a movie comfortably without glasses, to see anything small, like something on my phone, I needed assistance.

Once I could read the message, my head jerked back.

I didn't bother to fight the grin as I scanned it one more time to make sure I read it correctly the first time. Even though it came from an unknown number, I knew exactly who sent it.

And you better believe I would be adding that number to my contacts.

How's your head?

Still attached, I wrote back with a snort loud enough to make Timber lift his head and give me the side-eye for interrupting his beauty sleep.

It had been three days since my cranium made contact with the corner of the texter's table. Three days of silence. Three days of me reliving that kiss over and over in my mind.

Three days of wondering if Chase had been doing the same.

Three days of hoping the man would take me up on being a fuck buddy even though I hadn't officially offered, only hinted.

And I had assumed Chase could take a hint.

Was that why he was texting now? To finally open up dialogue between us?

Like two humans and not one human and one unbearable grumpy grizzly?

My head injury was a good reminder that I should wait until Chase made the next move, not me.

It took another full minute but my phone finally vibrated again within my fingers. *I guess that's a positive.*

I'm surprised you think so. As much as I found Chase to be attractive, I would still be satisfied with a platonic friendship. The man needed someone in his corner. Someone who also understood the most important aspects of his life. *Have you forgiven me for kissing you yet?*

Have you forgiven me for cracking open your skull?

Depends on if you started beta-reading my book. I pretty much figured he'd used it to start a fire by now.

I counted ten heartbeats before I got Chase's next text: *It's good.*

"Whoa," I whispered, then apologized to Timber for disturbing him again. He groaned and stretched out to take up even more real estate. "I'm so glad I bought a king bed just for you, your highness."

I pulled my attention from the four-legged bed hog and back to the two-legged man I wished was hogging my bed. *Only good?*

So far. Actually, I think it's your best one yet...

"Listen to this, Timber. C.J. Anson says this is my best book yet. How about that?" I didn't even get a glaring eyeball that time.

You remind me a lot of that P.I.

I frowned. *Is that supposed to be a compliment or an insult?*

He's YOUR character, you tell me.

I tipped my head back against the headboard and grinned up at the ceiling.

Yes, the man was as boarded-up as a Blockbuster Video store, but I occasionally got a glimpse of the man he used to be. Or whom I assumed he used to be.

Then I would say it's a compliment, since under his bumbling ways Dexter is a genius.

I don't think you're bumbling or a genius, came the reply.

My grin got bigger. *You don't know me well enough yet to have been truly dazzled by my geniusity.* I added a big grin emoji on the end for good measure.

What the hell? That's not even a word.

We're authors. We're allowed to make up words. Man shrugging emoji.

No. Angry face emoji.

I chuckled. *Okay, then... how about this? Blinded by my brilliance.* Man wearing sunglasses emoji.

Still questionable. Eye roll emoji.

Let me prove it to you. Praying hands emoji.

I don't need proof. I need to get back to reading, even though I should be writing. When I'm destitute due to not getting my next book done, I'm blaming you. Man cursing emoji.

Shock face emoji. *If you're desperate, I can loan you money. Even though you probably still out-earn me a million-times over despite not putting out a new book in years.* Dollar sign emoji. Dollar sign emoji. Dollar sign emoji.

I might be teasing him but it had to be true.

Public records showed what he paid for those two hundred acres. That information had been easy to find online. Of course, the house he sold on Long Island most likely paid for the mountain property and still left him enough money in the bank for the improvements he had done to it.

The man would survive. Monetarily, anyway.

The great C.J. Anson said I'm the best writer EVER.

Let's not get carried away.

I quickly texted, *I can now die happy since all my dreams have come to fruition.*

"Oh shit." I didn't think first before sending that.

Should I apologize? Should I wait to see how he responded to that first? Maybe it wouldn't be that big of a deal.

I got nothing but silence in return.

Shit. Shit. Shit.

I stared at my phone, hoping I didn't just screw everything up, willing him to write the next text even if he called me a callous asshole.

I chewed on my bottom lip as minute after minute ticked by.

9:33.

9:34.

9:35.

9:36.

I couldn't wait any longer. I hit the phone icon at the top of our string of texts.

It rang and rang and rang, then went to voicemail. "Shit!"

I sent another text instead of leaving a message. *Sorry for being an accidental dick.*

Two more minutes went by. I should just cut my losses and go back to watching my movie.

Unlike me, who's a dick on purpose? popped up on my screen with a man shrugging emoji.

You said it, not me, I typed back, adding an upside down smiley face emoji.

But you were thinking it.

You can hear my thoughts all the way up on your mountain?

Of course, because you're loud even when you're just thinking.

I snorted softly so I wouldn't disturb my dog's much-needed rest. He had a rough day today from chasing bunnies in his sleep. *Then, can you disregard all those thoughts I had about you?* Praying hands emoji.

Which ones?

The ones where we were both naked. At the same time. Doing some questionable but very satisfying things.

Silence again.

I quickly typed out another message so I wouldn't sound like such a perv. *You know how it is for us authors... Our imagination sometimes runs wild.*

The only thing was I didn't have to imagine Chase naked. I knew *exactly* what the bare bear looked like. I had locked that tidbit away and revisited it often.

More silence.

We're the only two gay men in Eagle's Landing, I reminded him.

Just because we're both gay doesn't mean we should be friends.

I didn't say anything about being friends. I was aiming for the gold and would accept being friends as a participation trophy if I failed to win.

It doesn't mean we should have sex, either.

It could be a stress-reliever, or a good way to fight writer's block.

Why would you want to fuck me? I'm a miserable prick, remember? Or have you forgotten that?

But I've SEEN your prick. Heart-eyes emoji.

It was cold in the water. Turtle emoji.

I KNOW. That's what I'm saying. Eggplant emoji.

Bigger isn't always better. Wincing emoji.

Speak for yourself. Mouth zippered shut emoji.

I am, he responded back.

You're a bottom? I asked and followed with three shock-faced emojis.

Goodnight.

WAIT!

Give it up, Peabody.

Never, Foster. I barked out a laugh and once again woke up Timber.

I stared at my phone and waited.

That couldn't be it. Our conversation was actually going well. I now held out hope that things were improving with him. Even better, between us.

I quickly asked *Have you always been out?* to try to keep the conversation going.

It took forever to get a response but my heart raced when it finally came through.

Since fifteen. When I told my parents I like other boys.

And? I wanted to keep him talking.

I jumped out of my skin when my phone actually rang. I couldn't slide my finger across the screen fast enough to answer it. I held my breath as I put him on speakerphone.

For a few seconds I thought he dialed me by mistake since there was nothing but more silence.

The man was nothing if not predictably frustrating.

His deep voice rumbled through the phone. "At first they told me I was confused and just going through a phase." He barked out a harsh laugh. "I'd *outgrow* it."

Holy shit. He actually gave me a piece of personal information. Was I really breaking down his walls?

Even better, he *called* me. Or was I really asleep and only dreaming this? One more fantasy in a long list of them.

"Timber, am I sleeping or is this really happening?" I whispered.

"What?"

I shook my head. "Nothing." *Shit. Don't blow this, Rett.* "Does that mean your parents weren't supportive?"

He released a soft sigh on the other end of the phone. "They were eventually, but it took some time. After a while, they realized it wasn't a phase I was going through due to teenage hormones and would outgrow it. Especially after I married..." His voice drifted off.

I wasn't sure if Chase was aware of it, but he spun the wedding band on his left hand often. The one he still wore even though he was no longer married and was officially a widower. I was sure though, in his heart, he'd always consider himself a husband to the love of his life.

I'd probably do the same if I had lost my soulmate.

"When you got married." I said it in a way that completed the sentence instead of leaving it hanging.

I wouldn't force him to say his husband's name. Not since the memory was still so raw.

"Yes," he answered. "Getting married convinced them that I was never changing my mind. At first they thought it was my decision to be gay, to be different. You and I know that's not how it works."

So true. People who thought it was a choice were dead wrong. And if the people surrounding them didn't accept that, it could be deadly.

One day someone's sexual preferences wouldn't matter and nobody would find themselves marginalized but that wouldn't be in our lifetime, unfortunately. Plenty of bigots still remained out there who wouldn't accept anyone different from themselves.

That was one reason why I had kept my sexuality secret from the residents of Eagle's Landing. I didn't want to risk my relationships with them. While some would be accepting, I worried some would not. Even though that wouldn't be a *me* problem, but a *them* problem, I'd still have to deal with any prejudices.

Chase's, "They're okay with it now," brought me back to our conversation. "They were very supportive when I lost..." He sucked in a breath. "When I became a widower."

"Are they close by? Or were they close by when you lived in Jericho?"

Maybe I shouldn't have mentioned the town he used to live in, it might remind him that I knew more about him than he wanted me to.

He had come to Eagle's Landing to be anonymous. I had ruined that for him.

After a slight hesitation, he answered, "No. They retired a while ago to Panama, believe it or not. It was more affordable than staying here in the States. I visit when I can and call them often. They've finally figured out how to video chat without being on mute the whole time or cutting off their heads so I'm looking at their chests while we're talking. They're living their best life as ex-pats and enjoying their retirement. I'm happy for them."

"Yes, I would certainly describe you as a happy guy," I told him dryly and then regretted it instantly. I was trying to get him to open up, not slam shut like a disturbed clam.

"On that note..." came the grumble through my phone.

He was trying to end the conversation. It was too soon. I scrambled to think of something else to say. "How many red pens have you run dry?"

A small noise came through the phone. "All of them."

"Oh, look at that. You *do* have a sense of humor."

"I wasn't joking."

I laughed. A second later, I panicked. "Wait. Really?"

Was he smothering a chuckle? Was that actually possible? No. Couldn't be. Should I ask, or just keep my mouth shut and hope I heard what I heard?

Mouth shut was always the safest bet. Especially when it came to me.

"I said it was your best work yet. I wasn't lying."

"I could kiss you right now!" *Damn it.* I quickly dialed in my excitement. "Metaphorically speaking. I'm not pushing my luck again. I had a headache for two days from last time I kissed you and it made it difficult to write."

I waited. For an apology. For sympathy. For something.

All I got in return was quiet.

And more quiet.

Finally he said, "I'll bring it back to you when I'm finished."

Would it be rude to ask how soon he'd be finished?

I didn't want to rush him but I was curious about what he red-penned. "Or just shoot me a text and Timber and I can come pick it up. I don't want to inconvenience you."

"I'll just drop it off next time I'm in town."

Was it because there would be less temptation that way? The two of us wouldn't be alone up in the woods in his cabin?

Hmm. "I'll be here."

The phone went dead.

"Well, hot damn, Timber. The man not only texted me, he *called* me. And, even better, he likes my latest book. I think I'm making progress with him."

Timber raised his head and gave me an exasperated look, then dropped it back to the mattress with a groan.

One thing was for certain, I couldn't stop grinning. Even through every gory part of the Stephen King movie I was watching.

CHAPTER 13

Chase

I GLANCED up at the apartment over The Next Page. It was late but I was hoping Rett would still be awake. The light peeking between the blinds indicated he most likely was.

This was a bad idea.

It would be smarter to leave the manuscript tucked under his truck's windshield wiper.

I glanced to my right and over my shoulder to where I parked my Bronco behind the bookstore. The small paved area was big enough for two parking spots. To the left of the parking area, where I currently stood, was a small grassy yard surround by chain-link fence. Not an area really big enough for Timber to get exercise but most likely good enough for the dog to do his business in bad weather.

I could leave the thick envelope on his Chevy, leave it on the rear stoop to the store or quietly creep up the steps and leave it at the apartment's door on the second level. Then cross my fingers he would find it before the next rain.

Or I could climb those steps and knock on the damn door.

I hadn't warned him I was coming.

I hadn't even told him I finished the beta-read.

But then, I hadn't planned on getting so restless up in my cabin tonight that I needed to go for a drive.

To the bookstore.

Ultimately, to Rett.

Ever since that damn kiss, he'd been in my thoughts.

My mind flashed back and forth between when our mouths were melded together to the injury on the back of his head I'd given him.

Guilt consumed me.

For letting him kiss me, for enjoying it, then for panicking and shoving him away. Worse, that same guilt soaked into the center of my bones due to the fact I couldn't stop thinking about him.

I figured if I finished reading through his manuscript and got it back to him and out of my sight, I'd be able to go back to my regularly scheduled programming.

Being alone, miserable and feeling sorry for myself.

And basically not letting anyone get close to me for fear of losing what remained of my heart if I took another major loss.

After Thomas's death, I was knocked off my axis and my whole world had tilted upside down. To protect myself, I wanted to solely concentrate on my career and my family by keeping in touch with the occasional video chat.

My plan had been to keep life as simple as possible until I was prepared to tackle the more difficult stuff. Rett could easily take my desire for simplicity and turn it into a very complicated matter.

If I let him.

Despite trying to resist, I now found myself standing at the bottom of the steps, staring up at the unlit wood deck off the back of the apartment.

I inhaled a deep breath of night air and filled my lungs completely. Being late June it was warm but not humid. I was sure that was coming around the corner.

I was only putting off what I came here to do. To return his manuscript with my recommended changes.

Yes, that was the only reason why I had driven ten minutes into town.

Sure it was.

I had no other reason to be here.

None at all.

I gritted my teeth and hiked up the steps.

His deck might be small but it was cozy with a couple of chairs, a small table, some string lights that were currently off, a couple of tall potted plants and even one of those canvas canopies overhead to give him shade in the heat of summer.

The rear of the building faced a side street that was currently quiet. I'm sure it stayed that way all day long, since Eagle's Landing wasn't a bustling town, it was a sleepy one. Another bonus to buying the cabin.

Just blissful peace and quiet.

At least until Rett.

I pounded on the door with a tiny half-circle window at the top. I couldn't hear his footsteps. Instead I heard Timber going nuts barking and growling behind the door and could see the top of Rett's head in that decorative window as he approached. All while yelling at the German Shepherd to "cool his jets."

After a click of the deadbolt, the door was cracked open and Rett's bare but hairy leg jammed into the gap, most likely to keep the Shepherd from squeezing out.

Or biting a possible intruder.

Once Rett's face appeared in the space between the door and the frame and he saw it was me, his eyes widened and the door swung open enough for Timber to rush out and onto the deck. The dog immediately did circles around me, wagging his tail and yipping in excitement. I winced when the high-pitched shrieks pierced my ears like an ice pick.

I had no idea that dogs could be so damn dramatic.

Since Rett didn't turn on the porch light next to the door, behind him the brightly lit apartment made him appear as a dark silhouette. When he stepped back, I could finally see him much more clearly. "What are you doing here?"

My throat was as dry and scratchy as sandpaper when I swallowed. My gaze rolled over him from his messy bedhead all the way to his bare feet. He only wore a loose pair of dark boxers, maybe black or navy, and a stretched-out, threadbare T-shirt that advertised the local bar, The Roost. It was so old, one nipple flashed me through a small hole and it had a questionable kidney-shaped brown stain right above his navel.

"Were you sleeping?"

He shook his head. "No, but I was chilling in bed with a beer and a movie."

"I didn't mean to interrupt."

He shrugged, drawing my attention to how the old T-shirt hugged his broad shoulders and clung to his biceps. "The beer's now flat and the movie sucks."

I rolled my lips inward until the urge to grin passed.

"Are you just going to stand there, or are you coming in?" He swept his hand toward the interior in invitation.

Stepping into his place might not be smart.

Just hand him the envelope, Chase, then get the hell out of there.

Rett tilted his head. "I'm not going to bite you."

But I want to bite you. I lifted the manilla envelope. "I'm just returning this."

His eyes flicked down to his manuscript and back up to my face. His brow furrowed. "You could've returned it in the morning."

"I didn't want to wait."

"I've got plenty of time to get it to my editor. I'm not planning on releasing it for six months yet."

"Like I said, I didn't want to wait."

"Apparently. Since it's after ten."

"Is it?"

One of his dark eyebrows rose. "You don't know what time it is?"

"I lost track."

"Come in," he insisted, gave me his back and walked away from the open doorway. He called out over his shoulder, "You want a beer?"

Did I?

I did, but I wasn't sure if I should. The man was tempting enough, but for me to add alcohol? That might make my steel resolve turn into molten metal.

It was bad enough seeing Rett in his skivvies made liquid heat roll through my veins.

My attention caught on the smooth roll of his hips as he moved away from me. I made sure Timber followed me inside before shutting the door.

My heart pounded in my chest since I was stepping into a situation I wasn't quite comfortable with. I focused on the apartment instead to try to kill the ants crawling under my skin.

The bookstore was a pretty good sized building, so it made sense that his home above it was also spacious. I scanned everything in my view, and I was right. It was larger than my cabin. The walls were covered with photos, both of family and wildlife, along with some general nature shots.

It made me wonder if Rett dabbled in photography. That also made me realize I didn't know a lot about him. Only the basics.

The area right inside the door was open-concept, just like my cabin, but more polished and modern. The living room area had a built-in gas fireplace with a large screen TV mounted on the wall above it. Opposite that wall sat a large, comfortable-looking leather sectional couch. Right in front of that on the floor was a large circular dog bed.

Taking it all in, I trailed Rett into the next open area, which was a decent-sized kitchen. It was clean and neat. Anything left out on the counter seemed to have its place. No dirty dishes filled the sink. No empty glasses set out on the counter. No food was left out besides some bananas hanging from one of those holders. I thought that was one of those kitchen gadgets people bought but never used.

Apparently, I was wrong.

Rett opened the fridge and reached in to grab something. And as he did, I let my gaze wander the backside of him, pausing on his ass and how the thin cotton of his boxers pulled tight over his very firm, perfectly-shaped cheeks.

I ripped my eyes away because I shouldn't be eyeing him up like he was a tempting treat.

When he turned after closing the fridge door, he had two bottles of Sea Dog Sunfish Ale in his hands. He twisted the top off of one and offered it to me. I stepped closer and plucked it from his fingers, checking out the label.

"Have you had Sea Dog before?" he asked.

"Once. I tried their blueberry beer."

"Oh, that's the best. Made from wild Maine blueberries. I have Rick order in cases of this brand so I can get it locally."

"Rick?"

"He owns The Roost. Have you stopped in there yet?"

With a shake of my head, I answered, "No."

"It's a sleepy little bar."

Just like the sleepy little town.

"Rick's a good guy."

I heard the unspoken "unlike you" loud and clear.

I tipped the bottle to my lips and the cold light ale slid down my tight throat. It tasted really good, smooth and refreshing. I might have to stop in at The Roost to pick up a couple of six packs for myself.

I wasn't a big drinker but sometimes I liked a good beer. Sea Dog would be the perfect brew to sit out on the porch, kick up my feet and stare out over the lake while listening to the local wildlife.

I needed to say something, instead of only standing there like a brain-dead idiot. "How's your head? Is it healed?"

He took a long swallow from his own bottle, set it on the counter next to the fridge, then stepped in front of me.

With neither of us blinking, we stared at each other for a few seconds, and just when I was getting antsy and was about to step back to give us some space, he turned to give me his back and slid his fingers into his hair to part it. I could still see the evidence of the injury.

Damn. "That left a mark," I murmured.

"Luckily, it's small. It'll fade."

The man was certainly optimistic about it. But then, he seemed optimistic about life in general.

When he turned back to face me, we once again stood boot tip to bare toe. I swore neither one of us breathed as we stared at each other, just inches apart.

"Why are you here?" he asked huskier than normal.

"I told you why." I sucked down two more large mouthfuls of the ale. I was hoping it would douse the heat rising from my gut.

"When did you finish it?"

"Does it matter?"

He nodded.

Of course it did. He was trying to analyze my thought process and actions. "This morning."

"And here you are at," he twisted his head to look at the digital clock on the stove, "almost ten-thirty at night."

"I…" I had no good excuse.

His head tipped to the side. "You…"

"I disturbed your evening," I concluded.

Because I certainly wouldn't admit I had been thinking about him until my skin was ready to split.

I wouldn't tell him I had jerked off in my shower this morning, thinking about that kiss.

I wouldn't tell him I had almost done it again tonight. I also wouldn't tell him that was why I climbed into my Bronco and parked behind his bookstore before I could talk myself out of it.

No. I wouldn't tell him any of that.

"I figured if I gave it to you tonight, you could get an early start on doing edits in the morning."

He lifted his chin and narrowed his eyes, seeing right through me to the truth and not the lie I just spouted.

My fingers curled tighter around the now sweating bottle. To break his spell on me, I lifted the beer to my mouth and guzzled the remainder. Since I was standing close enough to reach the small kitchen table nearby, I set my empty bottle on it without shifting my feet even an inch.

"Another?"

Yes. I wanted another kiss.

I nodded.

I breathed a little easier when he moved away from me to grab another Sea Dog from the fridge. Twisting off the cap, he came back to me, but he didn't stop until we were once again toe to toe.

On purpose. Because he *knew.*

Instead of offering me the beer, he held it snuggly against his chest, making me reach for it.

"Why are you here, Chase?" Not only was his question husky this time, it was weighed down with more unsaid questions than the one he actually asked.

I wrapped my hand around the cold bottle, but could only feel his warm fingers gripping it under mine. The back of my fingers brushed against the heat of his chest through the thin cotton.

I cleared my throat. "I told you."

"What aren't you telling me?"

Too much that I wasn't willing to share.

When I pulled on the bottle, trying to take it from him, he kept it pinned to his chest and came with it. Without even meaning to, I hauled him into me.

Until we were so close, our breaths merged.

"Why are you here, Chase?" he whispered, his Adam's apple slowly rolling up his throat, then rolling back down.

"I don't know," I whispered back. I knew why, I just didn't want to admit it. I was afraid to allow myself to have what I really wanted from Rett. What he offered willingly. What I could willingly accept. "It was a mistake."

"We all make mistakes."

I knew that all too well.

However, some mistakes you couldn't recover from. I hoped this wasn't one of them since I already had enough for a lifetime.

"Why are you here, Chase?"

"How many times are you going to ask me that?" I attempted to make my question come off as annoyed. I failed. Instead, it sounded slightly desperate.

"As many times as necessary until I get the truth."

"I gave you the truth."

"You gave me a convenient excuse. But deep down that's not why you came here."

Why was he so damn frustrating? Truthfully, I was doing it to myself since I came to him, not the other way around this time. "How do you know?"

"Even though you're trying your damnedest to hide it, I can see it in your eyes as plain as day."

Shit. I broke our eye contact. "You're imagining it."

"Bullshit. I recognize it because I want the same as you."

"I just want to be left alone."

"But here you are, in my apartment. Late at night. Using a very thin excuse to be here."

"I shouldn't have come." Truth.

"But you did, so now what?"

"I should leave." Also truth.

"Before you get what you came for?"

I downed the second bottle of Sea Dog in two gulps.

Rett shook his head and grabbed another beer out of the fridge, twisted off the cap, tossed it on the counter with the rest of them and then handed me my third beer.

I didn't hesitate to take it from him.

I was trying to fortify my walls with it. But, of course, that was just another failure, since they were slowly beginning to lower.

He tipped his head toward my third beer. "You drink that as fast as the other two and I'm not letting you go anywhere for a while."

This man was frustrating in more ways than one.

Keeping my eyes locked with his, I raised the bottle, put it to my lips, opened my throat and downed the whole thing in one swallow.

His mouth slowly curled into a grin, then he nodded.

I nodded, too, and set the empty bottle down next to the other dead soldiers.

I shot out my hand, grabbed his T-shirt and yanked him toward me, hoping the thin cotton didn't tear and knock us both off balance.

It didn't but it did slam Rett into me. Before he could catch his breath from the collision, I dipped my head and dropped my mouth to his. Not kissing. Not yet.

Simply breathing him in.

Working up the courage to do what I wanted to do to the man pulled against me. Chest to chest. Toe to toe. Mouth to mouth.

And now…

Erection to erection.

"I said I'd never kiss you again. You're not going to knock me out again this time, are you?" he whispered against my lips.

"No, because this time, *I'm* kissing *you* since this is the only way to shut you up."

"Well, it's not the only way, but—"

I knew the other ways, but we'd start with another kiss. One to make up for the last disaster. Thanks to my hang-ups.

With one hand, I grabbed him behind his elbow and with the other, I dug my fingers into the back of his neck, crushing our mouths together, along with everything else.

The second his mouth opened with a groan, his tongue tangled with mine.

There was not a damn thing gentle about our kiss. It was raw. Rough. Purely sexual. It wasn't sweet or intimate, nor did it give off romantic *forever* vibes.

The kiss we shared was for *right now*. That was it.

It was only to prove to myself that I could have physical contact without emotional attachment. That I could give him what he wanted, take what I needed, and move on.

Maybe even prove to us both that we were all wrong for each other.

We wouldn't be good as fuck buddies. We wouldn't be good as friends with benefits.

And we...

Fuck.

He fisted the hair at the back of my head so tightly, I wasn't able to move away even if I wanted to. His other hand trailed down my spine to find my ass and dig his fingertips into my denim-covered flesh, pulling me even tighter against him. His hard cock ground against mine.

When he groaned into my mouth, I greedily accepted it and gave him one in return. Though, I hadn't meant to.

I didn't want to let him know how much I wanted him. How much I needed this physical contact. How much I was enjoying this kiss. The one that was planned, not the one sprung on me when I wasn't ready.

Tonight, I was ready.

I was also ready for more.

I kept telling myself if what happened tonight went farther than a kiss, it would mean nothing. It would be for nothing but sexual relief.

We were only satisfying our base needs.

For the last three days I kept telling myself that we could keep it to sex, that it didn't have to go any farther than that. Just some simple, very needed physical contact.

No attachments. Nothing more.

No risk of emotional damage.

No risk of further destruction to my already scratched and dented heart.

He slid his hand up my ass again, stopping at the waistband of my jeans, then drove his fingers between the denim and my *hot-as-hell* skin.

His touch seared me, stoked the fire licking in my belly. Made me tilt my head and take his mouth more thoroughly, shove my tongue deeper, taste every corner.

The catch of his breath... The way his cock slid along mine... The way he pulled on my scalp until it made my eyes sting... The way his fingers played along the crack of my ass...

Everything he did lit me up from the inside out. It caused those flickering flames to become a roaring bonfire.

Driving me to want more. Need more.

I jerked him around and, with our bodies still crushed together, I began to walk backwards, careful not to break our connection. He stayed with me every damn step of the way as I moved us from the kitchen toward the hallway that had to lead to his bedroom.

I realized then, while I had prepared myself mentally for the kiss, I had not prepared myself for anything that might come of it.

I brought nothing with me. No condoms. No lube. Nothing.

If he didn't have any of that, we were dead in the water.

And if he did have all of that, who had he used those with in the past?

Nobody in this town from what it sounded like. He was forced to go elsewhere. Did he risk bringing another man home and hope that no one saw them?

He said he wasn't "out" in Eagle's Landing. I understood why but that meant if he was having sex, he had to travel for it.

Why did I even care? Why was I fixated on who else Rett might have had sex with or who he might still be having sex with.

A "fuck buddy."

Maybe he had them in every nearby town and wanted to make me one, as well, because I'd be closer and more convenient.

I stopped leading when he took over, using the grip on my hair and ass to tug me along since I didn't know which door led to his bedroom.

He backed down the hallway slowly and we somehow managed to keep the kiss going. Our lips not separating once.

I couldn't get enough of his mouth on me, the way his tongue fought with mine for control, the deep rumble that rolled from the back of his throat.

My cock throbbed, my balls became heavy. My heart pounded like a bass drum at a hard rock concert. For a split moment, I hoped my reactions weren't from a panic attack.

Now was not the time for one of those. When I lost my sight, when I lost my hearing, when I lost all sense of where I was. When everything became overwhelming and all I wanted to do was squeeze my eyes shut and curl up into a ball until it passed.

He released my hair and ass, reached behind him to shove open his bedroom door wider and finally, I yanked my mouth away.

Something brushed against my leg and I assumed it was Timber but I didn't look because I couldn't pull my eyes from Rett's.

His pupils were so wide it made his eyes appear almost pure black. His chest heaved at the same rate as mine. A flush rose from the stretched-out neckline of his shirt and colored his throat. His lips were parted and quick puffs of air escaped.

"Holy shit," he whispered shakily.

I agreed. *Holy shit.*

Every time we had accidentally brushed it had been like lightning crackling along my skin. It had both scared and worried me since I never had that reaction before.

Not with anyone.

Not even with…

The steel walls slammed down, shutting that thought out. I could not think about *him* when I was standing in the bedroom of another man. *With* another man.

I couldn't.

I wouldn't.

Not if I wanted to live with myself afterward.

CHAPTER 14

Chase

As soon as Rett tugged me into his bedroom by hooking a finger into my belt loop, he used his foot to nudge Timber back out of the room and quickly shut the door behind the dog, locking him out.

While I understood the need for that, apparently his dog did not. Hearing Timber's overly dramatic meltdown was like a bucket of ice water being dumped over my head.

But before I could break away, return to reality and head back to my cabin, Rett had me shoved against the door with our fingers interlocked and pinned on either side of my head. He went nose to nose with me, staring me right in the eyes with a determined look on his face.

"I can't," I forced out, trying to talk myself out of going any further with him.

It would be a mistake. It would give Rett more power over me than I was ready or willing to give him. I also feared that if I opened the door between us, he would barrel through it like a bull.

"You already did," Rett murmured as he pressed his forehead to mine and squeezed my fingers.

"I just… I can't…" I was going to regret this no matter how much I wanted it.

"It was only a kiss."

Yes, it was only a kiss. It was also so much more than that. It was a promise of what could come next. It also made me want to do so many things to Rett.

I tried to pull free but Rett's grip tightened. "It was only a kiss. Spontaneous, but meaningless."

So untrue. He was trying to keep me from panicking and shutting him out. But no matter what he said, in no way was the kiss meaningless.

It made me hard, heavy and aching for him. I hadn't felt anything similar to this in the last two years since I wouldn't allow it. Right now, I was feeling a bunch of shit.

And all of that worried me.

I could not get attached to this man or any other.

I couldn't.

It was safer to be by myself. Not to mention, so much easier.

But kissing him made me realize how much I missed intimacy, too.

I missed being held, being kissed and skin to skin contact. The excitement during intimacy and the satisfaction afterward.

I most likely could have it with Rett, but at what cost? Not only to me, but to him.

"You're overthinking this," he whispered. "It's only two men enjoying each other's company."

The man could be irksome with how astute he was. "I'm not sure I'm enjoying it."

"Because you're letting your guilt eat at you."

"I can't let myself want this. I want you, but I can't…"

"It's not cheating, Chase."

"To me that's what it feels like." Despite trying to hide it, my whisper sounded tortured. A war was being waged, both in my head and in my heart. No matter what, I needed to be honest with Rett. He knew I was struggling but he didn't exactly know why. "I love him. I'll never not love him. Despite him being gone, no one else exists for me. No one. It's only ever been him." I inhaled deeply, filling my lungs to capacity before finishing with, "I'm sorry. I shouldn't—"

"If he knew, don't you think he would want you to move on?"

"If *he* knew? He'll never know, but I will. I'll have to live with myself."

"He would never want for you to cut yourself off from others. Or not let yourself go back to living your life the way it should be lived. He would want you to be happy. He'd want you to remember the good times between the two of you but not dwell on his loss."

"How do you know that? You never knew him." My brow dropped low and my anger bubbled up from deep inside me. I tried to separate our hands but he only tightened his grip on our interlocked fingers and pinned me harder against the wall using his body.

I was sure I was stronger than him and could shove him away if I tried. But doing that had been a disaster last time. My goal wasn't to hurt him, but to keep myself from getting hurt.

"You're right, I don't know him. But I'm guessing he was a decent man if you loved him that much. And most decent people wouldn't want their loved one to be bogged down in grief for over two years. Here's the thing… I'm not trying to take his place, Chase. I would never do that. What you had with him is yours to keep forever. What you'd have with me is something new. Different. It could be light and fun and nothing serious. There's nothing wrong with letting yourself have that. To have more than what you're allowing yourself to have. My guess is you're flagellating yourself for something you had no control over."

He was right, but that didn't make it any easier.

This was my hang-up. Not Thomas's. Not Rett's. Mine and mine alone.

Maybe if I hadn't lost my husband in the way I had, I would be handling it differently.

Maybe if I hadn't been the one to find him.

Maybe if I had known what led up to Thomas making that devastating decision.

Maybe if I had been paying closer attention. If I had checked in with him more often...

Maybe...

So many damn maybes.

All of them too late.

Yes, I needed to move on, when in truth, I'd rather go back in time. I wanted a "do-over." To make sure I did everything in my power to let Thomas know he was wanted and loved, that I was there for him no matter what. To make sure he was taking care of himself. To make sure he was okay before I left that day, instead of only assuming...

He had slipped. But then, so had I.

No matter what, right now, it wasn't Thomas gripping my hands, it wasn't Thomas pinning me to the door. It wasn't Thomas with his forehead pressed to mine.

No, that would never happen again. We would never again share any of these types of moments.

I'd only have the memories. Until I lost those, too.

A whispered, "Chase," made me open my eyes that I hadn't even realized I'd closed. It brought me back to Rett's bedroom and the situation I was in currently.

With Rett.

So opposite of Thomas.

Rett was like a beaming ray of sunshine in contrast to Thomas's dark and stormy clouds.

My guess was Rett's good days outweighed the bad, while Thomas's bad days had outweighed the good.

Only none of that had been his fault.

Damn it, it hadn't been mine, either. So, why did I torture myself so much? Why couldn't I enjoy the man I currently was with without the guilt weighing heavily on me about the man I lost?

"Just give us tonight."

And then what? "If I do, what would you expect afterward?"

He pulled his head back so we could see each other's faces more clearly. "Absolutely nothing more than you'd be willing to give," he said in a way that disappointed me.

It shouldn't but unexpectedly, it did.

He was willing to take whatever I was willing to give him and nothing more.

While that was what I wanted, it also wasn't fair to him. And I had no idea why he'd expect nothing beyond us having sex tonight.

Unless that was a lie. Or… completely normal for him. He could simply be someone who could separate physical attraction from emotional attachment.

Unfortunately, I'd never been one of those types. To me, sex and intimacy went hand in hand. Sex wasn't just an act, it always had meaning for me. I'd never been into random hookups or one-night-stands. Not when I was younger and definitely not now.

Even so, he was willing to go into this with no expectations and be okay when he got nothing else from me. But could I be the same?

I'm not sure if that was possible. One more valid concern that niggled at me.

Worse, how awkward would that be down the road if things went horribly wrong? With both of us residing in the same town. Both of us in the same career.

Both of us attracted to each other like two damn magnets.

"I'm not sure if I've ever dealt with someone before who overthought things the way you do."

I never was like that before… Before things drastically changed in my life. I had missed details and now I couldn't risk missing any more.

However, I was beginning to worry he knew me better than I knew myself. I thought that would be impossible but I could be wrong. "You have no idea what I'm thinking."

"Actually, I do. It's clearly written all over your face."

I immediately shut down my expression, causing a slow smile to spread over his face. It wasn't because he was happy or amused, he was trying to grin and bear my unbearableness.

I knew that only too well.

As much as I had loved Thomas, some days had been difficult to live and deal with him. Toward the end, it ended up being more often than not. I shouldn't have been blind to that sign, too, but I had been busy. Caught up in my latest book release and dealing with all the "noise" that went along with it.

Book tours, signings, talk shows, you name it. Anywhere and everywhere my literary agent and publisher could book me to increase sales and boost their profits. I had been run ragged and forgot to pause long enough to check in with Thomas.

I opened my mouth to apologize to Rett but snapped it shut before that apology could formalize. He might be annoying due to being pushy but at his core I could see he was a good man.

He deserved so much better than me. Even for one night. "I should go."

"But you won't."

I hardly knew him but somehow, he knew me all too well. He had a gift or something. "You're very sure of yourself."

"And you're very unsure of yourself."

I was never like that prior, but, *damn it*, he was correct once again. That fact made him even more irritating. "That's why I should go."

He finally released our interlinked hands and bracketed my face within his warm fingers, lightly brushing his right thumb across my cheek and beard. "It's actually why you shouldn't."

His touch did things to me I didn't want to explore and I forced myself to keep from rubbing my cheek against his palm. To keep from encouraging him to continue to caress me.

I was barely keeping myself together as it was.

I was afraid if I allowed him to comfort or console me, I might just break down and shatter. If I did, I might not be able to put the scattered pieces back together again.

"Give it a chance. That's all I'm asking. If it's awkward or the chemistry that I think we have turns out to not exist, then fine, we can simply remain friends."

"We're not friends now."

The grin on his face turned genuine. "We are. You just don't realize it."

Damn, he was handsome as hell. And, of course, he knew it.

A smile. A touch. A few words. He didn't have to work hard to draw me in.

That also scared the hell out of me.

If I wasn't in the particular spot I was in in my life right now, I would be on him like white on rice. But I knew I was messed up. I knew *why* I was messed up. And despite wishing otherwise, I couldn't do a damn thing about it.

I had willingly jumped down Thomas's deep, dark well thinking I could help pull him back out. I obviously failed and did not need to drag anyone else down along with me. I didn't want to be responsible for taking a happy, very content guy like Rett and make him as miserable as I was.

All because he wanted to have sex with me.

And because I wanted to have sex with him.

My lips twisted downward. "Only sex. No expectations other than that, right?"

"I said I would take what you're willing to give me."

"Why would you be okay with the bare minimum?"

He shrugged. "Because right now I have nothing."

That was hardly true. "You have plenty." He had a bookstore, his author career, a great apartment, a town who was supportive, and a loyal dog.

"You know what I mean."

I absolutely did.

I was staring at a man who had a boatload less hang-ups than I had. I couldn't fault him for that.

"Fine," came out of me on a whisper so weak, I could hardly hear it myself.

His eyebrows shot up his forehead. "What?"

I grimaced, sucked in air and said, "Okay," but it wasn't much louder.

My heart raced as I waited for a bolt of lightning to strike me dead for cheating on a man who was no longer alive. Stupid, I knew. I wished I could get that nagging guilt out of my head, but I couldn't.

"I didn't hear you."

I leaned in closer, until we were nose to nose and repeated, "Okay."

As soon as his eyes widened and his mouth opened, I captured it with my own.

Two pounding heartbeats later, my cock had once again turned into steel, and our tongues were dancing a tango.

With his hands bracing my hips, he rocked his back and forth, grinding his cock against mine, driving me a little out of my mind. But that was exactly what I needed. To forget everything else but the man I was kissing.

The man I was about to fuck.

Damn. Who was fucking whom? I hadn't considered that. Not when I drove down my mountain, not when I drove through town, not even when I parked my Bronco next to his Chevy truck.

I really didn't think it would ever get this far.

Once again, I was wrong. It was about to go farther than I expected.

When he took over the kiss and pushed my tongue from his mouth and back into my own, I was beginning to think this might not work out anyway. If neither of us wanted to bottom, that could put a wrench in this whole thing.

And the way he was kissing me made me think he was not normally a bottom.

I wasn't, either.

That could be a problem.

I'd been married to Thomas—and more recently, celibate—for so long, I was rusty when it came to the ins and outs of dating. Or in this case, a hookup.

I was pretty much starting all over again and would have to fumble my way through it.

Would it be worth it?

I jerked when he pinched one of my nipples, drawing me from my wandering thoughts.

Damn. He didn't have to say a word to make me aware I was overthinking the situation once again. I set my concentration back on the man himself.

By letting Rett take control of the kiss for a few moments, I realized it would be worth it. Our mouths seemed to be made for each other. They fit perfectly with no awkwardness.

Simply kissing him made the fires deep in my gut burn even brighter and hotter. Made me want to throw him on the bed, climb on top of him and fuck him until we were both nothing but a quivering, sweaty mess.

I didn't want to make love.

I didn't want to have "neat" or polite sex.

I wanted to plunge deep into the man, fuck like wild animals— with teeth and nails and audible encouragement—and get us off before leaving depleted and satisfied.

Basic but animalistic coupling.

Once we both got off, we'd shake hands afterward and go back to being fellow authors and...

Possibly friends.

I'd give him that because I couldn't afford to give him anything more.

However, I'd deal with that later. Right now, I was ready to lose myself in the man I was kissing. As well as use this time to forget everything causing static in my brain on a daily basis.

For a short time, I wanted to shed the chains weighing me down and forget everything else.

I'd have no writer's block, no smothering family, no Thomas.

Only Rett.

His mouth, his cock, his ass, his positive attitude, even his *dorkwardness*. I wanted it all.

I fisted his shirt and when I shoved him backward—not to push him away but to move him closer to the bed—I heard the cotton of his worn T-shirt tear.

I ended the kiss, immediately sucking in mouthfuls of air to catch my breath while ripping that shirt up his torso and over his head. I dropped it onto the floor and before he could reach for mine, I reached behind myself to grab my own shirt in the middle of my back and yank it over my head, too, before dropping it at our feet.

"Okay," I whispered again, my voice as strained as my throbbing cock.

"Okay," he echoed, also in a whisper, but shaky. His body vibrated against mine when I used my bare chest to bump him backwards. One step... two steps... three steps until the back of his legs hit the mattress.

But I didn't stop moving until we both tumbled to the bed behind him, my weight pinning him down. Beneath me, his erection was hard and hot, searing my hip, even through my jeans and his boxers.

A rogue thought of taking him into my mouth and sucking him until he was a boneless, whimpering mess ripped through me.

I stared down into his deep brown eyes that went from half-closed to wide open. "What?"

I narrowed my eyes on him and grinned.

"Fuck," he whispered. "What's going on? I've never seen you grin before. Should I be scared?"

Instead of answering, I slid off him and back to my feet, grabbed his boxers at both of his hips and ripped them down his legs.

Jesus.

His hard cock was long and had a hefty girth. The crown had a shine to it, most likely from me smearing the precum when I yanked off his boxers.

Even though he lay on his back on the bed, his feet remained planted on the floor. I nudged his thighs wider with my knees and sank down onto my own, thankful his bedroom had thick carpet.

I was way past the age of wanting to kneel directly on concrete or wood.

When Rett lifted his head, I noticed a slight flush had risen from his chest all the way into his cheeks. Planting my hands on his muscular thighs, I shoved them even wider and shuffled closer until I was tightly sandwiched between them.

As soon as he reached for his erection, I knocked his hand away and had his cock in my fist, tugging it, milking it, until an almost-clear droplet appeared at the slit.

"Holy shit," he breathed, watching me watching him.

I kept my eyes on that glistening pearl, tempted to whisk it away with my tongue, and continued to stroke his girth, the skin silky against the roughness of my fingers.

As a writer, my hands never had callouses before. Since moving up to the cabin and chopping countless cords of wood, my hands were now as rough as a lumberjack's. I didn't know if that sensation was better or worse for him but he apparently didn't mind it, since with every stroke upward, his hips mimicked my motion in reverse.

With every upstroke, his hips lowered. With every downstroke, his hips rose.

With a groan, he continued to pump into my fist. "Jesus, Chase. It's not going to take much for me to come. I'm like a goddamn lit firecracker and the fuse is burning down."

I lifted my gaze from his cock to his face. "What you're saying is, you don't want me to touch you."

"Screw that! Of course I want you to touch me. I've fantasized about this moment since the first time you walked into my bookstore. See? That's the problem. Because I *have* fantasized about this moment, and now that it's really happening… I'm not going to lie…" His head flopped back to the bed, breaking our eye contact. "I'll be like a twelve-year-old boy having a nocturnal wet dream."

"Then, you don't want me to lick your cock or suck the head clean?"

He went completely still and after a second, his head popped back up. "Only if you insist."

Once again our gazes locked, and while they were, I lowered my head and took him into my mouth.

I wanted to make sure I kept my eyes open for this. While sucking him. Even when it came to fucking him. I wanted to keep my brain straight and not allow it to mix up who I was with and who I wasn't.

I did not want to forget for one second that this was Rett. I needed to make sure it was only the two of us in the room.

No one else belonged here with us.

Just you and him, Chase. No one else. Take this time and let yourself forget. Let yourself enjoy this. Enjoy him. He's willing. He wants this. He wants you.

Show him how much—despite how you come off—that you want him, too.

Unbury the old Chase, the whole one from before, and temporarily bury the broken one.

Even if it's only for tonight.

Give him this.

Give this to yourself.

It'll be another step toward healing, no matter how much you think you should continue to suffer.

He was right. You punish yourself over something you didn't have a lot of control over. You thought you did, but you were proven wrong.

When I opened my throat and practically swallowed him to the root, his hips surged off the bed and his fingers twisted in the sheets on either side of his hips.

"Holy shit," he groaned.

Again, I took him as deep as possible, almost to the sac, only stopping right before I'd choke or gag. He blew out a loud breath, followed by another groan. That encouraged me to continue working my mouth up and down his hard length, sucking and licking, even using my teeth to scrape along the sensitive head.

For a few seconds, I concentrated on the crown by running my tongue around the edge, sucking on the tip for a few seconds to collect the tang, before using the flat of my tongue to follow the path of the thick, pulsing ridge along the underside.

The thin, satin-like skin tasted slightly salty. Wrapping two fingers around the base, I squeezed until the veins popped before taking his whole length into my mouth again.

This time he whimpered and slammed both palms onto the mattress as his cock, hips and legs twitched around me.

His next words sounded winded and were broken up between each bob of my head. "If you make me come..." I took him all the way in. "I won't be able to fuck you..." I let him slip from my mouth until I hovered over the meaty head. "At least for a while..." I paused as he finished, "I don't know about you, but it takes me a lot longer to recover now that I'm in my forties."

It was the same with me, but...

I released him. "You're not fucking me." We might as well get that straight now and not wait until it was too late. Just in case it became a major issue.

When his head lifted, dark eyes landed on mine and stuck. I stared back, waiting for him to challenge what I said.

I shouldn't have been surprised when he didn't. That made me guess that even if he didn't bottom regularly, he would make an exception tonight.

For me.

Otherwise, he might lose out on having sex completely.

He wanted this more than I did, that was clear. Even though, right now, I was willing to give him what he wanted. But for him to get that, I planned on taking what I wanted in exchange.

When his head flopped back to the bed, I drew the corners of my mouth down to keep them from lifting into a grin.

After hooking my arms under his thighs, I used my shoulders to shove his knees into his chest.

His head popped up again. "What…"

I ignored him, instead focusing on what was only inches from my face.

Starting just under the rim of his crown, I traced the tip of my tongue down his length, followed the seam of his sac until I got to where it met his perineum. I pressed my mouth there and sucked.

"*Hooooly… shiiiiit…*"

Keeping my arms looped around his legs, I wrapped one hand around his cock and began to work it and cupped his sac, lifting it out of the way.

Then I got to work.

Driving him fucking crazy.

Pumping his cock with my fist, gently working his balls within my fingers, and running my lips down his taint until I got to his puckered hole.

He had no idea I was showing up at his door tonight. He had no time to prepare for what we were about to do, but I didn't care.

I wanted what I wanted despite the consequences. If I was going in, I was going all in.

My hunger for the man on the bed roared inside me.

I found myself completely insatiable. Starved.

As soon as I ran my tongue around his puckered rim, the floodgates opened and a rogue wave roared over me and through me. Pulling me under and drowning me in nothing but thoughts of Rett.

At that moment, I got what I wanted. What I so desperately needed… No past. No future.

I was finally present in the here and now.

CHAPTER 15

Rett

HOLY SHIT.

Holy shit.

Hooooooolllllllllly... shiiiiiiiiit.

I lifted my head to peer down my body between my two bent, spread legs to see Chase in *my* bedroom on his knees on *my* floor licking *my* ass.

I didn't remember this being anywhere in any of my fantasies.

I certainly wasn't complaining. This was so much better than I ever dreamed. And, bonus, he was so damn good at it.

My only regret was this hadn't been preplanned.

For a second a smidge of self-consciousness took over.

I hadn't prepped. I hadn't done any manscaping, so I was as furry as an *out-of-control* weed patch. That meant everything he was seeing, touching and tasting was *au naturel*.

He was getting the "real Rett" many hours after my last shower.

But, *hey*, if he was okay with it, then I had to be, too. I wanted to enjoy what he was doing without worries niggling at the back of my brain.

I hadn't asked him to do that, so everything he was doing was completely on him. If I would've known, I would've told him to wait until next time. But...

I was afraid there wouldn't be a next time, only a "never again." And that would be a damn shame.

Between him fisting my cock, playing with my balls and tickling my ass with his tongue...

I was about to blow. All he had to do was push my Start button with that skilled tongue of his and...

Damn... there it was... *aaaaaaand* there I went...

Going... Going... Gone.

Fireworks filled my brain and belly, and I might have even whimpered as my hips surged off the bed and my cock became a fountain, painting my stomach with warm strings of cum.

He continued to stroke me with a lighter grip, purposely avoiding my now overly-sensitive head. A few seconds later, once he had drained me dry, every muscle that went tight when I came, now no longer existed.

I had turned into nothing but a boneless, empty sack left on the bed.

Staring up at the ceiling in a super-satisfied fog, I became semi-aware when his tongue withdrew and his hands released my still twitching cock and now empty sac.

I simply breathed, recovering from what just happened and looking forward to what was to come next. It had been far too long since anyone other than myself had made me come. Now I wondered why I waited.

Well, I knew why. Random, nameless hookups had never been my thing. And dating... Forget it. It was just about impossible where I lived. It also took more effort than I had time for.

I gathered the strength to lift my head and stare at the man I think fate had plans for. What might have made me wait.

If that was true...

Was fate playing a cruel trick on me? Why would I want to be with someone like…

Chase.

Hot, yes. Sexy, absolutely. Pleasant to be around, absolutely not.

The cloud that hung over his head was too dark for me. The weather could change, sure. But would it?

I inhaled deeply through my nose and then pushed it all back out. Was he worth the work, potentially as frustrating as it might be?

When he stood up, unfastened his jeans and shoved both them and his boxer briefs down his thick, muscular and nicely furred legs, I pursed my lips and let my gaze slide over him now that he was completely naked.

Was he worth the work? I couldn't honestly answer that. He'd been too closed off to tell and I didn't know how his personality had been before he lost his husband.

Maybe he'd always been like this and he'd never change. I hoped that wasn't true and beneath his fractured surface was a seed worth growing.

However, there was no guarantee.

What if I tried to help him and all I got was resistance? Would it just cause us to despise each other? Was trying worth that risk?

He stroked his erection and for a split second I wished it was my hand doing it. Before I could sit up and reach for him, he stopped me cold with, "Condoms and lube? Where do you keep them?" as he glanced around my room.

Umm… "You don't have any in your wallet?"

His answering, "Don't you?" told me my answer.

I closed my eyes and shook my head. Now we were both naked and neither of us were prepared to take this any further.

Figures.

"You keep no condoms or lube in your place?"

He had the gall to sound annoyed when *he* was the one who showed up unexpectedly?

I opened my eyes so I could glare at his scowling face. "You came here to fuck me and didn't bring any?"

"I didn't come here to fuck you," he growled, standing there naked with his dick in his now still hand.

I sighed. "Right. Sure you didn't. Keep lying to yourself."

His jaw got as hard as his erection. My educated guess was that it wouldn't be hard for long and I was about to miss out.

Damn it.

Then it hit me where I kept some. My truck. From when I used to meet up with other men in other towns for drinks or dinner or... my favorite "dessert."

I did a quick inventory of my glovebox in my head. How old were those condoms? Did I still have enough lube? I wouldn't know the answers until I went down to check.

I glanced at my cum-painted stomach and now flaccid cock.

Not only was the man difficult to deal with, so was trying to have sex with him!

I clenched my teeth and lifted a hand. I was impressed when he understood my non-verbal signal and slapped his hand in mine to help haul me to my feet.

After snagging my old T-shirt from the floor, I scrubbed it down my abdomen, wiping away the evidence of my ejaculation.

I swore Chase could ruin a wet dream.

"Well?"

Again... *He* had the balls to sound annoyed? "Really? You're acting like I'm the one at fault here?"

"Who doesn't keep condoms and lube around?"

I paused pulling on my boxers, lifted my head and glared at him again. "Do we want to make a bet that your cabin has none, either?"

Of course that got him to pin his mouth shut.

"That's what I thought. Why buy lube when lotion works just as well? Plus, leaves me silky smooth." I made a jerk-off motion with my fist, then tipped my head toward my nightstand on the opposite side of the bed that held a huge bottle of lotion. The family-sized one with the pump I bought at Costco. I didn't get there often but when I did, I also stocked up on tissues.

Those were sitting by the bed, as well.

With one raised eyebrow, his eyes sliced from my nightstand back to me.

I grumbled my warning, "No judgment," and finished sliding my boxers on.

"Where are you going?"

"In my boxers? Nowhere. But after I pull on a pair of jeans, I'm going out to my truck to check my glovebox for the needed supplies."

"You keep some in your truck."

Funny, because that didn't sound like he was asking, it sounded like he was confirming a suspicion.

"Yes. Because my five-fingered friend is my only partner around here. At least... Until tonight." I raised both eyebrows at him. "If you would've warned me you were coming..."

"I didn't come here for sex."

"Of course. We're sticking to that story." I shook my head, snagged my discarded jeans from earlier off the chair next to my closet, yanked them up my legs, found a T-shirt without any cum stains and pulled that over my head. When I glanced back at Chase, he'd been watching me.

His cock was now as deflated as mine and his hands were planted on his naked hips.

"Why the hell do you look annoyed? I'm the one who has to get dressed and run down to my truck. I'm the one who's getting bent over and getting a cock rammed up my ass. I'm the one getting the short end of the—" I glanced down at his cock. "You're right, the water had been cold. There's nothing short about that. At least you have that going for you."

I didn't wait to hear his response. Instead, I ripped open the bedroom door, dodged Timber rushing in, acting like he had almost died because I had shut him out, and strode out of my apartment, only pausing at the door to slip on my flip-flops.

I was down at my truck and back within minutes. I grabbed what I found and figured I'd look at it closer once I was back inside.

I was relieved when I finally had enough light to read the expiration date on the box of condoms and to see how full the tube of lube was. Thankfully, we were set. The condoms were still good and the tube three-quarters full.

Except going out into the fresh air had made me rethink things. Rethink the unbearable bear waiting for me in my bedroom.

Once again, I wondered if it was worth grappling with a grumpy grizzly to get to the cuddly teddy that could be at his core.

Deep down I thought he could be.

Without breaking stride, I kicked off my flip-flops and headed back to the bedroom to find Chase perched on the edge of my bed with Timber sitting in between his legs, his tongue hanging out of the side of his mouth, giving the naked man on *my* bed googly eyes.

Once again, proving the dog I raised since a puppy, fed expensive food twice a day, bought birthday and Christmas presents for *and* took on daily walks was a traitor.

One handsome man walks in my door and my four-legged companion turns into Benedict Arnold.

Why didn't my *formerly* loyal dog have more discerning taste?

Oh wait. Maybe I should ask that of myself.

"Timber," I called. "Out."

Timber didn't move.

Of course he didn't. Not when he had someone scratching him under his chin.

The expression on my dog's face went from adoration to ecstasy.

Great. I should be the one in the middle of ecstasy.

"Timber, out!"

I ignored the man who raised a single eyebrow at me, and concentrated on the dog with selective hearing. When I got closer, I tossed the condoms and lube on the mattress and spotted a tennis ball peeking out from under the bed. I snagged it, showed it to Timber, then whipped it out the door.

With a shrill bark, Timber shot out of my bedroom at warp speed. I slammed the door behind him and sighed.

When I turned back to the bed, I barely caught it in time when Chase's lips pulled up slightly and for a shocked second, I thought he might smile. He managed to catch his reaction and hide it.

I rolled my eyes. "How can I both like someone and dislike someone so much at the same time?"

"I keep asking myself the same question."

"And yet, here you are."

He tipped his head to the side. "Here I am."

"Just a reminder, since you showed up here uninvited, I'm not responsible for any..." I also tipped my head and widened my eyes in a silent message.

"I'm aware."

"That doesn't bother you?"

"If it did, I wouldn't be sitting naked on your bed waiting for you to come over here so I can show you how much I won't be bothered."

"*Ooooh.*"

"Yes, oh."

One side of my mouth pulled up. "Now I like you a little more than five minutes ago."

"I'm relieved."

"You will be. But... uh..." I lifted a *wait-a-minute* finger. "Let me grab a towel." I headed into the full bathroom attached to my bedroom, snagged one from the linen closet and when I came back out with it, I tossed it at him. He caught it against his chest, removed the bedspread and tossed it onto the floor, then spread out the large towel as I stripped off my clothes.

By the time I was naked, I was hard once again.

I wasn't the only one.

Once he sat back down on the edge, I moved to stand in between his legs in the same spot where Timber had been. "Should I get on my knees so you can scratch me under my chin?"

"Will your leg twitch like Timber's?"

Ah, yes. There it was. A hint of a sense of humor.

That alone made me think, yes, this would be worth it. *He* would be worth it. I would just need a little understanding and a whole lot of patience.

"My leg has the potential of twitching but not from chin scratches." His dark eyes rolled up from my erection, now perpendicular to the rest of my body. "Impressive, right?"

"You call that impressive?"

I barked out a laugh. "Not the size—though, now you'll give me a damn complex—I meant the ability to recover so quickly."

"*Ah.*"

"*Ah?*"

"You're not going to need it," he explained.

"Yes, you already made me aware of that fact," I said dryly.

"Do you have a problem with that?"

"Normally, I might. Tonight, I'm making an exception for you. I hope you appreciate it."

He surged up from the bed, making me take a step back. When his hand snaked out, curled around the back of my neck and yanked me to him, it slammed me into his chest.

He immediately put his mouth to my ear, the wiry hairs tickling me, to murmur, "I appreciate it."

A shiver shot through me.

It wasn't only his voice that turned me on, it was everything about him. The power in which he held onto me. The breadth of his shoulders and chest. The dark hairs that covered his torso, lower stomach and thighs. His thick erection pressed to mine.

While his personality might be lacking, everything else was not.

Even better, with the way he looked at me like he was a hungry lion and I was an injured gazelle, I realized I might have unleashed a beast.

I was perfectly okay with that.

I could take gentle or rough. Words or silence. Quick or slow. I was fine with whatever Chase dished out as long as I was getting a piece of whatever he was serving.

I wedged my hands in between us to plant them on the thick

carpet that decorated his chest, to find both of his nipples. When I brushed the pads of my thumbs over the pebbled tips, he took my mouth again.

This time when he took full control, he kissed me like he was trying to eat me in one swallow. But before I could get lost in that kiss, he ended it, twisted us around and pushed me onto the bed.

I landed with a bounce. "Ass up or ass down?"

"Ass up."

I moved to the center of the bed and sat on the towel. "I need you to remember it's me you're fucking. I'm not going to be a hole you're pretending is someone else's. If that's what you want, then we aren't doing this." When he said nothing... "Chase..."

He nodded.

"That decides it. Ass down. If you don't like it, the door's behind you. If your head is elsewhere, I'd rather you just leave than use me as a substitute." I held my breath as I waited for his response, which came in him grabbing the container of Tush Cush and tossing it into my lap. I held it up. "Before I open this, I need to hear it from you."

"With the way your mouth runs, I'd have a hard time pretending you're anyone else."

"So, what you're saying is, I should talk the whole time to make sure you remain present in this room with me and don't end up in your head with someone else."

"What I'm saying is... shut up."

An unrestrained laugh burst from me. But that laughter quickly faded as he climbed onto the bed. I quickly shifted toward the headboard, made sure the towel was still tucked under me so we wouldn't make too much of a mess on my sheets, then I popped open the cap to the lube.

As I squeezed a generous amount on my index and middle fingers, Chase was tearing open a condom. While I prepped myself with the Tush Cush, Chase watched.

Closely.

That gave me a reason to make a show of it by planting my feet on the bed and lifting my ass to spread the lube generously around my hole, dipping my fingers inside. Once I had enough lube shoved in there, I plunged my fingers in and out in a seductive, hopefully not awkward, manner.

I must have achieved my goal since, as he watched, his hand slid up and down his length, the condom forgotten in the other.

When I turned it into an even bigger display, adding little moans and groans along with a few hip thrusts, he shook his head, rolled on the condom and snagged the Tush Cush from my fingers. "Are you ever normal?"

"Life's too short to be normal. I can fake it when I need to."

He applied the lube generously all over his latex-covered cock and when he was done, he closed the cap and placed it on my nightstand so it would be close by.

Smart thinking.

It had been a while since I'd been the receiver since that wasn't my preference. I didn't hate it, I just preferred being the plunger instead of the one being plunged.

On his knees, he shuffled between my bent legs, grabbing my ankles as he did so and like when he rimmed me, he pushed my knees into my chest. I loosened my muscles in preparation when he dragged his middle finger down my taint to my anus, and without warning, plunged it inside.

"I'd prefer—" His finger curled and stroked my prostate. "Nope. You're good."

With his finger still deep in my ass, teasing my most magical spot, he leaned over me and took my mouth.

Okay, I could get used to this.

He kept kissing me as he slipped his finger from my hole, wiped it on the towel and then shifted forward. He slid the head of his cock down my perineum until it was right at his target. Where he wanted it.

Where I wanted it, too.

A bump, a nudge, a knock at my back door. Then he was pressing forward while deepening the kiss that had me guessing if he was only doing it to keep me quiet.

I relaxed the ring of muscle, welcoming him inside.

He took that opportunity to slide in deeper, taking it slow and careful. Pulling back, shifting, pushing forward, working his way inside me while stretching me in the process.

The farther he went, the more full I felt, the more distracted I became, making me only half participate in the kiss.

But when he was finally fully seated, when he could go no further, when his balls were smashed to my ass, he stopped kissing me and lifted his head and stared down at me.

His expression was guarded, his eyes unreadable and he was no longer moving. He simply breathed and stared.

It actually started to worry me.

Was he regretting this already?

"Are you with me?" I asked.

I was relieved when he answered with a, "Yes." I was also a little annoyed that he sounded slightly surprised about it. However, he caught me off guard when he asked, "Are you good?"

Surprise, surprise. He was checking in on me. I hadn't expected that from him and was pleased he cared enough to ask. "I'm good."

"I'm not gentle."

"You could've fooled me."

"I won't be gentle," came the warning even though he didn't explain further. But then, he didn't need to, I heard what went unsaid.

There was a time and place for rough sex. The same as there was for gentle lovemaking. This would not be the second scenario. However, he didn't have to warn me because I was fine with the first.

Only he didn't know that.

He remained still until I assured him, "I won't break."

CHAPTER 16

Rett

WHILE I TOLD him I wouldn't break, a few seconds later I began to think I was wrong. I could very well be breakable since the man reminded me of a grizzly in mating season.

He was ramming his cock inside of me as hard and as fast as he could. For a second, I was thankful to be generously lubed up.

Because... *Whoa.* Whatever emotional turmoil he was going through, he was using it to fuel his actions. Or at least, that was my assumption. It could be he always fucked like this.

Once his big paws clamped tightly around my wrists and pinned them down to the bed, he brushed his beard along mine, the resulting sound reminding me of running a fingernail across a strip of Velcro. He continued brushing those coarse wiry hairs down my throat, scraping my skin, making me even harder as he went.

He shifted back up, nabbed my bottom lip within his teeth and bit down so hard, I thought he made me bleed. When he released my lip, I ran my tongue over it to check to make sure he hadn't broken the skin.

He hadn't.

Biting along my throat, he followed the same path he had dragged his beard.

He sank his teeth into my shoulder, deep enough to send a rush of endorphins through me. My moan changed into a groan when he clamped down on my flesh at the same time I lifted my hips to meet him thrust for thrust.

Yes, a wild animal inside him had been unleashed. He hadn't had sex for at least two years. For me, it had been over a year.

Both of us were more than ready for this. For a connection that only occurred while having sex with a partner. While going solo could get the job done, that was all it did. Any personal connection was missing.

He continued to slam his cock into me, his balls slapping my ass with each forceful pump.

When he began to nip a trail along my chest, to give him better access, I moved my legs out of the way by wrapping them around his hips. Taking one nipple into his greedy mouth, he sucked hard and scraped his teeth along the tip, causing me to groan and arch my back in encouragement. He went back and forth from nipple to nipple, alternating using his mouth and his teeth.

Oh yes, kissing me wasn't the only way to stop me from talking as he was quickly finding out.

However, because he had my hands pinned to the mattress, I couldn't play grab ass or fist his hair, which I was dying to do. By jerking my arms, I indicated he should let me go, but he ignored that and continued to drive me out of my damn mind. Fucking me. Sucking me. Biting. Scraping his beard and teeth along my now sensitive, heated flesh.

Then... it just stopped.

My wrists bore a majority of his weight as he pushed himself up until his face hovered over mine. A lock of his shaggy hair fell haphazardly over his forehead and I wanted to push it out of his dark, brooding eyes so I could see them more clearly.

To try to get a read on where he was at in his head.

Even though one eye was partially covered, I could see he was not looking through me but actually at me.

Relief swept through me when I realized I wasn't being used as a substitute for the lost love of his life. It was clear in his face he remained aware of who he was with.

At least at this moment. I only hoped it stayed that way the closer we raced toward our final destination.

"Chase..."

He gave me a single shake of his head, released my arms and drove his fingers into my hair, using his tight grip to tilt my head back with force and stretch my throat until it was completely exposed. I expected him to clamp his hand around it and squeeze. I found myself slightly disappointed when he didn't. Even though I'd never been into that type of stuff, I wasn't opposed to trying new things.

Instead of getting as rough as I thought he might, he took my mouth again. Kissing me hard. Kissing me deeply. Kissing me until I was breathless once more.

He railed my ass over and over, the drag of his cock over my prostate making my precum leak at a quicker pace, smearing the silky fluid between us and all over our skin. The way his weight pressed on my erection alone might actually make me come again.

With every one of his thrusts, I matched the motion, sliding my cock between the press of our bodies. Until I teetered along a very sharp edge.

One wrong move... No, one *right* move and I'd be gone.

And of course, that next move was all it took. I came and made a mess all over again.

After ripping my mouth from his, my lungs heaved as I gulped air. Chase's hips weren't the only thing pumping, so was his chest. He was struggling to breathe just as much as I was. But his was short, shallow pants. I could see it in his eyes—even though now he was avoiding mine—that he was almost there himself.

Once he clenched his teeth together and grimaced, I knew that was all he wrote...

He surged up, propping himself on his arms, closed his eyes, dropped his head forward, thrust two more times and when he blew out a rush of air, he came.

Every muscle tensed as he remained deep inside me, the sensitive nerves that surrounded my hole letting me know when his cock finished pulsing, when he was done coming.

Even after that, he stayed fully seated for surprisingly longer than I expected.

Was he afraid to pull out or was it that he was trying to hang on to that connection as long as possible? It could be a combination of both.

I waited patiently, leaving it up to him to move when he was ready since I was fine where I was. I didn't mind his weight on me and my only urge was to tuck my fingers under his chin and lift his face so I could see more of it. See if I could read what he was feeling because I had no doubt he was hiding it.

Of course, that wasn't shocking, even though a bit disappointing.

When he finally lifted his head, his expression was guarded and his jaw shifted sharply. Maybe he was masking his guilt of allowing himself this, this moment with me. Someone other than the person he loved with all his heart.

Because that part was obvious.

No matter what, tonight was a huge step for him. Two years was a long time to be stuck in hell, so I hoped what we did tonight would help break the cycle of him flip-flopping back and forth from depression to anger and push him into the next stage of grief: acceptance.

Not that I had the balls big enough to think that having sex with me wielded that much power. My ego wasn't that inflated.

Speaking of inflated... Chase's cock was beginning to do the opposite. Soon he would have no choice but to pull out and take care of business.

When he shifted, I murmured, "Hold on," and twisted my torso as much as I could toward the nightstand, since my lower half was still pinned beneath his solid weight.

Snagging the box of tissues with one finger, I slid it toward me. As soon as I could get a good hold of it, I flopped back to the bed and held the box up for him. "You're going to need these."

Without a word, he pulled a few tissues from the box, then slowly slid out of me and removed the condom, carefully tucking it into a tissue and using the rest to wipe himself off.

I needed to do the same but not where I currently was. I rolled from the bed, taking the towel with me so I wouldn't leave anything behind and went into the attached bathroom to clean up.

Quickly going through the motions, I wiped away the excess lube and cleaned myself off, worried that before I was done and went back out, Chase might have hightailed it out of my apartment.

I held my breath while opening the bathroom door and released it as soon as I saw Chase still there. In my room. Actually sitting on the end of the bed with his eyes on me.

Still without saying a damn thing, he got up and moved around me to head into the bathroom as I exited. All while making sure to avoid us touching.

While he was in the bathroom, I yanked on my boxers and sat cross-legged in the middle of the bed, waiting. I had no idea what would happen next. Where we would go from this point.

He could stay. He could go.

I wasn't going to push him either way. I would give him enough space for him to figure out what he wanted on his own. He needed to be the one willing to take this journey of healing and acceptance. I was willing to help him along the way but I couldn't force him.

If I did, all he'd do was dig his heels in and resist. Maybe even back off and shut me out.

So, yes, tonight had been a step forward, but that didn't mean it was a solid one. He could still stumble backward.

As soon as the door opened, a naked Chase approached the end of the bed. "You good?"

Him checking in with me again confirmed that he cared about others. The razor-wire topped fence he had constructed around himself was only to protect him. He was living the old idiom, "once bitten, twice shy."

"I'm fine. Are you?" When he didn't answer, I knew he was emotionally wobbly. No surprise. "It's not cheating, Chase. No matter how it feels right now."

"You don't have to tell me that again. I know what it was and what it wasn't."

Oh yes, someone was a bit touchy. "But do you?"

"Stop thinking you know me better than I know myself. You don't know me."

"No, I don't know you as much as I'd like to. If you'd let it happen."

"As friends?"

I jerked one shoulder up. "Friends. Or more."

"I don't want more."

I swept a hand over the bed. "We just did more. And if you say it was a mistake, I'm letting Timber back in the bedroom to bite your ass."

"He won't bite me."

That wasn't a lie. "Because you've corrupted him."

"He's needy. Just like his owner."

My eyebrows shot up my forehead. "*Oooh*. Are you making a *joke?*"

"Actually no. I was being serious."

I slapped my bare knee and did a laugh-snort. "You *are* making jokes!"

He sighed, grabbed his boxers from the floor and yanked them up his thick, darkly-furred legs.

I was surprised when he didn't do the same with his jeans.

However, I didn't say a word so I wouldn't spook him like a mole peeking his head out of his tunnel in the daylight.

I had to handle this whole "after-sex" thing carefully.

I climbed off the bed. "I'm grabbing some water. Do you want some?"

"I have to go."

"No, you don't. There is nothing and nobody waiting for you up at that cabin." I tipped my head to the bed. "Sit down. Let me grab you a bottle of water." *Then we can talk.*

Of course, I wouldn't say that last part out loud, either, giving him a reason to freak out and split.

Without waiting for an answer, I headed to the kitchen, and, of course, as soon as I opened my bedroom door, Traitor Timber practically barreled over me when he rushed to get to Chase. I cursed under my breath and retrieved two cold bottles of water from the fridge.

I found when I got back to the room that Chase wasn't petting a disappointed Timber. No, he sat on the edge of the mattress with his head down, his elbows planted on his thighs and his hands dangling between his spread knees. He stared at his wedding band, spinning it as was his habit.

I bit back the words wanting to spew from me because I reminded myself for the hundredth time that one, I needed patience with this man, and two, everyone handled grief differently and on their own timeline.

I offered him the water. "You held back."

He snagged the bottle from my fingers and, with a furrowed brow, lifted his gaze to my face. "What are you talking about?"

"You warned me twice about how you wouldn't be gentle. Why tell me that and not follow through?"

He cracked open the lid on the water, tipped his head back, drawing my eyes to his working throat as he swallowed a third of it.

When he was done, he wiped the back of his wrist over his mouth. "Are you saying you're disappointed?"

"Let's get this straight right now... I am *far* from disappointed. Having sex with you was more satisfying than I would like to admit. I actually wished it had sucked so I wouldn't be tempted to have sex with you again," I teased. "Even so, there was no reason to hold back."

"I didn't."

"Bullshit."

"If you want the truth—"

"I always want the truth." The only people who preferred lies were people too fragile to handle the truth. That wasn't me and never would be. To me, lies could cause more damage than facing the truth head on.

The truth might be painful but at least it was real.

"Here's the truth... I pulled myself back because I was beginning to lose control. I was afraid of hurting you."

I was afraid of hurting you. One more piece of evidence that proved deep down he was a caring man. I just needed to peel away the tough, scarred layers to get to the true Chase.

"Unless you're into some kinky bondage or even blood or breath play, you aren't going to hurt me. Or freak me out. I don't mind it rough. Though, I also enjoy the gentle moments that go hand in hand with shared intimacy. Either way, the most important part when it comes to sex is that it's *good*. We should be able to agree on that if nothing else."

"Was it good?"

"Yes," I answered.

"Then stop complaining."

I sighed. "I wasn't complaining. I'm just telling you that you didn't have to hold back with me."

"It was our first time together and I wanted..."

I ignored the part about this being our first time together. By focusing on that I might spook him. "You wanted?" I prodded.

He clammed up.

Shit. I messed up, anyway.

He was done, beginning to shut down completely. I could see it in his face and the way his fingers came close to crushing the bottle of water. Feelings were creeping up on him and he didn't like it.

However, he didn't get up or get dressed to leave. He stayed sitting on my bed with my disloyal dog at his feet. That made me think he wanted something else from me and was afraid to ask for it or simply take it for himself.

On the other hand, I could be completely wrong. That happened every once in a while.

But I'd never know what he wanted or needed if he wasn't willing to discuss it. Anyway, I couldn't imagine Chase Jones wanting to speak candidly like that. It was safer for him to remain at the surface and not do a deep dive.

For him, diving deep might take him to a dark and scary place.

I might not like that he was so closed off but I understood it.

Again, I needed patience and if I didn't have that, I should tell him to go home and then leave him alone. Those small, but significant, signs I kept picking up on gave me hope he wanted to get free from the emotional quagmire he was currently wallowing in.

Since he had already shut down, I figured I'd go for it. It couldn't hurt. "You mentioned our 'first time.' Are you staying so we could have a second time later?"

He scrubbed a hand over his mouth and stared at me. Of course, not in a good *I want to suck your dick* type of way.

Before he could shoot down the idea of staying, I continued, "You're thinking I'm crazy for wanting you to stay. And maybe I am."

"I'm not sure why…" His voice drifted off before he finished his thought.

"Honestly, I'm not sure, either, since you're about as personable as a rotting tree stump."

Well, damn. I actually witnessed an elusive lip twitch from him.

It struck me right then and there, my new goal in life would be to make the man smile. And not a fake one, either. A real honest-to-goodness genuine smile. Or, even better, make him laugh.

Why I gave a shit about this man's happiness…

Maybe I needed as much therapy as he did.

He finished off his bottled water, then took his time screwing the cap back on. Once he was done, he got to his feet, set the empty bottle on my dresser and came over to me. While his expression was serious, his eyes held confusion and I felt that to my very core.

He wanted me. He wanted to stay. But his heart and mind were once again waging a war against each other.

When he stepped bare toe to bare toe with me, I whispered, "Stay. Forget everything outside of this room for one night. Give yourself that and give yourself a break for once. You deserve it and no one will judge you for taking advantage of some companionship and intimacy. Especially me. You know why? I need it as much as you do. It might not have been two years for me, but still, it's been too long. You might not want to admit you need it, too, but I have no problem admitting it for myself. I need it, Chase, and you have what I need. So, I'm asking for you to stay."

"All night?" The soft, deep rumble did things to me no man's voice had ever done before.

"For as long as you're comfortable." Even if he only stayed for a few more hours, it would be another step forward. "I'm here for you for as long as you want it."

"I still don't know why…" Again, the doubt was there. Before I could explain why once again, he gave me a single nod and said, "Okay."

My mouth dropped open when he shocked the hell out of me.

Then he took advantage of my open mouth and claimed it all over again.

WARM BREATH SWEPT over my skin. I moaned and rolled over…

Only to go eye to eye with a male a lot hairier than Chase.

My shameless dog was in the middle of the bed, lying on his back,

214

all four feet in the air, his head tipped in my direction and his eyes on me.

He grinned.

I frowned.

So much for spontaneous sex this morning. My own dog was a cock block.

I stretched myself from my hands to my feet, and felt a little discomfort. It wasn't a lot but enough to remind me that Chase and I had sex twice last night. The second time he'd loosened up enough to show me some of what he was into.

He had even stayed afterward when I thought he'd bolt.

I rose up on my elbows and glanced at the other side of the bed...

Empty.

Somehow he had managed to slip out sometime between me falling asleep and now. All without waking me. That was a feat in itself, especially when I had a damn dog.

"Where'd he go?"

Timber flopped over on his side, glanced at me and then yawned big.

"You let him go without waking me up?"

Traitor Timber did a little *woo-woo*.

"You couldn't do that when he was sneaking out?"

My dog licked his chops, then sneezed.

I flopped my head back on the pillow and stared up at the ceiling, curious as to what time Chase left.

I had no doubt it was not long after we had sex that second time.

Last night, Chase seemed starved both times.

For attention. For simple physical contact.

For even more complex intimacy.

I was willing to give him that and so much more.

Whatever he wanted, I would offer. He would only need to accept it.

While last night proved we had a physical connection, what was still missing was the emotional bond. Something I knew better than to expect, but still held onto a sliver of hope that one day it might be there.

I wanted more from a man who might not be willing to give it. I tried to convince myself that it was because Chase was the first gay man who lived close since I moved to Eagle's Landing.

Having a convenient sex partner would be perfect. However, for some damn reason, now that I had a taste of him, I wanted more than just a friend with benefits. I wanted to continue to peel back his protective layers to discover who he was at his core and maybe help him find himself again.

But first, I should make an appointment and have my damn head examined. Because anyone in their right mind wouldn't take a man like him on as a challenge.

Not a damn one.

But then, us writers were a bit weird. We had to be. We listened to the voices in our heads and wrote down everything they said.

That couldn't possibly be considered normal.

I sighed, scrubbed my hands down my face, then rolled out of bed. "C'mon, Traitor. I'll let you out."

Timber jumped from the bed with an excited bark and waited impatiently by the bedroom door as I glanced around to see where my boxers ended up after Chase tore them from me that second time.

I had no idea where they were. Unless he took them as a trophy. A reminder of how good our night was together.

I snorted.

At least it was good sexually. Emotionally and conversationally it was a bit lacking.

I assured myself that would come eventually, once he pushed free of the grief and guilt that weighed him down.

After pulling a clean pair out of my dresser drawer, I yanked them up my legs.

First, Timber. Then shower.

Soon after that, and most importantly, a pot of damn coffee. I would need an extra mug or two of caffeine to function today.

Maybe later, I'd shoot Chase a text to check up on how he was doing. But for now, I'd leave him alone.

I only hoped he wasn't beating himself up over it. Since he seemed to be a bit looser during the second round of sex, I took that as a good sign.

Even then, he still held back.

Baby steps...

Timber rushed by me when I walked out of the bedroom, glancing around to make sure Chase wasn't still in my apartment and waiting for me to wake up.

Of course he wasn't.

But what was waiting for me on the counter was the manilla envelope with my manuscript. I had forgotten that was the excuse he used to show up last night.

Once I let Timber outside, I headed back over to it, sliding out the pages that made up my first draft.

The words written in red ink across the top of the cover page caught my eye. *Not much to say except... Don't change a damn thing.*

I was not expecting that kind of note from Chase aka C.J. Anson.

I ran a fingertip over his handwriting. It was made up of sharp slashes and hardly readable, reminding me of a doctor's.

I flipped through the pages only to find a few missed typos marked and some very minor grammar tweaks. Other than that, not much else.

Again, a huge shocker.

I figured he'd slash chunks of narrative, making my manuscript look like a murder scene with all the red.

With a smile, I slapped the manuscript back on the counter, then whistled all the way into the shower.

Yes, I'd be checking in with Mr. Chase Jones later today.

And now I couldn't wait.

CHAPTER 17

Chase

STANDING at the edge of the lake, I stared out over the water without seeing a damn thing. I was exhausted from last night since I didn't get a wink of sleep.

Not before having sex with Rett. Not after.

The guilt of lying in Rett's bed had been crushing, so I left. To avoid him trying to convince me to stay, I snuck out after he'd finally fallen asleep. I didn't want to have to explain myself or get into a disagreement about me not staying the whole night.

I couldn't.

I just couldn't.

What made it worse, as annoying as he was, I *liked* Rett. As much as I didn't want to, I *liked* him.

If I only wanted to find someone for sex, I could've found that elsewhere. A nameless stranger in a nearby town. It wasn't difficult to find an anonymous hookup. Apps were available for that.

But I didn't want anyone else and that bothered me. I was also aggravated at myself since I thought I'd never want anyone again.

After losing Thomas, I vowed to remain celibate for the rest of my life. Mistakenly telling myself I wouldn't need anyone. That he had been my one and only. That I wouldn't care about anyone the same way as I had my husband. That I could spend my remaining days alone and I'd be just fine.

The hard truth was, I was far from fine.

I was far from anything, except confused.

While the thoughts in my head were jumbled, one thing was clear...

Having sex with Rett last night made me realize how empty I was inside and what remained of my former self was a ghost.

I twisted my wedding band around my left ring finger. It shouldn't be cold metal. It should be searing me, burning my flesh for breaking my vows. To Thomas. To myself. To our union.

Clearly I was weak by allowing my attraction to Rett to drive me to break my personal vow of never being with anyone again.

I spun my ring faster.

And faster.

"Fuck!" I jerked it off my finger and whipped it as hard and as far as I could. "*You* did this to me. You! You didn't only hurt yourself, you damaged me beyond repair! Why the hell would you think that was okay? That leaving me would be okay? It's not. You destroyed yourself and you destroyed me along with you."

My knees could no longer hold me and folded under the crushing weight. They sank into the soft earth along the lake's edge and I curled over myself, trying to ease the unbearable ache in my stomach and chest.

I screamed until my voice cracked. Until my throat was raw. Until my vision swam before me from the tears I could no longer hold back. I couldn't stop my chest from cracking open, exposing the hole where my heart used to be.

By Thomas easing his own pain, he left behind the person he loved with a devastating and damaging loss.

My chest heaved with a scream that had no beginning and no

end. I could no longer catch my breath as sobs wracked my body. Until I had nothing left to escape.

I was cracking open and the hollowness inside being exposed.

I lost track of time as it all came crashing down on and around me.

It wasn't until my thoughts began to clear, when I could breathe again, when I had nothing left to expel, I realized what I had done.

Something I shouldn't have.

I straightened and scanned the lake. "Fuck!" My curse was amplified across the flat water. "Fuck!"

Why the hell would I do that? I just threw away an important part of my marriage. The symbol that bound us. The ring he had picked specifically for me. The only reminder I had left besides his ashes, some photos and memories.

I surged to my feet and bolted into the water, not wanting to take the time to strip off my clothes. I had no idea where it landed, but I needed to retrieve it before it got sucked into the muck at the bottom and could never be found again.

I wasn't coming out of that water until I did.

Until I had it within my fingers.

Starting where I thought it might have landed, I dove under the chilly water. My boots immediately became heavy buckets and my clothes water-logged, the weight dragging me to the bottom.

Even with my eyes open, I couldn't see in the murky water so I raked my fingers through the mud, searching by touch.

Nothing.

Nothing.

And a whole lot of nothing.

My water-filled boots made it impossible to kick my feet and a struggle to swim. I worried the ring had landed in the water where it was too deep.

But, *damn it*, I didn't know where it ended up. I only knew it was no longer where it belonged. On my finger.

Jesus. I wasn't getting out until I found it. Even if I ended up in a watery grave.

I continued to frantically search. With every rake of my fingers through the mud, it made the water even cloudier, now making it impossible to see even a few inches in front of my face.

Panic clawed at my already raw throat and my heart pounded uncontrollably against my chest. I hyper-focused on the search, not caring about anything other than finding what I lost, what I recklessly threw away.

Every solid object my fingertips brushed against was a slimy stone or a sharp rock. The bottom was covered with what seemed like thousands of them. If it wasn't a rock, my fingers skimmed across sticks or patches of rotting vegetation.

I found nothing smooth and circular. The symbol of infinity. Of forever.

We promised each other just that.

Thomas broke that promise.

Even so, I knew I needed to forgive him or my own "forever" would be stuck in grief. I needed to allow myself to let it go. Last night proved that and had become a turning point.

That didn't stop me from wanting back the ring Thomas gave me. He slipped it on my finger on our wedding day because he loved me as much as I loved him.

And no matter what he did or why, I still loved him and I would until my own end.

My lungs burned, my eyes were no longer useful. My fear of never finding it drowning me the same as the cloudy lake.

Any tears shed were immediately washed away by the water. But what couldn't be washed away were my regrets.

My body began to fight me, demanding for me to surface and take a breath. But I couldn't. I couldn't stop. Not yet. If I did, I'd lose track of where I'd already searched. I wouldn't take a breath until I found it.

It had to be here somewhere.

While the natural instinct to survive tricked my brain into thinking I should plant my boots against the bottom and push my way to the surface, my broken heart tried to convince me to simply give up and let the loneliness and excruciating pain be washed away forever.

A war was being waged.

And it didn't matter whether my heart or my mind won, I'd still be dealing with a loss.

However, my choice was taken from me the second something clamped tightly around my chest, tugging me sideways.

I struggled to escape whatever had a hold of me. The constrictive band around my chest and under my arms tightened even more and I clawed at it, desperate to break its hold.

An arm.

A human arm.

Was I delirious from a lack of oxygen? Was I losing the last thread of my sanity?

When my head broke the surface, I gasped, then coughed out some of the water I had inhaled, but my lungs still fought to pull in my next breath.

I blinked, trying to see who was dragging me from the lake.

Of fucking course.

My lungs gurgled as I barely managed to suck in enough air to talk. "Let... me... go..." My voice had an unnatural rasp to it.

"I'm not letting you go until we're out of this goddamn water," he yelled, a mix of fear and anger coloring his tone. Even with my blurry vision, I couldn't miss the sharpness in his jaw and annoyance in his eyes.

I could fight him, but if I did, I might drown Rett, too. "I can't get out yet!" *Jesus*, even my yell sounded like I was still underwater.

"You're getting out! You're as cold and stiff as a frozen side of beef."

I attempted to jerk away and try to break his grip. "I'm not done!"

He didn't respond or release me until we were both on our knees in the shallow water at the edge, both of us winded, trying to draw in the air our lungs demanded. At this point, I couldn't tell if it was tears or lake water running in rivulets down my cheeks.

"What the fuck were you doing?"

Oh yes, he was pissed. "I lost… something."

"In the lake?"

There, too. I nodded because it took too much effort to speak right now. If I forced it, I might break down and sob like a baby.

I didn't want Rett to see me cry. I didn't want him to see how desperate and destroyed I was, even though my gut instinct told me he already knew the extent of it.

With no strength left to get to my feet, I remained where I was and only glanced up when I heard, "Take my hand. Let me help you out of there."

Let me help you…

Unlike me, he now stood on the more solid shoreline with his hand extended. "Take my fucking hand, Chase. I can't carry you!" he shouted. "You need to help yourself, too. I can't do it for you. I can only help."

My first instinct was to tell him I didn't need his help when that was the farthest from the truth.

I needed help. A lot of it. And for whatever reason, this man was willing to be the one to do so. I just didn't understand why he'd want that hassle.

A shiver from deep within my bones ripped through me and my teeth began to chatter uncontrollably.

"Give me your damn hand now, Chase. You're going to go into hypothermia. Your lips are already turning blue."

Somehow I gathered up enough strength to slap my hand into his and he tugged me to my feet. Those same feet squished in my boots with every step I tried to take out of the water and onto more solid land.

But I was tired. Drained. With barely enough energy to move. That didn't stop Rett from turning into a draft horse powerful enough to physically tow me away from the lake and my lost wedding ring.

What I might never find again. What could be lost for all eternity.

That possibility made me anchor my feet and lean back, forcing Rett to a stop. "I need to go back in."

"For what? You were about to fucking drown, Chase. I'm not letting you do that. Not on my watch."

"I'm not trying to drown. I need to find it." I really didn't want to tell him what I carelessly threw away like the idiot I was.

"Find what?"

When I shook my head, lake water flung from my hair. "What are you doing here?"

"Find what?" he asked again.

"Why are you here?" I repeated.

"Answer my question first and I'll answer yours."

I was embarrassed to admit, "My ring."

His gaze automatically dropped to the hand he refused to release, even though I kept yanking on it to get free. His dark brown eyes, bloodshot from the lake water and surrounded by wet, spiky black lashes, flicked back up to me. "How did it get lost? You're still dressed and in your damn boots! Unless you started swimming fully clothed after I caught you skinny-dipping?"

His anger edged with aggravated sarcasm was so thick I could taste it. "Don't worry about how I lost it. The important part is I need to find it." I coughed again and my lungs still rattled slightly. I spat more lake water out on the ground.

"Not right now you don't."

"You can't dictate what I do."

He yanked my arm so hard, I almost lost my balance. "I can and I will since apparently you're incapable of thinking straight."

"Who the fuck do you think you are?" I half-shouted, half-coughed as I put all of my weight into rearing back.

"Fine. Go fucking drown."

I wasn't expecting him to give up so easily or to release my hand so suddenly. Because of that, I fell backwards and landed on my ass in the grass halfway between the lake and the cabin.

Stunned, I sat there, shaking from the cold, my teeth knocking together, my skin numb and every inch of me soaking wet. My feet had turned into frozen cinder blocks in my boots.

I ground the heels of my palms into my eyes when they began to sting all over again.

I took a few deep breaths to try to clear my lungs and collect my roller coaster of emotions. "I'm sorry," slipped from me before I could stop it.

"Who are you apologizing to? Me? Thomas? Yourself?"

I avoided both his eyes and his questions.

Strong fingers clamped around my jaw and lifted my face. "Chase…"

When I finally looked at him, he shook his head, squatted in front of me, wrapped a hand around the back of my neck and squeezed. "We need to get you inside, out of those clothes and warmed up."

His tone was much softer than it had been.

Pity. That was what it was.

Even though it was summer, the water always had a bite to it since the lake was fed from a fresh underground spring. Whenever I took a swim, it was a quick, invigorating one. I usually only stayed in until I couldn't take the temperature any more.

To be chilled to the bone, I must've been searching for the ring longer than I realized. Or maybe it was because I'd been scrambling around at the bottom instead of swimming at the sun-warmed surface.

I could hardly stomach what I read in Rett's eyes under his deeply furrowed brow. "Let me help you." His whispered plea was raw and tangible and only fueled the unbearable ache inside me.

"Why? Why the fuck would you want to help me? I'm…" *Fill in the blank.*

Whatever word I followed it with wouldn't be good but would, most likely, be fitting. But he didn't need me to finish.

"Yes, you are and luckily for you, I understand why." He stood up and held out his hand again. "Come on. You're shivering. You're going to break your teeth from all that clattering. And if you lose all your teeth, I might not want to kiss you." His lips twitched slightly before he pressed them flat.

When I took his hand, he once again helped haul me to my feet and, without another word, we trudged up to my cabin and inside. Straight away, he drew me into the bathroom and turned on the shower.

While the water warmed, he stripped me of my clothes since my fingers were stiff and shaking so badly, it seemed impossible for me to unlace and pull off my boots. Even for him, it was a struggle to peel off my wet jeans.

Once I was naked, he pulled the shower curtain aside and nudged me under the spray. The hot water running over my hair, down my face and over the rest of my body began to bring me back to reality.

Especially after Rett shoved the curtain aside again and, now naked himself, squeezed in. My brain had to be mush since I didn't consider how he'd been fully clothed in the chilly water, too, even if it hadn't been as long.

The shower stall was only big enough for one person, so Rett had to wedge himself behind me. Pressing himself to my back, he wrapped both arms around me and planted his hands on my chest, letting the water run over us both, warming us. A simple act of comfort not sexual in any way.

Closing my eyes, I relished the touch of his skin against mine, the press of his body, the way he securely held me. Between breathing in the steam, his body heat, and the warm shower water, I quickly came back to life. It wasn't long before the shivers stopped, my teeth no longer chattered and my muscles loosened.

During all that, not one word was exchanged, not one expectation required. I simply basked in his silent support and understanding.

Eventually the spray of water stopped and the slide of the shower curtain made me open my eyes. With a gentle nudge, he urged me to step out.

I reached for the towel hanging on the rack, but Rett grabbed it first, rubbing it over my skin, warming me up even further.

Making me almost feel human again.

And that scared me.

I was afraid the wall I had constructed around me was the only thing left holding me in one piece and if I lowered it...

If I lowered it, there might not be anything left for Rett to save.

Because it was clear... That was what he was trying to do.

I still couldn't fathom why.

Once I was dry, he pulled another towel off the stack in the narrow doorless closet and dried himself off quickly, strategically using his broad body to block me from exiting until he was done.

Obviously, he wanted to keep me in view.

"Timber?" came out of me on a croak. Between my screams and the dirty lake water, my throat would be paying for a while.

"You like my dog more than me."

From what I knew of the man, I could imagine him saying something similar if he was teasing. Today those words were tinged with hurt and maybe a little sadness.

I caused that.

Me.

Rett still believed I didn't like him. But then, not once had I given him a reason to think otherwise.

Despite my reluctance and my fear of letting someone get close to me, I needed to fix that. But I wasn't sure if I could.

Truthfully, I shouldn't encourage him on his current path of trying to help me. In the end, it might end up hurting him worse than I already had. I wanted to prevent him from slicing himself on one of my jagged shards.

He deserved much better than someone like me. Someone wearing his tragic past like a cloak. And instead of shedding it, I only pulled it more securely around me and wore it like a shield.

Unfortunately, that shield didn't protect me. Not one bit. If nothing else, it was destroying me from the inside out.

I stared at the pile of wet clothes on the bathroom floor. His and my clothes combined. Surrounded by a puddle that reminded me of the lake he pulled me from.

Rett saved me when I would've let myself drown.

I turned my eyes to him. "Where's Timber?" I asked again.

I don't know why I cared, maybe it was only a distraction from what I had done. From Rett saving me. From life in general.

"If you listen carefully enough, you can hear him outside whining on the porch, waiting to be let inside."

"Where was he?"

Rett shrugged one bare shoulder. "As soon as I got here, he chased a squirrel into the woods."

"You weren't worried about him running off?"

His lips curved into a half-crooked smile. "No. Usually after a little bit he remembers who loves him, takes care of him and where he belongs. He doesn't go far."

"He's loyal to you."

"Yes." Rett tilted his head as he looked at me. "And now to you, too."

"I'm not anything to him."

"You are more to him than you realize."

"That doesn't make any sense."

"As you well know, Chase, sometimes life doesn't make sense. But you deal with it in the best way you can because you have no other choice."

"You always have a choice."

"But some of those choices—even if made only for yourself—can affect others. So if you care about others, you might only have one. But in the end, is only having one choice really a choice at all?"

My heart skipped a beat. Did Rett know somehow?

He couldn't. He knew Thomas had died, but not how or why.

I suggested, "Why don't you go let him in?"

"Because I don't want to leave you alone."

"I'm fine," I lied.

"You're far from fine."

He could leave me alone and go let his dog in, but he felt he had no choice.

He proved himself right.

Again.

CHAPTER 18

Rett

I DIDN'T WANT to leave him alone. Even for the few seconds it would take to open the door and let Timber inside. Nevertheless, I had faith my dog could help pull Chase from his funk.

Something had driven the man to throw his wedding band into the lake. I feared that reason was me and what we did last night. The guilt had to be weighing heavily on him even though, in reality, he had nothing to feel guilty about.

But seeing him thrashing around at the bottom of that cold lake and then fighting me when I tried to pull him out...

It proved his reality was coated in anger, depression and guilt. If he didn't pull free of that, I doubted he'd survive.

My guess was he had kept himself as numb as possible since losing his husband to prevent going under forever and last night that changed when he was forced to confront his feelings.

Apparently, that confrontation had been unbearable.

I might not be a mental health professional but I'd done a lot of research when it came to the human mind and how we reacted to certain events, like death. All due to being an author and writing mysteries. Accuracy when it came to the reactions of characters was important to me.

After reading every C.J. Anson book he'd ever written, I knew it was just as important to him.

But he was too close to see it when it came to himself.

Once we had dry towels wrapped around our waists, I made him accompany me outside to wring out our sopping wet clothes and toss them over the rocking chairs and railing to dry, as well as let my whining and pacing dog into the cabin.

German Shepherds tended to dial in to their owner's emotions and today was no exception. Timber restlessly paced between me and Chase, constantly checking on us both.

I watched closely when Chase ran his fingers along Timber's silky back and then dug his fingers into the dog's thick scruff like he was holding on for dear life. Those actions made it clear that he still warred with his emotions. And might for a while yet.

I needed patience and understanding. Luckily for Chase, I had plenty of both.

Once I brewed a pot of coffee and handed him a steaming mug, I leaned back against the small counter in his kitchenette. I studied him over the rim of the ceramic mug as he stood at the window looking out toward the lake.

Where he'd "lost" his wedding band.

I was sure if I left, he'd go right back into that water. Most likely to never come back out.

I wouldn't be able to live with myself if I allowed that to happen. That meant I was going nowhere until I knew he was stable enough to be left alone. However, I could no longer stay silent. "Chase... Tomorrow will always come, with or without you. As you know, you giving up won't affect you the same as it would the people you leave behind."

Even though he hadn't told me how Thomas died, I had a good guess.

"I don't have anyone left," he mumbled.

"You have family. You have fans who love you even though they might not have ever met you. And... You have me."

"I didn't ask for your opinion or your help."

"Maybe not."

"No maybes about it."

"Let's get this straight... I don't care if you don't want my help. Or even my opinion. I'm going to give it to you anyway. And you know what you're going to do? You're going to fucking accept it. Remember that whole conversation about choice we had in the bathroom? In this instance, I'm only giving you one choice... to accept my help. Of course, to you that may feel like no choice at all."

He turned, shooting a glare in my direction while squeezing the steaming mug so tightly his knuckles paled. "I'm not sure who the fuck you think you are to come barreling into my life like this—"

"You know who I am and I know what you're going through."

"You don't."

"I lost my brother—"

"I lost my fucking *husband*. It's not the same."

"It's not exactly the same, no, but we both lost someone we loved. Someone who was a part of us. It's similar enough that I can still understand what you're going through."

"You can't."

I bit back a sigh. *Patience, remember? Patience!* "Grief can be heavy. Why don't you let me help you lighten it?"

He scraped a thumbnail across his forehead and tipped his head down until his chin rested on his chest, rising and falling quicker than normal.

He was about to unravel. Again.

I quickly set my mug behind me and pushed off the counter, trying not to step on Timber's toes as he frantically circled me.

When I got to Chase, I plucked the coffee mug from his fingers and went back to set it on the counter next to mine. Not wasting any time, I returned to him.

His hands were now clenched into fists as he struggled to keep himself together and fight back the tears.

Today was his breakthrough. He was finally releasing everything he'd kept bottled up inside. It might hurt like hell right now, but when it was over, I had hope he would feel better and see his future more clearly. As well as realize he had people in his life who loved and cared about him.

Who wanted him to remain on this Earth. Who wanted him to be happy and whole again and no longer fractured into pieces.

As soon as his body hiccuped, he clenched his teeth and turned away from me.

To hide his falling apart. To hide those tears.

I knew what it was like because in the past, I had shed them myself. And like most men raised to believe that crying showed weakness, the truth was, doing so was cathartic.

He needed to allow himself this. He would never be able to move on and heal if he didn't face everything ripping him apart. Especially if he only ignored it and kept it packed away.

However, he wasn't the only one hurting, I hurt for him, too.

I wished I could help ease his pain, even if only a little. Despite my wish, this was a path he needed to take himself. I couldn't do it for him. I could only walk alongside him and stay within reach in case he needed me.

Timber stood between us, his head tilted as he listened to Chase's attempt at smothering his sobs. I nudged my dog out of the way and pressed my naked chest to Chase's bare back. Hooking an elbow around his neck and an arm around his middle, I pulled him into me.

Immediately, he tensed, every muscle once again turning to concrete. Enfolding him in my arms felt like hugging a concrete statue.

It would take time to rid himself of everything he kept locked up deep inside. He might not realize it now, but every minute of that extraction would be worth it. A little short-term suffering could ease the long-term pain.

As we stood at the window, I embraced him for what seemed like hours, when in actuality it might've only been ten minutes.

Even after his cries turned silent, his tears were still deafening.

Once his breathing finally shallowed and he relaxed in my arms, he began to slip to the floor, no longer having the energy to hold up his own weight.

I went with him, not willing to break our connection. I wanted him to know I was there for him as long as he needed me.

Placing my lips at his temple, I vowed, "You can fight me all you want, but I've got you and I'm not letting you go."

I wasn't going anywhere. Wild grizzlies would have to rip me away.

AFTER DIGGING THROUGH HIS CABINETS, I found a jar of pasta sauce and a box of spaghetti, so that was what I made him later that night, once I could convince him to eat. We ended up eating outside on the porch overlooking the lake.

More like, I ate and he picked at his food. A happy Timber scarfed down some of his leftovers.

Even though I caught Chase staring at the water, he made no more mention of his wedding ring. That didn't mean he wouldn't go back in to search for it the second I left.

So, I didn't.

After washing the dirty dishes, I scrounged around for something more acceptable for Timber to eat besides pasta, then helped an emotionally-drained, physically-exhausted Chase into his bed and crawled in after him.

All without any resistance or a word of complaint from him.

Not even when I curled myself around him, pressed my nose into the back of his neck and held him all night.

Once his breathing turned slow and steady, I finally relaxed enough to allow my eyes to close. I was out in less than a minute since he wasn't the only one emotionally exhausted.

When I woke up, I woke up alone.

Shooting straight up in bed, it took me a few seconds to gather my bearings. Once I did, I realized...

No Chase. No Timber.

Shit.

My assumption was, if Chase went back into the lake, Timber would be running the shoreline barking at him in excitement.

Unless my dog saw a damn squirrel and ran off again.

Shit.

I rolled out of bed and rushed to the window. No dog to be seen. More importantly, not one ripple in the lake.

Was I too late, or was I too early?

I quickly dug a pair of dry, clean boxers out of Chase's top dresser drawer and yanked them up my legs.

My nostrils flared when it hit me...

The smell of bacon. And coffee.

My stomach growled and I breathed a little easier since Timber had zero skills at cooking.

I grinned and as soon as I yanked open the bedroom door, the smell of breakfast hit me right in the face.

Chase being up and cooking could mean he was feeling better this morning.

Of course, where he stood at the stove, Timber sat right next to him, staring up at him in longing, his tongue hanging out and a long string of saliva clinging to it.

My dog was pining for a piece of something he was forbidden to have. "No bacon for him."

Chase, only dressed in loose gray cotton shorts that clung nicely to his ass, glanced over his shoulder. "Too late." He went back to flipping the crackling bacon in a cast iron skillet with a fork.

"Then I guess you'll be on doggy diarrhea duty."

"I don't think so since he's leaving with you."

"Oh, I'm not invited for breakfast?" I asked, stepping up behind him and secretly glaring at my dog for eating pork.

"After breakfast," he responded, removing the bacon from the pan and setting the crispy strips onto a paper towel-lined plate to drain some of the fat.

"Smells good," I murmured as he cracked eggs one-handed into the same pan he'd cooked the bacon. "But all that bacon grease might harden my arteries." Chase wearing those ass-clinging shorts was about to harden something else.

As he monitored the eggs in the pan, I curled my arm around his waist and pressed a kiss to his warm skin at the center of his bare broad back.

He jerked, then put the fork down and turned in my arms to face me. I thought he'd push me away, but, instead, surprised the hell out of me when he wrapped his arms around me. "Thank you."

Holy shit. I wasn't expecting gratitude, either. "For what?"

"For yesterday. For last night." He sighed. "For putting up with me when you don't have to."

The second Timber whined because he wasn't getting any attention, Chase released me and turned back to the stove.

Thanks, dog, for ruining that moment. "Has he been out?"

"Yes."

Damn. "You're good with him. You should get a dog."

"I don't want a dog."

"They make the best companions." And so would I.

"I'm fine here by myself."

"Why are you so stubborn?"

"Just to annoy you."

Since he wasn't facing me, I couldn't tell if he was teasing or being honest. Two weeks ago I would not have even questioned it. It would've been the second one. This morning, it might actually be the first. "Well, you've succeeded. You can stop at any time now. It's exhausting."

"You don't have to be here."

"You're right. I don't. But I am, so don't be a dick."

Grabbing a spatula from the counter, he flipped the eggs, let them cook for a few seconds, then put two perfectly fried eggs on each plate, along with four strips of bacon.

When he was done, he carried both plates over to the table with Timber on his heels, leaving a trail of drool in his path. "Can you grab us coffee?"

After grabbing us two mugs, we sat down to eat breakfast like yesterday hadn't even happened. It was both reassuring and worrisome at the same time.

Could this be the calm before another storm? Or had last night finally been his turning point? Was it possible he was finally ready to move forward with his life and work toward happiness?

Sitting across from each other, he avoided my eyes and concentrated on his food, eating more enthusiastically than he had last night with dinner.

That could be a good sign.

"It's good," I murmured before shoving another forkful of fried egg into my mouth.

"It's over-easy eggs and bacon. A monkey could make it."

Maybe. But a monkey didn't make it, Chase actually made *me* breakfast. He hadn't kicked me out the door last night, he let me sleep while he took my dog out and cooked me a meal.

I didn't want to make a big deal out of it, but to me, it was a *huge* deal. And I appreciated this turnabout.

As soon as we were both done eating, he grabbed our empty plates, then came back for our mugs. Once he refilled them both, he tipped his head toward the door. I figured he wanted me to leave now that we were done.

"Let's sit outside."

Well look at that, I was wrong.

I nodded, trying not to get too giddy, and followed him out onto the porch, moving our still damp jeans from the two rocking chairs to the porch railing so we could sit.

Once we settled in the rockers, we sipped our coffee in companionable silence while Timber explored and marked the yard. Luckily, remaining in my view.

For a second, I could see us sitting out here every morning together, sharing silence and the surrounding nature, while sipping on coffee before we both started writing for the day.

I shouldn't get ahead of myself. I didn't want to jinx it. I also didn't want to be disappointed.

Chase was the first man in a long time I had any serious interest in.

Like Chase, I should look into attending therapy because I had to be nuts to take on him and his issues.

Unfortunately, the heart wanted what the heart wanted, no matter what the mind kept saying. Or warning me about.

Out of the corner of my eye, I could see Chase focused on the calm lake before us. "Tell me about him," I urged softly.

He took a long sip of coffee and when he was done, he turned toward me with a furrowed brow. "Why?"

"I want to know you better and he's a big piece of you."

"I'm surprised you want to get to know me better after how I treated you."

I lifted and dropped one shoulder. "Like I said last night, I understand how hard this loss is for you. Losing my brother was hard, too." I added, "And unexpected." What I assumed Thomas's loss was for Chase.

It couldn't be because of a long, drawn-out illness. His loss had been sudden with no time for Chase to mentally prepare.

"Have you talked to anyone?"

He turned to face the lake again, effectively avoiding my eyes. "The person I used to talk to is gone."

"I meant a professional."

"No. A therapist won't undo what's been done."

Maybe not, but they could still help him manage his grief. "Sometimes it's good to talk it out. My guess is that you've been keeping his loss close to the vest by not talking about him or whatever happened."

He tipped his mug to his lips, guzzled down the rest of his coffee and placed his empty mug on the floor next to his rocking chair. Dragging his fingers through his hair, he watched Timber exploring the edge of the tree line.

His chest slowly rose when he took a deep breath and I almost fell right out of my rocker when he actually began to talk…

Of course, I listened.

"We met in our early twenties. I was a junior at Brown University and he was working a frozen custard stand on the boardwalk in Ocean City, Maryland, where me and a few of my buddies went for spring break."

"He wasn't also in school?"

Chase shook his head, but remained focused on Timber who was on the trail of some fascinating scent. "No. He struggled in high school so he gave up on going to college."

He paused as if waiting for me to ask more questions, but I was doing my damnedest to keep my mouth shut and avoid asking a barrage of questions. Admittedly, a difficult feat for me. Especially when I wanted to know more about why Thomas struggled in school.

I had my guesses.

"We hit it off right away and practically spent all of spring break together. By the end of the week, I couldn't imagine never seeing him again and it was the same for him, so we began a long distance relationship while I finished school. It was a struggle to be apart but we managed to spend most of my breaks and summers together…"

Chase went on to tell me the summer after he graduated, he wrote his first book while working a job he hated.

After Thomas read the first draft, he told Chase the world needed to read it, too. He insisted Chase had real talent and his words should be shared with others. That spurred him to query an agent and ten months later, after almost giving up on hearing back, he finally received a response.

The agent requested the full manuscript and after he read it, immediately wanted to represent him and also said that the big name publishers would be fighting over the book.

His agent was right.

It turned out his manuscript went up for auction, the publishing rights were purchased for an insane amount of money, including a six-figure advance, and his author career snow-balled from there.

He gave up his crappy job, and pursued his dream of writing full-time.

Some of this I already knew from searching online, but I let him tell his story how he wanted and at the pace he was comfortable with. Amazingly enough, I managed not to interrupt once.

That could have to do with me biting my tongue every time I was tempted.

"Thomas moved in with me as soon as I found a place after graduation. He always supported me both emotionally and financially while I continued to write. It didn't take long until I made more than Thomas and could return the favor."

Just like that, he stopped talking. Simply stopped. As if that was the end of the story. I knew better than that.

Remembering how they met was one thing, but not dealing with the rest…

I prompted him with, "You met and fell in love. You were supportive of each other… Sounds perfect."

He twisted his head and his dark brown eyes bore into me. "It wasn't perfect."

No relationship ever was, but I was trying to get him to continue.

Even though I knew there was a lot more story to be told, if this was all he'd give me today, I'd take those crumbs and hope he'd open up more later.

This could very well be the beginning of us sharing our lives with each other. Both past, present and future. Even if only as friends.

Of course, I wanted more but I wasn't sure if Chase would ever be ready for that.

"I'd never been with anyone else."

Whoa. That was one confession I hadn't expected to hear. "No one?"

He shrugged. "I'd kissed some men..." Then shook his head. "No, not men... *boys* in college before I met Thomas, but that was all. It never went further than making out, but those kisses helped confirm I was gay. When I met Thomas, I knew right from the beginning he was 'the one' and it felt right to take it further. So... we did. Along the way we became inseparable and also learned from each other, fell deeply in love and eventually... got married. It should've been perfect."

"No matter how good a relationship is, Chase, it will never be perfect. My suspicion is that if a relationship seems perfect, then it's most likely fake. That couple is hiding something. We all have our ups and downs. We all have our bad days. No matter how much we might love someone, plenty of moments will exist where that other person disagrees with, annoys or frustrates us. It's only human nature."

"Of course we had our bad moments. We were both passionate and we tended to argue over stupid stuff. But we didn't hold grudges and typical disagreements weren't our main problem."

"What was?"

When he scrubbed his hands down his face, I figured we were getting to the part that would be the most painful. I was tempted to find a roll of duct tape and seal my mouth shut so I wouldn't say anything that would stop him from talking.

When Timber ran up the steps, he came to me first for a quick scratch under the chin and then moseyed over to Chase to sit between his legs. The man buried his fingers in my Shepherd's thick double coat as he scratched, causing Timber's eyes to half-close in pure ecstasy.

Was I a little jealous of my dog? Hell yes. Not because Timber wanted another man's attention but because my dog was getting the physical attention I longed to get from Chase. But petting my dog when I was unsettled always seemed to soothe my soul and I didn't want to deny the same benefit to Chase.

Brushing his fingers down Timber's neck and back, he turned his dark eyes to me once more. "What I'm about to tell you goes no farther than us."

I nodded, mentally bracing myself.

His Adam's apple jerked up and then fell when he swallowed hard. "I need to hear you say it."

"What you tell me won't go any farther than my ears."

He stared at me for a few seconds and when I nodded to reassure him, he returned the nod. Turning his attention back to my dog, he continued. "Thomas had always struggled with depression. At first, he hid it from me. He was worried I wouldn't want to be with him if he was taking meds to control it. Basically, he was embarrassed. But then that embarrassment, or his shame of not being 'normal,' all stemmed back to how his parents treated him. They would not accept that he was gay. They would also not accept that he struggled with depression. They thought he'd snap out of both."

"Impossible."

I hated hearing stories about parents who were unaccepting of their own child. I'd been one of the lucky ones. It was a good reminder for me to call my parents later and thank them for being so understanding. They had no idea how easy they made my life by simply loving me unconditionally.

"Right. But no one could tell them that. They were uber-religious and he knew they wouldn't accept him like that. So, he faked being straight until he met me. He never let anyone see the real Thomas. He unwillingly had to play a 'part' to survive. It wasn't until after we fell in love that he finally began to shed some of the shame that had been deeply ingrained in him. He wore it like a cloak no matter how much I tried to help him remove it. Even so, I was there for him and supported him accepting himself, too."

This sounded familiar...

Chase was to Thomas the same as I wanted to be for Chase. If he'd let me.

"How old was he when he began to suspect he was gay?"

"When he was twelve or thirteen... He had questions, of course. But his biggest mistake was going to his parents. Something any child should be able to do." Chase frowned and shook his head, still petting Timber, whose head was now propped on his thigh. "His parents were appalled. They said being gay was a sin and that he needed help. The depression began after his parents forced him into conversion therapy as a fucking child." His fingers tensed on Timber's back, making my dog's eyes open, especially after Chase shouted, "A fucking child!" It echoed over the lake. "He couldn't be cured or fixed because he wasn't sick or broken! At least not then. He suffered through that hell and it permanently damaged him. That bullshit should be illegal everywhere. Just because we don't conform to someone else's beliefs doesn't mean we're broken and need to be fixed. We need to be accepted and respected for who we are."

Conversion therapy was the worst. I was once again grateful I had accepting and loving parents. I couldn't imagine being treated like there was something wrong with me and I had to be repaired like a broken vase.

"Chase, you're preaching to the choir here." I reached out and grabbed the hand he wasn't using to pet Timber and gave it a squeeze. "I was fortunate in the fact I didn't have to deal with any of that. Was I bullied about it in high school? Yes. I tried to stay as low-key as possible, but there was always one kid or another that tried to make me feel shitty, that made fun of me, or said ignorant things. But my parents supported me, they loved me no matter who I was, and they still do. My parents didn't suspect but when I came out to them, they acted like it was no big deal. They told me they'd love me no matter what. They wanted me to be happy no matter who I ended up with. If they're disappointed about anything, it's the fact I'm in my forties and I'm still single."

I lifted his hand to my mouth. When I brushed my lips across his knuckles, his fingers twitched in mine.

He had been so closed off for so long, it seemed that any kind of caring touch surprised him. That made my heart ache.

"Why *are* you still single?"

Damn it, I made the mistake of talking about myself and my parents, giving him the opportunity to latch on to that and avoid continuing his own story.

"Quite simply… I haven't found the love of my life yet and I don't want to settle." I gave him a short, but truthful, answer because I needed to steer the conversation back to his relationship. It shouldn't be about me. "It would be nice if one day LBGTQ+ youth wouldn't have to come out at all. That everyone would be automatically accepted for whoever they are. That love and sexual attraction were strictly tied to individuals, not gender expectations. We need to lift up our youth, not tie them down so they struggle with life and suffer any permanent and debilitating damage. That sounds exactly like what happened to your husband."

CHAPTER 19

Rett

"When Thomas finally confessed what happened to him when he was younger, I did all kinds of research on conversion therapy to try to understand why he was suffering, why he struggled to get through every damn day."

I didn't know everything about conversion therapy, but I knew enough. Being a part of the LGBTQ+ community, I was aware a lot of states had banned it because it had been proven to be totally ineffective and ended up doing more harm than anything else.

The fact that people thought it was possible for someone to change their sexual orientation or gender identity, usually by force, enraged me as it probably did Chase. Those youth were not accepted by their own family and community as they existed and were repeatedly told something was wrong with them, that they should be ashamed for who they were attracted to or loved.

The fact was, trying to "convert" a child's sexual orientation or gender identity increased the chance of depression and tripled the chance of driving that youth to commit suicide. A high number even succeeded, a tragedy in itself.

"That program broke him. His parents rejecting him for who he was devastated him. As soon as he was old enough to get out of their house, he left and never talked to them again."

I couldn't imagine not being accepted for who I was and being forced to become someone else. By sending him to take part in that barbaric practice, Thomas was told by his own flesh and blood he'd be rejected unless he changed an integral part of himself, even though it was impossible.

Like Lady Gaga's song stated, "*Baby, I was born this way.*"

From what Chase said, Thomas played the part of being reformed until he could escape. But by then, the irreparable damage had already been done.

This harmful so-called "therapy" should be considered a criminal act and outlawed in every damn state. The fact that it hadn't been yet was appalling. Anyone who forced a child into conversion therapy should be the ones ashamed, not the youth trying to live their own truth.

"When he took his meds, he was the Thomas I fell in love with. Unfortunately, when life was going well, when he felt good, what he called 'normal,' he tended to stop taking them. I watched him like a hawk but not closely enough, apparently. Because I missed it. I missed the damn signs that he was spiraling into a dark hole." He tightened the grip on our interlaced fingers, to the point of bordering on pain. "Unfortunately, I had been on a tight deadline and locked away in my office to get all the words down. I missed those signs even though he was way more important to me than any amount of money or success. He was definitely more important than my fictional characters. If he had only reached out... just said *something*... I would have turned off my computer, stepped away from that damn book, told my agent and publisher to fuck off and I would've done whatever I needed to do to save him. Honestly, I thought he had finally found his peace once we got together. That his life with me, for the most part, was happy and content. That we were solid." His words caught in his throat and he roughly cleared it. "I was so fucking wrong."

I didn't encourage him to continue. I wanted Chase to only tell his and Thomas's story if he was ready. I could already see in his face how much of a toll this was taking on him.

Even so, telling this story could be cleansing for him.

"If only I'd recognized his struggle. Why didn't I? Was I so damn busy? Was everything else sucking up my time and pulling my attention from him? Nothing... *Nothing* was more important to me than Thomas. Not one damn thing. And for a moment, I forgot that. I forgot because I thought he was okay. He acted okay. I was wrong. He was suffering while plastering on a smile. Using it as a mask to hide the truth from the world. A mask to hide it from me, the one person who would be there for him when he wasn't okay. All he had to do was say something. All I had to do was pay attention. And in that moment I let my guard down... That was all it took. One slip on my part. One slip on his."

My breakfast churned in my stomach. I wanted to take Chase in my arms and relieve his grief and his guilt. While a simple hug wouldn't be able to do it, I hoped continuing to listen would at least help somewhat.

"That day..." He squeezed his eyes shut and swallowed. He kept them closed when he continued, most likely reliving *that* day. "That day I had a meeting with my PR firm to discuss the plans for my next release. On my way home I got stuck in the backlog behind a crash and was worried I'd be late for our dinner reservations. As soon as I got into the house, I called out to him." Chase shook his head, opened his eyes and turned them toward the lake. "He never responded. I rushed upstairs, took a quick shower, figuring he was out back waiting for me to get home..." He pulled in a long, slow breath and released it along with the words, "When I opened the closet to grab my dress clothes..."

When Chase paused, my breath seized. My fingers were

cramping from how tightly I held his hand. Because I knew what was coming and it filled me with dread.

I *knew*, but that didn't mean I was prepared.

If I wasn't prepared simply hearing what had come next, I couldn't imagine how unprepared Chase had been when he actually lived those life-changing moments.

I could barely hear his whispered, "I found him. He was in there."

I closed my eyes, *trying* to imagine what Chase discovered, *trying* to imagine how devastating it would be to find the one you loved like that...

But unless you lived it, could you really imagine it?

"If I had been home sooner..."

I opened my eyes and jerked on his hand so he'd look at me. Once our eyes met I asked, "You think it was your fault? For being late?" more harshly than I should have. I couldn't help it because my first urge was to yell and shake him, for blaming himself for something out of his control, for a desperate action someone else took, but I bit it back because it would do more harm than good.

"No, it was more than that. Being late was only one thing. When I look back now, there was a list of things leading us to that moment, for him to do what he did. That morning, he kissed me longer than normal when we said goodbye. Only, I didn't know it would be for the last time. I was in a rush and became impatient because he wouldn't let go. But *I* forgot. *I* forgot to pause and check in with him. That's on me.

"Somehow I missed that he had stopped going to therapy and taking his meds. I didn't ask and I should have. In the end, I don't know why he gave up. Why he decided to stop living. I would've done anything I could if he'd been open with me about his latest struggle. If he would've simply talked about it with me. We had fought so many other battles together. But this one... This one he fought alone."

Chase untangled his hand from mine and scrubbed it down his

shorts. His mouth opened but it took a minute before anything more came out.

"He fought alone. And he lost. He. Fucking. Lost. Because of that, I lost, too. I'm nothing without him. Nothing. When he took his life, he took mine along with it, leaving only a shell behind. An empty fucking shell."

As much as I wanted to insist what he was saying wasn't true— that he wasn't nothing, he wasn't only a shell, he was so much more —I wouldn't discount what he said. If that was how he felt, then that was what he believed. He owned that and I wasn't going to steal it from him.

However, there were other ways to convince him otherwise. To show him that he still had a life to live. That others still valued him.

His family. His fans. Me.

"Why?" His question was strained and agonizingly raw. Every ounce of that single word was felt deep into my very soul. "Why would he want me to find him? Why would he do that to me?" His voice cracked along with my heart.

I didn't know what to say, what to do to ease his pain. It ran a lot deeper than I originally thought since he felt responsible and blamed himself.

I wasn't sure if that would ever change.

I didn't want or need to ask for more details on his husband's suicide. I could guess it had to do with why the doors had been removed from the closets and never replaced. Something not normally done. Making him say it out loud wouldn't be fair to him. If he wanted to tell me, to dig up more from where he kept it buried, I'd listen. No matter how hard or uncomfortable it would be for us both. Him for reliving that nightmare. Me for living it along with him.

Even though I was willing to listen to whatever he said, no matter how difficult it would be to hear, I wasn't expecting his next words to chill me to the bone.

"I'll never unsee the scuff marks on the back of the door from him kicking. I don't know if it was just an instinctive reaction from him…" Chase shook his head again like he was trying to shake that memory free. "Or if he regretted his decision and was fighting to live. I'll never know because I didn't get home in time to save him. And because he didn't leave a note, he gave me no closure. Not even an 'I love you' or an 'I'm sorry' for leaving me. Not an apology for knowing I'd be the one—not a stranger—to find him. He *knew* that and chose to do it there and in that way regardless. The person who loved him the most found him. The person who loved and accepted him despite his faults and issues. The person who had been supportive and promised to stand by his side through thick and thin. The person who vowed to stay with him through it all, including sickness and health."

The hand that wasn't buried in Timber's coat bunched into a fist.

"I said my vows because I meant every damn word of them. I thought he did, too. I'm not going to lie… There were a few times I considered joining him. To ensure we'd be together forever. For the longest time, I didn't think I could go on without him. But then, I thought about how I felt afterward. Completely gutted. Betrayed. Destroyed."

While suicide ended the agony for the one taking their own life, it was only the beginning of the same for those left behind. Sometimes the person couldn't see past their own suffering to realize that fact.

"So, here I am. For the last two years, doing my best to survive despite the fact all I wanted to do was give up. Yesterday you reminded me of the reason I didn't end it after I found him. I didn't want to do the same to my family. To the people who loved me and who I'd leave behind."

While what Thomas did wasn't Chase's fault, the guilt still weighed heavily on him. I'm sure he suffered from nightmares from finding the man to whom he pledged his heart.

When silence encompassed us, I waited to see if there was anything left for him to say, for him to unbury.

After it seemed he was done, that he had emptied out everything he was willing to rid himself of, I finally spoke. "Life has a way of bulldozing us over, Chase. Sometimes we get buried. Other times we get up and brush ourselves off. But doing so takes a lot of energy. Some people get to the point where they no longer have enough energy to keep going, to keep pushing. To wade through the darkness to find the light. Especially if that light is merely a flicker."

I wasn't sure if what I said would help, but right now I felt helpless and I had nothing else to give him. As an author, you'd think I'd know the right words to say. Unfortunately, that wasn't how it worked. Fictional characters were just that and a living, breathing person's suffering couldn't begin to compare.

Once I rose from the rocking chair, I moved Timber out of the way so I could go to my knees at Chase's feet. After wrapping my arms around his waist, I lay my head in his lap. It wasn't exactly an embrace but it *was* a physical connection. Whether he needed or appreciated me holding him or not, I didn't know. However, I needed it myself after everything I'd just learned.

"I'm sorry you had to deal with that. I'm sorry you lost the man you loved. But you were right, your loss was nothing like mine. I miss my brother so much that it still hurts years later, but his death was caused by an untimely and unfortunate accident. Thomas's was intentional. By easing his suffering, he handed it off to you. He might not have even been aware that would happen."

"Probably not, since he wasn't thinking clearly. I found out later he stopped taking his meds and going to therapy for a while because he mistakenly thought he was better." When he went to spin his wedding band, of course, it wasn't there.

I sat up, grabbed his hand and pressed my lips to the ring of pale skin circling his finger. The indentation left behind would eventually fill out and the skin would tan enough to match the rest of him. Or one day another ring could very well replace it.

Chase closed his eyes and whispered, "I'm afraid of forgetting him."

"You don't need your ring to remember him."

"Touching it is a habit. A way for me to feel closer to him."

"It's habit now, but even without your ring, I promise you won't ever forget him. You couldn't, Chase, even if you tried because he left his mark here." I pressed my fingers over his heart. "We don't forget the ugly and we don't forget the beautiful. We tend to forget the mediocre. And from what you've told me, your love was far from mediocre."

"No matter how strong our love was, it couldn't heal the damage already done."

Unfortunately, in this case, that was true. "Sometimes love isn't enough, no matter how strong it is, and that's not your fault. You loved him more than anyone and I'm sure he knew that. Think of all the good years you surrounded him with your love and acceptance."

He nodded and blew out a breath, turning his dark eyes down to me, still on my knees, clinging to him to show my support. "I've never told anyone any of this. I didn't think I'd ever be capable of it. I'm not even sure why I told you. But one thing I do know, I never want to talk about it again."

"I'll take it as a compliment that you were comfortable enough around me to tell me. Thank you for sharing so I could understand what you're dealing with."

He had opened up to me and I considered that a huge step. For him and for us.

Of course, I realized there wasn't an 'us.' But him telling me what he did meant he trusted me enough to do so and proved he valued my friendship, so I was taking that as a positive step forward. I hoped things would continue to grow between us from here on out.

We could work on the rest as slowly or as quickly as Chase wanted. I was willing to give him all the time he needed. However, if he didn't want the same as I did, if he wanted us to remain platonic, I would accept that, too.

I was simply grateful to find someone I could relate to living so close.

As soon as he stood and drew me to my feet, he went over to

stand at the railing. Where the sun was in the sky caught my attention.

Shit. It was getting to be late morning and I needed to go open The Next Page before someone in town worried that something had happened to me. I didn't want to leave him, though. Truthfully, I wasn't *ready* to leave him. He just ripped himself open and was still exposed.

I grimaced. "I need to go open the bookstore, but I don't want to leave you alone."

When he turned to face me, his expression was solemn but he did seem to be okay. At least on the surface. I hoped it wasn't an act. "I'll be fine."

"I'm sure you will, but I won't. Promise me you won't do anything stupid. If you promise me that, I'll promise to find someone with either a waterproof or underwater metal detector so we can find your ring."

He gave me a lopsided smile that really wasn't a true smile and didn't quite reach his eyes. "I promise not to do anything stupid."

I shook my finger at him, forcing my own grin so I wouldn't look worried. "I'm going to hold you to that."

Before I could put my hand down, he grabbed my wrist and yanked me into him, circling his arms tightly around me, catching me totally off guard.

He pressed his forehead to mine and we stood in that embrace for a surprisingly long time.

Eventually, Chase whispered, "Thank you."

If that didn't warm my thumping heart, nothing would. "You don't have to thank me," I whispered back, meaning every word.

"Yes, Rett, I do."

"You don't have to thank me."
"Yes, Rett, I do."

That exchange not only made my heart melt, it left a crack behind. Chase followed those words with taking my lips in a tender kiss. Afterward, he again clung to me for the longest time. We simply shared a space so he could emotionally recover from the damage done by him discussing that day.

I stood in his arms for as long as he needed it, until he eventually released me, even if reluctantly on both of our parts.

Him opening up to me could be Chase's chance at a new beginning. Of course, he'd never forget Thomas, both their love and their ending. But maybe the sharp edges surrounding that tragic end would soften and he'd allow himself to heal, instead of continually beating himself up over something he never had control over. Even though he mistakenly thought he did.

If Thomas hadn't done what he did that particular day, there was no guarantee it wouldn't have happened another time since depression was a daily battle.

My heart skipped a beat when, before I left, he asked if I would return later.

Chase Jones was no longer pushing me away, but pulling me closer. Our connection might be tentative and fragile at this point, but it did exist.

I was now confident it would only get stronger.

I would throw an overnight bag into my truck before heading up to his cabin tonight, just in case…

The excuse I told myself was that I didn't want to have to borrow Chase's clothes again to come home like I had this morning. Another good reason to pack a bag was to bring along swim shorts. Because after calling Harry at the hardware store, I had scored an underwater metal detector.

With it, I planned on searching for Chase's wedding ring.

For his sake, I hoped I could find it. But then, I was determined not to give up until I did.

Just like I was determined not to give up on the man himself.

CHAPTER 20

Chase

ALMOST EVERY NIGHT for the past three weeks, once Rett closed down the store for the day, he'd load himself and his dog into his truck and trek up the mountain to join me. In all that time we did nothing but talk and spend our nights together, sharing both dinner and a bed.

What we did not do was have sex.

After stirring up and releasing everything I'd been holding inside, I wasn't ready. He respected that, even though I had spotted lube and condoms in the overnight bag he brought with him.

I had volunteered to come down to his place and spend the night a few times, but he was fine with staying with me in my cabin, a place safe from curious eyes. It turned out he was worried about small-town gossip, even when there was nothing to gossip about. Yet.

Tonight that would change. I was ready to move forward with intimacy between us since my head was in a better place than three weeks prior.

Only he wasn't aware of my plans.

I no longer looked at him as an annoying pest trying to tear down my walls. Because no matter how much I resisted, he somehow had succeeded to break through my barriers.

In those three vital weeks, I had opened my heart and welcomed him in to start filling that void.

It wasn't love. For now it was respect, a solid friendship and valuable companionship.

Not once had he pushed for sex. Instead, he patiently waited for me to be ready.

I hadn't pushed him for sex, either, because I was waiting for the time to be right. However, I was done waiting.

More importantly, I didn't want to move forward with anybody but Rett.

One reason I waited was I was well aware sex with him could get sticky. Even without him admitting it out loud, he obviously wanted more than a friendship with benefits. He didn't have to say it because I could see it in his actions, his reactions and in his choice of words. Also, in the way he looked at me.

Not once had he said no when I invited him to spend the night. Though, I expected him to eventually refuse out of frustration since I wasn't giving him what I was sure he wanted and waited for.

So yes, he hinted but didn't push. What he did was leave the door cracked and when I was ready to open it, he'd be waiting on the other side.

Even though I still couldn't fathom why he'd want a relationship with me, I appreciated the fact the man had an endless supply of patience and understanding when it came to dealing with me, my past and my issues.

I honestly didn't believe I was worth the effort. He begged to differ.

I smirked. Maybe he was a little touched in the head. That possibility made me think we might be good together.

Together.

Was I really considering another relationship when I swore to myself I was done with them? Especially when it came to a man I'd only known a few months and during most of that time I kept pushing him away?

The second I heard his truck making its way up Coleman Lane, I finished the last sentence in the current chapter I was writing and closed my laptop. I was now very familiar with the grunts and groans of his Chevy when it climbed my mountain.

Despite attempting to patch some of the deep crevices and holes, as soon as we got a good storm, the rain would wash away the soil and stone I used. I decided it wasn't worth my effort. Unless I paid to have the whole dirt road paved—which would cost a fortune—I'd have to live with it the way it was. Or more like, *we* would since Rett coming to the cabin had turned into a nightly thing.

Not once in the past two weeks had he slept in his own bed. If he did, it was due to him sneaking in a nap during the day.

Once I tossed my ring into the lake and after the next morning expelling everything bottled up inside me, the words seemed to flow much easier from me. I was relieved to finally get back into my writing groove and I had Rett to thank for it.

As I glanced at my still empty ring finger, I waited for Timber to come tearing around the cabin and onto the porch for his expected ear and butt scratches. Another routine that had become habit. Surprisingly, one I actually looked forward to.

I never thought I'd be so damn invested in a dog. As well as his owner.

But this evening it wasn't only Timber rushing around the corner. What I first thought was a black bear cub followed on his heels, attempting to bite his tail as the Shepherd trotted toward me.

I squinted. What the hell *was* that?

"What the hell is that?" I shouted my question as Rett trailed the two animals at a much slower pace. "You got another dog?"

"No."

No? "What is it, then?"

"I mean, yes, I got another dog. But not for me."

The black puppy had a blocky head, a shaggy coat and massive paws. I was right with my first guess. A puppy parading around as a black bear cub.

"Her name is Onyx."

"You didn't tell me you were getting another dog. Is she house trained?" Last thing I needed was a puppy doing its business all over the interior of my cabin.

"Since she's ten-weeks old, I'll give you one guess."

Great. "And you expect her to sleep in my bed tonight?" That wasn't going to happen, even if he said yes. I was not waking up in a wet spot. At least not the kind of wet spot most straight men preferred.

"Not yet. I brought a crate and a dog bed along with me."

He did what?

The puppy managed to finally get her jaws around Timber's tail and she started playing tug of war with it. Timber seemed as patient with the rowdy puppy as Rett had been with me.

"Onyx!" Rett scolded as he climbed the stairs and approached me at the small table where I worked outside.

I had already received a couple of bids on adding a large all-season room that would almost double the square footage of my cabin. Until then, while the weather was nice, I continued to work out on the porch.

"Onyx," I repeated in a huff.

Rett cursed as he pried open the puppy's jaws from around poor Timber's tail. "You can change it if you don't like it."

I blinked. "Why would I change the name of your dog?"

With a sigh—since Onyx now had a hold of the bottom of his pant leg and was ripping on it with gusto, all while growling, of course—Rett plopped into the seat next to me. "Because she's yours."

I stared at him like he'd lost his damn mind. Because he had. "I'm sorry... what?"

"You don't have to be sorry, just thank me."

I shook my head. "For what?"

"For getting you a loyal companion."

"You must have knocked that thick head of yours hard enough to make you forget that I told you I didn't want a dog."

"She's a puppy."

"That will grow into a *dog*." I needed to dial down my rising voice as well as my panic of possibly being responsible for another living, breathing thing.

Rett flipped a hand toward the lake. "You like to swim in that cold-ass water. In case you're unaware, Newfies *love* to swim. You shouldn't swim alone and now you won't have to."

"Why would I need a dog to go swimming with me?"

"What if you drown?"

"That answer is simple. I drown. What's a dufus-looking puppy going to do?"

"Drag you out of the water."

"You have a lot of faith in that twenty-pound puppy that's all paws and hair."

He ignored that. "I brought you supplies, too. You're welcome."

"I didn't thank you and I don't need supplies because I don't want a damn dog."

Rett shrugged. "Too late."

"Does it shed?"

"Does a dog have hair? I included a shedding comb and a brush in the bag of supplies. I'll grab it from my truck later."

He would do what? "Does it drool?"

Rett shook his head. I wasn't sure if that was a negative answer or him being impatient.

"How big is it going to get?"

"Can you just say thank you?"

"No."

"It's only two words."

"And that," I pointed to the puppy now chewing on a chair leg, "is at least a ten year commitment."

"One you'll thank me for later."

"You mean once all of my furniture is destroyed by teeth marks? Sure I will. Don't be surprised if you find a puppy tied to the front porch of your store."

He sighed. "Then I will load her into my truck again and drive her back up here."

"I don't want a dog."

"You've made that clear."

"Then you should respect my decision."

"If it was a valid one."

"Rett."

"Chase. Trust me on this. I promise you'll thank me later."

"With bags of lit dog shit on your welcome mat?"

"I thought we were long past the part where you're a complete asshole."

I tilted my head and raised my eyebrows at him. "We are?"

He huffed, "If we're not, can you hurry up and get there?"

I sighed and once the puppy stopped gnawing on my wood chair, she came over and flopped into a sloppy sit in front of me.

I stared at her. She was damn big for a ten-week-old puppy. "How big is she going to get?"

"Oh... Uh..." He rubbed his forehead and avoided my eyes. "I don't know... A hundred pounds... or so?"

I picked my jaw up off the wood-planked floor. "*Or so?* Why the hell would you think I'd want a dog that will be almost half my size when full grown and probably out eat me?"

"Because I see how good you are with Timber." I opened my mouth, but he stopped me with a raised palm. "Take it from me, Onyx will be good for you."

"I can't afford to feed her."

He rolled his eyes. "Oh please. You told me how much the advance was for the book you're working on. I don't want to hear that you can't afford it. Onyx could eat filet mignon every night and you'd still be okay financially."

"Why are you being so damn stubborn?"

He turned toward me with a raised eyebrow. "*Me?*"

"Yes, you."

His second eyebrow joined the first halfway up his forehead. "Have you looked in the mirror?"

"Yes, and what's reflected back at me in that mirror is a perfectly reasonable guy."

Rett snort-laughed. "*Ooooo*-kay, then. I see someone's delusional this evening."

"Yes *he* is, since *he*, without asking me first, brought me a hundred-pound dog that will eat me out of house and home."

"Oh my god," Rett muttered, dropping his head and shaking it. "You win. I'll take her back to the breeder tomorrow."

He would do what?

I pursed my lips and stared at the puppy as I considered my options. I could kill Rett for overstepping once again, I could send Onyx home with him and have him take her back to where she came from or...

I groaned. "Fine. I can take her for a test drive."

"She's not a car."

"She'll probably be as big as one."

"On the days you don't take a dip in that ice bath, you can take her hiking with you. She'll also be a good snuggler on cold winter nights and—"

"Isn't that what you're for?"

When I cut him off, his mouth had been open and after my question, it still hung there. No words came out.

Damn. I actually made the man speechless for once. I thought that was impossible.

When he was capable of speech again, he said, "I'm not here every night."

"Aren't you?" In the past three weeks, he didn't sleep next to me for only two. He was splitting hairs.

"Don't act like you don't ask me to come here every night and I've forced my way into your life against your will."

"Rett…"

He lifted a hand and grinned. "Okay, I'll admit… I didn't believe that lie myself."

One side of my mouth pulled up.

His mouth dropped open again. "Whoa. Is that a grin I see?"

"No."

He rose from his seat, came to stand in front of me, and nudged my legs wider apart with his knee so he could step between them. "Now who's lying?"

My half-grin turned into a smirk. "I really didn't want a dog, Rett."

"Too late."

"I'll keep her if you're going to help take care of her."

"I have no problem with that."

"That means more time up here."

"Jokes on you. I have no problem with that, either," he repeated, the smile on his face spreading.

I grabbed his hips and pulled him closer. "I've been thinking…"

He groaned. "Should I be concerned?"

"Only if you didn't bring condoms and lube with you. If you didn't, then yes, you should be concerned. As you probably know, using spit just isn't the same."

He fisted my hair, used it to tip my head back and turn it left to right, as he squinted at me. "What happened to Chase Jones? Did aliens take him and replace him with someone else? Someone who grins and makes jokes, even as horrible as they are? Do I even know this stranger sitting before me?"

I shrugged. "The point is… I'd like to get to know you better."

"You've known me for months."

"Naked."

His mouth formed an O. "*Ooooh.*"

"Starting tonight."

"*Oooooooh.*"

"So, if you didn't bring lube you might be saying *ouch* instead of *oooooh*."

"If I didn't, Harry's Hardware isn't that far away."

A chuckle slipped from me before I could rein it in. "Are you talking WD-40?"

"Wow. Look at you. Totally hilarious. Really, who is this new Chase? I'd like to get to know him better, too."

"I'm ready for a fresh start. Thanks to you."

His smile disintegrated. "Me?"

I tipped my head. "You."

"No, Chase. You're the one responsible for your change, not me."

"If it wasn't for you, I'd still be," there was no other word for it, "miserable."

"I'm glad I could help, but I can't take the credit."

"If it wasn't for you, I'd still be stuck in my personal hell," I said more firmly this time.

"I... don't know what to say."

"Say you brought lube and condoms."

"Of course I did. I'm no fool."

"Then we're good."

He pulled away, his eyes serious and his brow furrowed. "Are we, Chase? Are we good? Are you *really* ready for this?"

"It's all I've been thinking about."

Those same eyes narrowed on me. "For how long?"

"At least a week."

"And you're only wanting to have sex with me now? We've been sleeping next to each other every damn night."

"Think of the anticipation as foreplay."

"More like edging. I've been waiting..."

"I know."

"I want this more than you know."

"I want this, too. But I wanted to make sure I was in the right head space first. It wouldn't be fair to you if I wasn't. Like that first time."

He searched my face. "Do you consider that first time a mistake?"

I had to be careful about my choice of words. I didn't want to hurt Rett in any way, shape or form. "No, it wasn't a mistake. It was the first step to lifting me out of my dark pit of despair."

"And you're out of it now?"

He didn't seem to believe me. "Don't you think I am?"

"No, not completely."

I'd give him that. "I'll never not love or miss him, Rett. I've always been upfront about that."

"I know. It would be selfish of me to think otherwise. I wouldn't want that, anyway. What you two had together was special. It might not have been perfect, but it was certainly true love."

"Thank you."

"For what? Recognizing that truth?"

"Not being jealous over my love for my husband."

"Never. Here's the thing... Knowing you can love that hard, that completely, gives me hope that one day you could love me just as much."

All the air in my lungs vanished. I could hardly breathe when an invisible band tightened around my chest. I stared up at him, unable to form any words.

Finally, when I could, I only managed to breathe his name. "Rett..."

His eyes shut for the second it took him to blow a breath out of his nostrils. "Forget I said that. I shouldn't have."

I swallowed down the lump in my throat. A lump formed from the fear of disappointing him. "You might be expecting too much from me."

His fingertips brushed along the wiry hairs covering my jawline. "I don't think so. Don't sell yourself short."

"I'm not. I just don't want to hurt you."

"Then don't."

An easy answer to a complex issue. "I wish it was that simple."

"It can be. If it becomes difficult, it's because you made it that way, Chase. You have the power. I've handed it to you for a reason."

"I appreciate that more than you know, but you didn't have to do that."

"Yes, I did. And look where we are right now because of it."

"And where are we?"

His brow wrinkled when his eyebrows lifted. "Well, it sounds like you're about to get laid."

I rose to my feet, making him take a step back. "Actually, it sounds like *you're* about to get laid."

"Tomatoes, *tomahtoes*. As long as we're making sauce…"

"We'll be making a white sauce, not red."

He blinked, rolled his lips inward, then he threw his head back and burst out in laughter. It was full and rich and came from deep inside him, echoing around the clearing surrounding my cabin.

When that glorious sound hit my ears, it made me smile in both pleasure and relief. I had been afraid that by being around me, I had dampened his joy in life. That me being a miserable prick had made him that way, too. Despite it being his choice to spend time with me.

Again, I didn't understand why he'd stuck it out, but I was damn glad he did.

If it wasn't for him…

No doubt… If it wasn't for him I'd be a wretched, lonely recluse. I had already been headed in that direction. The whole reason I bought this property. My plan was to hide from everyone. *Hell*, hide from life.

I owed him a lot for being stubborn and not giving up on me. I wasn't sure if I'd ever be able to pay him back in full. That didn't mean I wouldn't try.

"Why aren't you kissing me yet? Are you afraid of catching something?" he teased.

Yes, feelings.

I swallowed that truth back down. I feared it might be too late.

Those two nights he hadn't stayed with me in the first few weeks, I had actually missed him.

Really missed him. Imagine that.

It surprised me just as much.

The man had quickly become a habit. One I wasn't sure I wanted to break any time soon, or ever. I enjoyed our conversations. I enjoyed sharing my evening with him. I enjoyed seeing him sitting across from me at breakfast, sipping on coffee and chatting about his plans for the day while he also glared at me when I slipped Timber a bite of bacon or sausage.

When it came down to it... I just enjoyed being with him.

I couldn't forget that the night we had sex was enjoyable, too. It would've been a lot better if I had allowed myself to enjoy it instead of only going through the motions.

Tonight my head would be more in the game than it had been that night. Amazingly enough, my time with Rett had me feeling halfway human again.

If I wanted to admit the truth, it was more than halfway.

He and Timber barging their way into my life had done more for me than any therapist every could. The man seemed to have some sort of magical power.

However, there was no freaking way I was telling him any of this. I'd never hear the end of it.

Of course, right now, he had better things to do with his mouth. I'm sure he would agree.

CHAPTER 21

Chase

KEEPING my lips attached to Rett's in a very thorough, very deep and *very* arousing kiss, I walked him backwards toward my bedroom, using his hips to steer him as he gripped my face tightly with both hands.

If he tripped, we were both going down. Hopefully neither dog got in our way.

As soon as we went through the door from the porch into my cabin, I had pulled off his T-shirt, not paying attention to where it landed—apparently on Timber's head—until Rett made a noise at the back of his throat. Still refusing to break the kiss, I peered out of the corner of my eye and witnessed Onyx snag it, whipping it back and forth while trotting around proudly like she scored a prize.

I had no doubt Rett would need a new T-shirt after today. I didn't know much about puppies but I did know they could be destructive. A good explanation for why Rett had brought a crate along and not only a dog bed.

If we were finally going to have sex, I didn't want to be worried about the puppy destroying my home and distracting me.

Tonight I wanted to give Rett every ounce of my attention. Tonight I would show him how much I appreciated him and everything he'd done. Tonight I wanted to get lost in the man I was falling for, despite my resistance.

He deserved all of my focus and more.

It was about time he got something out of our "relationship" instead of it only being one-sided. He'd been the giver and now...

It was my turn.

When he pulled free of our kiss, he jerked his head back so he could see my face. "Why are you grinning?"

I pinned my lips together and shook my head. "No reason."

With a twist of his lips, he shot me a suspicious look. "You're up to something."

I shrugged. "I'm not, but that puppy will be. Can we put her somewhere to keep her out of trouble while we get into trouble?"

Rett wiggled his eyebrows. "*Mmm*. We're getting into trouble?"

"That had been the plan but you surprising me with a puppy I didn't want might ruin it."

He raised a finger between us. "Can you put a cork in this while I go get the crate and set it up? Or will that ruin the mood?"

"The mood will be ruined if she shits on the floor."

He grimaced. "You're right. Be right back."

As soon as I released his hips, he rushed past me toward the back door. I followed him to help bring in, not only his overnight bag since we'd need the condoms and lube he usually packed, but all of the puppy's supplies.

Someone went a little overboard with everything he brought. That meant we ended up taking several trips out to his truck and back to haul in all the canine loot. I had no idea dogs needed so much stuff.

Luckily, it didn't ruin the mood since Rett was working bare-chested. In fact, I had a hard time keeping my eyes off him to concentrate on digging out the toys, bowls and everything else the puppy would need.

A puppy that was apparently staying.

Rett put a big circle-shaped dog bed under the window in my bedroom and set up the large wire crate next to it. Once he lured the puppy inside the cage with a treat, he quickly closed the door and latched it.

"Just block out any whining," he instructed.

"From you or Onyx?"

He turned to face me with a single lifted eyebrow. "Remember when you said I wasn't funny enough to do stand-up?"

My lips twitched. "No."

"Uh huh. Well, I do. And you had no room to talk then and still don't. Don't give up your day job."

Timber climbed into the dog bed, circled it several times and finally flopped down with a groan while the puppy began the whining I was supposed to ignore.

I wasn't sure that would be possible. Was sex with ear plugs a thing? I guessed it would be if I owned a pair. "Do you have ear plugs in your bag?"

"Quiet, Onyx," Rett scolded over his shoulder as he approached me. "Actually, don't give up your day job, anyway. You're too good at what you do. You'd disappoint all of your readers and possibly cause a riot."

"I aim to please."

"That's all a man has to hear…" He grinned, wiggled his eyebrows and pointed to the bulge in his jeans.

"Have you been hard this whole time?"

"Not the whole time, but most of it. Are you saying I'm so small you haven't noticed?"

"Are you fishing for compliments?" I countered. The man was not small. He wasn't huge, either. He was just right.

"I know what I have," he announced proudly.

"Then you'll know the only reason I missed it was because I was put to work hauling in supplies for a four-legged creature."

"Well, now you can work on this three-legged creature." He jerked a thumb toward his chest.

A laugh burst from me.

"Damn," he whispered.

"What?"

"You don't know how good it is to hear you laugh."

I thought the same thing earlier when he'd done the same. "The truth is it feels good to laugh. Once again I have you to thank for that."

He stepped toe to toe with me and grabbed a fistful of my T-shirt. "If you keep thanking me like that, I'm going to get a swelled head... Oh wait," he grabbed my hand and pressed it to his erection, "too late."

I laughed again but didn't remove my hand. I cupped his denim-encased length instead. Hot, hard and so damn tempting.

But, yes, it felt good to finally laugh. And smile. And want to kiss the words right out of someone's mouth.

No, not just anyone. More specifically, Everett James Williams. A man who did not give up on me when I needed it the most.

"Since you have a grip on my shirt, why don't you take it off for me?" I suggested.

He purred, "Gladly."

After he yanked the shirt over my head, he tossed it on top of my dresser. I needed to get out of the habit of dropping clothes on the floor or leaving shoes out. Otherwise, with a puppy in the house, I might have to buy a new wardrobe.

I glanced at my open closet. I should also start thinking about re-installing the doors and see if doing so triggered me. No matter if it did or didn't, the cabin needed to be puppy-proofed if Onyx was staying.

No, not *if*, I already knew she was. My hope was she wasn't the only one staying.

I wasn't ready for him to move in, of course. It was way too early for that. While we'd slept together a lot recently, tonight would be only the second night we had sex. However, I did hope him staying over more often than not continued.

These last three weeks made it clear Eagle's Landing could now be officially called home. A permanent place to start over. A new place to restart my life.

I should probably make an effort to make some acquaintances in town so I wasn't labeled the weird, anti-social "writer" on the mountain. Not everyone knew I was author C.J. Anson yet, but eventually they would.

"My favorite animal…" Rett murmured as he raked his fingers down my chest and then followed the dark trail of hair until he paused at the waistband of my jeans. He began to unfasten them.

I tilted my head in question.

"A bare bear," he answered.

I brushed a hand across my hairy chest. "You like my carpet?"

"I love your carpet. It's the perfect fluffy pillow for my head when I fall asleep on your chest."

"So, I shouldn't shave it?"

Rett gasped dramatically. "Don't you dare."

"It gets hot in the summer."

"Baby, it's hot all year round." He added a sexy little growl to the end of that.

Wait… The corner of my eye twitched. "Baby?"

"You don't like it?"

I wasn't sure.

"You've never been called that before?"

"No."

"Just 'asshole?'"

"For a long time, that's what fit."

"Thankfully, things have changed."

"I'm sure you're relieved."

Rett wrapped his hand around the back of my neck and his mouth hovered over mine. "You have no idea."

He was wrong for once. I did have a good idea.

"If you don't like me calling you baby, then, since we're both supposed to be experts with words, we should be able to come up with something better. Like 'boo.'"

"A simple 'Chase' works but we can take 'baby' for a test drive, too. However, don't you dare call me 'boo.'"

He chuckled against my mouth. "Are we done talking now so we can get down to the important business, *Chase?*"

"You're the one who talks too—"

He stole the rest of my words when he captured my mouth. I let him have it for a few seconds before taking it back. "Pants off," I ordered.

His eyes lit up and he took a step back so we'd both have room to remove our shoes, socks and jeans. After our clothes ended up in a messy pile on top of my dresser, we stood facing each other naked.

My gaze swept down him from head to feet. Even though we hadn't had sex for a while, we had seen each other naked just about every day. What I was seeing wasn't anything new but seeing him totally naked still stopped me in my tracks every damn time.

Everything about the man was gorgeous. His appearance, his personality, his outlook on life.

Whether I knew it at first or not, he was exactly what I needed to get out of my funk. To return to some sort of normalcy. To be able to breathe easier without feeling like I was suffocating.

His patience and determination was the icing on the smart, attractive and funny cake. A cake I was hungry to eat.

I would still love and miss Thomas for the rest of my life but I had made room for Rett, too. Luckily, he didn't seem to mind sharing that space, another reason to really...

Like him.

He had found a place in my heart and filled some of that emptiness.

I deepened my voice and ordered, "On the bed."

His mouth curling into a smile was a clear "yes," but him shaking his head told me he didn't want that. "No, not yet."

"Then wha—" I swallowed the rest of that when he slid down my body and landed on his knees.

He was about to swallow something, too.

"Okay, then…"

He raised his eyes to mine and asked, "You sure?"

With a nod, I answered, "I'm okay with this delay."

He chuckled again and wrapped two fingers around the base of my aching cock. "You sure?" he asked again. "Because I don't want you to—"

I quickly cut him off. "I'm sure. Take your time."

His shoulders shook as he took just the tip into his mouth.

Sweet baby Jesus.

I tensed the muscles in my legs and locked my knees. The sight of him on his knees at my feet with my cock in his mouth…

My breath hitched and my heartbeat quickened.

And as he manipulated my cock with his warm, wet mouth and tongue…

Holy shit.

When I threw my head back and my eyelids slid closed, my fingers brushed through his silky hair and I resisted the temptation to curl my fingers and grab a handful.

I previously told him I could be rough. That hadn't been a lie, but interestingly enough, I didn't feel that same urge with Rett. At least, not yet.

He said he could take it and I'd keep that in mind for the future. But tonight wasn't only about sweaty skin slapping together until we both reached release. Tonight was about strengthening the connection between us. Developing an—what I hoped—unbreakable bond.

Establishing a relationship and an even more solid friendship.

Maybe that was why Thomas's loss hit me so hard. He had not only been my husband, the man I loved and cherished, he'd been my best friend. A mirror to my soul. I could tell him anything. And I had.

Rett had stepped up, more than willing to provide that necessary outlet for me. Someone who wasn't afraid to tell me when I was being an ass or when I was wrong.

He had no fear of hurting my feelings. He told me the truth, no matter how much it might cause a sharp blow.

I valued his honesty and his outlook.

I valued *him*.

It only took me a while to see it clearly and now that I had...

We had arrived here. To this very spot and this very moment in time.

Yes, what we were about to do could be considered merely sex, but we both knew tonight would be much more than that.

Another step forward. For me. For us.

Another stitch to close the gaping wound left behind after Thomas's unexpected death.

The pain was no longer as sharp. The hurt not so deep.

According to the website Rett sent me on the stages of grief, I finally moved into the acceptance stage.

Speaking of acceptance...

Rett was practically swallowing my cock whole. A few times I had bumped the back of his throat, but that didn't stop him. He continued to suck me deep and hard, causing my fingers to flex in his hair to the same rhythm of his mouth.

He squeezed the base using one hand and tugged my balls gently with the other as his mouth moved up and down my harder than hell cock.

I got lost in the squeezing, tugging, licking and sucking.

When my legs could no longer hold my weight, when my knees started to fold, when I was having a tough time thinking about my next chapter, the new puppy, where Rett and I went from here, anything and everything to prevent me from coming down his throat...

I groaned, "Rett." I was at my limit.

It had been so long...

Weeks since I last fucked Rett and before that a couple of years. My tolerance was low. My patience was even lower.

It didn't help that Rett was highly skilled. I was surprised I lasted this long.

I twisted my fingers in his short hair as best as I could and tugged on it, indicating he should release me and get up since I was teetering dangerously close.

"I don't want to come in your mouth." I shook my head after I realized what I said. "I mean, I do. Just not right now."

My pulsing cock glistened when it slipped from between his lips. His lips were shiny, too.

"Get up." I grabbed him behind the elbows and encouraged him to his feet, before I was tempted to say, "Screw it" and finish in his mouth.

If I did that I knew I'd regret it afterward. I wanted to be inside him in a connection much deeper than simply getting a blowjob.

Between the heat in his eyes, the swell of his mouth, the slight color in his cheeks...

My head spun with how much I wanted this man.

Really wanted *this* man.

And he had waited.

He waited for me to catch up. Without one damn complaint, too.

He climbed into my bed almost every night, knowing that the only physical touch he was getting from me would be us spooning or simply holding hands. Or him propping his head in my lap while we watched movies or shows on the flatscreen in my bedroom.

In all that time, we did not kiss. We did not play or tease. Even once we settled to go to sleep at night, the extent of our physical connection was him spooning me or him resting his head on my chest.

He waited when he didn't have to.

He waited when he most likely didn't want to.

He waited. For me. For this.

His wait was over.

I would give him what he wanted and take what I needed.

If he needed more than that, I would do everything in my power to give it to him. Even if that meant flaying myself open and offering him my heart and soul.

He deserved that along with my gratitude.

"What's the matter?"

I focused on Rett's frowning face. "Absolutely nothing."

"Chase…"

I didn't like the look in his eyes. The mix of growing doubt and disappointment.

"You're just standing there. Are you having second thoughts?"

He was misreading my hesitation. "Absolutely not. I know exactly what I want." I grabbed his hand and yanked him toward the bed. "You."

CHAPTER 22

Chase

WHEN WE GOT to the bed, I used Rett's hand to spin him around. The second I let it go, I planted both palms onto his broad chest and shoved.

With a grin, he fell backwards and landed with a bounce on my mattress. The unrestrained chuckle spilling from him pulled a smile from me.

With his feet still touching the floor, his knees bent on the edge of the bed and his head raised, his dark eyes, crinkled in the corners from laughter, took me in. His head wasn't the only thing raised. His thick, hard cock lay across his hip, the glistening pearl of precum balancing at the slit tempting me.

"Where's your bag?" I asked.

"By the back door."

Even though my cabin was small, right now the back door seemed too far away. "Don't move."

"And miss this? I'm not going anywhere."

After taking a mental snapshot of him lying naked and fully erect on my bed, I forced myself to walk away to grab his overnight bag.

It might be time for him to start leaving a few things at my place so he wouldn't have to keep hauling them along every time he stayed over. It also might be time for me to stock up on lube and condoms since tonight was only the first night of hopefully many more nights together.

I just couldn't blow it.

But I sure could blow him.

A soft snort burst from me at my unexpected juvenile thought. I threw his bag on the kitchen table—safely out of reach from destructive teeth—and dug through it to find what we needed.

Suddenly it hit me... Why my body hummed like a live electrical wire. It wasn't only from sexual arousal, but from the thrill and anticipation of...

Not fucking, but actually *making love* with Rett. Our first night together had been simply sex, but tonight I wanted it to be different. I didn't want him to think I was using him since that was farthest from the truth.

I rushed back to the bedroom with the condoms and lube, tossing them on the mattress next to Rett, so they'd be close.

His eyes went wide when, without even a pause, I dropped to my knees at *his* feet. "Chase..."

"I owe you more than I'll ever be able to repay you."

He reached for me. "You don't owe me anything and you don't have to do that tonight."

I ignored his outstretched hand. "You're right, I don't. But I want to." Plus, it would give me a little time.

If I buried myself inside him right now, I would probably disappoint the both of us. Worse, embarrass myself. I really needed to harness Rett's endless supply of patience so I could use it myself.

It might help if I concentrated on something other than stuffing my cock into one of Rett's holes. Giving him head first might do that.

"I'm not going to argue," he stated and his head flopped back onto the bed. He waved a hand around over his lower stomach. "Do what you feel is necessary." He feigned an impatient sigh.

"Are you sure?" I smothered my grin.

His head lifted slightly. "Don't worry about me. I'll deal with it."

Cupping his erection in my palm, I lifted it from his hip, a string of precum now dangling precariously.

I licked my lips and then licked him, letting his salty tang coat my tongue.

He moaned and lifted his hips off the bed. My eyes flicked from his cock to his face. His own were shut tight and his jaw tense.

"I haven't even done anything yet."

One eyeball popped open and pointed my way. "Don't worry about me. Just go ahead and do whatever torture you're planning."

I shook my head. "If you insist."

"I do."

Once I took the tip into my mouth, he sucked in a sharp breath. With his cock pulsing in my palm, I sucked the crown, then used the flat of my tongue to trace the underside along the thick ridge. When I reached his sac, I pulled one ball into my mouth and sucked on it gently before doing the same with the other, scoring another drawn-out groan from him.

"*Jeeeeesus*, Chase." His raspy response and his fingers clenching the bedding encouraged me to continue. Nonetheless, I could do better.

I lifted my head only long enough to say, "Grab the lube."

If he was barely hanging on right now, before I hardly did anything, he was going to be in for a big surprise.

His head shot up off the mattress and his mouth was slightly parted as he stared at me. "What are you planning?"

"Grab the lube," I repeated.

His hand shot out to the location where it was tossed and without looking, he patted the bed until he found it. As soon as he had it in his possession, I held my hand out above his stomach. "Lube up my fingers."

"*Oooh.*"

"Are you going to be okay with that, too?"

He popped the cap open, "I'll manage," and squeezed out a generous amount on my index and middle fingers.

Using the tip of my tongue, I followed the seam of his sac, followed along the ridge and when I got to the crown once more, I swallowed him as far as I could handle. I couldn't deep throat quite like he could, but I could make it up to him in another way.

Using my slick middle finger, I ran it around the outer ring of his anus, then dipped it slightly inside, working the lube in and out until it was well distributed before my second finger joined the first.

"Chase."

I loved hearing my name coming across his lips, especially with how he was moaning it. I challenged myself to get him to the point where he was chanting it mindlessly. Maybe even using it when he begged me to finish him off because I'd driven him to the point where he couldn't take anymore.

My own cock flexed as I imagined hauling him to the peak of a mountain and shoving him over.

We'd get there.

With my mouth working the top half of his erection and my fist working the lower half, I sucked him as hard and as deep as I could while my two fingers worked in and out of him.

His hips drove up as my mouth sank down. His inner walls clenched and his ass rose with each stroke of my fingers over his prostate.

Teasing. Coaxing. Encouraging.

"Chase..."

I ignored his whimpered plea and continued on my quest to drive him out of his mind. To leave him on the bed totally drained and having to recover from how hard he came.

Keeping the plump crown in my mouth, I swirled my tongue around the rim and swept away the continuous flow of precum caused by stimulating that magical, walnut-sized spot.

I didn't let up, not even for a second. Not even when his fingers curled in my hair and he began pushing and pulling on my head, wanting to control my pace.

I let him.

This was all for him tonight. My goal was for him to feel wanted and to have no doubt how much I appreciated him. Words were simply not enough.

Using my own fist as a bumper, he couldn't shove his cock too deep. When I glanced up, his eyes were still squeezed shut and his mouth moved as if he was talking but nothing was coming out.

A shock of desire surged through me from my scalp all the way to my toes. It was dangerous watching him. I was afraid that alone could make me explode.

I was conflicted. I needed to hurry this along so I didn't come before I got to seat myself deep inside him, but I also didn't want to rush. He deserved better than that.

Keep yourself together, Chase. For Rett.

I gave myself a pep talk, trying not to hear the sounds coming from the man I just wanted to flip over and drive my cock into. Trying not to see his reactions. Trying not to pay attention to the uncontrollable responses of his body.

I tried to ignore it all.

Impossible.

When Rett's fingers dug into my scalp, almost to the point of pain, he started mumbling my name over and over until it all blended together.

Achieving the first part of my goal, I was ready to move on to the second.

I plunged my fingers in and out of his ass and sucked on his length as hard as I could, causing his hips to hop around.

"Chase..." came out on a ragged breath. "Chase..."

I didn't want to take my mouth off him long enough to verbally encourage him to let go, so I repeated those words in my mind as quickly as he said my name.

Let go. Let go. Let go.

"*Aaaah, shiiiiit,*" he cried out. His hips shot up, almost dislodging my buried fingers, and hot, salty semen coated my tongue, filled my mouth. I almost failed to keep up with swallowing his non-stop coming.

When he was done, when he had nothing left to give, he melted back into the mattress and relaxed so much it was like he disappeared into the bed. With amusement, I realized he reminded me of one of those cartoon characters after it had been run over by a steamroller.

Once he finally let go of my head and gave me my freedom, I slowly withdrew my fingers and mouth. Staying on my now aching knees, I straightened and glanced at him sprawled across my bed.

If it wasn't for his rapid breathing, I might have thought I sucked the life right out of him.

An impressive feat, if possible.

I was so damn hard that I ached and couldn't wait to plunge into him, but clearly he needed a minute. I decided while he was recovering, I'd attempt slipping out of the room without waking the puppy or Timber, and head to the bathroom to wash my hands.

When I returned, Rett had an arm flung over his eyes and wore a very lazy smile. "I didn't think I'd experience anything better than my Autoblow AI, but… uh… Your mouth comes pretty damn close."

Autoblow AI? I'd have to google that when I got a chance. Or better yet, have him give me a demo.

"Just close?" I razzed, standing at the edge of the bed between his spread thighs.

When he flung his arm off his face, it flopped heavily to the bed and he stared up at me, his eyes still not fully focused. "While the other week it was good, tonight it was even better. Let's just say I wouldn't complain if you did this again later."

I raised an eyebrow. "Later?"

"Tomorrow night would be fine, too."

"I'll make a note of it."

"Also, jot it down on your calendar for the rest of the week." His gaze landed on my aching erection bobbing straight out from my body. "That looks uncomfortable."

"It is."

"Did you want help with that?" he asked with an eyebrow wiggle.

"I could use some assistance," I admitted.

"I don't mind volunteering."

"That's good because you're the only one here."

"Are you saying you're stuck with me?" he asked, pretending to be offended.

"I wouldn't quite say stuck, no."

"*Wellllll*, if there was someone else you've taken a fancy to…"

Taken a fancy to? Did I miss us teleporting back to the Regency era?

"Have you *taken a fancy* to start writing historical romance? Do you have a secret pen name you've been hiding?"

Rett wrinkled his nose. "No. Forget balls, carriages and horrendous body odor. I'll stick to murder, mayhem, and hard-to-solve cases."

"*Mmm*. Same. Slide up the bed."

As he did so, I climbed onto the mattress and followed him by walking on my knees as he slid up to the headboard.

When he tucked a pillow under his head, I told him, "You're not going to need that. At least not for your head."

"Oh. Where else am I going to need it?"

When I held out my hand, he jerked the pillow from under him and handed it to me.

"Head down, ass up."

He didn't hesitate to flip over and when he did, I stuffed the pillow under his hips to lift them. "That's also a good place for it," he confirmed.

"Spread your ass cheeks. Show me where you want me."

A flush spread from his neck and slightly down his back. I'd never seen that before, but then, before Rett, I never had sex with anyone other than Thomas. I was sure I would discover a lot of new things with Rett, both in bed and out of it.

I looked forward to both expanding my horizons and maybe even my close-knit circle.

With a hand clamped on each ass cheek, he exposed his tempting little hole to me, still shiny from the lube. More would be needed before I took this any further.

"Next time I'll eat that first." Before I slathered it with inedible lube.

The bed shook violently at my announcement. From shock, surprise or wonderment? Maybe all three.

"Will you be able to manage that, too?" I asked.

"I can manage anything you throw at me, baby."

Baby.

I still wasn't sure about that endearment. I never saw myself as anyone's *baby.* Lover or husband, yes. Baby? I'd either have to get used to it or find him an alternative. But not right now. I had much more important things to do.

Like Rett.

I grabbed a condom out of the box, ripped open the wrapper and took my time rolling it down my throbbing cock that had its own heartbeat. I lubed myself generously, along with adding more in and around his puckered hole.

"Are you ready?" I asked in a rough whisper when I was through prepping and had moved into place.

"*Yesssss.* I'm so damn ready." He had his head buried within his crossed arms, but it popped up. "Are you going to be rough tonight?"

"I wasn't planning on it. Why?"

Silence.

"Rett…"

"Take me how you normally like it. Don't hold back on my account."

"I wanted tonight to be…" *Special.*

"We can make tonight however we want to make it. After all, it's *our* night. This is *our* beginning. We can do things however we want to. That means fucking me how you like to fuck. I don't want you holding back. I want all of you, Chase. The good, the bad, the beautiful and even the ugly. I want the real Chase. The man he used to be as well as the man he recently grew to be."

I considered what he said and, of course, he was annoyingly right. Again. The man was rarely ever wrong.

Yes, this was *our* beginning. We could build our relationship how we wanted it. How we both needed it.

We could start a foundation tonight, officially shifting from friends to lovers. Eventually moving from lovers to something more when the time was right.

Neither of us were in a rush. We had no pressure. We had plenty of time to figure it all out and do it right.

Now that he knew almost everything about me, he'd be better equipped to deal with my "moods" if and when they sprung up. I couldn't promise him I would never slip back into the darkness, even if temporarily, but it would help me immensely to know he'd be waiting to help lift me back out.

In turn, I wanted to be there for him, to support him in every aspect of his life, especially with his business and his writing. Since he helped me stand straight and true again, I would be there for him whenever he needed to lean on me.

He had been my pillar, now I wanted to be his.

Getting lost in my thoughts had cooled the lava rushing through my veins enough so I no longer worried about coming undone within the first thirty seconds of being inside him.

As always, Rett's patience impressed me. He wasn't pressuring me to "hurry up." He wasn't complaining about me taking my time. He waited for me to be ready.

He didn't have to wait any longer.

I was ready and it was time.

I shifted forward and gently drew one hand down his spine and over his ass while holding my cock in the other. Separating his muscular cheeks, I rubbed the crown up and down over his glistening hole.

Seeing him relaxed and open like that had me not wasting any more time. I placed the head of my cock at his opening and nudged forward. He stretched around me as I buried myself inside him. With a shudder, his spine arched slightly and I kept pushing until I was fully seated.

I breathed through my urge to ram into him over and over, and gathered myself enough to ask, "You okay?"

"Yes," came muffled from where his head was tucked in his arms. "I'm more than okay."

His response helped me relax and settle for a few seconds.

However, my urge to pound him into the mattress until I came was quickly ramping up. I fought it, reminding myself not to do that tonight.

Rocking my hips, I found a steady, gentle rhythm.

My movements had the opposite effect than intended. Instead of getting into it, getting lost in what we were doing, Rett was tensing.

I gritted my teeth and held back. Tonight wasn't only for sex, it was for us to connect, for sharing and intimacy, I reminded myself.

"If you aren't going to give me one-hundred percent, Chase, at least give me fifty. Right now, it feels like you're only giving me ten."

"Sorry," I mumbled. He was right. Of course!

With a deep inhale, I closed my eyes and began moving again.

I started slow, then gradually ramped it up, taking him faster and deeper. Until the room filled with the sounds of slapping skin, harsh grunts and deep groans. Until his fingers gripped the bedding like he was afraid his head would be driven into the headboard.

Until he was crying out my name, encouraging me to take him harder. Until a sheen of sweat coated his skin. Until beads of perspiration dropped from my chin and pooled in the small of his back.

I did not let up and he did not ask me to.

Every time I rammed forward, he slammed his ass into me, meeting me thrust for thrust.

Staying in position, he turned his head on the mattress enough so he could watch what I was doing.

I fell over him, nipping along his spine. Scraping my teeth along his shoulder blades. He had to dig his knees deeper into the mattress to stay in place and to keep from being shoved higher up the bed with each pounding thrust.

I licked the sweat from the back of his neck, then sucked on that tender spot where his shoulder and neck met. With one hand planted on the back of his head, I pinned it down to help keep him in place. My fingers instinctively curled, grabbing his hair so tightly, it had to make his scalp sting.

But I did not let up.

Not yet. Not unless he told me to.

I was riding this high and taking Rett along with me. Every movement, every noise, he made spurred me to take it further.

"That's it, baby. That's it. Just like that," he encouraged.

He was taking everything I was giving him and even asking for more.

He was unbreakable.

But was I?

Pressure built in my lower belly and my balls pulled tight. The urge to come rushed through me, trying to pull me under and make me surrender.

I didn't want to come like this, with him face down. Unfortunately, in my haste, I hadn't thought that through.

When I paused, a noise of complaint rose from him. I adjusted our legs and rolled us to our sides. I looped my bottom arm around his waist, holding him close. The other I draped over top his waist, dragged my fingers up his stomach and as soon as I found one hard-tipped nipple, I twisted it at the same time as I sunk my teeth into the firm flesh of his shoulder. Not as deep as I would normally, to the point just shy of breaking the skin, but hard enough for him to twitch against me and groan.

However, I still held back, afraid of hurting him, since I didn't know the edge of his limits. Not yet. It would take some time and a lot of exploration to discover how far we could take things and to find what worked between us and what didn't.

We'd get to that point eventually, if that was what he really wanted. I would need to test just how rough he'd be comfortable with.

Thomas had a high pain tolerance and always wanted it as rough as he could get it. Now that I thought about it, all the brainwashing done to him when he was a teen could've made him believe he deserved to be punished. How many times had he been lied to by being told that God would punish him for being gay? Sadly, countless.

When in reality, that was farthest from the truth.

Me leaving behind welts and bites, scrapes and bruises, and everything else he begged me for whenever we had sex, could have fed into that without me even knowing.

When Thomas told me everything he went through during conversion therapy, he said he was told he'd go to hell for being gay. He had also been called depraved, a sinner, and so many other degrading insults and names. The participants promised if he complied, his life would be so much better. He'd be accepted, loved and welcomed into heaven. All he had to do was think and act differently. All he had to do was "change."

An impossible feat.

They expected him to change into something he wasn't. A person he'd never be. Instead, he was forced to fake compliance so he could escape the torture.

For shit's sake, I should've recognized all of that, too. Unfortunately, it was one more thing I missed in a list of them.

I was determined to do better when it came to Rett. While I learned from my mistakes with Thomas, I realized I could do more.

By being more aware. By being more present. It was the least I could do for someone I cared about.

Rett moving my hand from his lower abdomen to his cock brought me back to the present and the bed. He was hard again, the head slick from precum. I fisted it and began to stroke in time with my thrusts.

"Will you come again?" I whispered against his ear.

"Yes. Please make me come again."

He began to squirm with every deliberate draw of my cock over his prostate. With every pump of his cock with my fist.

Closing my eyes, I pressed my nose to the back of his neck, sucking in air as quickly as I could. Being one with Rett, I got swept away to a new time, a new place, a new life.

This was home now. This town, this cabin, this man. I had finally found myself after being lost.

I no longer was drowning in guilt.

I had hope.

I had peace.

I had Rett.

My life was now becoming full again after being agonizingly empty for the past two years.

His hips twitched and his cock pulsed as he grunted and I captured the strings of cum in my palm.

Him coming rocketed me right to the peak. I slowed my thrusting, taking him more gently now. Grabbing his hair, I twisted his head to seal his lips with mine.

Then... I tumbled over the edge and went into a free fall.

My own grunt-turned-groan was captured between us as I thrust one more time and came.

When I finally landed, I reluctantly released his mouth but continued to hold him tightly with my cheek pressed to his, both of us simply breathing and sharing a space.

At first, I didn't want anything to do with him. I wanted him to leave me alone. But now... We fit together more perfectly than I ever expected.

We fit together perfectly. Period.

For once I was the "big spoon" and I wanted that to last as long as possible.

I didn't want to move. I didn't want to break our connection.

Unfortunately, I would have to.

When he twisted his torso a little more, I caught the soft look in his eyes and his very kissable lips curved into a just as soft smile.

I checked in with him. "Are you good?"

"Definitely."

Thankfully, I hadn't hurt him and had done the exact opposite. "Ready for me to pull out?"

He trailed his warm fingers over my cheek, across my lips and then scraped his fingernails along my beard. "No, not yet. Stay."

"I won't have a choice soon," I warned.

"Wait until you have to."

"I don't want the condom to spill."

"I'm not worried if it spills. Like you, I haven't had sex with anyone except you for at least the last year."

I already knew that, I did. But to hear it again warmed me from the inside out.

Unfortunately, that wasn't the only thing warming me. Between the two of us, I swore our combined body heat was the same temperature as the sun.

The ceiling fan wasn't quite cutting it when it came to cooling us off. It was one thing to melt with sexual satisfaction, another to melt from overheating.

I peeled myself away from his back, secured the condom within my fingers and warned him I was pulling free.

Once I did, I removed the full condom and knotted it, as Rett flopped onto his back with a long, drawn-out sigh. I yanked a couple of tissues out of the box next to the bed, wrapped up the used condom and wiped off my fingers.

With a long groan, he stretched. "I'll go clean up, then take the dogs O-U-T."

"How about if I take the dogs O-U-T while you clean up?" I suggested.

"I accept that offer."

We both rolled off the bed, and he immediately pulled on his boxers before tossing me mine. I snagged them mid-air and yanked them up my legs while he released Onyx from her crate. Timber was already on high alert the second Rett told him they were going "out." This time not spelling it out.

The puppy would need to learn that word, too. The puppy would need to learn a lot of things. Unfortunately, since I knew hardly anything about puppies, I was going to break it to Rett later that he would be responsible for Onyx's training. That would be the penance for surprising me with a dog I didn't want.

When Timber rushed out of the bedroom in his excitement of heading outside, the puppy was on his tail. Literally holding onto his tail and being dragged behind the much larger Shepherd.

I scratched my ear and shook my head. She was going to be a handful.

I stared at the other handful in my life as he headed to the bathroom. I needed to head out the door, too.

"Rett," I called out.

He paused in the doorway and glanced back over his bare shoulder at me. It took me a second to collect myself because seeing him standing there—handsome, sexy and freshly fucked—made me not only lose my breath, but my train of thought for a second. I also realized how lucky I was for him sticking around and helping me through my darkest time.

He didn't have to do that, he did it anyway. Because of that, I owed him the truth and I needed to be upfront about what was going on in my head.

"I know we've known each other for a few months and have only gotten closer in these last few weeks, but I hope I made it clear tonight how much I want you. How much I appreciate you being in my life. How much you mean to me. With that said..."

"With that said...?" he prodded with his expression cautious.

I didn't want to put him off by saying what I was about to say, but it needed to be said so there was no misunderstanding. "I hope you agree that we still need to take this slow."

His concerned look fled and a grimace replaced it. "I guess I need to cancel the tux rental, then. I'll lose my deposit." A grin appeared. "Sorry... Yes, I agree, we need to take it slow."

Since that grin reached his eyes, I had no doubt it was genuine and he wasn't hiding his true feelings from me. Still, I wanted to be sure. I didn't want to assume anything since I had made that mistake before. "That won't be a problem?"

"Baby, I've been taking it slow since the day I saw you across the diner. Despite being a grumpy grizzly, I wanted you then and planned on having you. I just didn't know the mountain I'd have to climb to get you or whether it was worth the work."

"Was it worth the effort?"

"It took a while... But, yes, that difficult climb was worth it."

I nodded and, with a wink, he disappeared.

Still sporting that handsome grin.

THE SECOND MY eyes opened I realized it was way too early for me to be awake.

I probably woke up because of all the lumber being sawed in my bedroom.

Unsynchronized, of course.

Rett was glued to my side, with one arm and one leg thrown over me, pinning me to the bed.

He always slept like that. As if he was afraid I'd sneak out and disappear forever.

I didn't blame him since that was how I left Long Island. I didn't tell anyone I was leaving until I was already gone. At the time I didn't want anyone talking me out of my plans to move to Eagle's Landing.

While I was glad I did it the way I did, I somewhat understood Rett's worry. However, I would have to assure him he had nothing to worry about.

I wasn't going anywhere. I found my place here and even though I thought I'd never find my happy again, I did.

I carefully extracted myself from Rett and got out of bed, trying not to disturb him or the dogs.

After taking the dogs out for the last time before we fell asleep, Rett didn't stick Onyx back in the crate like he should have. She was now curled up with Timber in the dog bed. Both canines were snoring louder than the two-hundred pound human asleep in my bed.

I shook my head. He bought me a damn Newfoundland puppy.

It could be he thought the puppy would be a bridge for us to bond. A joint "project" for us to work on to bring us closer together.

I didn't know. It could be Rett didn't even know, either. However, he seemed to be pretty intuitive when it came to our relationship and what was needed.

Since I needed water and to use the toilet, I practically tip-toed toward the door. I paused when something caught my eye. The small, shallow dish I kept on my dresser to throw spare change into. It was sitting right next to our now neatly folded pile of clothes.

I ignored the change and plucked the object that grabbed my attention from the dish.

It took two weeks but Rett had finally found my wedding band using the borrowed underwater metal detector. Every day after he closed The Next Page and before we sat down to dinner together, he'd go out for at least an hour and search while I prepared our meal and kept Timber occupied so he wasn't standing on the shore yapping non-stop at Rett being out in the lake.

Timber didn't like to swim, so he wasn't happy when either of us went into the water. I considered buying a small rowboat so the damn dog could be out there with us and stop his high-pitched screams from blowing out our eardrums.

Turning the ring slowly within my fingers, I studied it. I then glanced at my empty finger before turning my eyes to where Rett slept, now spread out on his back with one arm flung over his head, the other across his chest and soft snores rolling out of his gaping mouth.

Directing my attention back to the gold band, I very carefully placed it back in the dish.

I had expected the second it was back in my hands, I would immediately slide it back on my ring finger. When Rett handed it to me the evening he found it, I surprised both of us when I didn't. I still had no plans to return it to its former spot.

Especially after tonight.

While I didn't want to get rid of it—it was still an important symbol of my marriage with Thomas and would always hold meaning—it no longer belonged on my finger. Instead, I decided to buy a gold chain and wear it around my neck so it was always near my heart.

With one last glance back at the man in my bed, the two dogs— everything that consisted of my future—a smile grew across my face and I headed out to the kitchen.

CHAPTER 23

Rett

I COULD SEE it in his face.

I could feel it in his attitude.

He was happy. Truly happy. That alone was worth dealing with Chase during the times when he wasn't. Thankfully, that didn't come as often anymore.

He got to a point where he now socialized in town and everyone knew he was C.J. Anson. He'd even done a few readings at the bookstore and they were well attended.

Even better, he no longer struggled with writer's block.

For the most part, Chase was a different man now than when he first came to Eagle's Landing. Fresh air, small town support and a man who loved him more than he'd ever know could do that to a person.

When I suggested we attend the annual Christmas party at The Roost, surprisingly he agreed. No hemming and hawing, and no prodding was needed. I had actually slapped a hand to his forehead to check for a fever.

In response, he pushed my hand away and told me, "If that's what you want, Rett..."

Of course that was what I wanted. I wanted to be seen in public with the man I had fallen in love with. With the man I now lived with. With the man I expected to spend the rest of my life with.

The date I "officially" moved in with him was a bit fuzzy. It just happened. Every week more and more of my stuff ended up at his place and so did Timber's.

I decided to keep my apartment empty and not rent it out. It was a good place for us to stay if a nor'easter whipped up and buried the area in snow, or if the power went out up at the cabin for an extended period of time. The backup generator could only be used for short power outages.

Plus, keeping the apartment available gave me a place to do my baking and plenty of extra storage since the cabin was still tight quarters. Especially for two men and two big dogs. It wouldn't be much better even after the proposed four-season room was added on next spring.

I'm not sure how we managed it, but somehow we kept both being lovers and living together under wraps for the last few months.

And here it was, now mid-December.

Everything between us had fallen into place. Not so easily at first. It took a little time and patience, but we achieved it.

Of course we still hit bumps in the road. But nothing we couldn't handle by working together to get past it.

Chase and I, Timber and Onyx, made up our little family. Others might think it untraditional, but it was perfect for us.

I manned the bookstore and wrote there during the week, while Chase continued to pen his novels at the cabin. On the weekends, we both put our writing aside and went hiking, swimming and even took day trips.

After coming home one evening and finding two shiny new four-wheelers in a shed Chase had delivered a few weeks prior, we also began riding around the property. Having the dogs follow along burned off some of their pent-up energy. We even added platforms on the back of the four-wheelers and once tired, the dogs would hitch a ride.

They loved every second of it. So did we.

Purchasing those two ATVs hardly made a dent in Chase's most recent book advance. I guessed those were the perks of hooking up with a famous author who sold millions of copies of his books.

He was always cautious when it came to mentioning the royalties he made, but he quickly learned I wasn't jealous of his success. If anything, I was proud of him. I only wanted the best for him, no matter what it was.

I glanced around the bar, packed full with every local in the area. Unless someone was sick, everyone made an effort to show up at one point or another during the evening, even if they couldn't stick around for very long.

An extensive food buffet was set up, colorful blinking lights filled the bar's interior and a fully decorated Christmas tree sat in a corner. Beer and drinks flowed freely and the song choices included a mix of both holiday and regular tunes. The music had to be loud to be heard above the din of voices since gossip, news and personal views were being shared at every table and in every corner.

When my gaze swept over the crowd, it landed on Chase working his way through and around small groups of gathered people on his return from the restroom. He'd get pulled to a stop here and there with people greeting him or wanting to know how his latest book was coming.

He would smile and nod, shake hands and give some of the women or girls a requested hug. If he was uncomfortable doing any of that, he hid it well.

When he finally made it back to the small high table where I sat waiting for him, the first thing he did was pick up his pint glass. I couldn't pull my attention from his thickly corded throat when it undulated as he swallowed down half of his draft beer.

"Too much peopling already?" I teased.

"It can be a bit much," he admitted and brushed away a fleck of foam caught on his upper lip.

He no longer looked like a wild lumberjack. His hair was back to being trimmed on a regular basis and his face clean-shaven so he'd look neat and professional. I kind of missed the rugged mountain man look. His PR team didn't.

What I would not allow him to trim was his chest hair, no matter how much he complained about it being too hot. I'd be bummed if I couldn't get lost in that thick rug every night. It made the formerly grumpy grizzly bearably cuddly.

"What are you grinning about?"

I lifted my gaze from his neck to his face. "Nothing."

He gave me a look that clearly said he didn't believe me. No surprise. I shrugged.

His mouth opened and quickly snapped shut when Dolly materialized out of nowhere to stand next to him. She squeezed Chase's shoulder. "I'm so glad to see you here, Chase!"

"I'm glad to be here."

I raised an eyebrow and cleared my throat. Now *I* didn't believe him.

The mayor's wife turned toward me. "You told me you were bringing a date!"

Oh shit. Here we go... "I did."

"Well, handsome, where is she? I can't wait to meet her. I promise we won't scare her off."

Of course they wouldn't. That would be impossible.

"*He* is right here," I announced, flipping a hand toward Chase.

He turned into a concrete statue right before my eyes.

Dolly clicked her tongue. "I thought you meant a real date. I was hoping you finally found someone."

Several times, we had discussed "coming out" to the locals, we just hadn't discussed when. He was leaving it to me to decide. I figured tonight was the perfect opportunity. It would be better if they saw and heard the truth directly from us instead of learning a twisted version from the local phone tree.

Dolly squeezed my forearm. "We'll find you someone. You, too, Chase. No need to be lonely up at that isolated cabin of yours. Oh! There's Margaret! I have to give her an update on Sasha's baby. Have fun, boys, and try not to get too drunk tonight."

"You, too, Dolly," I answered, not hiding my amusement as she beelined over to Hardware Harry's wife.

I slipped from my stool and offered my hand to Chase. With a frown, he stared at it like it was a snake with three heads. "Are you sure you want to do this tonight?"

"If I wasn't, I wouldn't have spilled it to Dolly first."

"After that you'll never be able to jam that cat back in the bag. You know that, right?"

"Of course, I do. Take my hand," I insisted.

"I'm not sure this is smart, Rett," he said under his breath.

"Maybe. Maybe not. But we can't hide who we are to each other forever... Take my hand."

He considered my extended hand hovering between us. "Warning... If I take it, you'll be taking my heart along with it."

Whoa. "And do you have a problem with that?"

"If I did, I wouldn't do this..." He slapped his hand in mine and interlocked our fingers. "You're always annoyingly right. Tonight *is* the perfect time." After a deep, audible inhale, he turned us toward the center of the bar where the tables had been cleared to make space for dancing. "Let's do this."

I nodded and gave him a smile. "Let's do this."

"Just be aware, I hate dancing. I'm taking one for the team."

"No surprise about the dancing. We can fake it through a few slow songs."

He tugged me along behind him until we joined a half dozen older couples shuffling their way around the dance floor to the classic *At Last* by Etta James.

The song was perfect for this very moment.

Once we found a spot where we wouldn't be in anyone's way, Chase faced me and pulled me into him. "Ready?" he whispered.

"Never more ready," I whispered back.

He curved one hand around the back of my neck and placed the other at the small of my back and tugged me even closer. Hooking my arms around his neck, I sandwiched myself against him from our chest to our hips, leaving no doubt who and what we were to each other.

Our "bromance" was no longer that. Once the *B* was dropped it became much more serious.

I refused to look around to see if any and all eyes were on us. I assumed they were since even over the music, murmurs and whispers could be heard swirling around us. We couldn't quite make out what was being said, but no one approached us. No one shouted anything derogatory. No one escorted us to the exit.

I hoped that was a good sign. While things seemed okay at the surface so far, it would be a while before the flutters in my stomach disappeared.

With his cheek plastered to mine, he murmured, "Ignore them," in my ear. "They'll either get used to it or they won't. They'll either accept us or not. If they don't, that's on them, not us."

"This is small town America," I reminded him. One reason I had kept being gay to myself all these years. But then, I had no reason to "come out" until now.

Now I had every reason and that reason was currently dancing with me.

"Small town America will never change if someone doesn't try."

"Are you saying we're pioneers?" I teased.

"Hardly. This is a pale comparison to what others have done before us to pave the way and what others will do after us. Tonight is only a slight blip in a long journey others have traveled."

Who was this man? "Well look at that, guess who's right for once?"

His chuckle vibrated against me and his hold tightened. "Well, you have me beat. One point for me versus your million."

"You have a lot of catching up to do."

"I've got time."

We remained on the dance floor, moving slowly in our little bubble and ignoring the rest of the world, when the song changed to Mariah Carey's *All I Want for Christmas is You*. A more holiday appropriate song.

When I sang the chorus to Chase, he just shook his head and said, "You already have me."

"I just hope you'll let me share your heart with Thomas."

"You already do," came the deep rumble. "Thank you for being willing to share it."

I stopped dancing and with a tilt of my head, locked gazes with him. "I'm nothing but honored to share it with him. Even though he's gone, I hope you know that love will never be taken away from you. You hold it in here." I patted his chest over his heart and under his shirt, I could feel the wedding ring he now wore on a chain around his neck. "We can love more than one person in our lifetime. It isn't an either/or situation. Our hearts are capable of expanding so you can add all the people you want there. There isn't a limit on love. It's endless, even after death." I let that sink in first, then added, "Now, tell me I'm right so I can up my score by another point. I don't want you closing that gap."

He shook his head and huffed, "You're too damn right."

"Ha! Of course I am." I stepped into him again, began moving and then it hit me… "Holy shit, I forgot to tell you something important!"

I didn't actually forget but I wanted to get him worked up before I revealed what I wanted to say. Plus, this way, he'd be paying closer attention.

He pressed his cheek to mine once again as we circled in place, our hips rocking back in forth with the rhythm of the music. "What? Did my agent finally get you a contract with one of the big five publishers?"

"No," I answered. Getting a publishing contract wasn't a do or die situation for me. I was already content with how my author career was proceeding. "It's more important than that."

"I'd consider that pretty damn important."

Of course he would. He'd never been anything but traditionally published. "Not as important as this."

As soon as he tensed with impatience, I turned my face just enough to hide my grin until I could get it under control.

"Well?" he finally prodded when I didn't give him what he wanted right away.

I cupped the back of his neck and put my mouth to his ear so no one would overhear us. "Pay attention to what I'm about to say."

"Rett…"

"Chase…"

"Jesus Christ," he growled.

"I…"

He sighed, his fingers gripping my waist tighter. "You…?"

"I love you."

His feet stopped moving abruptly and that also pulled me to a halt. We once again stood still in the middle of the dance floor.

"You're telling me this now? Here?" His expression flip-flopped from amazed to confused to… I didn't even know what. I couldn't keep up with his sudden flux of emotions.

"Yes, why not?"

"You couldn't tell me this later, after we got home?"

"Do you want me to take it back for now?"

He jerked his chin back and stared at me, a frown line now creasing his brow. "You can't take it back now. Too late."

"Sure I can. They're my words. I can take them back if I want to."

"No, Rett. That's where you're wrong." Locking gazes with me, he said, "Now they're *my* words and I'm not letting you have them back. Ever."

Then he kissed me right there. In the middle of the dance floor, in the middle of The Roost, in the middle of Eagle's Landing.

That kiss was the best ever and one neither of us would ever forget.

~

THE SKY WAS a blend of orange, yellow, and red as the sun began to fall behind the mountain. The higher we climbed, the more worried I got about hiking back down when we were done. Besides the threat of being attacked by carnivorous wildlife, we could twist an ankle on a rock or trip over a fallen tree.

The dogs explored ahead of us, but remained in our sights. Luckily, Onyx was a quick learner and easy to train. It helped Timber was a good teacher, too. If she ever wandered too far, his herding instinct kicked in and he got her back where she belonged.

When we finally reached the summit, I swore I lost a lung somewhere along the trail. How Chase wasn't huffing and puffing like me, I had no clue.

I guess my workout routine wasn't as good as his.

However, today we didn't climb the mountain for exercise.

Around New Year's, we had a conversation about what to do with Thomas's ashes. Up to that point, I hadn't been aware Chase had them in his possession. I had always assumed his husband had been buried in a cemetery back on Long Island.

It made sense that Chase wouldn't want to leave Thomas behind and would want him with him always.

While discovering Chase still had his husband's ashes hidden away had been a surprise, finding out he wanted to spread them on the property, surprised me even more.

We had been lying in bed late at night watching a movie about a woman coping with losing her husband to suicide when he brought it up. Being winter at the time, he mentioned about waiting until the weather turned nicer.

I was all for that recommendation since winter weather could be unpredictable. "Do you want to do it by yourself?"

It took him a few moments of considering his answer before he gave it. "I don't know if I can."

I appreciated the fact that he never hid how vulnerable the loss of his husband had made him. It made me love him even more. It showed he was far from cold and distant—my first impression when I met him—but instead, how extremely loyal and how deep he could love.

When he was "in," the man was "all in."

"Well, you don't have to. I'll be there for you either way. I can go to the summit with you if you want. Or I can stop along the way and let you head to the top by yourself, if you need to be alone. No matter what, I'll be waiting for you. Whether down here at the cabin, partway up or at the top standing by your side."

In the end, he wanted me to be with him. So, now I stood at what might be a thousand feet above sea level, attempting to suck oxygen into my straining lungs.

"You okay?" Chase asked, concern causing his brow to crease.

"I'm… good," I lied, so he wouldn't worry.

"You sure?"

I nodded and took a sip from my water bottle. "I'm ready whenever you are." I watched him carefully pull the urn out of his backpack. "Are *you* ready? If you're not, Chase, we can do this another time. It doesn't have to be today. It doesn't even have to be tomorrow or in this decade. I don't even mind if you want to keep his remains in the urn and display it where you can see it."

Swallowing hard enough to be visible, he dropped his backpack on the ground and hugged the plain stainless-steel urn to his chest. "I appreciate that but we're here now. Let's do this."

"You can change your mind."

"No." He turned his dark brown eyes to mine. "I'm not going to change my mind. About anything."

I studied him a few more seconds. His determination to get this over with today could be seen in the tightness of his jaw. "Okay." I just didn't want him to regret his decision afterward. Once he threw the ashes into the wind, there was no getting them back.

I helped him remove the cremains from the urn and open the bag, then I stepped back to give him his space.

His lips moved as he said something—possibly goodbye—and then opened the bag. Turning it over, he shook out the ashes. The breeze picked them up and swept them away in a cloud of dust.

Ashes to ashes. Dust to dust.

My heart ached as he stood there for the longest time. My guess was he was hiding his tears from me even though I, too, experienced a sharp sting and some blurry vision. But if he needed that privacy, if he needed to take a moment or even hours, I could wait. I was a pro at that now.

When he extended his hand behind him and toward me without turning, I moved forward, grabbed it and came around to face him, careful not to get too close to the edge of the rock formation on which we stood.

While the tears might now be dry, the proof they had existed remained.

"It was time to let go."

I didn't agree or disagree since that wasn't my decision.

"Remember what I said at the Christmas party? He'll always be here." I pressed my hand over his heart the same way I did that night. It beat slow and steady under my palm. Completely shattered once, it was now close to being whole again.

"I know. Even though I say this often, it needs to be said again here and now... I appreciate everything you've done to help me get to this point. For sticking by my side no matter how much I resisted, no matter how I treated you."

"I appreciate you not slugging me while I helped."

He yanked on my hand, turning me around before pulling me back against him, so we both faced the valley and the lake below us. Wrapping his arms around me, he leaned his chin on my shoulder while we stood together and took in our home.

After what might have been fifteen minutes of us simply standing in silence, he said softly, "I have something important to tell you."

My heart seized. With a thump, it restarted and began to beat rapidly. "I've heard this somewhere before."

"Yes, you have."

"Does it have to do with a contract and a big fat check?" I asked.

"No, but it does have to do with a commitment."

"Too late. You can't send Onyx back to her breeder. No give backs."

He shook his head. "She's not going anywhere. Neither is Timber. And... neither are you."

One side of my mouth pulled up. Besides my racing heart, my blood was rushing through my veins in anticipation. What he was about to say could be what I'd been waiting for.

"I love you, Rett." After he whispered those three very small but very important words to me, I knew right then and there I was finally done waiting. Especially after he added, "Now and forever."

We had not only physically climbed a mountain and reached the summit today, we did it in our relationship, too.

EPILOGUE

FINDING THE LIGHT

Chase

I PULLED the Bronco in front of The Next Page and shut off the engine. Since it was almost closing time, I had no idea why Rett wanted me to drive all the way into town instead of just telling me whatever he needed to tell me on the phone or when he got home.

As soon as I climbed out of the Ford, Onyx began barking in excitement as she bounced around the back cargo area. I had to install a cargo net to keep her back there since she thought, even as a ninety-pound puppy, she could still fit in my lap when I drove.

She was far, *far* past that point, even if she wasn't aware of it and she wasn't even done growing yet.

I wasn't afraid to admit, she was the best gift I'd ever received. After Rett, of course.

As soon as I let her out of the back of my Bronco, she rushed to the front entrance of the bookstore and once again began to dance and bark non-stop to be let inside.

I grimaced when each bark pierced my brain. Before I could reach for the door, it was flung open and Onyx only paused for a fraction of a second at Rett before barreling past him to find Timber.

"Well, hello to you, too," he called out to her, shaking his head. "Hey, baby," he greeted me.

Unlike Onyx, when I stepped inside, I paused for more than a split second. I stopped long enough to plant a solid kiss on Rett's lips. "Hey."

He closed the door behind me and I followed him over to the front counter.

"Okay, spill. What was so important that you dragged me down here?"

"Don't act like coming down here's a chore," he huffed.

I sweetened my tone. "It's never a chore to come see you."

He rolled his eyes. "Look at you, from a grumpy grizzly to a teddy bear in a little over a year." He patted himself on the back. "I have some skills, don't I?"

"I'll agree with that, but I'm sure we're thinking about two different kinds of skills."

"Oh, do we want to go upstairs for a quickie?"

That was a question that didn't need to be asked, but... "I want to find out what's so important first."

He headed behind the register, bent down and when he straightened, he placed a large box on the counter with a groan. "These were delivered to the store this morning. Once you sign them, I'll put them on the shelf."

After he opened the flaps on the cardboard box, I grabbed a hardcover edition of my latest release. The cover was stunning, especially with the dust jacket. "Only hardbacks?"

"Paperbacks are coming soon, too."

I nodded. "I'll get them signed as soon as they come in."

"A bunch of both are already spoken for."

That was good news.

"By the way, the word on the street is, this is your best one yet."

I raised an eyebrow. "The *street*?"

Rett tipped his head and grinned. "Dolly."

Of course. The woman had been a fan prior, but now that she

knew I was the author, she was obsessed. I swore she did a better job of spreading the word about my book releases than my PR team did. We needed to take her and the mayor out to dinner sometime soon to show our appreciation.

I had fallen in love with Eagle's Landing, just like I had fallen in love with Rett. While there might've been curious looks and plenty of chatter about us during and after the Christmas party last year, not one local had anything bad to say. We had been accepted as a couple—more importantly, as a *gay* couple—without any issues.

All the townspeople had been nothing but warm and openly accepting. Thankfully, no one looked at us any differently.

It was refreshing, to be sure.

Rett continued with, "I also heard that all the major critics and reviewers are raving about it."

"Is that what you heard?"

He rolled his eyes again. "Like you don't know that. I'm sure you're getting hourly updates from your agent."

I shrugged one shoulder. "He's texted me a few times." While my books paid the bills, they weren't the most important thing to me anymore. The man standing in front of me was. "Speaking of Randall, have you heard anything from him directly?"

I had been hounding my agent to take Rett on as a client. While Rett preferred to keep publishing his own books so he could keep creative control, he said he'd consider writing a series for a top five publisher *if* he could land a decent deal.

I had no doubt he could, we just needed to get his talent in front of the right people.

"Yes."

"And?" I held my breath while waiting for him to answer. I didn't want him to be disappointed if the proposal he sent Randall was flat-out rejected. Even though Rett's writing was stellar, it was hard to land a good literary agent and even harder to get a solid contract with a healthy advance.

"And..." He smiled. "He wants us to do a collaboration."

A collaboration? "He said nothing to me about that."

"I asked if I could propose it to you instead of him. He would like a spin-off series combining both of ours. He said with both of our names, he'd be able to sell it without a problem. He's already shopping the idea around to test the waters."

"He wants me to write a series with you?"

"More like, he wants me to write a series with you. You're more well-known than I am. My guess is he wants to go that route to get my foot into a door that hardly opens."

If that was what needed to happen, I'd do it. Our writing styles would mesh perfectly. "So, Foster & Peabody would be working together to solve crimes and take down bad guys." I liked the sound of that.

"Foster would be the straight man to Peabody's comic relief."

That could be interesting.

He came around the counter to stand next to me. "It would be similar to the collaboration between Williams and Jones."

"You mean Williams and Anson."

"No, Williams and Jones. It makes sense, right? To team up to write since we're already teaming up in real life?"

I pulled him into my arms. "Absolutely. Partners in business, partners in life."

"Wait. Does that mean I need to sign over half the store to you?"

"No."

"Are you sure? You could cover half the expenses."

I laughed. "I see what you did there, sneaky."

"What?" His question dripped with fake innocence.

"I've seen your spreadsheets. Good thing you love this business because any financial advisor would tell you to board it up and cut your losses."

"But cutting my losses would only be the easy way out."

A deeper meaning was behind that statement. He could've easily cut his losses with me. But he stuck it out, no matter how much of an asshole I was to him.

When the man got his teeth into something, he did not let go.

Like Onyx and my damn socks.

"So, what do you think?" he asked.

"I want to do whatever makes you happy," I answered. "If you want to write a series together, I'm on board. If you want to keep doing the indie thing, I'll support you on that path. If you want me to help shoulder the burden of this store, I'll do that, too. Whatever you want, Rett."

He splayed his fingers along my cheek. "Would I sound greedy if I asked for all of that?"

"No. You gave me my life back. In turn, I want to give you the world."

Rett had done the same for me as I had done for Thomas. Or tried to, anyway. Even though I failed, Rett had been determined enough to achieve his goal.

The man had gumption I wish I could harness and sell. If I could, we'd be living large on a private tropical island with our feet in the sand and cold cocktails in our hands.

Though, if that happened, I'd miss our little cabin that had become our home.

It would take some convincing for me to move anywhere else. It might not be a tropical paradise—especially during winter—but it was *our* paradise. One we created together.

It couldn't get any more special than that.

"I don't need the world, baby. I just need you." He placed a soft kiss on my lips. Before I could take it deeper, he stepped back. "Now, let's go celebrate with dinner at The Eagle's Nest and drinks at The Roost. Let's let someone else do the cooking and the dishes for once."

"Ah. *That* was why you lured me off the mountain and away from my laptop."

"*Mmm hmm,*" he murmured.

"You always have an agenda."

He wiggled his eyebrows. "That I do. Are you complaining?"

"Hell no, because it gave me you and a future to look forward to."

"See? Step one, approach the new grumpy guy in town. With caution, of course, because he bites. Step two, force him out of the past and back into the present. Step three, make him fall in love with me."

"That wasn't difficult to do."

"Which part?"

"Making me fall in love with you. I'm just surprised you fell in love with me first."

"It proves I should've went to therapy."

I snorted. "You won't get an argument from me about that."

"Ah, but look at us now. We're perfect."

Perfect was a bit of a stretch. "Hardly, but close enough."

"Close enough," he agreed. "Together we can get through anything."

"Somehow I don't find you being right about that so annoying this time."

"Progress!" he said on a laugh.

I grabbed him and hauled him against me to give him a kiss that smothered that laugh.

That night we celebrated in another way.

We didn't do it by going out for dinner and drinks.

We did it by staying in.

"A person's tragedy does not make up their entire life. A story carves deep grooves into our brains each time we tell it. But we aren't one story. We can change our stories." ~ Amy Poehler

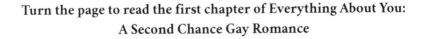

**Turn the page to read the first chapter of Everything About You:
A Second Chance Gay Romance**

Sign up for Jeanne's newsletter to learn about her upcoming releases, sales and more! http://www.jeannestjames.com/newslettersignup

EVERYTHING ABOUT YOU

**Turn the page to read the first chapter of
Everything About You: A Second Chance Gay Romance**

About the book:

*I had given him everything. He turned around and left me with
nothing...*

It was your smile.
Your laugh.
The color of your eyes.
The way you looked at me when no one else was looking.
The way you held me.
The way you kissed me.
It was everything about you I loved.

The flattening of that smile.
The silence of your laughter.
The loss of your lips.
The way you left.
The way you destroyed it all.
The way you destroyed me.
Destroyed us.
It was everything about you I hated.

Everything about you.
I wanted.
Needed.
Hoped for.
And that day you not only broke my heart.
You fucking crushed it.

Note: Everything About you is a standalone gay (M/M) second chance romance. **Please refer to the content note at the beginning of the book before buying or reading. You can access that page by using Amazon's "Look Inside" feature or downloading the free sample. This info can also be found on my website here:** https://www.jeannestjames.com/everythingaboutyou. *As always, this book doesn't have a cliffhanger and an HEA is guaranteed.*

EVERYTHING ABOUT YOU:

A SECOND CHANCE GAY ROMANCE

Chapter One

Ronan (Now)

I STABBED the up arrow button on the lobby elevator in my building. My breath quickly returning back to normal and the sweat starting to dry on my body. I looked forward to washing that sweat and grime from my skin once I got upstairs.

Maybe even doing more than that under the warm spray of the shower.

The numbers lit up one after the other as the elevator car traveled down from the sixth floor.

Ding. Five.

Ding. Four.

Ding. Three.

The buzz and click of the outer lobby door unlocking behind me had me glancing over my shoulder to see if I needed to hold the elevator for whoever just entered.

I pulled the sweaty T-shirt from over my shoulder where I had tossed it, and used it to wipe my face, because clearly I was seeing things. Sweat must have gotten into my eyes. Or maybe I was lightheaded because I hadn't eaten anything since much earlier today.

Or...

Or... I was really seeing who I thought I was.

But that couldn't be. I had to be imagining it. Imagining him.

Maybe I was having a stroke or some medical issue and needed to sit down. It was true that I hadn't been running outside as much as I should be and it could be my blood sugar reacting to the intense cardio session.

Or I was simply delusional.

The man who had walked through the front entrance paused in the vestibule lined with the residents' mailboxes. He appeared as if he had just rolled out of bed, even though he wore a suit. It was wrinkled like he'd slept on a park bench.

He couldn't be homeless since he had the code to the front entrance and that was changed once a month. That meant he had to be a current resident, even though I had never spotted him in the building before.

However, not only did he look out of sorts, he was talking to himself. Just like the homeless man who often slept on a bench in Point State Park. The one who occasionally bathed in the fountain and also fished out the change thrown in by tourists and locals alike.

Funny, I never once had my wish come true after throwing a penny into a fountain, but maybe it worked for other people.

I couldn't hear what the man was saying because of the second set of doors separating the vestibule from the lobby, but even with his head tipped down, I could clearly see his lips moving. He could be wearing earbuds and talking to someone on his cell phone.

Or he could be having a full-blown conversation with himself as he dug deep into his pants pocket. Most likely for his mailbox key.

Even after drying the sweat from around my eyes, he still looked so familiar.

Too familiar.

The elevator dinged as it arrived on the main floor and the doors whooshed open. Mr. and Mrs. Callahan from the fourth floor stepped out with their little yappy, ankle-biter Pomeranian, Mr. Pibbles.

I side-stepped to give the older couple room to pass and also so that little fucker didn't take a chunk out of my ankle.

Mrs. Callahan's gaze swept over me and I knew exactly why.

I was wearing nothing but black silky shorts that, when sweaty, clung to my assets, along with running sneakers, ankle-high sports socks and a Penn State U baseball cap.

It also didn't help that my skin wasn't a perfect shade of pale and I sported a wide assortment of tattoos covering my torso and arms.

However, it wasn't the first time they'd seen me after a run and, unfortunately for them, it wouldn't be the last.

Mr. Callahan held the elevator door for me even though it looked like he was sucking on a lemon while doing so.

They were lovely people.

By lovely, I meant judgmental assholes.

Even so, we needed to coexist since we all lived in the same building. Instead of flipping him the bird, I gave him a nod and said, "I'm not going up yet, but thanks," then took a quick glance over my shoulder again toward the vestibule.

The newest resident must've found his key since the metal door to one of the mailboxes now hung wide open while he rifled through a fistful of mail.

Shaking his head, he continued to talk to himself. The only time he glanced up was when the Callahans walked past him with Mr. Pibbles yapping in warning. Mr. Pibbles didn't like strangers.

Hell, Mr. Pibbles didn't like anyone except for the Callahans. And even that was questionable.

As soon as the couple and their orange yap rat stepped out onto the sidewalk, the man shut the mailbox and turned...

And the revolving Earth came to a complete and abrupt stop, as if someone had jerked up the emergency brake.

My heart seized. My lungs emptied. My soul decided to flee the lobby without me.

But my mind... My mind began to spin like a Tilt-A-Whirl with a drunk carny at the controls.

"Oh shit." When my heart kick-started, I yanked my baseball cap lower to hide my face and quickly tugged my damp T-shirt over my head and torso as I hurried into the nearby stairwell.

I made sure the steel door didn't slam behind me and for a second pressed my back to the wall next to it.

I wasn't sure what the hell to do. I certainly wasn't ready to face him.

This couldn't be reality. He couldn't live in the same building as I did.

It couldn't be him. No fucking way!

He left Pittsburgh twelve years ago after he graduated, why the hell was he back now?

My only guess was that it wasn't Tate. That it was someone who looked like him. A doppelgänger.

I was freaking out for nothing.

I was being a foolish idiot.

But to be sure, I slid my back from the wall to the door, flipped my baseball cap backwards, then turned, bent my knees and popped my head up enough to peek out of the little fireproof window.

I watched as he headed over to the elevator and jabbed the button ten times in quick succession. While he waited impatiently for the doors to open, he shuffled from one foot to the other.

Twelve years.

It had been twelve fucking years since I last saw him.

But it was like yesterday.

We both looked different but also the same.

Definitely older. Debatably wiser.

But he looked worn out. Beat down.

As if the easy life he was supposed to be living turned out to be not so easy.

I watched him until he stepped into the open elevator car and the doors shut behind him, whisking him away.

I continued to stare at the empty spot where he previously stood because I had a hard time pulling myself away.

I could only chalk it up to shock.

Once I finally forced my feet to move, I sat on the third step and dropped my head into my hands to try to wrap my head around who I just saw. Unsure why he was here. In Pittsburgh. In the same damn building where I lived. Unsure why any of this was happening.

For a moment in the silence, I was transported back.

To when I had hope.

Dreams.

Expectations.

And, of course, to when those were all crushed.

~

Ronan (Then)

I SPREAD myself out in the seat with an arm casually hanging over the back of the empty one to my right. I might be a freshman but I came to Duquesne with the intent to not act like one. To not be seen as a boy fresh out of high school.

Instead, I wanted to feel like a man ready to seize the world.

It might not be true, but the saying "fake it until you make it" existed for a reason.

Because of that, I did my best to look confident and like I belonged, when really, deep down inside I was anything but.

I did really well in high school, which helped me earn scholarships and grants. But attending Duquesne University was a whole other world compared to high school.

It would be fan-freaking-tastic if the students here weren't so close-minded like they were at my high school in a small town right outside of Hershey, PA. My roomie in the dorm seemed to be cool so far, but I'd only known him for less than a week and I also hadn't told him I was gay.

Yet.

My hope was that if he got to know me first, by the time he figured it out, he'd discover I wasn't defined solely by my sexual preference. Being gay was just a small part of who I was as a person.

This morning I arrived earlier than usual for this first class—I hadn't been sure where the lecture hall was located—and settled myself in an empty row of seats.

I didn't want to be quite up front, but didn't want to hide in the back, either. There'd be no point since this was Multi-Genre Creative Writing. A class I wasn't forced to take but was interested in because I hadn't quite pinned down my major yet. I had no reason to hide in this class, unlike with my algebra course.

At this point I had no idea what I wanted to do with my life. I was leaning toward a business degree, so I had signed up for a core credit course along with a mix of electives to see if anything caught my fancy.

Since writing was a big part of most careers, I figured it couldn't hurt. While I was a pro at sending texts and casual emails, when it came to professional correspondence, I could use some work. Plus, how hard could creative writing be? Unlike algebra.

Here I was, sitting in the third row, waiting for the professor and watching the seats fill up around me. I had my old Asus laptop set up on the flip-up desktop, hoping my electronic dinosaur held a charge long enough to get me through my classes today. The battery on my three-year old cell phone with the cracked screen was slowly dying, too. I just couldn't afford to replace either *soon-to-be* paperweights.

That reminded me... I needed to find a job in which the hours would be flexible around my classes, studying and, of course, some partying. Since I was putting myself through school, the first and second were the most important. Partying, dating or hooking up with someone would be more of a reward for all my hard work.

I glanced at my flickering screen to skim over the syllabus one last time as everyone finished wandering in. When the chatter came to a halt, I looked up to see the professor wander in, drop off his briefcase on the table, write *Dr. Mario Louden* on the whiteboard and then turn to stand at the lectern.

Dr. Louden cleared his throat. "In case you're lost, this is—"

The door was thrown open with a bang and a student rushed in. He paused, made eye contact with Dr. Louden and grimaced.

"Mr. Harris, *this* is one reason why you are repeating this course. You've known what time this class starts since you got your schedule at least two weeks ago. There is no excuse for you being tardy."

"Sorry. Sorry," he muttered, adjusting the gaping-open backpack half hanging off his shoulder.

"I expect this won't happen again. Right, Mr. Harris? Otherwise, my suggestion is for you to drop out and find another class and instructor to insult with your tardiness, instead."

"I need—" The student shook his head. "I swear I won't be late again."

That sounded like a lie to my own ears, but I didn't give a shit about what was coming out of his mouth. I was more fixated on his actual lips and not the words being muttered from them.

He. Was. Absolutely. Beautiful.

A chunk of thick dark hair fell across his forehead and a flush had crept up his neck and into his cheeks.

I couldn't keep my eyes from my future boyfriend—maybe I'd go so far as future husband even—as he jogged up the steps with his head down. Unfortunately, he disappeared somewhere behind me.

Hopefully, he didn't notice me gawking.

And if he did… Oh well.

He would probably just think I'm staring at him because I thought he was rude to arrive late to class.

I heard the thump of his very heavy backpack hitting the floor a few rows behind me, a loud rustle and a slew of grumbles.

I wasn't the only one who noticed. So did Dr. Louden who stared past me to the future Mr. Ronan Pak.

325

I liked that. Another man taking my name. If he really pushed it, I'd let him hyphenate. Harris-Pak.

"Are you sure you're ready for me to start class, Mr. Harris?" Dr. Louden called out with one dark bushy eyebrow stuck high up his forehead.

A few sniggers and muffled laughs could be heard and I noticed everyone was turned around in their seats to check Mr. Harris out.

Correction. Mr. Harris-Pak.

A smile spread across my face and I pulled myself out of my fantasy to concentrate on today's lesson as our professor began to teach. I certainly didn't want him calling me out in front of the whole class for daydreaming.

Over an hour later, I was stuffing my shit back into my backpack, including my ancient computer—luckily, it hadn't let me down during class—and thinking about the next time I'd see Mr. Harris, since I didn't know his first name yet.

Yet. But I would.

I would make sure to get to class early on Friday and grab a seat toward the back so I could stare at my newest obsession without anyone knowing. Study him. Learn every detail to memory. For my fantasies.

When I stood, I heard a rush of feet coming down the steps behind me, so I waited and fiddled with my backpack, trying not to be too obvious.

I just wanted to get another look. Of the back this time, since I already liked what I'd seen of the front.

I was not disappointed as Harris jogged down the steps toward the front of the lecture hall. However, his backpack still gaped wide open and all the contents were at risk of falling out.

"Hey!" I called out in warning and quickly followed him down the steps.

He either didn't hear me or was ignoring me as he rushed out of the lecture hall and into the corridor.

I elbowed my way through a group of students standing around and talking, but more importantly, blocking me from my future husband. I got around them and headed out, hoping I didn't lose Harris.

I didn't.

Not because he was waiting, but because what I feared had happened. His backpack was now dumped on the ground and all the items inside had been strewn across the hallway like the contents of a smashed piñata at a birthday party.

What made me almost tear up a little was what looked like a new laptop on the floor.

An utter tragedy. What I would do for a new laptop like that…

Hopefully it wasn't broken and if it was, that it was insured.

Not my problem. My concern was with the broad-shouldered, narrow-hipped man, with a perfectly juicy peach for an ass, now squatting on the floor, collecting his belongings while everyone else walked around him and didn't bother to help.

This was my chance to introduce myself and be his knight in shining armor.

Squatting down while facing him, I began to gather pens, a rainbow of highlighters and various colored sticky notes.

My takeaway was the man carried way too much shit in his backpack. Who hauled around this much stuff? No wonder he couldn't zip it shut.

After my hands were full, I grabbed his backpack and tossed everything into it. If he wanted it organized, he could do that himself and once he was out of hallway traffic.

I stood and moved closer to my future lover, gripping the bag tightly. My brain was trying to trick me into thinking that holding his backpack was the same as holding him.

It wasn't. Unfortunately.

I waited as he stacked some textbooks, and what might be some fiction, into his arms and rose to his feet, his face flushed from either embarrassment or the exertion.

I held the backpack out to him. "Here."

After glancing around to see if he missed anything, his face lifted. And when he reached for his bag, I couldn't release my hold. Once he got a more solid grip on it, our fingers touched and a shock zipped up my arm and a tornado of heat swirled around my gut.

Our surprised gazes locked, and...

I forgot how to breathe.

His blue eyes...

Seeing them up close and personal caused lightning to zap me right in the middle of my chest.

His awkward, crooked smile caused a heaviness in my balls and I hoped like hell I didn't pop a boner right there in the corridor.

"Thanks," got caught in his throat. He cleared it and repeated it more clearly.

"No problem."

"The zipper's broken," he explained.

"Probably because you're hauling around half of your college career in that thing."

"I don't live on campus, so I..." He seemed to lose his train of thought but never once did he lose hold of my eyes. His were locked solid with mine. "I... uh..."

"Don't want to forget anything," I finished for him.

He nodded and that chunk of dark hair fell lower on his forehead. I curled the fingers of the hand not holding the backpack into my palm to avoid reaching out and pushing it off his eyebrow and back into place.

"You can't leave stuff in your car?" It wasn't like I really cared what he carried around like a pack mule, I only wanted to keep him there as long as possible.

"No car." His voice was much deeper than one would think by looking at him since he was on the slender side.

"How do you get to campus, then?"

"My bike or I walk. I sometimes catch a ride with one of my roommates, depending on our schedules."

A little tug had me finally releasing his backpack, even though I didn't want to. I wanted to hold him there, like a hostage. Take him for myself and keep him until he fell desperately in love with me.

Of course, I knew that wasn't realistic. But there was one thing I *could* get from him, if nothing else...

"Cool. By the way, I'm Ronan, but you can call me Roe."

His dark eyebrows pinned together. "Ronan?"

"Yeah, it's Irish. I look Irish, don't I?" I cocked my head and kept my expression serious even though I purposely put him on the spot.

I watched him panic about answering my question and possibly offending me. "Uh..."

I kept my lips from twitching and giving myself away. "I'm actually only half Irish. The front half. The back half isn't." I waited to see if he would ask me about the rest of my ethnicity since I certainly didn't even look half Irish. But he played it safe and didn't, so I asked, "How about you?" I wasn't ready for this conversation to end.

"I'm... I'm not quite sure..."

He scraped his fingers through his hair, messing it up even worse. To me, it made him appear even sexier. I'd love to see his hair like that when I rolled over in the morning and found his head on the pillow next to mine.

"I'm a mutt, I guess. A mix of European. Like German and—"

"I meant your name," I clarified.

"Oh." The redness in his cheeks intensified. "Tate. Harris. You can call me Tate."

When I grinned, I watched something cross Tate's face I was *not* expecting.

Interest. Cautious interest.

Hmm. Could he be gay? Or at least bi?

Could I be so lucky that my future husband actually liked men, too?

Nah, I was never that lucky.

I jutted out my hand. He stared at it for a second like I had just thrown him a curve ball. Then he adjusted his backpack over his shoulder more securely and placed his warm hand with its long fingers in mine.

And, *holy shit…*

I couldn't wait to get my next class over with since I needed to head to the computer lab and start printing our wedding invitations.

I hoped Tate wouldn't mind.

∽

Ronan (Now)

IN THE QUIET STAIRWELL, I dropped my hands and lifted my head, taking a deep, cleansing breath to push out the memories.

Out of all of them I couldn't shake, that had been a good one and I needed to stop before they turned to the painful, soul-crushing ones.

Rising to my feet, I pressed my lips together and set my jaw. I began the long hike up the stairs to the penthouse. And as I did so, I realized one thing…

There was no way in hell I was ready to go face to face with Tate Harris.

Not today and maybe not ever.

In the time between the last day I saw him and today, I'd been with plenty of men. But not one had ever been like him and I'd never loved any of them.

Because of that, I never had a loss as great as losing Tate.

After all these years, I thought I was over him.

Clearly, I was not.

Get Everything About You here:
mybook.to/EAY

IF YOU ENJOYED THIS BOOK

Thank you for reading Reigniting Chase. If you enjoyed it, please consider leaving a review at your favorite retailer and/or Goodreads to let other readers know. Reviews are always appreciated and just a few words can help an independent author like me tremendously!

Want to read a sample of her work? Download a sampler book here: BookHip.com/MTQQKK

ALSO BY JEANNE ST. JAMES

Find my complete reading order here:
https://www.jeannestjames.com/reading-order

* Available in Audiobook

Stand-alone Books:

Made Maleen: A Modern Twist on a Fairy Tale *

Damaged *

Rip Cord: The Complete Trilogy *

Everything About You (A Second Chance Gay Romance) *

Reigniting Chase (An M/M Standalone)

Brothers in Blue Series:

Brothers in Blue: Max *

Brothers in Blue: Marc *

Brothers in Blue: Matt *

Teddy: A Brothers in Blue Novelette *

Brothers in Blue: A Bryson Family Christmas *

The Dare Ménage Series:

Double Dare *

Daring Proposal *

Dare to Be Three *

A Daring Desire *

Dare to Surrender *

A Daring Journey *

The Obsessed Novellas:

Forever Him *

Only Him *

Needing Him *

Loving Her *

Tempting Him *

Down & Dirty: Dirty Angels MC Series®:

Down & Dirty: Zak *

Down & Dirty: Jag *

Down & Dirty: Hawk *

Down & Dirty: Diesel *

Down & Dirty: Axel *

Down & Dirty: Slade *

Down & Dirty: Dawg *

Down & Dirty: Dex *

Down & Dirty: Linc *

Down & Dirty: Crow *

Crossing the Line (A DAMC/Blue Avengers MC Crossover) *

Magnum: A Dark Knights MC/Dirty Angels MC Crossover *

Crash: A Dirty Angels MC/Blood Fury MC Crossover

Guts & Glory Series:

(In the Shadows Security)

Guts & Glory: Mercy *

Guts & Glory: Ryder *

Guts & Glory: Hunter *

Guts & Glory: Walker *

Guts & Glory: Steel *

Guts & Glory: Brick *

Blood & Bones: Blood Fury MC®:
Blood & Bones: Trip *
Blood & Bones: Sig *
Blood & Bones: Judge *
Blood & Bones: Deacon *
Blood & Bones: Cage *
Blood & Bones: Shade *
Blood & Bones: Rook *
Blood & Bones: Rev *
Blood & Bones: Ozzy
Blood & Bones: Dodge
Blood & Bones: Whip
Blood & Bones: Easy

COMING SOON!
Double D Ranch (An MMF Ménage Series)
Blue Avengers MC™

WRITING AS J.J. MASTERS:
The Royal Alpha Series
(A gay mpreg shifter series)

The Selkie Prince's Fated Mate *
The Selkie Prince & His Omega Guard *
The Selkie Prince's Unexpected Omega *
The Selkie Prince's Forbidden Mate *
The Selkie Prince's Secret Baby *

ABOUT THE AUTHOR

JEANNE ST. JAMES is a USA Today and international bestselling romance author who loves writing about strong women and alpha males. She was only thirteen when she first started writing. Her first published piece was an erotic short story in Playgirl magazine. She then went on to publish her first romance novel in 2009. She is now an author of over fifty-five contemporary romances. Along with writing M/F, M/M, and M/M/F ménages, she also writes under the name J.J. Masters.

To keep up with her busy release schedule check her website at www.jeannestjames.com or sign up for her newsletter: http://www. jeannestjames.com/newslettersignup

www.jeannestjames.com
jeanne@jeannestjames.com

Newsletter: http://www.jeannestjames.com/newslettersignup
Jeanne's FB Readers Group: https://www.facebook.com/ groups/JeannesReviewCrew/
TikTok: https://www.tiktok.com/@jeannestjames
Audible: https://www.audible.com/author/Jeanne-St-James/B002YBDE7O

facebook.com/JeanneStJamesAuthor

twitter.com/JeanneStJames

amazon.com/author/jeannestjames

instagram.com/JeanneStJames

bookbub.com/authors/jeanne-st-james

goodreads.com/JeanneStJames

pinterest.com/JeanneStJames

Printed in Great Britain
by Amazon

33527650R00193